THE
SHOTGUN
WEDDING

A HAVE BRIDES, WILL TRAVEL WESTERN

WILLIAM W.
JOHNSTONE

AND J. A. JOHNSTONE

PINNACLE BOOKS
Kensington Publishing Corp.
www.kensingtonbooks.com

PINNACLE BOOKS are published by

Kensington Publishing Corp.
119 West 40th Street
New York, NY 10018

PUBLISHER'S NOTE
Following the death of William W. Johnstone, the Johnstone family is working with a carefully selected writer to organize and complete Mr. Johnstone's outlines and many unfinished manuscripts to create additional novels in all of his series like The Last Gunfighter, Mountain Man, and Eagles, among others. This novel was inspired by Mr. Johnstone's superb storytelling.

ISBN-13: 978-0-7860-4412-2
ISBN-10: 0-7860-4412-8

First Kensington hardcover printing: May 2020
First Pinnacle paperback printing: December 2020

10 9 8 7 6 5 4 3 2 1

Printed in the United States of America

Electronic edition:

ISBN-13: 978-0-7860-4413-9 (e-book)
ISBN-10: 0-7860-4413-6 (e-book)

THE
SHOTGUN
WEDDING

CHAPTER 1

"You take the one on the right," Bo Creel said as he walked forward slowly, holding the Winchester at a slant across his chest. "I can handle the other two."

"Wait a minute," Scratch Morton said. "You mean their right or our right?"

"Our right. Your man's the one with the rattlesnake band around his hat."

"You mean the ugly one?"

"They're *all* ugly."

"Bein' dead ain't gonna make 'em any prettier," Scratch said, "but I reckon that's where they're headin' mighty quick-like."

Bo said, "We'll give them a chance to surrender. That's the only proper thing to do, seeing as we're duly appointed lawmen and all."

Scratch muttered under his breath about that, something that included the words "dad-blasted tin stars" and some other, more colorful comments, then said, "All right, Deputy Creel, let's get this done."

"Sure thing, Marshal Morton."

* * *

They continued up the dusty street toward the three hard cases standing in front of the Silver King Palace, the largest and fanciest drinking establishment in the settlement of Silverhill, New Mexico Territory. The gun-wolves wore arrogant sneers on their beard-stubbled faces. They were killers and didn't care who knew it. In fact, they were proud of their infamous deeds.

And clearly, they weren't the least bit worried about the two older men approaching them.

They should have been. They didn't know what ornery sidewinders Bo Creel and Scratch Morton could be.

At first glance, the two Texans didn't look that formidable, although they stood straight and moved with an easy, athletic grace not that common in men of their years. Both had weathered, sun-bronzed faces, which testified to decades spent out in the elements. Bo's dark brown hair under his flat-crowned black hat was shot through heavily with white. Scratch's cream-colored Stetson topped a full head of pure silver hair.

Bo looked a little like a preacher, with his long black coat, black trousers, and white shirt, and with a string tie around his neck. Scratch was more of a dandy, wearing a fringed buckskin jacket over a butternut shirt and brown whipcord trousers tucked into high-topped boots.

Both men were well armed at the moment. Bo had the Winchester in his hands and a Colt .45 revolver riding in a black holster on his right hip. Scratch carried a pair of long-barreled, silvered, ivory-handled Remington .44s in a hand-tooled buscadero gun rig. All the weapons were very well cared for but also showed signs of long and frequent use.

Bo and Scratch had been best friends since they met

more than forty years earlier, during the Runaway Scrape, when the citizens of Texas fled across the countryside before Santa Anna's vengeful army. Though only boys at the time, they had fought side by side in the Battle of San Jacinto, when those Texans finally turned around and, against overwhelming odds, gave the Mexican dictator's forces a good whipping. Texas had won its freedom that fine spring day in 1836, and a lifelong friendship had been formed between Bo and Scratch.

In the decades since, they had roamed from one end of the West to the other, enduring much tragedy and trouble but also living a life of adventure that perfectly suited their fiddle-footed nature. Every attempt they had made to settle down had ended badly, until finally they had given up trying and accepted their wanderlust. Along the way they had worked at almost every sort of job to make ends meet.

Every now and then they had even found themselves on the wrong side of the law.

But right now they wore badges, which was mighty uncommon in their checkered careers. Despite being handier than most with guns and fists, they had hardly ever been peace officers.

More likely they'd be *disturbing* the peace . . .

The "peace" of Silverhill was about to be disturbed, all right. Like most mining boomtowns, this could be a raucous, wide-open place, but there weren't many gunfights on Main Street in the middle of the day.

Bo hoped there wouldn't be this time, either, but he wasn't convinced of that. Not by a long shot.

Bo and Scratch came to a stop about twenty feet away from the trio of hard cases. The one in the middle, who had long, greasy red hair under a black hat with a Montana pinch, clenched a thin black cigarillo between his large, horse-like teeth and growled, "We heard the law was on the way. What in blazes do you old pelicans want?"

Scratch said, "We want you boys to unbuckle your gunbelts and let 'em drop, then hoist those dewclaws and march on down to the jailhouse. You're under arrest."

"Under arrest?" the redhead repeated mockingly. "What for?" The second man, short and stocky, with a walrus mustache, said, "It's probably got somethin' to do with that piano player you plugged, Bugle."

"Shut up, Tater," the bucktoothed redhead snapped.

The third man, who had the gaunt, hollow-eyed look of a lunger, said, "Now you've gone and told these lawdogs your names."

"We already knew who you are, Scanlon," Bo said. "There are wanted posters for all three of you in the files in the marshal's office."

"So we wouldn't have been inclined to just let you ride out of town, anyway," Scratch added. "But killing a man . . . well, that sort of leveled it off and nailed it down. You're goin' to jail, all right, and then, in the due course of things, to the gallows, I expect."

Tater looked up at Bugle and said, "See, I done told you we oughta start shootin' as soon as we seen 'em headed this way. Now it's gonna be an even break."

"An even break?" Bugle said. He seemed to like to repeat things. "How in blazes do you figure that? These two old fools ought to be sittin' in rockin' chairs somewhere, instead of bein' about to die in the middle of a dusty street!"

"Oh," Bo said, "I don't reckon we're quite *that* old."

Bugle's sneer twisted into a hate-filled grimace as his hands darted toward the guns on his hips.

Bo snapped the Winchester to his shoulder. He had already jacked a round into the chamber before he and Scratch started down here, so all he had to do was squeeze the trigger. The rifle cracked.

Bugle's head jerked back and the cigarillo flew out of his mouth as Bo neatly drilled a slug an inch above his right eye. The bullet made a nice round hole going in but blew a fist-sized chunk out of the back of Bugle's skull when it erupted in a pink spray of blood and brain matter. He went over backward, with his guns still in their holsters.

Beside Bo, Scratch slapped leather. The Remingtons came out of their holsters so fast, they were a silver blur. The cadaverous-looking gent called Scanlon was a noted shootist, but Scratch shaded him on the draw by a fraction of a second.

That was enough. Flame shot from the muzzles of both Remingtons. The .44 caliber slugs hammered into Scanlon's chest and knocked him back a step just as his fingers tightened on the triggers of his own guns. One bullet plowed into the dirt a few feet ahead of Scanlon. The other went high and wild. He caught his balance and tried to swing the guns in line for another shot, but Scratch, with time to aim now, calmly shot the gun-wolf in the head.

Meanwhile, Bo was realizing that he might have made a mistake in shooting Bugle first. The short, dumpy Tater didn't look like he'd be much of a threat when it came to gunplay, and Bugle was the one who'd shot and killed the piano player in the Silver King, after all.

But while Bo was busy blowing Bugle's brains out, Tater drew an old Griswold & Gunnison .36 with blinding speed and thumbed off a shot. Bo felt the heat of the round against his cheek as it barely missed spreading *his* brains on the street.

Brass sparkled in the hot, dry air as Bo worked the Winchester's lever and sent the empty he had just fired spinning high in the air. He slammed the lever up and fired again, but not in time to prevent Tater from getting off a second shot. This bullet tugged at Bo's coat, but this attempt was a narrow miss, too.

"A miss is as good as a mile," the old saying went. But Bo hadn't missed. His bullet shattered Tater's right shoulder and knocked him halfway around.

Tater was stubborn. Not only did he stay on his feet, but he also didn't even drop the gun. Grimacing in pain, he reached over with his left hand and plucked the weapon out of his now useless right hand.

Bo cranked the Winchester and fired his third shot. This one ripped through Tater's throat and severed his jugular vein, judging by the arcing spray of blood from the wound. He dropped to the dirt like a discarded toy. The other two hard cases hadn't moved at all once they hit the ground, but Tater flopped and thrashed a little and made a gurgling sound as he drowned in his own blood.

Then he was still, too.

The battle had lasted five seconds. Maybe a hair under. Echoes of the shots hung over Silverhill for a moment and then faded away.

"You hit?" Bo asked his old friend.

"Mine didn't even come close," the silver-haired Texan replied. "How about yours?"

"Close," Bo admitted. "No cigar, though. But that's because I misjudged old Tater. I thought Bugle was the more dangerous of the two."

Scratch shook his head. "Hard to be sure about such a thing, just from lookin' at a fella. I got to say, though, if I'd been in your place, I think I'd've made the same mistake. Comes down to it, those varmints are dead and we're still kickin', and that's all that matters, ain't it?"

"Yeah." Bo took cartridges from his coat pocket and thumbed them through the Winchester's loading gate to replace the rounds he'd fired. Quietly, he added, "Looks like folks are coming out of their holes."

The street and the boardwalks had cleared out in a hurry when it became obvious gun trouble was imminent. Nobody wanted to get in the way of a stray bullet, and you couldn't blame them for that. Now, up and down the street, people were stepping out of the businesses into which they had retreated and were peering toward the three bodies sprawled in front of the Silver King. A few even took tentative steps in that direction to get a better look. Before too much longer, a crowd would gather around the corpses, Bo knew, as the curiosity on the part of Silverhill's citizens overpowered their revulsion.

"Reckon we ought the fetch the undertaker?" Scratch asked.

"I'm sure Clarence Appleyard is already hitching up his wagon," Bo replied. "It never takes him long to get to the scene of a shooting."

"No, he's Johnny-on-the-spot. You got to give him that."

They turned and walked back toward the squat stone building that housed the marshal's office.

"Hell of a first day on the job, ain't it?" Scratch asked.

"Well," Bo said, "we knew the job might be dangerous when we took it."

They were passing the Territorial House, the biggest and best hotel in Silverhill, and before either man could say anything else, the front doors flew open and several figures rushed out.

Almost before Bo and Scratch knew what was going on, they were surrounded by a handful of femininity as anxious, questioning voices filled the air around them.

CHAPTER 2

The five young women who surrounded Bo and Scratch were a study in contrasts. Two were blondes, one had hair black as midnight, another was a brunette, and the fifth and final female had a mane of thick chestnut hair falling around her shoulders. One blonde was small, dainty, and curly haired; the other was taller, with her wheat-colored tresses pulled back and tied behind her head. The young woman with dark brown hair had an elegant but cool and reserved look about her, while the one with raven's-wing hair was sultry and exotic looking. Unlike the others, the tomboyish gal with chestnut hair wore boots, trousers, a man's shirt, and looked like she was ready to go out and ride the range.

The one thing they all had in common was that they were beautiful. The sort of beauty that made men take a second and even a third look as their jaws dropped. In a boomtown such as Silverhill, they were definitely diamonds in the rough.

With a tone of command in her voice, the cool-looking brunette, Cecilia Spaulding, said, "Everyone just be quiet!

Mr. Creel and Mr. Morton can't answer our questions if everybody is talking at once."

"That's easy for you to say," chestnut-haired Rose Winston shot back at her. "You heard all that shooting, same as we did. We just want to know if they're all right."

"I don't see any blood on them," the taller, more athletic-looking blonde, Beth Macy, said.

Bo figured it was time he got a word in edgewise. He said, "No, neither of us was hit."

"You killed the men you were after, though, didn't you?" Rose asked with a bloodthirsty note in her voice. "Those hombres who shot the piano player at the Silver King?"

"Seemed like the thing to do at the time," Scratch replied with a grin. "How'd you know what happened to that ivory pounder?"

"People were talking about it in the hotel lobby," Cecilia explained. "It was quite the topic of conversation . . . as violence usually is."

Jean Parker, the dainty, curly-haired blonde, sniffed and said, "It seems like a day can't go by in this town without a killing of some sort."

"You're exaggerating, Jean," exotic-looking Luella Tolman said. "Why, until today it's been almost two weeks since there was a real gun battle here!"

"Two weeks ago," Jean said. "You mean when that horde of Mexican bandits and that other gang of outlaws and those horrible gunslingers and those wild cowboys all converged on the town and we were nearly killed? Is *that* what you're talking about, Luella?"

"Now, ladies," Bo said, "there's nothing to worry about."

"Oh?" Cecilia raised a finely arched eyebrow. "Can

you guarantee that nothing like that will happen again, Mr. Creel?"

Rose said, "You should call him Deputy Creel now. He's a lawman."

"And Mr. Morton is the marshal," Beth said. She tilted her head a little to the side. "Although, for some reason, I would have thought it would be the other way around. No offense, Mr. Morton. But, anyway, with the two of them in charge of enforcing the law now, I'm certain what happened today was just an isolated incident. Silverhill will settle right down and actually become peaceful."

Bo wished he was as convinced of that as Beth seemed to be. He pinched the brim of his hat, nodded, and said, "We'll do our best to make sure that happens, ladies."

Scratch tipped his hat to the five lovelies but stopped short of bowing. Then he and Bo moved on toward the sheriff's office.

"Beth's right," Scratch said quietly. "You really ought to be wearin' this marshal's badge, Bo. I ain't sure why you insisted I'd be the marshal and you'd be the deputy."

Bo snorted. "It's bad enough we agreed to be star packers. I didn't want to be in charge."

"We could've told those fellas no when they came to see us yesterday."

Bo nodded slowly and said, "I've got a hunch that we may wind up wishing we had slammed the door in that poor young fella's face."

The Territorial House,
the previous afternoon . . .

Bo and Scratch were in their room in the hotel when a knock sounded on the door. Scratch was dealing a hand of solitaire on the table that also contained a basin and a pitcher of water, while Bo had his Colt taken apart and spread out on a towel he'd put on the bed so he could clean the revolver.

Scratch turned on his chair to look over his shoulder at his old friend and ask, "You expectin' company?"

"Not me," Bo replied. "It might be one of the girls looking for us for some reason."

Several weeks earlier, Bo and Scratch had set out from Fort Worth in the company of five beautiful young women: Cecilia Spaulding, Jean Parker, Luella Tolman, Beth Macy, and Rose Winston. The five of them were from the town of Four Corners, Iowa, and had known each other all their lives. They were mail-order brides, and Bo and Scratch had been hired by Cyrus Keegan, whose matrimonial agency had arranged the matches, to accompany them to their destination, the mining boomtown of Silverhill, in New Mexico Territory, and act as bodyguards during the trip.

That journey had been filled with excitement and danger, and things hadn't really calmed down once the group reached Silverhill. Actually, even more hell had started popping. Once Bo and Scratch, with some help from new friends, had straightened out that mess, they had decided to remain in Silverhill for a while. Cyrus Keegan had informed them by a letter delivered on the twice-weekly stagecoach run from El Paso that he didn't have any more work for them at the moment, and the two footloose drifters had taken an avuncular interest in the five young women, who had wound up not getting married, after all.

But as lovely as they were, none of them lacked for suitors.

Scratch stood up and went to the door, drawing his right-hand Remington as he did so. Caution was a habit of long standing with the two Texans. Scratch called through the panel, "Who's there?" and then stepped quickly to the side, just in case whoever was in the hall had a shotgun and decided to answer the question with a double load of buckshot.

Instead, a boy's reedy voice replied, "It is only Pablo, señores."

Bo and Scratch had gotten acquainted with the youngster since they'd been staying at the Territorial House. He ran errands and did odd jobs around the hotel. Bo didn't hear any strain in Pablo's voice, like there would have been if somebody had a gun on him and was forcing him to try to get them to open the door, so he nodded to Scratch, who turned the knob—but didn't holster the Remington just yet.

Pablo was alone in the hall, they saw as Scratch swung the door back. He gazed with big eyes at the gun in Scratch's hand, clearly impressed by it, but then quickly remembered why he was there.

"Some gentlemen downstairs wish to see you, Señor Creel, Señor Morton."

"Which gentlemen would they be, Pablo?" Bo asked from the bed.

"Señor Hopkins, Señor Carling, Señor Esperanza, and Señor Dubonnet."

Scratch looked at Bo and raised an eyebrow. Both drifters recognized those names. Albert Hopkins and W.J.M. Carling owned two of the largest silver mines in the area. Hector Esperanza ran Silverhill's largest and most successful livery stable. Francis Dubonnet's general mercantile store took up almost an entire block. All four men were wealthy and influential. Silverhill had no mayor and no official town council, but for all practical purposes, these men occupied those positions.

The former owner of the Silver King Saloon, Forbes Dyson, had been part of that circle, as well, but Dyson was six feet under now.

"What do a bunch of high rollers like that want with the likes of us?" Scratch asked.

Pablo shrugged. "They did not tell me, señor. They said only that they wished to speak with both of you. They wait in the lobby." The boy shook his head. "Hombres such as those four do not like to wait, señores."

"Well, they'll have to for a few minutes, anyway," Bo said. "I'm putting my gun back together."

"Tell 'em we'll be down in a spell and they shouldn't get their fur in an uproar," Scratch said.

Pablo's eyes widened again. He said, "I will tell them, Señor Morton. Perhaps not in those *exact* words . . ."

Scratch grinned and took a coin from his pocket and flipped it to the youngster, who snatched it out of the air and then hurried toward the landing. Scratch closed the door and turned to Bo, who was deliberately reassembling the Colt.

"Usually when the leadin' citizens of a place want to see us, it's to tell us to rattle our hocks and shake the dust o' their fine community off our no-good heels."

"And they say that in no uncertain terms," Bo agreed without looking up from his task.

"You reckon that's what these fellas want with us?"

"I don't know. There's been a lot of trouble since we got here, but none of it was really any of our doing and, anyway, it's been quiet for a while."

"Could be they've decided that trouble just sort of follows us around, whether it's our fault or not."

"Well, considering our history," Bo said, "you couldn't blame them for feeling that way." He stood up, slid the cleaned and reassembled Colt back in its holster, and reached for his coat. "Let's go ask them."

When they went down the stairs and reached the lobby, they found the four men looking impatient as they stood beside some potted plants. As mining tycoons, Hopkins and Carling dressed the part, with frock coats, bowler hats, fancy vests, and cravats. Hopkins wore a close-cropped beard, while Carling sported bushy gray muttonchop whiskers and a jaw like a slab of stone. Both men smoked fat cigars.

Despite owning the general store and being worth a small fortune, Francis Dubonnet usually wore a canvas apron and worked behind the counter, alongside his clerks. He had discarded the apron today in favor of a brown tweed suit. His wavy black hair was plastered down with pomade, and wax curled the tips of his impressive mustache.

Hector Esperanza also had a mustache, but it was a thin gray line on his upper lip. He was short, lean, leathery, and wiry and had a reputation as one of the best men with horses in the entire territory. He wore a brown tweed suit, as well, with a collarless shirt and no tie, and didn't look anything at all like the rich man he was. He had a pipe clamped between his teeth.

"There you are," Hopkins greeted Bo and Scratch.

"Sorry to keep you waiting," Bo said, even though he really wasn't. Texans were courteous when they could be, though. "What can we do for you?"

Carling said, "I'm not in the habit of talking business while standing in a hotel lobby."

Bo and Scratch exchanged a glance. Neither of them had any idea what sort of business they might have with men such as these.

Esperanza took the pipe out of his mouth and suggested,

"Why don't we go in the dining room and have some coffee?"

Carling and Hopkins scowled, but Dubonnet said, "That's an excellent idea."

The dining room was empty at this time of day. The six men sat down at a large round table. The lone waitress who was working hurried over to them, and Hopkins ordered coffee all around.

Then he leaned forward slightly, clasped his hands together on the fine Irish linen tablecloth, and said, "We'll get right down to business. Creel, Morton, we want you men to work for us."

Again, Bo and Scratch looked at each other. Bo said, "We don't really know much about mining, but we've guarded ore shipments before—"

Hopkins made a curt gesture. "Not at the mines."

"Well," Scratch said, "it's true we've clerked in stores and mucked out stables, but we ain't really lookin' for jobs like that right now—"

"We don't want to hire you to work at any of our own businesses," Esperanza said. "We want to hire you to work for the town of Silverhill."

"As lawmen," Dubonnet added.

"Specifically," Carling said, "we're offering you the job of town marshal, Mr. Creel, and we'd like you to serve as deputy, Mr. Morton."

CHAPTER 3

Silverhill had had a town marshal when Bo and Scratch arrived with the young ladies, but the man wasn't good for much of anything except locking up drunks when they got too loud and obnoxious. Then he had disappeared during the trouble a couple of weeks earlier, and no one knew what had happened to him until a man came forward to claim that he had seen the marshal riding out of town in the dead of night, obviously seeking greener—and less dangerous—pastures somewhere else.

Since then, the marshal's office and jail had been locked up, unoccupied.

Surprised by the unexpected offer, Bo and Scratch hemmed and hawed, explaining that they already had a job working for Cyrus Keegan's matrimonial agency back in Fort Worth.

"That's hardly suitable employment for a pair of men such as yourselves," W. J. M. Carling insisted.

"That's right," Albert Hopkins added. "You're frontiers-men, not . . . not nannies!"

Scratch scowled and started to stand up at that, but Bo put a hand on his arm and said, "Looking out for those young ladies is a mite more of a chore than that, Mr. Hopkins, and you ought to know it, considering everything that's happened."

"I meant no offense, but you know what I *did* mean, Creel. You're accustomed to action and excitement. Keeping the peace in a young and burgeoning settlement such as this promises both of those things."

The mining magnate was right about that. Just because Silverhill had been relatively quiet in recent days was no guarantee that it would stay that way. In fact, Bo was certain some new fracas would bust out anytime now. That was just the nature of things in a boomtown.

"You're already staying here, waiting for your next job," Esperanza said. "And because you've grown fond of those five señoritas, am I right?"

"We'd like to see 'em settled in good and proper before we leave," Scratch admitted.

Dubonnet spread his hands and asked, "Then why not take the job and see how it goes while you're waiting? That way, you make some money *and* help out the town."

It was a compelling argument, and as Bo glanced at his old friend, he could tell that Scratch felt the same way. Neither of them cared for just sitting around and doing nothing. They were a far cry from young, but they weren't nearly old enough—at least in their own minds—to be put out to pasture.

"It's something we might be willing to think about," Bo said, "but there's one condition."

"We're willing to pay you an excellent salary—" Esperanza began, but Bo cut him short.

"It's not about the salary."

"Wait a minute," Scratch said. "I wouldn't mind hearin' what you boys had in mind to pay."

"Seventy-five dollars a month for the marshal and sixty for the deputy," Hopkins said. "And we don't intend to negotiate, by the way."

"But we'll also pick up the expense of your hotel room," Dubonnet added. Hopkins scowled at him, as if he would have preferred that the storekeeper hold on to that card and not play it unless they needed it.

"That's fine," Bo said, "but my condition is that Scratch will be your marshal and I'll be the deputy."

The other five men at the table stared at him.

"And I don't intend to negotiate about that, either," Bo added.

"Bo, what in tarnation?" Scratch said.

Bo smiled at his friend and said, "That's just the way I want it. But if you don't want to go along with that, I don't blame you a bit, and we don't have to take the job."

"Hold on, hold on," Carling said. "We have no objection to that arrangement, do we, gentlemen?"

The other three community leaders shrugged and shook their heads.

"We always figured the two of you would work together," Carling went on. "I don't see how this changes things to any great extent. So what say you? Will you take the jobs?"

Scratch frowned for a second, then said, "Sure, I reckon. Won't be the first time we've pinned on badges, although it's been a while and it ain't that common." He paused. "I don't reckon you fellas'd say something to the folks in the cafés and the saloons about free food and drinks . . ."

At the dubious looks on the faces of Bo and the other men, Scratch held up his hands and quickly went on, "Nope, nope, that wouldn't be right. I realize that now. Just forget I said anything, gents. Your marshal needs to be a law-abidin', morally upstandin' hombre, and I figure on fittin' that bill."

With that settled, they sat and drank their coffee for a few minutes, but the other men were anxious to get back to their various enterprises.

Dubonnet pushed badges across the table to Bo and Scratch, followed by a pair of keys.

"Those unlock the door to the marshal's office," the storekeeper said. "There are keys in the desk that unlock the door to the cellblock and the cells themselves. If you gentlemen need anything else, let one of us know and we'll do our best to see that you get it. Is there anything else?"

Scratch looked at Bo, but when Bo just returned the look blandly, the silver-haired Texan said, "Nope, I reckon not. We're obliged to you for the faith you're puttin' in us. We'll try not to let you down."

"I'm certain you won't," Carling said as he got to his feet. "Perhaps we'll all be fortunate, and peace and quiet will reign in Silverhill."

That tranquil respite lasted almost twenty-four hours after Bo and Scratch took office as the settlement's lawmen.

Then three hard cases rode into town, tied their horses at the hitch rail in front of the Silver King, and went into the saloon. Bo was less than a block away, having just stepped out of the café where he had eaten lunch—paying full price for the meal—and he got a good look at the trio of hard-bitten strangers.

Bo had heard lawmen talk about how their instincts allowed them to spot owlhoots and killers. Bo wasn't a natural-born star packer, but he knew trouble when he saw it, and those three were bloody chaos on the hoof. He walked quickly back to the marshal's office, where Scratch was holding down the fort.

In point of fact, Scratch was holding down the swivel chair behind the old, scarred desk. The chair was tilted back so he could rest his boots on the desk. He swung his feet to the floor and sat up quickly, though, when he saw the expression on Bo's face.

"What's wrong?"

"Three hombres just rode into town and went into the Silver King," Bo said. "For some reason, they looked familiar to me . . . and I've got a hunch I know why."

He went around the desk to open the large bottom drawer on the right. Inside was a thick stack of wanted posters. Evidently, the previous occupant of the office had stuffed them in there as they arrived, probably without ever paying much attention to them.

The previous day, after he and Scratch had unlocked the stuffy office and opened the door and windows so it could air out, Bo had sat down and leafed through all those reward dodgers, out of idle curiosity more than anything else. And while he had been at it, he'd made sure there weren't any posters with his or Scratch's name and likeness on them.

Every time they had wound up on the wrong side of the law in the past, it had been because of a misunderstanding or because they'd been framed—or because Scratch had gotten too friendly with some woman without knowing that she was married to a sheriff or a politician. . . .

The important thing was that Bo was pretty sure they weren't wanted for anything in New Mexico Territory, but there was no telling where all these wanted posters had come from. There might be some in there from other states and territories.

Thankfully, he hadn't found any such incriminating documents, but while he'd gone through the posters, he had studied the faces of the wanted men they depicted, and some of them had stuck in Bo's brain.

Such as the outlaw on the poster he set in front of Scratch now. "Tater Malone. He was one of them." Bo continued flipping through the stack of papers he had taken from the desk. After a moment he dropped another one in front of Scratch. "And Newt Scanlon . . . And this fella here, Jed Bugle. The three of them rode into town together and went into the Silver King just a few minutes ago."

Scratch moved the reward dodgers around until they were side by side and studied them.

"Looks like they should've paid more attention in Sunday school," he said. "They been sinnin' right and left . . . bank robbery, stagecoach holdups, killin's . . ." He tapped a finger on each of the posters in turn. "Five hundred, five hundred, and eight hundred. That's eighteen hundred bucks for the three of 'em! That'd keep us in high cotton for a long time!"

"We've already got jobs," Bo pointed out. "Two of them, in fact. And if we go after these boys for the rewards, that'll be three jobs, because it would make us bounty hunters. Our jurisdiction extends only to the edges of Silverhill, and they haven't committed any crimes here, that I know of."

Scratch frowned and said, "We never have gone huntin' blood money."

"No, we haven't," Bo agreed.

"On the other hand, these are bad hombres. If we let

them go, they're bound to hurt more folks in the future, and I don't like to think about how we'd sorta be responsible for some of that."

"There's that to consider," Bo said, nodding.

"Plus, we just naturally don't like outlaws, even though we been accused of belongin' to that breed our own selves, more'n once."

"True enough. What do you believe we ought to do, Marshal?"

Scratch took a deep breath and said, "I reckon we ought to march on down to the Silver King and arrest those varmints. Not for the rewards, mind you, but because it's the right thing to do." He sighed. "Of course, chances are they won't come peaceable-like."

Bo was about to agree with that when the sound of rapid footsteps came from outside. The office door swung open a second later, and a townsman with a frightened but excited look on his face burst in and said, "Marshal, there's been a shooting!"

Scratch came to his feet and asked, "Whereabouts?"

The answer didn't come as much of a surprise when the man said, "Down at the Silver King." He stood there a second to catch his breath, then hurried on. "Some stranger took exception to Hobey Biggers's piano playing. Hobey was playing 'Dixie,' and the fella told him to stop it, and Hobey said if he didn't like it, he could go climb a stump . . . Hobey'd been drinking, you know, the way he does . . . and the stranger just up and hauls out a gun and shoots him!"

"Is Mr. Biggers dead?" Bo asked.

"Yes, sir. That man plugged him right in the ticker. You could tell by the way he hit the floor that he was gone."

Scratch said, "You saw all this yourself?"

The townsman nodded enthusiastically. "Yes, sir, with my own eyes! But I was by the side door, and when I saw Hobey go down like that and knew he was dead, I slipped out without any of those fellas noticing and came to fetch you lickety-split."

"Funny we didn't hear the shot," Bo commented.

"Well, it was pretty loud in there, right up until the time that hombre pulled the trigger. Then the whole place got quiet. Mighty quiet." The townie jerked a thumb over his shoulder. "You gonna go arrest those fellas?"

"Seems like we might ought to," Scratch said. "We got jurisdiction now, once they went to gunnin' down piano players inside the town limits."

"We sure enough do," Bo agreed.

He stepped over to the rifle rack and took down a Winchester, checked to see that it was loaded, and then joined Scratch in walking out of the office. The man who had come to tell them about the shooting hurried off to spread the word. Within seconds, the townspeople who were out and about began hunting cover in anticipation of bullets flying.

Bo and Scratch looked along the street, saw the three wanted men saunter out of the Silver King, three blocks away, and stop short before going to their horses.

"Looks like they noticed us," Scratch said.

"Yeah, but they're not trying to get away. Appears they're just going to stand there and wait for us."

"Well, then . . . I reckon we'd best oblige them."

Now, with the shooting over and the three outlaws dead, Bo and Scratch returned to the marshal's office. Bo put the reloaded Winchester back in the rack, while Scratch went to the potbellied stove in the corner and picked up the coffeepot that had been left sitting on it to stay warm. He sloshed the contents back and forth and said, "Little bit left. You want some?"

"Might as well," Bo said. He hung his hat on a nail driven into the wall, while Scratch filled two tin cups with the strong black coffee he had brewed earlier in the day and brought them over to the desk.

Scratch sat down, thumbed his hat back on his head, and said, "You know, this is a good thing. There was bound to be some more trouble sometime, but now we've got it out of the way and things can go back to bein' peaceful."

"Yeah," Bo said as he nodded and picked up his coffee cup. "I'm sure that's exactly the way it'll work out."

CHAPTER 4

Cecilia Spaulding strolled along the aisles of Dubonnet's Mercantile Emporium. Since Silverhill was a mining boomtown, much of the store's space was taken up by tools and equipment and tough, sturdy clothing for the men who worked in the mines.

But there was a small area devoted to ladies' fashions, and while Cecilia was certain the garments in this part of the store were hardly up to date with what was stylish back East, she still enjoyed browsing through them. Four Corners, her hometown in Iowa, hadn't exactly been Paris or New York, either.

She was holding up a green dress with a froth of lace at the collar when a man said behind her, "You'd look mighty nice in that, Miss Cecilia."

She recognized the voice, so she didn't get in any hurry to turn around. Instead, she said coolly, "I didn't realize you were an expert on ladies' fashions, Mr. Craddock."

Hugh Craddock moved around her so she couldn't help but see him standing there, large and formidable looking. He was older than her but not excessively so, in his middle thirties. He had the vitality of a younger man about him, as well. His curly brown hair under a pushed-back tan Stetson, his regular features, and the slight cleft in his chin made him undeniably handsome, but the self-confidence in his expression bordered on arrogance and mitigated his attractiveness. Especially to Cecilia, who had no use for arrogant men in general and Hugh Craddock in particular.

Craddock wore range clothes, but they were expensive and showed no signs of wear. He owned a successful ranch southwest of Fort Worth, and although he normally worked his stock alongside the cowboys who rode for his brand, he dressed well for pursuing the woman he intended to marry: Cecilia Spaulding.

They had first encountered each other in Fort Worth, in the office of Cyrus Keegan's matrimonial agency. Cecilia had been there with her friends, preparing for the trip to Silverhill, while Craddock had come to complain about the match Keegan had arranged for him. Miss Susan Hampshire had come to Fort Worth to marry Craddock, but when they met for the first time, Craddock had flatly rejected the idea, claiming that Miss Hampshire had deceived him by pretending to be younger that she really was.

From the first time Craddock had laid eyes on Cecilia during that chance meeting, he had claimed to be in love with her and had insisted that *she* was the woman he was actually meant to marry. Cecilia hadn't felt the same way at all, and the fact that Craddock had followed all of them to Silverhill and continued to stick his nose into her affairs hadn't made her change her mind about him.

Besides, she had met Susan Hampshire, too, and thought that the woman was lovely and very nice. She was about the same age as Craddock and would have made a perfectly fine wife for him, if he hadn't been so blasted stubborn.

Craddock gave Cecilia one of those maddeningly self-assured grins of his and said, "I don't pretend to be an expert on much of anything, Miss Cecilia, and certainly not ladies' fashions. But I know when something will look good, and take my word for it, you'll be beautiful in that dress. Of course, you're beautiful in anything you wear—"

"That's enough flattery, Mr. Craddock," she said, cutting him off.

"You can call me Hugh. I think I've told you that once or twice—or twenty times—before now."

Cecilia didn't respond to that. She turned away and moved on along the aisle to a display of hats, several of them adorned with feathers or ribbons. She picked one up and pretended to look more closely at it while she wished that Craddock would just go away.

He was nothing if not persistent. He stepped around her again and said, "I've heard there's going to be a social at the town hall in a couple of weeks. It would be a pure pleasure if you'd attend with me, Miss Cecilia."

"A social?" she repeated, interested in spite of herself. "I hadn't heard anything about it."

Craddock made a face. "Oh, shoot. I probably shouldn't have said anything about it, since you and your friends are supposed to be the guests of honor. I think some of the leading citizens of the town feel bad that the festivities a few weeks ago didn't quite go the way they were intended to, and they want to make it up to you."

"Yes, bandit raids and attempted robberies and bloody gun battles do tend to throw a crimp into any festivities," Cecilia said dryly.

"Well, anyway, I'd certainly be pleased if you'd be my guest for this get-together, Miss Cecilia—"

"If the other ladies and I are to be the guests of honor," she interrupted him, "I don't believe it would be proper to restrict myself to the attentions of one gentleman. The only fair thing to do would be to dance with as many different gentlemen as possible."

Craddock's jaw tightened at that. Anger sparked in his eyes as he said, "You're making fun of me, Miss Cecilia."

"Not at all," she said. "You do a fine job of that yourself, Mr. Craddock."

She left him there fuming and walked toward the big double doors at the front of the store. For a change, Craddock didn't trail after her like a lovesick puppy.

She almost felt sorry for him, Cecilia thought. It must be a terrible thing to be completely smitten with a person but not have that interest returned.

That sympathy lasted only a second, though. Whatever "suffering" Hugh Craddock was enduring, he had it coming.

She had succeeded in putting him out of her mind completely by the time she reached the high porch in front of the store, which also served as a loading dock. A wagon, probably from one of the mines in the nearby hills, was parked in front of the store as a couple of clerks loaded crates of supplies into the back of it. The driver was nowhere in sight. *Probably off in one of the saloons, getting a beer*, she thought.

Cecilia went down the steps at the end of the porch. A man approached the store from the other direction, but she didn't pay any attention to him as she turned to cross the street and go back to the hotel. She had only a vague impression that he was large—and her nose wrinkled at the gamy, unwashed smell that came from him or his garments, or both.

At that moment, one of the clerks loading the wagon stumbled, and the crate in his hands slipped from his grip and crashed down in the back of the vehicle. Startled by the noise, the four horses hitched to the wagon lunged forward against their harness so violently that the clerk yelled as he was thrown over backward and landed among the supplies already loaded.

Normally, the brake would have stopped the wagon and the team from going anywhere. But the driver, perhaps anxious to get that beer, had forgotten to set the brake, and the horses pounded toward Cecilia, only a few steps away.

She saw them coming and probably could have jumped back out of their path, but before she was able to make a move, someone grabbed her from behind, lifted her off the ground as if she weighed nothing, and swung her back to safety at the foot of the steps. An arm that seemed as thick as the trunk of a young tree remained clamped around her waist, and the smell she had gotten a whiff of a moment earlier surrounded her now, making her gag.

The man hadn't just grabbed her and pulled her out of the way. With his other hand, he had snagged the harness of the closest horse as it went past him and had hauled back on it, bringing team and wagon to an abrupt halt. That was quite a feat of strength, and even in her startled state, Cecilia realized that.

Forcing the words out past the tight grip, she said, "You can . . . let go of me now."

"Oh!" her rescuer exclaimed. "Oh, yeah." The brawny

arm fell away from her waist. "I'm plumb sorry, ma'am. I meant no offense—"

"That's quite . . . all right," Cecilia said. She was breathless from the combination of being grabbed, the near miss of being trampled, the strong odor filling her nostrils, and the sheer size of the man looming over her.

He stood well over six feet tall and had shoulders as broad as an ax handle. It was hard to tell how he was built, because of the ratty buffalo coat draped around him, but she assumed that thick slabs of muscle covered his back, shoulders, and chest. That had to be the case for him to have stopped the wagon team like that. A battered, sweatstained old hat was tipped back on a tangled thatch of brown hair, and a bushy brown beard covered his cheeks, jaw, and chin. He bore a distinct resemblance to the buffalo that had provided the material for his coat. He wore thick canvas trousers and old, scarred boots, and he was unarmed, as far as Cecilia could see.

She didn't want to delve under that coat to find out if he carried a gun. The stench would be horrible, she imagined.

"Are yuh hurt?" he rumbled.

"No, I . . . I'm fine," she assured him.

A man hurried toward them from the direction of the Silver King. He lifted a hand and called, "Hey! Hey, what're you doin' with my team, you big ox? If you're tryin' to steal that wagon—"

The horses had settled down now. The big man let go of the team's harness and turned toward the angry newcomer.

"That your wagon?" he demanded.

"Yeah, and you got no right to be messin' with . . . Whoa!"

He let out the startled exclamation as the big man took hold of him under the arms, lifted him off the ground, and started to shake him.

"What in blazes were yuh thinkin', goin' off and leavin' that wagon without settin' the brake? Somebody coulda got hurt! That pretty lady almost got trampled! Why, I oughta . . ."

Cecilia didn't hear the rest of the rant, because at that moment Hugh Craddock grasped her arm and turned her to face him.

"Miss Cecilia," he said. "Are you all right? I heard all the commotion out here."

"I'm fine," she said as she tried to work her arm out of his grasp. "It's nothing to worry about."

A few feet away, the big man was shaking the teamster so hard that the man's head jerked back and forth wildly. There was no telling how much damage the giant might have done if he hadn't glanced back over his shoulder and seen Craddock clutching Cecilia's arm. Evidently, he didn't like that, either, because he stopped shaking the teamster and flung him away. The man sailed a good ten feet through the air before landing on his back and skidding along the dusty street for a couple more yards before he came to a stop and lay there, stunned.

The big man swung around, took two stomping steps, and poked a sausage-like finger against Craddock's chest hard enough to make him jerk back.

"Are you botherin' this poor woman?"

Craddock's face darkened with rage. He let go of Cecilia, but as soon as he did, his hand dropped to the holstered gun at his hip. Cecilia saw that and moved quickly to put herself between the two men. She didn't want Craddock to hurt the massive stranger, who, judging by his slow, lumbering words, wasn't overly bright. She knew Craddock wouldn't draw his gun if she was in the way.

"I'm fine," she said again, and the words were directed at both men this time. "It was a near accident, that's all. No one is hurt."

Francis Dubonnet had emerged from his store to see what the ruckus was about, too. From the top of the porch steps, he said, "I'm not so sure about that, Miss Spaulding." He nodded toward the man lying in the street. "The driver from the Santa Clara hasn't gotten up yet."

Cecilia recognized that name. The Santa Clara Mine was one of the big, lucrative operations in the hills. She thought a man named Hopkins owned it, but she wasn't sure about that.

The driver groaned, so he wasn't dead. Dubonnet said to his clerks, including the one who'd dropped the crate and sparked the near disaster, "Go help him up. Make sure he's not hurt too bad."

"Sure, boss. That big fella was shaking him like a dog with a rat! Never seen the likes of it."

Dubonnet narrowed his eyes at the big man. "I know you. You work at the Minotaur, don't you?"

"Yup," the man said. With a hand that was so grimy with ingrained dirt it was almost black, he dragged his hat off his head and held it awkwardly while he nodded to Cecilia and went on, "They call me Roscoe, ma'am. Roscoe Sherman."

Craddock still looked angry. Cecilia put her back to him and summoned up a smile as she said, "Thank you for helping me, Mr. Sherman."

"Aw, shucks. 'Tweren't nothin'." Roscoe Sherman looked

embarrassed and uncomfortable now. Faced with this petite brunette, he had lost the self-confidence his huge size gave him. "I just seen them horses fixin' to tromple you an' figured I'd better get yuh outta the way."

"Well, I appreciate what you did." No one could ever actually get used to that smell, Cecilia thought, but at least it didn't seem quite so overpowering now. "Are you a miner?"

"Yes'm. At the Minotaur, like Mr. Dubonnet there done said. It's, uh . . . I reckon it's about all a fella like me is good for." He brightened. "But I'm mighty good at breakin' rocks and totin' rocks."

"I'm sure you are, Mr. Sherman."

"Aw, shoot, you don't need to call me mister. Roscoe's fine. That's what the fellas at the mine call me." He lowered his voice a little, although with his booming tones, he couldn't accomplish much in that area. "They call me some other things, too, but nothin' a fine lady like yourself could ever say."

Cecilia managed to smile again. "Well, I'm going to call you Mr. Sherman whether you like it or not."

He ducked his head and wiped at his nose with the back of the hand holding his hat. "Never said I didn't like it, ma'am."

By this time, Dubonnet's clerks had gotten the wagon driver on his feet and had helped him over to the vehicle. He stood there shaking the cobwebs out of his head and glaring at Roscoe Sherman. He found his voice and said, "I oughta get the law on you, you big lummox. You coulda killed me—"

Roscoe scowled at him and said, "You're the one who didn't set the derned brake. You're lucky I didn't put my boot right up your—" He stopped, drew in a breath, and went on to Cecilia, "Sorry, ma'am. Sometimes I rile up too easy."

Craddock snapped, "Well, you've done your good deed, and the lady thanked you. Why don't you go on about your business?" Without waiting for Roscoe to respond, he turned back to Cecilia. "Now, about that town social we were discussing . . ."

Cecilia lifted her chin. It was true that she was grateful to Roscoe Sherman for what he had done. She thought she might have been able to get out of the way of the startled horses on her own, but if she hadn't . . . if she had stumbled and fallen, say . . . that could have been very bad for her indeed.

For the most part, though, she had been nice to this hulking, smelly miner because she knew it would annoy Hugh Craddock. She knew that, even though it meant admitting to herself that she was capable of being rather petty at times. Craddock just annoyed her so much. . . .

Still, none of that explained what she did next. She interrupted Craddock by saying, "Speaking of that social . . ." She turned to Roscoe Sherman and went on, "In gratitude for what you've done for me, Mr. Sherman, I think it only appropriate that I ask you to be my escort to the social."

CHAPTER 5

Bo had been a couple of blocks down the street when he heard the loud, angry voices. Several days had passed since the shoot-out with the three outlaws in front of the Silver King, and during that time the settlement had been peaceful. He and Scratch hadn't even had to lock up any drunks.

Despite that, the Texans continued to take their new jobs seriously. One of them was usually in the marshal's office, while the other strolled around town, nodding politely and exchanging small talk with folks, mostly for the purpose of letting everybody know that the law was around.

Now it sounded like trouble was trying to break out again, although Bo hadn't heard any shots yet, just yelling. He didn't break into a run, but he didn't waste any time walking up the street toward the commotion.

As he came closer, he saw a crowd gathered in front of Francis Dubonnet's store. One man was being helped up out of the street by a couple of Dubonnet's clerks. Several other people stood beside a wagon at the end of the store's porch, including a towering figure Bo didn't recognize.

He saw someone he did recognize, though, as the big

man moved aside a little. His pace increased as he realized that Cecilia Spaulding was in the middle of the commotion, whatever it was.

Bo arrived just in time to hear Cecilia ask the giant to be her escort to the upcoming town social. He and Scratch had just heard about the social this morning. Hector Esperanza had told them about it while they were at the livery stable, checking on their horses. Bo didn't think it was a bad idea, necessarily—but he had seen trouble break out pretty often at gatherings like that, even if it was just a couple of cowboys drinking too much spiked punch and getting into a fight over a gal.

Looked like this social might start a ruckus long before the fiddler ever rosined up his bow. Hugh Craddock's expression clouded up to rain, and he exclaimed, "What! You can't mean that, Miss Cecilia!"

"Oh?" she responded to him with an icy note in her voice. "And why shouldn't I attend the social with Mr. Sherman?"

"Well . . . well . . . look at him!" Craddock blustered. He waved a hand at the big, shaggy gent in the buffalo coat. "You can't go with an oaf like that."

"I don't cotton to name-callin'," the big man rumbled. "Whether it's me bein' called names or somebody else."

Cecilia nodded and said, "That's a very admirable attitude to have, Mr. Sherman."

"But he stinks!" Craddock burst out.

That was true enough, Bo had to admit. He was hanging back some, and he had no trouble smelling Roscoe from where he was. The others were even closer. But there had been plenty of times in his life when nobody would have mistaken him for a rose. That didn't necessarily mean a whole lot.

"That's none of your business, Mr. Craddock," Cecilia said, even chillier now. She turned a bright smile toward the hulking figure. "How about it, Mr. Sherman? Will you do me the honor of escorting me?"

Roscoe looked like he would have rather been somewhere else, but he shuffled his feet and said, "I reckon I can't refuse a lady like you, ma'am." He scratched at the beard jutting out from his chin. "It just come to me that I don't know your name."

"It's Cecilia. Cecilia Spaulding."

She held out a pale, dainty hand. Roscoe hesitated, then reached out tentatively, as if he were about to pick up a rattlesnake. His filthy hand completely engulfed her clean and manicured one, but he clasped it only for the briefest of seconds, then let it go, looked down at the ground, and muttered something unintelligible that sounded like an apology.

"I'm very pleased to meet you, too," Cecilia said.

Hugh Craddock made a disgusted sound, threw his hands up in the air, and turned on his heel to stalk off. Bo was glad to see him go. Craddock was a troublemaker, had been ever since he had first met the rancher back in Fort Worth.

"I don't know exactly when the social is," Cecilia went on, "but I'm sure you can find out. I'm staying at the Territorial House. You can call for me there that evening. Does that sound all right to you?"

Roscoe was starting to look lost and confused now. He swallowed hard, making his beard bob, and jerked his head in a nod.

"I reckon. If'n you're sure that's what you want."

"It is."

"I can, uh . . . oh, shoot." Roscoe closed his eyes and

rubbed his temples, as if all this thinking was making his head hurt. "I can clean up a mite, if you figure I should . . ."

"That would be very nice," Cecilia told him. "You won't forget, will you?"

"No, ma'am . . ." Roscoe glanced around, looking for all the world like a man searching for a way to escape, Bo thought. The big man's gaze landed on Francis Dubonnet, and he said hurriedly, "Yuh got a package here I'm supposed to pick up. For Mr. Carling, I mean. It's come in, ain't it?"

"That's right. I do," Dubonnet said. "Come on in. I'll get it for you."

Roscoe nodded to Cecilia and said, "So long, ma'am. Miss Spauldin'. I'll be seein' yuh."

"You certainly will," Cecilia said. As Roscoe clumped up the stairs to follow Dubonnet into the emporium, Cecilia turned to Bo and went on, "Hello, Mr. Creel. I didn't see you come up."

"Hard to see much of anything with that man mountain filling up the scenery," Bo said. "What just happened here?"

Before Cecilia could answer, the man who had been lying in the street when Bo first saw him bustled over to them and said, "Marshal, I want you to go in there and arrest that big ox."

"It's Deputy," Bo corrected. "What did he do?"

"He blamed near broke my neck, that's what he did!"

"After your carelessness nearly caused a serious accident," Cecilia put in. "Perhaps I should pass that information along to your employer."

"No, no, you don't need to do that," the man said hastily. He started backing away. "I'm sorry for what happened, ma'am, I sure am. I'll never make a mistake like that again, I promise you."

Sniffing, Cecilia turned away from him. "It was just an accident, Mr. Creel," she said to Bo. "But no one was harmed."

"I'm glad to hear it. You don't want to make an official report?"

"Oh, no, that's not necessary."

"What about Craddock?"

Cecilia's lips thinned for a second as she pressed them together. "Mr. Craddock was being his usual persistent self," she said. "He thought I should go to the social with him."

"And he didn't care for it when you said you'd go with that big galoot instead." Bo chuckled. "I can understand you wanting to put a burr under Craddock's saddle, Cecilia, but I don't know if going to a dance with that hombre is the best way to do it. He smelled a mite . . . ripe."

"That's nothing some soap and good hot water can't fix." Cecilia looked like she was pondering something. "In fact, if that wild beard and hair were trimmed . . . and if he had some different clothes, instead of those filthy old things he had on . . . Mr. Roscoe might actually be presentable. It's hard to say. There's so much . . . obscuring what he really looks like . . ."

"Maybe so," Bo said, thinking that there was nothing some women liked better than a challenge, especially when that challenge involved taking a man and remolding him into what she thought he should be. Evidently, Cecilia was that sort.

Only he couldn't help but think that in the case of the massive, lumbering miner named Roscoe, she might be biting off more than she could chew.

* * *

Inside the building, Dubonnet led Roscoe Sherman to the back of the store and went behind the counter to rummage through some bundles stored on the shelves underneath it. He came up with a package wrapped in brown paper and tied with twine and set it on the counter with a solid thump.

"This is it, isn't it?" he asked. "From some bookseller back East?"

"Uh . . . I reckon," Roscoe said. "Nobody told me who it was from or what was in it. Said just to fetch it."

"Well, it's addressed to Mr. W. J. M. Carling at the Minotaur Mine." Dubonnet pointed to the writing on the paper, then shoved the package across the counter toward Roscoe. "I'll just charge it to the Minotaur's account."

"Nope. The boss gimme money to pay for it when he sent me into town," Roscoe said. He dug around in the pocket of his canvas trousers for a few seconds before coming up with a coin. "He said this here gold eagle would cover it."

Dubonnet frowned at the ten-dollar coin Roscoe slapped down on the counter next to the package, as if leery of picking it up after it had been that close to the big man's person. Business sense won out over fastidiousness, of course, and he scooped up the money.

"That's right. Thank you, Roscoe."

"Yes sir," Roscoe said, bobbing his head as he picked up the package and tucked it under his arm. "I'm mighty obliged to yuh."

"That's quite all right."

Still bobbing his head, as if he had trouble stopping once he started, Roscoe turned away and shuffled toward the door. He hummed to himself. He was well aware that all the customers he passed on his way out of the store turned away from him. Some of them even made faces when he went by. That didn't bother him.

The wagon that had been parked in front of the emporium was gone, along with its careless, belligerent driver. Roscoe was glad to see that. He didn't want to have any more trouble with the fella.

But Miss Cecilia Spaulding was also nowhere in sight, which was both a relief and the cause of a brief pang of sadness. The way she had asked him to escort her to that town social had taken him completely by surprise. He should have told her that he couldn't do that, but looking at her in that moment, it had seemed to him that the most important thing in the world was not disappointing her.

Now he was in a fix, and he didn't see any way out of it.

He'd have to ponder that, he told himself, but for now he needed to get back to the Minotaur. It would take the rest of the afternoon just to ride back into the hills to the mine, especially since he planned a brief stop along the way.

He had left his mule at one of the hitchracks along the street. When he reached the big, ugly brute, he tied the package of books to the saddle, then tugged the reins loose and swung up. Nobody bothered him as he rode out of town. A few people frowned at him in disapproval because he was so filthy and unkempt, but just like the reactions of the people in the store, he didn't care about that. He pointed the mule to the northeast, toward the rugged hills where the silver strike had been made.

This wasn't really scenic country, but there were a few pretty spots here and there. An hour after leaving Silverhill, when the settlement was far out of sight behind him, Roscoe reined up at one of those spots. The trail had been climbing for a while, and to his left, a little valley fell away, green with vegetation, dotted here and there with cactus roses, leading to a flat that glimmered off into the north in a haze of distance and purple sage. After regarding the view for a moment, Roscoe turned the mule and let the animal pick its way down the slope. When he stopped again, he dismounted, untied the bundle of books, and sat down on a rock. He took off his ragged old hat and set it beside him.

His thick, blunt fingers weren't made for tasks as delicate as untying the knots in the twine, but he managed it with surprising deftness. When he had the wrapping paper loose, he pulled back part of it and reached into the bundle to pull out one of the books. He placed the rest of them beside him on the rock, with his hat, and then looked at the one he held, running the fingertips of his other hand over the leather binding. His chest rose and fell in a sigh of contentment. He lifted his head, looked out over the valley again, and said, "A new edition of Lord Byron's poems, Mary. I'll see if I can find your favorite."

Then he opened the book, began turning through the pages, and stopped when he reached the one he wanted. His voice rang out, powerful and mellow, as he read "So We'll Go No More A-roving."

CHAPTER 6

Rose Winston leaned on a hitch rail and gazed long-ingly at the batwing doors of the Silver King Palace across the street. The way they flapped back and forth when someone went in or out seemed to call to her, entic-ing her to push them aside and enter the shadowy confines of the saloon herself.

"What in the world are you staring at?" Beth Macy wanted to know. She had walked up without Rose realizing she was there.

"You ever just wish you could stroll right into a saloon, go up to the bar, and order a drink like a man?"

"Not really," Beth said. "But I don't suppose there's any-thing stopping you, if that's what you really want to do."

Rose snorted as she straightened from the hitch rail. "Cecilia'd never let me hear the end of it. She'd be scolding me from now on about how it's not ladylike to do such things."

Beth smiled and said, "Not being ladylike has never stopped you before, has it?"

"You're a fine one to talk," Rose shot back at her. "You may be wearing a dress right now, but I've seen you in trousers and on horseback plenty of times, riding astride just like a man!"

"Just like *you*, you mean!"

Both of those accusations were true. Rose had grown up on a farm outside of Four Corners, so she had been around horses and other animals from the time she could walk, and since coming west, she had discovered that she was also good with a rope and a gun.

Beth's father, a former army officer, hadn't coddled his daughter while she was growing up, either. She had learned to drive his buggy for him when she was just a girl, and she had proven to be good at handling teams of horses or mules hitched to wagons. Both young women were headstrong and didn't like to be left out of anything that interested them.

"I don't think you actually want a drink," Beth said. "You just don't like being told that you can't go in there and order one like a man."

"Well, it's not fair!"

"Plenty of things in life aren't fair. You should have learned that by now."

Beth might have continued the discussion, but at that moment a sound caught her attention, and she turned to look toward the eastern end of town. She lifted a hand to shade her eyes as she peered into the distance. It didn't take long to spot the dust cloud rising from the trail outside of town. As she and Rose watched, the sandy-gray column drew closer.

"It's the stagecoach!" Beth said.

The stagecoach made twice-weekly runs between El Paso and Silverhill. There had been a great deal of talk about the railroad building a spur line to the settlement. Construction on that line had gotten under way recently.

When the railroad arrived in Silverhill, more than likely telegraph wires would, too.

For the time being, though, the stagecoach was the main method of communication between Silverhill and the outside world. Because of that, the coach's arrival was always greeted with enthusiasm and excitement from the citizens.

That wasn't exactly the reason Beth was happy to see it coming, though, and Rose knew it. She laughed and said, "You want to moon over that handsome shotgun guard some more, don't you?"

"What? I don't know what you're talking about!" Beth's vehement denial didn't ring true. She turned pink and looked uncomfortable.

Rose went on, "I've seen the way you stared at him the last few times the coach has stopped here in town. You always manage to be somewhere close to the station when it's due so you can get a good look at him."

"No I don't. I just . . . it just so happened . . . I'm not going to talk about this. It's just crazy!"

Beth lifted her chin defiantly and stalked off. Rose noticed, however, that when she left, she went in the direction of the stagecoach station. Beth could make whatever claims she wanted to, but Rose knew what was going on.

The coach slowed as it reached the edge of town. The driver kept the reins taut and the team moving at a sedate pace, since it wasn't safe for the horses to race unchecked along the busy street. Rose went around the hitch rail and leaned back against it, resting her elbows on it, as she watched the stagecoach roll past her.

The driver was a stocky, barrel-chested older man with a drooping gray mustache. The shotgun guard was much younger, in his mid-twenties, with a brown hat shoved back on a shock of sandy hair. He held a double-barreled coach gun, with the butt resting on the seat beside him and the twin barrels pointing at the sky. Both men wore long dusters.

The guard glanced over at Rose as they passed and nodded to her, but it was just a polite gesture, nothing more. His expression was all business. He took his job seriously. Rose thought he actually *was* handsome, as she had said to Beth, but he wasn't the sort of hombre who appealed to her. He was too stiff necked and stodgy. She liked a man who liked a little excitement . . . not that she was actually very experienced in such things. But she wanted to be.

After the stagecoach had gone past, Rose turned to look again toward the Silver King. The clatter of hoofbeats drew her attention as several riders drew up in front of the saloon. As Rose watched, all but one of them dismounted and headed inside. She recognized them as punchers from the SJ Ranch, located thirty miles north of Silverhill, where some decent cattle range could be found, instead of the rugged hills, where silver ore lurked, buried in the earth.

One of the cowboys stood beside the hitch rail for a moment instead of going into the saloon with his friends. He turned, looked diagonally across the street, as if he had sensed Rose looking at him, and locked eyes with her. The two of them stood there like that for several seconds, and then he started across the street toward her. That drink he had ridden to town for seemed to be forgotten, at least for now.

Rose recognized him as he came closer. He was a lean, darkhaired young buckaroo about her age. His range garb included a leather vest with pockets decorated with silver and turquoise conchas. A black-butted Colt rode in a holster slung on his right hip. He took off his black hat, which had a thin layer of trail dust on it, as he approached her.

"Miss Rose," he greeted her. "Do you remember me?"

"Of course I do," she said. "You won the big horse race during those festivities that went all wrong."

When the mail-order brides had arrived in Silverhill, instead of the arranged marriages they had been expecting, they had discovered that dozens of men from all around the area—miners, cowboys, teamsters, store clerks, almost anybody who was male, single, and had a pulse—had signed up for a series of competitions, which had included the horse race she mentioned. The winners of those competitions hadn't been guaranteed that one of the young ladies would agree to marry them—but as prizes for their victories, they'd been awarded first chance and the inside track on courting Rose and her friends.

She went on, "Your name is . . . Stan, I think?"

"Steve," he said, correcting her.

Actually, she knew good and well what his name was, but it was better to let him think he hadn't made that much of an impression on her. Otherwise he was liable to get a swelled head about it.

"Steve Hargett," he continued, holding his hat in front of him. "I ride for the SJ brand."

"I remember. Your foreman is Mr. Plummer."

"Yes'm. It's mighty nice to see you again." He paused. "Have you, uh . . . has anybody been courtin' . . . ? I mean, you're bound to have plenty of suitors—"

"Not really," Rose interrupted him. She made a little sound of disgust. "Seems like a lot of the men around here don't know what to make of it when a girl can ride a horse and shoot a gun just about as well as they can."

"Well, that sure wouldn't bother me," Steve Hargett declared. "I was really lookin' forward to getting to know you. I mean, after I won the horse race and all . . ."

"And then everything went to hell, didn't it?" Rose asked with a smile.

"It did, for a fact."

"But you're here now," she told him. "I didn't know if I'd ever see you again."

"You didn't think I'd ride back down here to, uh, claim my prize?"

Rose raised an eyebrow and asked, "Just what do you think that prize is, *Steve*?" She drew out his name like that so he could tell that she wasn't really all that impressed with him.

"I figured I'd take you to dinner," he said. "In some nice restaurant, if we can find one here in Silverhill."

That answer surprised her a little. She nodded toward the saloon and said, "What about your friends who went in the Silver King? Weren't you planning on having a drink with them?"

He grinned. "Those hairy-legged boys can get along without me, I reckon. Anyway, all the time we were ridin' to town, I was hopin' I'd run into you, Miss Rose. And I was really hopin' you hadn't gone and got yourself hitched already."

"Well, I haven't. And I accept your invitation to dinner, Mr. Hargett." It wouldn't hurt anything to be nicer to him now. He was good looking, but he also had a bit of a wild, "Go to the devil" sparkle in his dark blue eyes. Rose liked that attitude. Steve Hargett struck her as being a lot more interesting than, say, that dull shotgun guard Beth had her eye on.

"I think I'll mosey on down to the barbershop and get cleaned up a mite," Steve went on. "And then I'll figure out where we're going to eat, and I'll come by the hotel and pick you up later on. Does that sound all right to you, Miss Rose?"

"I suppose so. You don't have to call me Miss Rose, you know. I'll answer to just Rose."

He smiled and said, "You could never be 'just Rose' to me, ma'am."

Rose felt her face getting warmer. Was she *blushing* at his flattery? Suddenly, she felt annoyed with herself, and it didn't get any better when she heard herself saying, "I'd better put on a nice dress . . ."

"You wear whatever you want. I'm sure you'll look mighty fine . . . Rose."

Danged if he wasn't smooth. She nodded and said, "All right. I'll see you later. Around dusk?"

"I'll call for you at the Territorial House." He held his hat over his heart and nodded. "Good-bye for now."

"Good-bye," she said.

Then, as he turned and walked off toward the barber-shop, she looked around quickly to make sure none of her friends were standing around and watching her make a simpering fool of herself. Thankfully, she didn't see Cecilia, Jean, or Luella, and Beth was down at the stagecoach station, mooning over that shotgun guard.

It was Beth's fault she'd acted like that, Rose told herself.

Whatever ailment Beth had, it must be catching.

Steve Hargett figured he would get just a shave and a haircut, but the barber pointed over his shoulder with a thick thumb and asked, "You want a bath, son? Got a tub of water back there that's only been used once, and I can have the Chinaman heat it up for you."

Steve looked at the curtain-covered doorway to the shop's back room and considered the suggestion.

"I can have those duds washed for you, too," the barber went on, gesturing at Steve's dusty range clothes.

"No, I don't reckon there's time for that," Steve replied with a shake of his head. "But maybe the Celestial fella could sort of knock some of the dust off of them?"

"Sure," the barber said. "He can brush off your hat real good, too. Then a shave and a haircut and plenty of bay rum, and you'll be a plumb gent instead of a scruffy cowpoke."

Some of his friends would take offense at a comment like that, Steve thought, but he didn't. All he could think about was how he wanted to impress Miss Rose Winston. She was just about the prettiest girl he'd ever seen, and something about her made his heart race.

"Let's get it done," he said. "How much?"

The barber thought. "Lessee . . . four bits apiece for the shave and haircut . . . Bath's normally a buck . . . And there's the Chinaman cleanin' up your clothes . . . I'll give you a good price, kid. Dollar and a half for everything."

That price actually seemed kind of high to Steve, but he didn't feel like arguing. He dug a handful of coins out of his pocket, picked through them until he had the right amount, and paid the man. Then the barber yelled at his Chinese assistant in some lingo that Steve didn't understand.

"The boy'll heat a few buckets of water and bring them in," the man told Steve. The "boy," who was middle aged and gray haired, bobbed his head. "Leave your clothes on the chair back there and he'll take care of 'em."

Steve nodded and went through the curtain. The big tin washtub took up most of the back room, along with a

ladderback chair in one corner and a short three-legged
stool in another. Steve sat down to take off his boots, then
unbuckled his gunbelt and hung it over the chair's back.
He stripped out of the dusty garb and piled it on the chair,
then placed his hat on top of it.

The water in the tub was cool but not ice cold, he discovered when he stepped into it. That hot water would feel
good when the Chinese man got around to bringing it.
Some soap scum floated on top of the water. Steve swiped
it aside as he sat down. He leaned back and closed his eyes.

Instantly, a vision filled his mind's eye . . . a vision of
Rose Winston. He sat there in the tub, thinking about her,
glad that some other hombre hadn't swooped in and dabbed
a loop on her in the time since he'd last been in Silverhill.
Of course, that hadn't really been very long, but as lovely
and wonderful as Rose was, any man who had a lick of
sense would move fast in his courtship and try to get her to
agree to marry him.

A little voice in the back of Steve's brain tried to warn
him that he had gone plumb loco. He had never given any
thought to getting married and settling down. He'd always
ridden high, wide, and handsome where the gals were
concerned, romancing saloon girls and cantina señoritas
from Laredo to Santa Fe.

Anyway, what could a fella like him offer a wife, really?
It was true, some of the hands who rode for the SJ were
married. The boss provided quarters for them and paid
them a little better, since he believed that married men
were a mite more stable and dependable than wild young
cowboys. And that was true, from what Steve had seen.
But still, it wasn't much of a life for a woman, unless her
husband could work his way up to being foreman someday.
And those opportunities didn't come around all that often.

No, if he really wanted to be fair to Rose, he ought not to rush her into anything, but rather try to figure out some other path for him to follow, something that might actually put enough money in his pocket so that he could provide a decent life for her.

There was one possibility, he mused, but he didn't really like the idea. . . .

He was thinking about that very thing when the curtain slid back and somebody stepped into the room. Steve figured it was the Chinese man with the hot water, but then the curtain snapped shut again. Steve opened his eyes, and considering what he had just been pondering, seeing the man who had just come in made startled words leap out of his mouth.

"Speak of the devil . . . "

The newcomer grinned as he turned from the curtain toward the washtub. His hand dropped to the gun at his hip and palmed it out. He thumbed back the hammer and held the gun so that the barrel pointed casually at the man in the tub.

"That's right, Steve," he said. "And I've come to collect on our bargain."

CHAPTER 7

Beth waved her hand back and forth in front of her face to clear away some of the dust as she approached the stagecoach, which had pulled up and stopped in front of the station.

Silverhill's stagecoach station was an adobe building with thick wooden vigas that stuck out from the top of the front wall and were supported by wooden pillars. Brush had been laid across the vigas in a latticework fashion to form a shady arbor, under which chairs had been placed. To the right of the building was a long shed with an attached pole corral, where extra horses for the stagecoach teams were kept between runs.

The passengers had already disembarked by the time Beth got there. The driver stood at the back of the vehicle, where he had unfastened the canvas cover over the boot and opened it so the passengers could retrieve their bags. A couple of men in tweed suits and derby hats reached into the boot and took out carpetbags and sample cases. Those would be traveling salesmen of some sort, Beth knew. Drummers.

The next man to get his bag also wore a suit, but he had

a Western hat on his graying head. A rancher, perhaps, or maybe a mine owner or an engineer, although he looked a little too well-to-do for that last possibility.

The fourth man off the stage was well dressed in a dark suit, too, but he had no hat, which was uncommon on the frontier. Dark haired and sleekly handsome, he lifted a carpetbag out of the boot and then reached inside to take out a smaller black leather bag. Unless Beth was mistaken, that was a medical bag.

Two ladies stepped up last, although describing them that way was probably a stretch. In their feathers and finery, and with their faces painted a bit too much, there wasn't any mistaking their profession. They smiled and laughed as the driver said, "Lemme get those for you, ladies," and reached into the boot to haul out their carpet-bags.

As Beth watched them walk up the street toward the saloons, where they would no doubt seek employment, she told herself sternly that she had no right to feel superior to them. Everyone had their own story in life, and it wasn't up to anyone on this earth to judge them. Unless they broke the law, of course.

All those impressions occupied only a matter of seconds, and then Beth turned her attention to the real reason she had come down here, although she wouldn't have admitted it. She watched as the shotgun guard unlocked the box under the driver's seat and took out the express company pouch. The pouch contained letters and other mail from back East, and sometimes it carried money or other valuables, as well. That was why a shotgun guard always rode along on the coach.

With the double-barreled Greener under his arm, the guard took the pouch into the station. The driver ambled up alongside the coach and put a hand against the door to steady himself. At first, Beth thought it was just a casual gesture, but then she saw the way his chest rose and fell rapidly as his breathing increased. With trail dust coating his features, it was hard to be sure, but she thought his face had turned gray, too. He was in some sort of distress.

Without any more warning than that, the driver groaned and slumped against the coach, and his knees buckled. Beth's eyes widened as she watched the man collapse.

She had always been coolheaded in moments of trouble. Her father, who had been a decorated young officer in the Mexican War and then had commanded a Union cavalry regiment during the War Between the States, had taught her how important it was to keep one's wits about one. When she saw the stagecoach driver fall to the street, she knew immediately what she needed to do.

Her head whipped around. She spotted the hatless man walking away from the station. She called, "Doctor! Doctor!" then hurried to the driver's side and dropped to her knees.

He was lying facedown in the dust. She was a strong young woman, so when she took hold of his shoulders, she was able to roll him over onto his back. His eyes were wide, too. He opened and closed his mouth, but nothing came out except a few strained gurgles. His left arm was drawn up, and that hand was clenched into a fist, which he pressed against his chest.

She leaned over him and said with as much confidence as she could muster, "You're going to be all right, sir. Just rest. Help is on the way."

She hoped that was correct.

Heavy footsteps sounded behind her. She thought it

might be the man with the medical bag, but to her surprise, the shotgun guard knelt next to her and said, "Fred! Fred, what happened?"

The driver struggled to find his voice. He managed to croak out, "Monte . . . By the great . . . horn spoon . . . it hurts!"

Beth couldn't take the time to think about how big and attractive the young man called Monte was as he knelt beside her, but it was impossible not to be aware of his physical presence. She said, "He just turned gray all of a sudden and leaned against the coach for a second, then collapsed."

"He's been complaining about his chest hurting, off and on," the guard said with a grim frown on his face. "But he swore up and down that it was nothing to worry about."

"Step back, please," a new voice said briskly. "I need some room here to examine this man."

It was the man with the medical bag. Beth looked up at him and asked, "You're a doctor?"

"That's right. Dr. Arliss Chapman. Now, if you don't mind . . ."

"Of course, of course." Beth started to stand up, but the shotgun guard made it to his feet first and took hold of her left arm to give her a hand. She was grateful for the strong grip and didn't mind it, but he let go of her as soon as they were both standing. They moved back to give the doctor room to kneel beside the fallen driver. A number of bystanders were starting to gather around, but they didn't come too close.

"I hope he's going to be all right," Beth said quietly.

"Yeah, me, too. Fred's a good hombre. We've been making this run together for a while."

"Yes, I know," Beth replied, then wondered instantly if she should have said that. It was pretty much an admission that she had been watching the stagecoach—and the men on it—when it arrived in and departed from Silverhill.

A man Beth recognized as the manager of the stagecoach station came out of the building and asked, "What's going on here, Monte?"

"Something wrong with Fred, Mr. Mitchum," Monte said as he nodded toward the fallen driver. "But there's a sawbones tending to him."

The doctor had loosened the driver's clothing and pulled the shirt back so he could slip a hand inside it and feel the heartbeat. After a moment he leaned over and placed his ear against the man's chest. When he straightened, he opened the leather bag, which he had placed on the ground beside him, and took out a small metal case. He opened the case and extracted a small cloth-wrapped capsule of some sort.

Leaning closer to the driver, he held the capsule under the man's nose and gave it a sharp squeeze to crush something inside the cloth.

"Lie there and take deep, slow breaths of these fumes," he told Fred. "That medicine should begin to ease your pain in a few minutes."

The station manager edged up behind the doctor and asked, "Is he going to be all right, Doc? It's his ticker, isn't it?"

"He appears to be suffering from some sort of heart malady, yes," Dr. Arliss Chapman replied. "I can't really say at this point if he's going to recover. But it would help if there's somewhere he could be put to bed, so he can rest . . ."

"There's a room in the back of the office with some cots

in it, where the drivers and guards sleep when they lay over here for the night."

Chapman nodded. "That will do. At least it's close by." He looked around at the bystanders. "Some of you men give me a hand here."

"You heard the man," a deep, resonant voice said from the back of the crowd. "Let me through, and I'll help, too."

People stepped aside to give Scratch Morton room to reach the doctor and the driver. The silver-haired Texan pointed to a couple of the men he passed and jerked his head for them to follow him.

Monte surprised Beth by turning to her and saying, "You mind hanging on to this for a minute?" He held out the shotgun toward her.

Beth didn't hesitate. She said, "Of course," and took the double-barreled weapon from him. He stepped forward and bent to take hold of one of the driver's arms. Scratch got Fred's other arm, and the two men Scratch had "volunteered" out of the crowd took the driver's legs. They lifted him and carried him under the brush arbor and into the station. Mitchum and Dr. Chapman trailed behind and vanished into the adobe building, as well.

Beth stood there holding the shotgun. She figured it wouldn't be long before Monte came back to retrieve the weapon.

She was right about that. He strode out of the station a few minutes later, and with the duster's hem swinging around his knees, he came over to her.

"Thanks," he said as he took the Greener from her. "I probably shouldn't have just handed it to you like that. Reckon I wasn't thinking."

"Why do you say that?" Beth wanted to know.

"Well, most gals don't like guns. They're scared of

them. And a scattergun like that is kind of heavy, too. I'm sorry if it strained your muscles."

"It didn't," Beth said, "and I didn't mind a bit. You don't need to apologize." She smiled. "I'm not like 'most gals.' I could handle a shotgun by the time I was ten years old. My father believed it would be a good idea if I was able to defend myself."

"Reckon I probably ought to remember that," he said with a faint smile of his own.

Beth changed the subject by asking, "How's your friend?"

Monte shook his head. "The doctor doesn't know, but he says it's a good sign that Fred's still alive. According to him, a lot of times when a fella goes down hard like that, he doesn't live more than a minute or two. So I hope there's at least a chance he'll be all right." He paused. "Mr. Mitchum's fit to be tied, though."

"The man who runs this stage station? What's he upset about, other than one of his employees being stricken like that?"

"He's short a driver," Monte said, "and the stagecoach is due back in El Paso tomorrow. Plus, there's no telling how long Fred will be laid up, if he even makes it."

"Oh. Yes, I suppose that would be a concern."

Even as Beth said that, a crazy thought began to percolate in the back of her mind.

Along with the other men who had carried the driver into the station, Scratch came out of the building. He paused to ask, "Are you all right, Miss Beth? When I saw you right in the middle of this commotion, I got a mite worried for a minute."

"I'm fine, Mr. Morton," she said. "I mean, Marshal."

"Shoot," he said with a grin, "you know you can just call me Scratch anytime you want to."

"I just happened to be close by when the driver collapsed," she explained. That wasn't strictly true—it wasn't happenstance that had led her to be here—but the real reason wasn't anybody else's business.

Scratch turned to Monte and said, "You're the guard, ain't you?"

"Yeah, Monte Jackson." He tucked the shotgun under his left arm and stuck out his right hand. Scratch clasped it and shook.

"You're gonna have to find a new driver."

"That's just what Mr. Mitchum was saying," Monte replied with a sigh. "You don't know anybody who'd want the job, do you, Marshal?"

"Well, there was a time I'd have been willin' to help out, myself. I've been a jehu more'n once, and rode shotgun, to boot, when Bo was handlin' the reins. But these days . . ." Scratch tapped the tin star pinned to his shirt. "We got too many responsibilities right here in Silverhill. And I'm afraid I don't know anybody else who'd want the job. Nearly all the able-bodied men in these parts are either workin' in the mines or tied up with somethin' else."

"I just thought I'd ask," Monte said. "If you do run into anybody who'd want it, send them to talk to Mr. Mitchum, would you?"

"Sure thing," Scratch agreed. He clapped a hand on Monte's shoulder, added, "Best of luck to your pard," and then headed back up the street. The crowd had already thinned out after the stricken man was carried into the building, so Scratch didn't have to disperse the bystanders.

Monte started to turn back toward the station, but Beth stopped him by saying, "I know someone."

He frowned. "What?"

"I know someone who could drive the stagecoach," she said. She couldn't believe she was doing this, but she supposed that if she was going to be insane, she might as well be plumb loco, as Scratch might put it. "It's not an able-bodied man, though, like the marshal was talking about."

"Then who is it?" Monte asked.

"It's an able-bodied woman," Beth said. "Me."

CHAPTER 8

Sometimes when Dr. Arliss Chapman was tending to a patient, he took off his coat and rolled up his sleeves. There had been no need to do that in this case, however, because there really wasn't much he could do for the stagecoach driver.

Outside, he had administered amyl nitrite to relieve angina pectoris and heart paroxysm, and it seemed to have helped. The effectiveness of that procedure had been established within the past few decades by European physicians, beginning with the Scot Dr. T. Lauder Brunton, and Chapman had read numerous articles about it in medical journals. For several years now, he had been carrying the cloth-wrapped glass capsules in his medical bag and he had had occasion to use them more than once.

Once the stagecoach driver had been brought inside and placed on the cot, Chapman had taken his stethoscope from the bag and had listened carefully to the rhythm of the man's heart. It had been fairly steady, which had led Chapman to believe that either the driver had not suffered an actual heart paroxysm or else it had been brief in duration.

It was impossible to say at this point how much damage had been done to the heart itself.

The driver appeared to be resting comfortably at the moment, not fully asleep but in something of a dazed state. The station manager stood in the doorway, with a worried look on his face. Chapman closed his bag and motioned for the man to go back into the office. Chapman followed and eased the door closed behind him.

"Fred's going to be all right, isn't he?" the man asked.

"His condition is stable for the moment. Beyond that, I can't really say. As I mentioned earlier, the fact that he never fully lost consciousness and has survived for this long is promising. Heart paroxysm often kills very quickly."

"I sure appreciate what you did for him, Doc—"

"Chapman. Dr. Arliss Chapman."

The man nodded, put out his hand, and said, "I'm Henry Mitchum. I run this station for the stage line."

Chapman shook hands with him. Mitchum went on, "If you want to give me your bill, I'll send it to the main office in El Paso and see to it that you get paid."

Chapman smiled and waved that offer away. "Please, that's not necessary. Since that gentleman is my first patient in Silverhill, I'd like to dispense with any fee. As a goodwill gesture, let's say."

"That's mighty kind of you, Dr. Chapman."

"What's the patient's name?"

"Fred Overton," Mitchum said. "He's been driving for the company for several years now."

"Well, he won't be doing any driving for a while," Chapman said. "The next twelve hours or so should tell the story. If he lives through the night, I believe he'll survive. But even if he does, his condition will require a great deal of rest. He won't be up to the exertion of driving a stagecoach for quite some time . . . if, indeed, he's ever able to do anything that strenuous again."

Chapman kept his voice low so the driver wouldn't be likely to overhear him through the door. Mitchum groaned loudly in dismay, however. Earlier, he had been fretting about having to find another driver to take Fred Overton's place, until Chapman had silenced him with a stern stare.

"You're sure about that, Dr. Chapman?"

"I am," Chapman replied crisply, not bothering to keep the annoyance out of his voice. The driver had almost died right outside this very office, and all Mitchum was worried about was how it would affect the business.

Mitchum sighed and nodded slowly. "I reckon you know what you're talking about," he said. "But it's sure liable to put me in a bind."

"I can't help you with that." Chapman started toward the door.

"Doc?"

Chapman looked back. He hated being addressed like that, but it seemed as if everyone west of the Mississippi River insisted on referring to physicians that way. Many of those east of the Mississippi, too, if he was being honest about it.

"I'm obliged to you for helping Fred," Mitchum went on. "I know I was carrying on about the business, but he's a friend, too, and I'm glad you saved his life. You must be a mighty smart man, to be a doctor and all."

"Well, I'm just glad I was close by and was able to lend a hand," Chapman said, mollified by the compliment, as usual. He had never run across a doctor who *didn't* like being told how intelligent he was, and he was self-aware enough to know that was true of him, too.

It did no good for a man to lie to himself about his own strengths—or his weaknesses.

"I'll come by this evening, after I've gotten settled into one of the hotels, and check on him," Chapman went on. "Make sure he gets plenty of rest. Someone should probably stay with him."

"I can hire a Mexican woman to do that, and to see about feeding him and such," Mitchum said. "And if you're looking for a hotel, the Territorial House is the best one in town. Kind of expensive, though."

"Well, I'll be looking for a house where I can set up my practice and have my living quarters, as well, so with any luck, I won't have to stay there for long."

"If I hear of a good place, Doc, I'll let you know."

Chapman nodded and went on out, glad to leave the office behind him. Business had always struck him as being a little . . . grubby. That was one reason he had gone into medicine. It was just cleaner and nobler.

He spotted the Territorial House up the street and walked toward it. It was a large, impressive building with a front porch shaded by a second-floor balcony. The hotel's name was painted in large letters across the front, just below the roof.

Chapman wasn't worried about being able to pay if he had to stay there for a while. He had come into a good sum of money before leaving Missouri, where he had lived for several years before setting out on this journey west. He had plenty to be able to afford to set himself up properly in this new town.

He wasn't sure why he had chosen Silverhill as the next stop on his journey, but looking around at the boomtown now, he decided it seemed quite promising. He had read something about it in a newspaper while stopping for a time in San Antonio. The story had made it sound populated enough to support another medical practice, but at the same time, the settlement had the isolation that Chapman liked. Big cities had always appealed to him, but so had smaller, out-of-the-way places like this. Yes, he thought, there was every chance in the world he could be quite happy and satisfied in Silverhill.

"Look at that," Luella Tolman whispered to Jean Parker as they sat on a divan in the lobby of the Territorial House. The divan was situated between two potted plants and had a good view of the front door, but Jean hadn't been paying much attention to who went in and out of the hotel. She had been reading a book, while Luella had been doing needlework.

Jean lifted her head as her friend spoke to her. She said, "Look at what?"

"Not what. Who. The man who just came in. He's going to the desk now."

Jean saw the well-dressed, dark-haired man. Unlike most Westerners, he wasn't wearing a hat. He carried a carpetbag in one hand and a smaller black leather bag in the other.

"Is that a doctor's bag?" Jean asked.

"It looks like one. Isn't he handsome?"

Jean didn't shrug, but she put a note of ambivalence in her voice as she said, "I suppose so."

She had a habit of keeping her actual emotions in reserve. Not as much as Cecilia did, but by no stretch of the imagination did Jean wear her heart on her sleeve. Because of that, she sounded almost bored as she responded to Luella's comment, but the truth was that she thought the newcomer was strikingly handsome. And he was just enough older than her—in his early thirties, she thought— that he had an air of maturity about him.

Plus, he appeared to be a doctor, which meant he had to be an intelligent man. That appealed to Jean, as well.

Luella put her needlework aside and said, "I'm going to go talk to him." She started to stand up.

Jean put a hand on her friend's arm. "Wait a minute. You're going to just waltz up to him and introduce yourself? That wouldn't really be proper, would it?"

"Oh, you worry too much about things being *proper* all the time, Jean. Don't you believe in just giving in to your impulses now and then?"

"I don't know," Jean murmured. "That seems awfully reckless."

Reckless or not, she knew Luella would do it. The dark, exotically beautiful young woman wasn't as wild as Rose and Beth, but she didn't mind taking chances now and then—a tendency that had landed her in trouble in the past.

Luella didn't have to march up and introduce herself to the newcomer, though. He had finished checking into the hotel and had gotten a room key from the clerk, and as he turned away from the desk, he paused when he saw the two young women sitting on the other side of the lobby. After a second, he smiled and started toward them.

"Oh, my heavens!" Luella said under her breath. "He's coming over here."

"Well, don't get in a tizzy about it," Jean told her. "It's not like he's a wild Indian or anything."

She tucked the book's ribbon marker between the pages where she'd been reading and closed the volume.

The stranger came up to them and set the carpetbag in his right hand on the floor at his feet. "Ladies, if I may be so bold," he said, "I'm new in town, and I was hoping I could prevail upon you to provide me with some information. I'm Arliss Chapman, by the way."

"*Dr.* Arliss Chapman?" Luella said.

"Why, yes! You've heard of me?" He chuckled. "I find that hard to believe, since there's nothing all that special about me."

"I wouldn't say that, but . . . No, it's the bag you're carrying. That's what made me think you're a doctor."

"Guilty as charged," he said. "And you are . . . ?"

"Not guilty," Luella replied. She held out her hand. "I'm Luella Tolman."

Chapman took her hand. He didn't kiss the back of it or bow, but he managed to seem courtly, anyway, as he held it for a moment.

"I'm very pleased to meet you, Miss Tolman. It is *Miss* Tolman?"

"Yes. Neither of us is married. This is my friend Jean Parker."

She should have introduced herself, Jean thought, but for some unexpected reason she couldn't understand, she had found herself speechless. Chapman reached to take her hand, too. She managed to give it to him.

"Miss Parker, what a great pleasure it is to make your acquaintance."

Jean found her voice. "Yes. Yes, it is. A pleasure to meet me." She gave a little shake of her head. "I mean, it's a pleasure for me. To meet you." She was ashamed of herself for being so flustered, but she couldn't seem to help it.

"You said you need some information from us, Doctor?" Luella prodded.

"Yes, as I mentioned, I'm a newcomer in Silverhill, and I was hoping that you could tell me the name of the best restaurant in town."

"Oh, that's easy. Harbinson's is where you want to go. There's a small dining room here in the hotel, and it's all right, but Harbinson's is better."

"I suppose Silverhill is small enough that I won't have any trouble finding it—"

"I have a better idea," Luella said. "I know that Jean was planning to dine there this evening, and if you wanted to meet her here in the lobby later, I'm sure she'd be glad to show you where it is."

Jean's head snapped around, and she glared at Luella in a mixture of anger and amazement.

Chapman didn't seem to be the least bit flustered by her reaction or to even notice it. He said, "I couldn't accept such a favor without repaying it. Perhaps you'll accept my invitation to have dinner with me, Miss Parker?"

"I . . . I don't know . . . I didn't—"

Luella interrupted Jean's pathetic attempts to form a coherent sentence. "She'd be very happy to."

"Excellent! I need to go freshen up from my trip. Traveling by stagecoach isn't the most fastidious way to get from one place to another, you know!" He took Jean's hand again. "I'll meet you here in two hours, Miss Parker. I look forward to it!"

Jean swallowed and was able to nod at last. "Yes," she said.

Dr. Arliss Chapman left them sitting there and went over to the stairs with more of a spring in his step than he'd demonstrated when he came into the Territorial House.

As soon as he was out of sight, Jean stared at Luella again and exclaimed, "Why in the world did you *do* that?"

"Oh, I just hurried things along a little," Luella said, with a wave of her hand. "He was going to ask you to have dinner with him, anyway. I don't doubt it for a second."

"But . . . but I thought *you* liked him."

"He's very attractive," Luella admitted, "but I saw the way he looked at you, and I saw the way *you* got all tongue-tied when he started talking to us, so it was pretty obvious that you like him, too. I don't mind bowing out when I know it's a good thing for a friend."

"You think it is?" Jean asked. "A good thing, I mean? "

"Dear, I think meeting Dr. Arliss Chapman is absolutely going to change your life!"

CHAPTER 9

In the back room of the barbershop down the street, Steve Hargett sat in the tub of cool water and cussed himself for not making sure that he'd left his holstered gun within reach before he climbed in.

Not that it really would matter if he had, he realized as he looked at the man pointing a Colt at him. Even if his own gun was right beside him, there was no way he could have gotten it out of the holster in time to beat a man who had already pulled his iron.

But then, Ben Wilcox eased down the hammer of the revolver he held and grinned broadly. As he slid the gun back into leather, he laughed and said, "Boy, you look like you're ready to shrivel up and die in there, Steve. Did you really believe I was gonna ventilate you?"

"I don't know," Steve said as he regarded Wilcox warily. "The last time we talked, you seemed pretty mad at me, like you wouldn't have minded putting a bullet in me."

For a second, Wilcox looked irritated. Then he smiled, but the expression didn't reach his eyes. He hooked the three-legged stool with a foot and pulled it over to him so he could sit down. He pushed his hat back and leaned forward, clasping his hands together between his knees.

"The only reason I had a burr under my saddle," he said, "was that you won't get off the fence, Steve. You've got a great opportunity just sitting there right in front of you, and you're too blasted stubborn to open your eyes and see it!"

Wilcox was in his mid-thirties, a decade or so older than Steve. He had an angular face and lank, thinning hair that was almost colorless. His dusty, shabby range clothes marked him as a cowboy, although the well-worn walnut grips of his revolver showed that it had gotten quite a bit of use, too.

Apparently, Wilcox hadn't followed him in here to shoot him, after all, so Steve blew out a breath and relaxed a little. He still didn't fully trust Wilcox, though. The older man was unpredictable and was known to have a temper. That was one of the things that had almost gotten him fired from the SJ. He was always blowing up at Rance Plummer, the foreman.

Before Steve could say anything, the barber's Chinese assistant came in carrying two buckets of water with little tendrils of steam curling up from them. He said, "Careful. Hot," to Steve, who scooted back as far as he could while the man poured the water into the tub. The hot water drifted around Steve and felt good—or at least it would have if Wilcox's unexpected intrusion hadn't had him worried.

The Chinese man set the buckets aside, picked up Steve's clothes and hat, and went back out through the curtained opening. When he was gone, Wilcox asked, "What are you gettin' yourself all spruced up for, Steve?" He grinned again. "Let me guess . . . You're goin' courtin'!

Is it that mail-order bride gal you entered the horse race to win? Some of the boys told me about how you're still sweet on her!"

Steve wasn't surprised to hear that. Wilcox's temper was a problem, but he still had friends among the crew, which was one of the things that had led to the problem facing Steve now.

"Don't worry about that, Ben," he said. "The reason I'm getting cleaned up doesn't have anything to do with our business."

"Well, that's just what I'm here to talk about. So far, you and me don't seem to *have* any business together . . . and that's why I followed you when I saw you coming in here. I'd like to change that."

Steve didn't want Wilcox to know that he'd just been thinking about the proposition that the man had made to him a week earlier. He said, "Dang it. Couldn't some of the other fellas work with you? I just wouldn't feel right about it. The SJ has been good to me. And Rance—"

"Rance Plummer rides your back and chews you out all day every day," Wilcox snapped. "Why you'd ever give a hoot in Hades about him is beyond my understandin'. And the SJ is owned by a syndicate back East. How can a man feel any loyalty toward a blasted *syndicate*?"

"Maybe so, but—"

"No buts about it!" Wilcox interrupted again. "You know I'm right, Steve. This is the best chance you'll ever have to actually get what's comin' to you. Otherwise you'll just keep on burning up in the summer and freezing in the winter, working yourself down to a nub for forty a month and found for the rest of your life." He paused. "And it's mighty hard for a man to support a wife on wages like that."

Steve felt his face getting hot, and the reaction had nothing to do with the heat of the water in the tub.

"Nobody said anything about a wife."

"Yeah, but a young fella like you, that's got to be a consideration. As for getting the other boys to help me . . . some of them have already said that they'll throw in with me. But I can always use another good man . . . and I'm convinced that man is you, Steve."

Steve felt himself wavering. He was just starting to court Rose Winston. The dinner she'd agreed to have with him this evening was the beginning. Things between them might not ever get to the marrying point.

But if he was honest with himself, he knew that possibility was in the back of his mind, and Wilcox was right about it being hard to support a wife on what a cowboy made. Especially when kids came along, as they inevitably would.

And the syndicate that owned the SF, why, those were just a bunch of stuffed-shirt, fancy-pants Eastern tycoons. They didn't know a thing about what it was like to work in a saddle nearly every day of the year, no matter how blazing hot or freezing cold it was. They never spent hours on horseback, soaked to the skin in a downpour or choking on a mouthful of dirt from a sandstorm. They just sat in their offices or mansions and counted their dang money. . . .

"Here's the thing," Steve heard himself saying. "I don't want anybody to get hurt."

Wilcox raised his eyebrows and demanded, "Who in blazes said anything about anybody gettin' hurt? All I'm interested in is the money!" He waved a hand. "Shoot, we'll go at it smart-like. We'll only take a few cows at a time, and with enough of us working together, Plummer might not even notice that some of those cows have gone missing!"

"I don't know about that. Rance is pretty sharp. And he's bound to notice come roundup time next year—"

"By then you'll have a nice little cache of loot saved up," Wilcox argued. "The smart thing to do before roundup comes around will be to draw your time and move on. Make a fresh start somewhere else, only you'll have some dinero to do it with. You might even be able to buy a spread of your own, where you and that wife of yours—assumin' you have a wife by then, of course—can make a mighty fine life for yourselves and raise a whole passel of young'uns. Now, you can't tell me that doesn't sound good to you, Steve."

"It sounds good," Steve admitted. "But if I move on and leave these parts, and so does everybody else who's helping you, won't that look suspicious?"

"What if it does?" Wilcox said with a shrug. "Nobody'll be able to prove anything. And you'll be long gone."

The hombre had an answer for everything, Steve thought. But still he hesitated. This was a big step Wilcox was asking him to make. Steve had always been a law-abiding sort. . . .

A look of impatience appeared on Wilcox's face. He said, "You're forgetting something, Steve. You know what I've got in mind, and there's an old saying about how anybody who's not with me is against me."

Steve shook his head. "I'd never say anything, Ben. You know that."

"Do I?" Wilcox rested his hand on the butt of his gun. "I reckon I'm not quite as sure of that as you are, pard."

Steve knew a threat when he heard one. His face warmed again, but with anger this time.

"I told you I wouldn't spill anything," he snapped. "As long as we worked together before, it seems to me you ought to take my word for that."

"I'd like to," Wilcox said, "but I'd feel a whole heap better about it if we were working together again. And I know it'd be better for that gal you like, too. What's her name? Rose? Rose Winston?"

Steve stiffened. Was Wilcox threatening *Rose* now? Was that what that question was really trying to get across to him?

Steve glanced at the gunbelt hanging on the chair back. Maybe if he made a fast enough lunge at it, he could get his Colt out before Wilcox could draw. . . .

No, that was hopeless, and he knew it. He was no gunslinger. Wilcox wasn't, either, but Steve suspected the man was faster than he was. And there was a chance he was wrong. No matter what it had sounded like, Wilcox might not have meant that last comment as a threat against Rose.

Wilcox smiled again, but it didn't do much to ease the tension in the room.

"I can see you're givin' it some serious thought," he said. "But the time for thinking is over, Steve. It's time to make up your mind. Are you in?"

Wilcox had him boxed in, Steve realized. Between his own ambition, his hopes that he might someday build a life with Rose, and his worry about what Wilcox might do if he didn't go along with the plan, there was no way out for him.

He sighed and nodded. "I'm in."

Wilcox clapped softly and said, "*Bueno*! I will be in

touch when the time comes and will let you know what you need to do. Until then, you just go on with what you'd normally do. Like havin' dinner with Miss Rose Winston this evening. The two of you have a good time, you hear?"

"Yeah," Steve said, his voice a little hollow with the anticipation—or was that dread?—of what the coming weeks might bring. "A good time."

CHAPTER 10

Each evening, not long after sundown, either Bo or Scratch made the rounds of Silverhill's businesses, walking up one side of the street and then back down the other.

This wasn't like the night rounds they made later, when they checked to make sure all the doors were locked, because during this stroll around the settlement, most of the places they passed were still open. It was more of a chance to gauge the mood of the town and remind folks that the law was on the job. Sometimes they could tell when trouble was brewing, just from a certain feeling in the air. From a practical standpoint, the law being out and about also gave people a chance to let them know if they thought something was wrong.

Today, as the light faded and shadows began to gather, a feeling of peace settled down with the dusk. The usual hubbub came over the batwing doors of the saloons Bo passed—men talking loudly, painted ladies in spangled dresses laughing, cards being slapped down, the click of poker chips, the rattle of a roulette wheel, the tinny strains of a honky-tonk piano player—but nothing out of the ordinary. If anything, the clamor was a little more subdued than usual.

Wagon wheels squealed as vehicles rolled away from the stores, carrying a few late customers. Horse and mule hooves thudded on the dusty street. Townspeople on the boardwalks smiled and nodded and sometimes shook and howdied with Bo as they met him, but no one had any complaints or concerns to pass along.

He reached the stagecoach station at the far end of the settlement and was surprised to see Beth Macy leaning on the corral fence and looking at the horses standing inside the enclosure. He tucked the shotgun he carried under his left arm and said, "Evening, Miss Beth." When she turned to face him, he pinched the brim of his hat. "I'm a mite surprised to see you down here."

"I was just looking at the horses."

"Yeah, I can see that. Mind if I ask why?"

"Are you asking as a deputy?" she said. "Am I doing something suspicious?"

"You know better than that," he chided gently.

"Yes, I do. I'm sorry. I've been arguing all afternoon, so I guess I'm a little on edge."

"Arguing?" Bo repeated. "About what?"

"About Mr. Mitchum giving me a job driving the stage-coach. And then, after I talked *him* into it, I had to argue some more with Monte Jackson, that muleheaded shotgun guard."

Bo couldn't stop his eyebrows from climbing up his forehead in surprise.

"Wait a minute," he said. "*You're* going to drive the stagecoach? You're the new jehu?"

"That's right," Beth replied with a smile.

"Well, that's just . . . I knew that old Fred Overton

collapsed earlier today and had some problem with his heart—Scratch told me about that—but I sure never figured they'd replace him with you!" He added, "No offense, but—"

"But a woman has no business driving a stagecoach, right?"

Bo shook his head. "No, I never said that. I've heard tell of several women who worked driving coaches. And now that I think about it, I can see why you'd be interested in the job. You did fine handling the team on the wagon that brought you ladies out here. A stagecoach is a mite different, but I'm sure you'll get the hang of it pretty quickly."

That response appeared to mollify her irritated reaction. She nodded and said, "I appreciate you saying that, Bo. I know it's sort of a crazy idea, but I thought it might be fun."

"Well," Bo drawled, "by the time you spend a few days wrestling with those horses and getting your teeth jolted by the bouncing and breathing in a few bushels of dust, it might not seem quite as entertaining. But if that's what you want to do, then good for you, I reckon."

She smiled. "Thank you. Although you make it sound pretty daunting."

"You said Monte Jackson didn't care for the idea?"

Beth blew out an exasperated breath. "He got so upset about it that I thought he was going to quit! Then poor Mr. Mitchum would have had to find a new shotgun guard, too. But in the end, he agreed that we could give it a try."

"I hope it works out," Bo told her. "If you need any advice, talk to Scratch. We've both been jehus in the past, but he was always better at it than I was."

"I'll do that," she said.

Bo nodded, bid her a good evening, and moved on. He

waited until he thought he was far enough away that she wouldn't notice before he shook his head. The whole idea was loco, he thought—but sometimes loco ideas turned out all right.

He was back at the Territorial House when he saw a familiar figure emerge from the hotel, accompanied by a man Bo didn't recognize. He raised a hand in greeting and said, "Hello, Jean."

"Good evening, Mr. Creel," Jean Parker said. She smiled and added, "I don't know if I'll ever get used to calling you Deputy Creel."

"It doesn't matter," he assured her. "You can call me anything you want. Just don't call me late for supper, as Scratch would say." Bo looked at Jean's companion. "I don't believe we've met."

"Arliss Chapman," the man said as he extended his hand. Bo clasped the long, slender, and surprisingly strong fingers. "And you'd be the law in these parts?"

"One of them," Bo said. "Bo Creel. Deputy town marshal."

Jean said, "Arliss should have introduced himself as *Dr.* Arliss Chapman."

That made Bo remember where he had heard the name before. He said, "You're the sawbones who took care of Fred Overton when he collapsed this afternoon."

"I was fortunate enough to be nearby and able to assist the man," Chapman said. "I plan to stop by the stagecoach station later and see how he's doing. But first, Miss Parker has been kind enough to agree to have dinner with me. She's going to show me the best place to dine in Silverhill. Harbinson's, I believe, is the name?"

"It's good, all right," Bo agreed. "Do you plan to stay on here in town, Doctor?"

"That's right. I intend to establish a practice here."

"I reckon Silverhill can always use another good doctor. You probably don't have a location for your office in mind yet."

Chapman shook his head. "No, I just arrived a few hours ago and haven't had a chance to start looking around yet. What I really want is a house that will provide living quarters as well as space for my office, examination room, and surgery. But I don't mind staying here in the hotel for a while, if necessary. If you hear of a good location that might be available, I'd appreciate it if you'd let me know."

Bo nodded and said, "I'll do that." Curious, he added, "Did you two know each other before?"

Chapman smiled broadly. "I never laid eyes on Miss Parker before I walked into the Territorial House this afternoon. But I'm a strong believer in not turning one's back on good fortune, and making her acquaintance certainly qualifies!"

Bo nodded and ticked a finger against his hat brim. "You two enjoy your dinner, hear? And welcome to Silverhill, Doctor."

He walked on and let them resume their stroll toward Harbinson's Restaurant. Dr. Arliss Chapman seemed like a good sort. From what Scratch had told him, the man was a capable physician, too. Fred Overton had survived, at least so far. Maybe he would have even if Chapman hadn't been around, but there was no way of knowing that.

Despite that impression, Bo worried about Jean having dinner with a man she barely knew. He had always gotten the feeling that she'd lived a somewhat more sheltered life than the other mail-order brides. He wasn't her father or even her uncle, of course, but he still didn't like the idea of anybody taking advantage of her.

Maybe Chapman was as nice as he seemed, and Bo wouldn't have to worry about that. He was going to keep an eye out for Jean's best interests, anyway.

A few minutes later, he was passing the mouth of an alley when a sudden scuffling sound in the shadows drew his attention. It sounded like a fight going on back there as feet scraped on the ground and somebody grunted with effort. Somebody might be getting robbed. Bo swung the Greener's muzzle in the direction of the commotion and barked, "Whatever's going on back there, hold it right now and come on out of there!"

He was alert for the sound of a gun being cocked. If he heard that metallic ratcheting, he planned to loose one of the loads of buckshot into the gloom.

Instead, to his surprise, a familiar voice called softly, "Don't shoot, Bo!"

"Rose?" he asked.

She seemed to materialize from the shadows as she came along the alley and stepped up onto the boardwalk. She wore a dress, which was a little unusual for Rose Winston. As she stood there looking uncomfortable, she tugged a little at the garment, as if it had gotten disarranged. When she had gotten that done, she tucked her chestnut hair back behind her ears. It looked a little mussed, too.

Bo gave her a hard look and asked, "What was going on back there, Rose? Somebody giving you trouble?"

"No, no, not at all," she replied, but her answer seemed a little too rushed to be entirely believable. "I was . . . I just . . ." Her voice trailed off as she found herself unable to come up with any explanation.

"You weren't alone," Bo said. He had lowered the Greener, but now he lifted the twin barrels toward the darkened alley again. "Come on out of there," he ordered sharply. "I know you're in there. I can hear you breathing."

That wasn't a lie. He did hear the faint sound of someone breathing heavily, as if they were upset—or frightened.

"Bo, please," Rose said as she took a step toward him and lifted a hand. "You don't have to do this—"

"I reckon I do. It's my job to keep the peace around here, and something's happened to disturb you. I aim to get to the bottom of it."

A man said from the shadows, "Take it easy with that scattergun, Deputy. I'm coming out."

The hombre who emerged from the gloom and stepped up onto the boardwalk next to Rose looked familiar to Bo, but in the poor light, it took a moment to place him.

Then Bo pointed the shotgun at the ground again and said, "I know you. You're one of Rance Plummer's crew. You ride for the SJ."

"That's right, sir," the young man confirmed. "My name's Steve Hargett."

That name jogged Bo's memory even more. He said, "You won the big horse race."

A quick smile flashed across Steve Hargett's face. "Yes, sir, that's right. I sure did."

Bo's voice hardened again as he went on, "You figure that gives you the right to come back here to Silverhill, grab Miss Winston off the street, and drag her into an alley?"

"No!" Rose and Steve exclaimed at the same time.

"You don't have to defend this young scoundrel, Rose. It's clear that he was trying to take advantage of you. You should've yelled when he grabbed you. One of us, either Scratch or me, is always close by—"

Steve sounded angry now as he broke in, "Mister, I would never do a thing like that."

"No? Rose came out of that alley, breathing hard and looking mussed up, and you expect me to believe she wasn't back there wrestling with you, trying to fight off your unwanted attentions?"

"That wasn't what happened at all!" Rose burst out. "*I'm* the one who dragged *Steve* back there."

Bo stared at her for a second, then realized he needed to pick his jaw up off the boardwalk. He found his voice and said with discomfort clamping its awkward teeth on him, "You mean it was your idea to . . . that the two of you were . . ."

Rose sounded embarrassed, too, but she forged on resolutely. "I reckon you've been in a few haylofts with a few girls in your time, Bo. You know that girls sometimes enjoy a little slap and tickle, too."

"We were on our way to get some supper, Deputy Creel," Steve said. "That's the gospel truth."

"I didn't know the two of you were even keeping company."

"Tonight was the first time. I mean, for us to have dinner together."

Bo grunted. "First time for a lot of things, I expect." He frowned at Rose.

"Don't look at me like that," she said. "You're not my pa."

"No, but I took money from Cyrus Keegan in return for a promise to keep you and those other young ladies safe."

"Well, I don't know about the others, but I'm fine," Rose insisted. Her chin had a defiant tilt to it now. "I just thought it would be fun to spark a little before we went on over to Harbinson's. And it *was* fun . . . until you came along and ruined it!"

Many years earlier, Bo had been married, and he and his wife had had a couple of children. Then, tragically, illness had taken all of them away from him. So no, he wasn't Rose's pa, and he'd never had to deal with any wild, headstrong mostly grown girl children of his own, but he imagined this was sort of what it felt like.

"Listen to me," he said. "If the two of you were on your way to Harbinson's, you just go ahead and skedaddle on over there. Then, when you've had your dinner, I expect you to walk Rose back to the Territorial House, Hargett, and I mean straight there. No stopping in any dark alleys along the way."

"Yes, sir, Deputy. I understand," Steve said.

"Yeah, well, what if I don't?" Rose demanded.

Bo fixed her with a steady stare and said, "Then somebody's liable to get arrested. There are laws in this town against disturbing the peace."

"We weren't disturbing anybody's peace!"

"Mine was disturbed . . . and I'm the deputy marshal."

"Oh!" Rose packed a lot of exasperation into the single word. She grabbed the young man's hand and added, "Come on, Steve."

As she tugged him along the boardwalk, the cowboy looked over his shoulder and said, "Straight back to the hotel, Deputy. I swear it."

Bo watched them until they reached Harbinson's and went inside the fancy, well-lighted restaurant. He wondered if they would run into Jean and Dr. Chapman in there. At least Jean was having dinner with a gentleman. Rose had defended Steve Hargett and tried to take the blame for herself, and Steve had sounded sincere when he promised that he would escort Rose straight back to the hotel after dinner, but Bo still didn't trust him.

To tell the truth, Rose *did* have a history of being impulsive and reckless. If he was being honest with himself, Bo knew she indeed might have been the one who prodded Steve back into the shadows for a little boy-girl wrestling.

He and Scratch had earned the money they had taken from Cyrus Keegan. They had gotten the mail-order brides safely to Silverhill, and that was all they had signed on to do. Anything they did after that was their own lookout.

But they had grown too fond of those five young women to do otherwise, and now they had taken on the responsibility of maintaining law and order in the whole town on top of that.

All of which added up to a stubborn hunch inside Bo that more trouble was on the horizon.

The stars had come out but the moon had not yet risen as a lone rider toiled up the slope of a ridge a mile south of Silverhill. The man let the horse have its head, so the animal could pick its way slowly in the darkness.

When they reached the crest, the man reined in as several other figures on horseback loomed up in front of him. Clearly, they had been waiting for him, and the one in front, a lean hombre with a wide-brimmed, steeple-crowned sombrero, said, "Welcome back, Lupe. Did you see them?"

"*Sí*," responded the man, who had come from Silverhill. He turned slightly in the saddle and waved an arm back toward the settlement, the lights of which twinkled brightly in an otherwise vast sweep of darkness. "They are there. All five of them. I saw each with my own eyes."

"Even—"

"Especially the one señorita."

"How does she look?"

"She looks well, amigo. Very well."

The leader sighed and then nodded in evident satisfaction, yet there was something unsettled about the sound.

"Something else," the man called Lupe said. "Those two old men . . . the Texans . . ."

"Creel and Morton?"

"*Sí*. They are still in Silverhill, and now they wear badges. They are lawmen. The town marshal and his deputy, from what I overheard in the saloons."

The leader drew in a deep breath. This was unexpected news. He knew from experience that the two old Texans were formidable enemies. But the obstacle they represented would just have to be dealt with.

"That doesn't change anything," he declared. "Not a thing. When the time is right . . . we strike."

CHAPTER 11

Two months later . . .

Bo and Scratch were sitting on the front porch of the Territorial House, Scratch with his chair tilted back so that his boots rested on top of the railing that ran along the porch. His hat was tipped down over his eyes as he snoozed on this hot afternoon. Bo had taken a tobacco pouch from his pocket and was packing his pipe for one of his infrequent smokes. Both Texans appeared quite at ease, although out of long habit, they were also alert for any signs of trouble.

A couple of months had passed since they had pinned on the tin stars, and Silverhill being the boomtown it was, inevitably a few problems had cropped up during that time. It would have been unrealistic to expect otherwise. Fights had broken out in the saloons from time to time, one of them an epic brawl between miners and cowboys that had all but destroyed one of the smaller establishments, known as the Bonanzer. That was the way it was spelled on the sign, and nobody had bothered to correct it.

Bo and Scratch had finally succeeded in busting up the ruckus and had arrested more than two dozen men. The cells in the jail had been packed to the gills for a night, until the next morning, when the local justice of the peace levied fines and damages and the combatants paid up.

That incident had led to increased tensions between the two factions for a while, but eventually the strain had eased. Now and then, a man from each side might engage in some fisticuffs, but it no longer seemed like total warfare was on the verge of erupting.

A couple of shootings had also occurred. Two cowboys had blazed away at each other following an altercation over a soiled dove, but due to their terrible aim, all they had done was burn a lot of powder and break a couple of windows as they emptied their Colts. It was pure luck no innocent bystanders had been struck by the wild shots, though, so Bo and Scratch had slapped the cowboys behind bars, and the judge had sentenced them to three days in jail—which had seemed longer to Bo and Scratch because the prisoners had never stopped whining and complaining.

The other, more serious shooting had resulted in a pair of fatalities, although only one from a gunshot wound. A miner had accused a professional gambler of dealing off the bottom in a game in the Silver King. The gambler had taken offense at that and had produced a derringer from a sleeve holster—inadvertently dislodging an ace of diamonds he had hidden up the same sleeve—and plunked a .32 caliber slug in the miner's brawny chest.

That wound had proven mortal, but not immediately. The miner had lived long enough to lunge across the table and thrust the knife he'd yanked from a sheath on his belt into the gambler's guts, not once but three times, ripping the man's belly wide open and creating a fatal mess on the Silver King's floor. Such violent eruptions were common in boomtowns, and Bo and Scratch considered themselves lucky that there had been only one so far during their tenure in office.

One more death had taken place, and it was even more disturbing.

One of the working girls from a house known as Lily's Place had been found one morning in the alley behind the blacksmith shop. The girl had gone by Florence, but of course nobody knew if that was her real name or not. Somebody had taken a knife to her, and the bloody result had been almost enough to turn Bo's stomach when he saw her. He hoped that most of those cruel injuries had happened *after* the slash across her throat that had ended her life, but somehow, he couldn't quite convince himself that was the case.

Of course, the life of a soiled dove was full of risks, and everybody knew that, but this was worse. As Scratch had commented to Bo, anybody who would do such a thing was just "plumb, pure evil," and Bo couldn't disagree with that sentiment.

More than likely, though, it had been an isolated incident, and as the nights had gone by without it being repeated, the lawmen had leaned even more toward that being true. Even so, they had patrolled the settlement more diligently for a while, paying special attention to the alleys.

They had also talked to Lily, the proprietor of the house where Florence had worked, and she had assured them that in the future none of her girls would agree to meet a man outside the house, which was what she believed had happened with Florence. Such things were against her rules, but they happened sometimes, anyway. Not now, though, since all the girls were so spooked by the brutal killing.

Bo and Scratch had also talked to the madams at the other two houses in town and had also spread the word to the saloons where the girls did more than just serve drinks. In the end, though, it came down to each of the soiled doves being careful on her own, and you never could predict what they would do, especially as time passed with no more incidents and they started to relax their vigilance, as inevitably happened.

So the Texans hoped the man responsible for Florence's death had moved on, even though that would mean he wouldn't get the justice he had coming for what he had done. Better that, maybe, than more girls dying.

But a troubling thought nagged at the back of Bo's brain: even if more girls didn't die in Silverhill, they probably would somewhere else, as long as a beast like that was alive.

He wasn't thinking about any of that today, however. The stagecoach was due in soon, and he and Scratch were waiting for it.

Bo had just fired up his pipe when Scratch swung his feet down from the railing and sat up. The silver-haired Texan thumbed his hat back and said, "Sounds like the stage comin'."

Bo had already heard the hoofbeats from the team and the rattle and squeal of the coach itself as it approached Silverhill. He shook out the lucifer he had just used to light the pipe and flipped the spent match into the street as he stood up.

"I reckon we ought to go down and meet it."

"Yeah, it's part of our job to keep up with who's comin' and goin' in town."

Scratch took his responsibilities as marshal seriously, just as Bo had figured he would. Rising to the challenge, so to speak. Scratch had always been the more carefree member of the pair from Texas, and they were both so fiddle-footed that normally they would have moved on by now. Two months was a long time for them to stay in one place, and they had been in Silverhill for almost three!

Maybe the time had finally come for them to settle down, Bo mused as they walked along the street toward the stagecoach station. They had tried such things before. A while back, they had even returned to their homes in Texas and come close to putting down roots there again. But in the end, it hadn't worked out, and they had wound up working for Cyrus Keegan, taking the job that had brought them to New Mexico Territory.

Before they reached the station, the coach rolled past them. Scratch waved a hand in front of his face to clear away some of the dust that swirled over them, and said, "Beth whips up them horses more'n ol' Fred used to."

"Yeah, but she's never late," Bo said. "She sticks right to the schedule or even beats it."

Scratch chuckled. "Which means that Fred ain't likely to ever get his job back. The stage line sets a heap of store by keeping on schedule."

Fred Overton had recovered fairly well from whatever ailment had befallen his heart that day. A month had passed by the time Dr. Arliss Chapman declared that Fred was fit to go back to work, although the doctor advised that he take it easier than in the past and, say, maybe drive only every other run.

Henry Mitchum, the station manager, had been even more adamant that the old jehu needed to rest until he was fully recovered. Beth Macy was doing a good job filling in, he had claimed, so there was no reason Fred had to rush back to work. In response to Scratch's comment, Bo said, "Beth may not want the job permanently, you know. After all, she came out here to get married."

"Maybe. But maybe she found something she'd rather do. Anyway, wrestlin' that coach back and forth to El Paso twice a week like she does, where's she gonna find a fella to marry?"

"She sits right next to a decent young fella most of the time," Bo pointed out.

Scratch glanced over at him. "Monte Jackson? That galoot's more likely to marry his shotgun! I've never seen any sign that he's got an ounce o' romance in his soul."

"We don't actually know him that well. Beth ought to, though, by now."

They didn't continue the conversation, because they had reached the stage station. Beth had already brought the coach to a stop and was standing beside the boot at the back while the passengers retrieved their bags.

Nobody would be able to find much of a resemblance between Beth as she looked now and the young woman Bo and Scratch had first met back in Fort Worth. Her long blond hair was tucked and pinned up out of the way, under an almost shapeless old brown hat with a floppy brim. More than once the Texans had seen her driving the stage at such a rate of speed that the wind pushed the brim up and flattened it against the hat's crown.

Instead of a dress, she wore a duster, baggy canvas trousers held up by suspenders, and a faded red shirt, and she had a blue bandanna around her neck. Her feet were thrust into high-topped boots. Dust coated her clothes and face.

Other than her relatively small stature and the lack of a bristly beard sticking out from her chin and cheeks and jaw, she almost could have passed for a man. Almost . . . But to Bo's eyes at least, some indefinable female quality still came from her. He would have known her for a woman anywhere.

He wondered idly if Monte Jackson felt the same way about Beth. The shotgun guard wasn't in sight, so Bo assumed he had already taken the express pouch filled with mail.

None of the passengers who had gotten off the stage looked particularly interesting. A couple of salesmen, a miner, a man in a somewhat shabby frock coat, who was probably a gambler. Maybe that last one had heard about the gambler who'd been killed in the Silver King, and thought there might be room in town for another dealer. Once the men had claimed their bags and moved on, Bo and Scratch walked up to Beth.

After they exchanged greetings, Bo asked, "Any trouble on this trip?"

Beth shook her head. "Just a lot of heat and dust. Oh, and we saw some scorpions and rattlesnakes."

Scratch said, "And you had Monte and that scattergun of his ridin' along to take care of them, if they needed it."

Beth let out a little snort and pushed back the right side of the duster she wore to reveal a holstered .38 caliber Smith & Wesson revolver.

"If a varmint bothers me, I'll shoot it myself," she declared.

"I do believe you would," Bo said with a smile.

During the trip from El Paso to Silverhill, he and Scratch had tried to teach the young women a little about handling guns, since that was often a very important skill to have on the frontier. Not surprisingly, Rose and Beth had taken to it quicker and easier than the others and had demonstrated some actual shooting talent, but Cecilia and Luella had done all right, too. Only Jean had seemed to be

absolutely hopeless in that area and had never been able
even to come close to anything she aimed at.

Monte emerged from the office and nodded to Bo and
Scratch. He said to Beth, "Mr. Mitchum wants to talk to
you."

"Is something wrong?"

"No, I don't think so." Monte paused, then added, "He
probably wants to give you a raise, he's so pleased with the
time we've been making lately."

"We wouldn't make such good time if I slowed down
every time you told me to," Beth replied with an edge of
tartness to her voice.

"Yeah, well, one of these days we're gonna bust an axle
or knock a wheel clean off, the way you keep that coach
bouncing and jolting over rough ground. Fred never
pushed it quite that hard."

"Fred was late sometimes, too," Beth shot back at him.
"I never have been . . . and I don't intend to be." She turned
to Bo and Scratch and said, "See you later, fellas," then
went into the office.

Monte watched her go. He had a scowl on his face, but
at the same time, Bo thought he saw a certain amount of
keen interest and admiration in the young man's eyes. Beth
might not be very feminine looking in that jehu's getup,
but she had an appeal that went beyond what she wore.

"She sure is hardheaded, isn't she?" Monte said a little
under his breath, as if he didn't care whether he got an
answer or not.

Bo gave him one, anyway. "I'd say she's determined."

"That's one way to put it." Monte shrugged. "But I'll
give her this . . . She can handle a team. Don't tell Fred I
said this, but she may be better at it than even he was."

Scratch said, "I don't reckon either one of 'em need to

know that. Might give Beth a swelled head, and then she'd try to make those runs from El Paso even faster, just to prove she could do it."

"And she already drives like a bat out of hell!" Monte exclaimed. "Although . . . I never saw a bat that looks quite like her."

As they walked away from the station, Bo said quietly to Scratch, "You still think Monte doesn't have an ounce of romance in his soul?"

"Well, after seein' the way he looked at Beth—"

"You noticed that, too, did you?"

"Yeah. And he had kind of an admirin' tone in his voice when he talked about her, even when he was complainin' about her drivin'. I guess it really ain't all that surprisin'. If I was forty years younger and spendin' as much time with a gal like Beth as Monte is, I'd probably be a mite smitten with her, too."

"Wonder if that's all it is," Bo said, "or if it's a little more serious than—"

He didn't get to finish that speculation, because at that moment, a flurry of loud, angry voices came from farther up the street.

From the sound of it, the peaceful, trouble-free afternoon in Silverhill was over.

CHAPTER 12

The commotion came from a knot of men gathered in front of the Territorial House. Bo and Scratch were still a block away, so they couldn't make out too many details, but judging by their rough work clothes, a group of miners had surrounded somebody.

Bo caught a glimpse of a tall, broad-shouldered figure in the middle of the clump, but before he could determine who it was, the yelling got even louder and more profane and the miners suddenly leaped at their intended victim, evidently intent on dragging him down and stomping him into the ground.

It didn't work out that way.

For a moment, the knot of men swayed back and forth, almost like a bizarre dance, and then two of the miners flew backward out of it, yelling as they flailed their arms but were unable to stop their flight. They landed on their backs and skidded along the dusty street.

Loud thuds of fists against flesh rose above the shouts. Another miner reeled back out of the fracas, with his hands clamped to what appeared to be a broken jaw. He made gurgling noises through it as he stumbled around.

Bo and Scratch stopped several yards away. Scratch frowned and said, "You reckon we ought to break that up?"

"I think if we're patient, it'll be over on its own in another minute or two," Bo said.

It looked like his prediction was going to come true. The man in the middle of the battle suddenly reared up, appearing even taller. He had hold of one of his attackers by an arm and a leg and hoisted the struggling man above his head. With a furious bearlike roar, he pitched the man into the other miners and laid three of them low.

That was enough for the other two men still on their feet. They backed away, and now, instead of brandishing fists, they held their hands in front of them, palms out defensively. The object of their wrath took a step, as if he intended to come after them, then stopped and settled for glaring darkly at them.

Bo recognized the man. He was the miner called Roscoe, who had plucked Cecilia Spaulding from in front of a wagon team that day a while back. Even though a couple of months had passed since then, Bo immediately knew who the man was. Once a fella had laid eyes on Roscoe Sherman, it would be difficult to forget the shaggy giant.

"Hold on there, Roscoe!" Bo called to him, even though Roscoe had stopped and now stood there on wide-planted legs, with his ham-like hands raised and clenched into fists. Bo went on, "I don't think these fellas want to fight anymore."

One of the miners who was still conscious turned and looked over his shoulder at the Texans. "You got to arrest this monster, Sheriff!" he said. "He don't need to be loose around normal people!"

Scratch said, "Judgin' by what I saw while we were comin' up the street, it was you and your pards who jumped him, mister. Are you sayin' I can't trust my own eyes? And it's Marshal, not Sheriff."

"It may have looked like we were gangin' up on him, but you seen what happened for yourself, Marshal. We knew it'd take all of us to bring him down, and even then, we couldn't do it!"

"Why did you even want to?" Bo asked.

"Because the big dumb ox makes the rest of us look bad! He does more work by himself than a whole crew does!"

Scratch said, "I don't see why that'd be a bad thing."

"Because the superintendent up at the mine fired some of us over it. Told us he didn't need us no more, because he's got Roscoe. That just ain't right! We've talked to him and tried to get him to slow down, but he's too dang dumb to understand!"

In a voice that rumbled like an underground cave-in, Roscoe said, "I just do what the boss tells me to do. Ain't that what I'm supposed to do?"

The miner who had been doing the talking turned to glare at him and responded, "Not if it costs good men their jobs!"

Scratch said, "I don't reckon you can ask a fella not to be himself. He's just doin' what he's told."

Several of the miners who'd been knocked down groaned and climbed slowly and painfully to their feet. The man with the broken jaw had sat down on the boardwalk and was rocking back and forth in pain. A couple of others were still lying senseless in the street.

Bo turned to one of the bystanders who had gathered

to watch the fight and told him, "Run and fetch Dr. Chapman. That fella there on the boardwalk is going to need some medical attention."

The man hurried away on that errand. Arliss Chapman had rented an adobe house at the edge of town for his practice and living quarters and was usually there during the day.

The first miner who had spoken up said to Scratch, "Are you gonna arrest Roscoe or not?"

"No, I'm not," Scratch snapped. "I don't care whether you think it was justified or not, you fellas jumped him, and to my way of thinkin', that's no reason to throw him behind bars. You varmints, on the other hand . . ."

"Hold on, Marshal," the miner said hastily. "There's no need for that—"

"Then skedaddle and stay out of Silverhill for a while," Scratch broke in. "If I see you again anytime soon, I'll be liable to forget I decided to give you a break."

The man pointed at his broken-jawed friend. "What about him?"

"Help him to the doc's," Scratch said with a jerk of his thumb in the direction of Chapman's house. "You'll probably meet the sawbones on his way here. Get your pards who ain't up yet on their feet, too, and help 'em outta here."

As the miners drifted away, Bo and Scratch cautiously approached Roscoe Sherman. The giant had relaxed a little as it became obvious that the battle was over, but he still looked wary, ready to start swinging those massive arms and fists again.

"Take it easy, Roscoe," Bo said, keeping his voice calm and level.

"Are you gonna put me in jail?" Roscoe asked with a frown.

"No, we're not," Scratch said. "Like I told those other

fellas, they're the ones who jumped you, and I'm not gonna arrest a man for defendin' himself."

"Good. I don't reckon I'd like bein' in jail."

Bo said, "You've never been arrested?"

Roscoe shook his head ponderously. "No, sir. I believe in followin' the law. I never set out to do nothin' wrong."

"Well, that's the best way to be, I reckon," Scratch assured him. "What are you doin' in town, Roscoe?"

"Came to pick up a package for Mr. Carling," Roscoe explained. "Them other boys follered me, I reckon. I didn't know they was gonna cause trouble."

Bo said, "As much work as they depend on you for out there at the Minotaur, I'm surprised the superintendent would take you away from that for something like picking up a package."

"Well, this is my day off. Mr. Carling, he don't believe in workin' his men seven days a week. I told the boss I wouldn't mind doin' it." Roscoe shook his head. "Most of the fellas, when they don't have to work, they come into town to get drunk or cavort around with immoral women. I never set no store by things like that, my own self."

Bo clapped a hand on the giant's arm and said, "Well, you're a good man, Roscoe."

That brought a beaming smile to Roscoe's face, or at least Bo thought so. It was difficult to be certain with all that tangled hair obscuring the big man's features.

"So I can go on to Mr. Dubonnet's store?" he asked.

"You go right ahead," Scratch told him.

Roscoe nodded and started to shuffle off. He stopped and looked back at the two Texans.

"Umm . . . how's that lady doin'? Yuh know, that real pretty lady who nearly got runned over by the horses last time I was in town?"

"Cecilia?" Bo said. "You remember what happened that day, do you?"

"Shoot, a fella would never forget meetin' a lady as pretty as her!"

"She's fine," Bo assured him. Hugh Craddock was still in Silverhill, stubbornly trying to convince Cecilia to let him court her, and she was just as stubbornly resisting his efforts. But Bo didn't see any reason to go into that with Roscoe, who seemed satisfied with the answer he had gotten to his question.

"Good," Roscoe said as he nodded. "I'm glad to hear it. When you see her, would yuh tell her I said hello?"

"Sure, Roscoe." As Bo watched Roscoe make his shuffling way toward the store, he said quietly to Scratch, "That fella is one odd duck."

"I never saw a duck anywhere near that big," Scratch said. He frowned. "That'd be kind of scary, wouldn't it, a duck that big? Wouldn't be no tellin' what a critter like that'd do."

Bo just chuckled at the idea, and they moved on.

Steve Hargett eased his horse up to the hitch rail in front of the Silver King and swung down from the saddle. Tonight that hitch rail likely would be full, but right now, late in the afternoon, a few spots were open. He tied his mount in one of them and then stood there beside the animal for a moment, gazing at the batwings.

He thought about going in there and having a shot or two of whiskey to fortify himself, but then he decided against it. What he had to do today was too important for him to muddle his mind with Who-Hit-John.

So instead of entering the saloon, he turned and angled

across the broad street toward the hotel instead. He didn't know for sure that he'd find Rose at the Territorial House, but that was the best place to start looking for her.

He hoped she would be there. He kind of thought it would be a good idea to have some other people around when he broke the news to her.

She would understand, he told himself. She had to. What he was going to do was for her own good. It just wasn't safe for the two of them to be involved anymore. Wasn't safe for *her*—and during the past two months, Rose Winston had become the most important thing in Steve's life.

He had just stepped up on the hotel porch when Jean Parker and Dr. Arliss Chapman emerged arm in arm from the front door. Jean recognized him, nodded, and said with a rather stiff note of politeness in her voice, "Hello, Mr. Hargett."

"Ma'am," Steve said as he took off his hat. "Good to see you again."

He knew that Jean didn't like him. None of the other mail-order brides did, except maybe Beth Macy, a little. Jean and Cecilia Spaulding and Luella Tolman all thought Rose could do better for herself than some scruffy cowhand like Steve. And they felt like that without even knowing the truth about what was going on at the SJ Ranch. If they ever found out about the rustling . . . !

"If you're looking for Rose," Jean went on, "she's not here. I believe she went down to the stagecoach station to watch Beth bring in the stage. She's probably still down there."

Steve nodded and said, "Thank you, ma'am."

Jean looked back and forth between Steve and Dr.

Chapman. "Have you two met?" she asked, surprising Steve a little.

Chapman said, "I don't believe we have." He put out his hand. "I'm Arliss Chapman."

"Yes, sir, Doctor, I know who you are," Steve said as he clasped the man's hand. "I'm Steve Hargett. Ride for the SJ Ranch. I haven't, ah, needed your services since you've been in town."

"Well, that's a good thing, isn't it?" Chapman said with a smile. "I take it from Miss Parker's comment that you and Miss Winston are, shall we say, keeping company?"

"Yes, sir. Rose has been kind enough to allow me to court her."

"Then you should be good to her," Chapman said. "She seems' like a fine young woman, and I know that Miss Parker here thinks the world of her."

Steve nodded and said, "Yes, sir," yet again. He felt like a grimy, uneducated dunce next to the suave physician. Which was a pretty accurate comparison, he told himself.

"It's good to meet you," Chapman said, and then he and Jean moved on, stepping down from the porch and strolling up the street. Steve didn't know where they were bound, but it was none of his business. He turned the other way, toward the stagecoach station. Maybe Rose was still down there, or else he would meet her on her way back to the hotel.

That was exactly what happened. He spotted her walking toward him, and she saw him at the same time. Instantly, a smile appeared on her face and her step got a little more of a spring to it, but then she slowed down and a slight frown creased her forehead. She must have noticed how grim and determined he looked.

She wore a dress today, something she had been doing

more often lately. Steve thought she looked beautiful, as always, with her tall, lithe figure and the waves of thick chestnut hair tumbling around her head and shoulders. Just the sight of her was enough to make his heart slug harder in his chest.

It was going a mile a minute with trepidation right now.

"Hello, Steve," she said as she came up to him. "Is something wrong?"

"What, uh, what makes you ask that?" he said.

"You just sort of look like you've got the weight of the world on your shoulders. Is there a problem out at the ranch?"

It was an innocent enough question, but she didn't know what she was asking, he thought. If she were aware of what was really going on, she'd be disappointed in him. She might even hate him.

But more than likely, she was going to hate him, anyway, once he'd told her what he had to say, he realized.

He should have been smart and never have allowed Ben Wilcox to rope him in on this mess.

"It's the chance for a big cleanup," Wilcox had said the night before, as he talked to Steve and the other four members of the rustling ring, all of whom had gathered beside one of the corrals at the SJ. It had been a dark night, with clouds obscuring the moon and most of the stars, and they had drifted out of the bunkhouse one by one when Wilcox gave them the high sign.

Steve said, "I thought we were just gonna keep on slipping off with a few cows at a time, so nobody will notice what's goin' on."

"Yeah, that was the plan," Wilcox said, "and it's been workin' all right for a while, but none of us knew the syndicate was gonna sell off a big bunch of stock. Next week

it's gonna be sitting right out there at that bed-ground, boys, just waitin' for us to drive it off. We can't pass up this chance. I've got a buyer lined up down on the border. We run those cows down there, collect the dinero we got comin' to us, and then we can shake the dust of these parts off our boots. Shoot, we'll be right there at the border. Easy as pie just to drift on down into Mexico and enjoy the good life down there for a while." Wilcox grinned, his teeth showing even in the darkness. "Tequila and warm, willin' señoritas, boys. It doesn't get any better than that."

Steve disagreed. He could think of things a lot better— but he knew Wilcox wouldn't care about any of that.

He took a deep breath and said, "I think you fellas are just gonna have to manage without me this time."

"What! Steve, don't be a fool. You can make as much from this one deal as you'd make in a year of punchin' cows. You can't really mean to say you'd pass that up!"

"Yeah, I'm afraid so. I'm out, boys. You go ahead and do what you have to do, but you can do it without me."

"I don't know if we can," Wilcox said with a hard edge knifing into his voice. "This job will be a lot easier with six men instead of five."

"I can't believe one man would make that much difference."

"He will," Wilcox snapped, "if he's liable to ruin the deal for everybody else."

Steve stiffened. The other men moved a little, surrounding him and closing in. The threat was obvious in their stance.

"Blast it! You fellas know I'd never talk! I'd be loco to do that. I've been just as guilty as any of you."

"So far, maybe," Wilcox said, "but it's all been penny-ante stuff up to now. Wouldn't get you sent to prison for

more than a year or so. What I'm talkin' about is a lot bigger risk . . . like five or ten years behind bars. I don't intend to spend a chunk of my life that way."

"I don't blame you, but what in blazes makes you think I'd ever say anything?"

Wilcox poked a finger into Steve's chest, hard. "That gal you've been sparkin'," he said. "If we deal you out of the game and leave you here, maybe you decide you want to settle down with her, but you feel too guilty about keepin' our secret. So you tell her, and she says you've got to tell the law. You really expect me to believe you wouldn't do whatever she wanted, Steve?"

With his jaw tight, Steve just stared at Wilcox. Like it or not, the man had a point. Steve would have a hard time denying Rose anything she really wanted—even if it meant testifying against his partners in this scheme.

"I might, just might, be able to trust your conscience, but we can't trust hers," Wilcox went on. "So you can see, it'll be a lot safer for us . . . for you . . . and for her if you just go along with this. Maybe sometime, after things have cooled off, you might be able to come back for her. Folks might be suspicious of you, but they couldn't prove anything. What it comes down to right now, though, is that you're part of this and there's no backing out."

Wilcox couldn't put it any plainer than that, Steve supposed. It wasn't just his life that was in danger, but it was Rose's, too, and he couldn't allow that to stand. She had to stay safe, and he could see only one way of guaranteeing that.

All that flashed through his brain in an instant as he stood there looking at her.

An impatient expression appeared on her face as she said, "Well? Are you going to tell me what's wrong or not?"

"There's nothing wrong," he said. He couldn't tell her the truth. All he could do was break the news that he was going away, that he wouldn't be courting her anymore or . . . or doing any of the other things they'd been doing, no matter how much they both enjoyed them. . . .

"Good," Rose said in response to his lie. She seemed pretty serious and solemn now, too, and as she glanced around to see if anyone was nearby, she went on, "I'm glad you came to town today. There's something I really need to tell you."

"All right, but wait a minute. First, I need to say—"

"No." Rose shook her head. "Whatever it is, it's not as important as the news I have." She glanced around again, leaned toward him, lowered her voice to a whisper, and said, "I'm with child."

CHAPTER 13

During their time in Silverhill, Bo and Scratch had dined on occasion at Harbinson's Restaurant, but the place was too expensive for them to eat there on a regular basis. The informal town council wasn't paying them good enough wages for that.

Sometimes they ate in the dining room of the Territorial House, but again, that cost enough that they saved it for special occasions. Most of the time, they took their meals at the Red Top Café, a building made from large blocks of sandstone, with a red slate roof, which gave the place its name. The food therewas good but inexpensive.

Bo went in there that evening to get his supper, while Scratch remained on duty at the marshal's office. When he was done, Scratch would come get something to eat.

When Bo went in the door, an L-shaped counter was to his left, with the longer leg of it running toward the back of the building. To the right were the tables, covered with neat blue-checked tablecloths. Blue-patterned curtains covered the windows on the front and side of the café. The place had a homey feel to it, and Bo always enjoyed coming in here.

He had a surprise waiting for him this evening, but not an unpleasant one. The woman working behind the counter, waiting on the half-dozen men sitting there, was in her mid-thirties, with dark hair pulled back and pinned into a bun at the back of her head. She wore a dark green dress with a white apron over it. As she poured coffee into customers' cups, using a thick piece of leather as a pot holder, she glanced toward the newcomer and smiled at Bo.

"Why, Miss Hampshire," he said, "what are you doing here?"

"What does it look like, Deputy Creel?" she asked as she placed the coffeepot back on the stove behind the counter. "I'm working."

Bo shook his head and said, "I didn't know you had a job here."

A man with a face like a friendly bulldog's called through the opening between the dining room and the kitchen where food was passed through, "She just started tonight." That was Ed Massey, the owner and cook.

Susan Hampshire said, "I'm not breaking some law, am I, Bo?"

"None that I'm aware of," he assured her. "I just wasn't expecting to see you, that's all."

"I had to do something. I couldn't stay here in Silverhill indefinitely without any income." She shrugged. "And I've just about exhausted the funds I brought with me when I came out here."

Susan hadn't been supposed to stay in Silverhill at all. After her disastrous meeting with Hugh Craddock in Fort Worth, when he had taken back his proposal of marriage and accused her of being too old for him, she had followed him out here for no other reason than to give him a piece of her mind. She had been on hand for the big celebration that had turned into a battle royal, and after that, Bo had figured she would catch the next stage to El Paso and head back to Vermont, where she came from.

Instead, something about this harsh but starkly beautiful area had caught her fancy, and she had stayed in town, living in a room at the Territorial House for a while and then moving into a boardinghouse, which was more affordable. But as Susan had said, her funds weren't limitless. If she was going to remain in town, she had to do something to earn a living.

Bo supposed working as a waitress at the Red Top wasn't a bad way of doing that. The café might not be fancy, but it was a respectable place. If a woman didn't have the money to open a dress shop or something like that, most of her other options weren't so respectable.

As he sat down on one of the stools at the counter, she went on, "What can I get for you?"

"A cup of that coffee, to start out with," he said. "Hate to ask it of you, since you just set the pot back down."

"Oh, no, that's not a problem," she said. She picked up a cup and saucer from a shelf on the wall and set it in front of him, then poured some of the strong black brew in it. With a smile, she added, "I've already discovered that topping off coffee cups is a never-ending job. Now, I assume you're here for supper, so what would you like to eat?"

Bo ordered a bowl of Ed Massey's beef stew, knowing that it was always good, and Susan delivered it to him a few minutes later, along with a hunk of bread on a small plate. Bo dug in and enjoyed the food.

He also enjoyed watching Susan move along behind the counter as she tended to the needs of the customers. Another woman, Massey's wife, Gwendolyn, waited on the tables. It was a smooth-running operation, and Susan seemed to fit right in.

That came as no surprise to Bo. He had spent enough time with Susan during the past two months to know that she was intelligent and levelheaded, and he could see with his own eyes that she was a hard worker.

He hadn't really intended to start keeping company with her, but he had been attracted to her from the first time he'd met her, on the train going from Fort Worth to El Paso. He hadn't known who she was, though, until both of them were here in Silverhill, and he hadn't pursued a relationship then, because he didn't figure he and Scratch would be staying around for very long. They would move on to whatever job Cyrus Keegan had waiting for them.

The thing was, Keegan hadn't had a job waiting for them, although he had mentioned in the letters he'd sent them that he was working on several different matrimonial arrangements, as he called them. So it had made sense for them to remain in Silverhill while they waited to hear something definite from him, and then this business of being hired as lawmen had come up, and so Bo had stayed in town, and so had Susan Hampshire, and since the two of them had hit it off from the first . . .

It wasn't like they were carrying on some hot and heavy romance. Bo was too old for any emotional drama. But they enjoyed spending time with each other, whether it was eating dinner together a couple of times a week or taking buggy rides in the hills. Scratch referred to Susan as Bo's lady friend, and Bo supposed that was true, for now, anyway.

He was sopping up the last of the stew with the final bite of bread when she paused on the other side of the counter from him and leaned forward.

"If you happen to be making rounds later, about the time Mr. and Mrs. Massey close up, I wouldn't object if you were to walk me back to the boardinghouse."

"I don't know if I ought to do that," Bo said. "You might distract me from my official duties."

"I think you'll be able to concentrate well enough on what you're doing."

"Well," Bo said, "I suppose that depends on what I'm doing." She smiled and lowered her eyes.

Bo chuckled and went on, "I'll be by around closing time."

"I'll be here," Susan promised.

Bo paid for his meal and then left the Red Top with some reluctance. Both he and Susan had jobs to do, he told himself, and besides, Scratch was waiting back at the office to get his own supper. He had mentioned already that he was going to one of the Mexican taquerias, where he could dine on the fiery cuisine he so enjoyed.

When Bo entered the office, though, he told his old friend about Susan's new job at the Red Top and said, "Why don't you go there? Be nice for her to see another friendly face on her first night on the job."

"I reckon I can do that," Scratch agreed. "Although I don't reckon Susan will have any trouble fittin' in there. She seems to get along with just about everybody."

"Except Hugh Craddock," Bo pointed out.

"Well, he's as crazy as a cow that's spent a week grazin' on locoweed. He'd have to be, to figure that she ain't worth his time. Seems to me any man'd be lucky to have a gal like Susan willin' to marry him, and he just up an' throws the chance away."

"Yeah," Bo said, "I've been thinking the same thing lately . . . about how any man would be lucky to have her."

Dr. Arliss Chapman was whistling softly to himself as he walked toward the house on the edge of town that was not only his medical office but also his home. Normally, he was a man who was satisfied with his life for the most part, accepting of his own successes and shortcomings and those of other people. Tonight he was more than satisfied. He was happy.

And *that*, he was convinced, was due almost entirely to Miss Jean Parker.

The process of finding a place to live and setting up his medical practice had consumed most of Chapman's time, as well as his thoughts, for the past couple of months. When he hadn't been dealing with those things, Jean had been a most welcome distraction. When he wasn't working, he was either spending time with her or thinking about her. His growing friendship with her didn't allow him to dwell on other, less pleasant parts of life. Only occasionally did his thoughts turn in those directions.

Tonight had been yet another very enjoyable evening spent in Jean's company. She was so refined, so witty, such a good conversationalist. And so beautiful, of course. Any man would have been honored and thrilled to have such a lovely companion on his arm. He certainly was.

And yet she wasn't *all* refinement. She had a fiery side, too, although she kept it well hidden most of the time. But when they were alone and he took her in his arms and kissed her, as he had earlier tonight, she returned his ardor with an intensity that left him shaking inside.

They were a good match, and he knew from what she had told him about her life that she had come to Silverhill to get married. Those plans hadn't worked out . . . but perhaps they had just been delayed. Perhaps she hadn't met the right man . . . until now.

The thought was growing stronger and stronger inside him.

Of course, he hadn't told her all that much about his own life, but there wasn't much to tell, really. And like all men, he had his little secrets, things that a wife didn't necessarily need to know. Jean would just have to understand about that, assuming she accepted his proposal. And assuming he actually decided that a proposal was in order.

All those thoughts whirling around in his head left him in a good mood, and so he whistled to himself as he headed home—"Beautiful Dreamer," a Stephen Foster tune that he had learned as a child from listening to his mother sing it as she played the piano. It transported him back to earlier times and filled him with memories and feelings.

Even with that tune in his ears, though, he heard the soft moan that came from a bench in front of the darkened store he was passing.

Chapman paused, looked closer at the bench, and saw the shape huddled on it. He said sharply, "Are you all right? What's wrong? I'm a doctor."

"Oh!" That was a woman's voice. "I . . . I'm sorry, Doc. I didn't mean to disturb you."

"You're not disturbing me at all. But if there's a problem, I'd like to help." Chapman smiled in the darkness. "That's what I swore an oath to do, you know."

"It . . . It's nothin'. Just a bellyache."

"Sometimes bellyaches are nothing, and sometimes

they're quite serious." Chapman sat down on the other end of the bench, not crowding her. "Tell me about this one."

"Well, it just . . . it just started sudden-like, you know? I was workin' when it came on me out of the blue."

"Working? Where?"

"At one of the saloons. The Red Devil."

"I'm not familiar with it," Chapman said. He'd been in the Silver King, but that was the only saloon in Silverhill he had visited.

"Oh, it's just a hole-in-the-wall. Nothin' fancy."

He had been able to tell from her speech that she wasn't an educated woman, so he wasn't surprised she worked in a saloon, and evidently a squalid one, at that. But she was still a human being in pain, so he said, "Why don't you come with me? My office isn't far away. I can examine you, and if the ailment isn't serious, I have some tonic that I'm sure will ease your discomfort."

"What if . . . it *is* serious?"

"Then you need medical attention, and you'll be right there in a doctor's office, won't you?"

She couldn't argue with that logic. She said, "Yeah, I guess so. What'd you say your name was?"

"I didn't, but it's Chapman. Dr. Arliss Chapman."

"Yeah, I . . . I think I've heard of you, Doctor. You really think you can help me?"

"I'm positive of it." He got to his feet and gently took hold of her arm. "Please, let me help you."

"A-all right." She stood up and started along the street with him while he maintained his light grip on her arm.

"What's your name?" he asked.

"J-Julie. Julie Hobbs." Her voice held a slight note of defiance as she added, "It's my real name, too. I may work in a saloon, but I don't do nothin' to make me ashamed of tellin' folks my real name."

"I'm sure you don't. How's the pain now?"

"It still hurts . . . but maybe not quite as bad."

"Good. We'll be there soon."

A few minutes later they reached his house, and he led the way inside. He already knew his way around by feel, so he didn't have any trouble lighting an oil lamp once the door was closed behind them. The curtains were pulled tight over the windows in the front room.

As the lamplight welled up, Chapman saw that Julie Hobbs was young. He had been able to tell that from her voice, too. The dress she wore wasn't short and spangled like the garb sported by the girls who worked in the Silver King, but it was cut low enough in the front to display a considerable amount of cleavage. She was a pretty girl, if one was willing to stretch the definition of *pretty* a bit beyond the usual. Her long light brown hair was worked into a braid that hung halfway down her back.

She summoned up a smile when she saw him, and that expression improved her looks considerably. Now she was genuinely pretty, Chapman decided, and the dress showed off her young body to advantage.

He picked up the lamp and said, "Come in here, please." He led her into the examination room. "Sit there on the table and let me take a look at you."

He helped her onto the table.

"Now, show me where it hurts."

She pressed her fingers against the upper part of her stomach, just under her bosom, and said, "Right here."

"Not lower down, on the right side?"

"No, sir. Just here. But it burns like fire."

Chapman nodded. "I was worried that your appendix

might have burst, but clearly, that's not the case. Have you had anything to eat this evening?"

"No . . . Well, Mr. Walsh, he's the fella who owns the Red Devil, he keeps a plate of meat and chili peppers and such sittin' out on the bar, so fellas can snack on it while they're drinkin', and I snuck some off of it. Mostly, I wait until I get home at night to eat supper, but I was hungry tonight and didn't think he'd mind."

"Have you done that before?" Chapman asked.

"No, sir. Tonight was the first time."

He smiled. "Well, that explains it. You're just having a reaction to spicy food you're not used to."

"You mean . . . I ain't dyin'?"

"Not at all, but it can be quite uncomfortable." He turned to a cabinet and opened one of the doors to reveal an array of bottles and pillboxes. He selected one of the bottles and worked the cork out of its neck. "Here, drink some of this. It'll put out that fire that's trying to burn you up from the inside out."

Hesitantly, she took the bottle from him, lifted it to her lips, and swallowed some of the liquid. She made a face and said, "It doesn't taste good."

"Not particularly, but it will help. A few minutes and you won't feel a thing."

"You reckon?"

"I give you my word." He corked the bottle and put it back in the cabinet.

"I guess I . . . I'd better be goin'. I need to get home."

She started to slide off the examination table, but he put a hand on her arm and stopped her. When fate presented a man with such a fine opportunity, he'd be a fool to waste it, Chapman knew.

"I'd prefer that you stay until we can be sure that tonic

is having the effect it's supposed to. If it doesn't fix you right up, we can try something else."

"I'm sure it's gonna be fine, Doc. How . . . how much do I owe you? If it's very much, I'll have to come back and pay you—"

"Please, don't worry about that right now. Just sit back . . . Yes, that's right. Take deep breaths. Relax. Now, isn't that starting to feel better?"

"To . . . to tell you the truth, Doc . . . it don't hurt no more . . . but I kinda . . . don't feel much of anything except tired. Like I could . . . just stretch out on this table . . . and go to sleep."

"Not yet," Chapman told her. "There's one more thing I need to do."

He kept his left hand on her shoulder while he stepped around the table and went behind her. He reached over with his right hand to a dresser with a cloth spread on top of it. A number of medical instruments lay on the cloth. He picked up a scalpel.

"Doc," Julie Hobbs murmured, "I'm startin' to feel bad again."

"We'll take care of that," Dr. Arliss Chapman said. He reached around her, plunged the scalpel into her throat, and pulled it straight across in a deep, clean cut. "There, just like I promised. You won't feel a thing."

Chapter 14

Cecilia was the only one of the mail-order brides who had her own room at the Territorial House. Jean and Luella shared a room, as did Rose and Beth. Beth was there only a couple of nights a week, though, because the rest of the time she was out with the stagecoach, on the way to or from El Paso.

When she was at the hotel, she generally got up before Rose, because the stagecoach pulled out for El Paso promptly at nine o'clock, and Beth liked to check the team and the coach well beforehand, then get something to eat before the long journey got under way.

This morning, though, when she sat up and saw the gray light of predawn peeking through the crack between the curtains over the window, she noticed that Rose wasn't under the covers on the other side of the bed, or anywhere else in the room.

She knew Rose had been there during the night. They had talked for a while before going to sleep. Rose had seemed distracted about something, Beth recalled. As she swung her legs out of bed and stood up, she wondered if Rose had sneaked out to meet Steve Hargett. The SJ cowboy had been in town the previous afternoon. Beth knew that he and Rose had had supper together.

Maybe they'd had a fight of some sort. That would explain why Rose hadn't quite seemed herself the night before. But it didn't answer the question of where she was now.

Beth started getting dressed. Rose was a grown woman, she told herself, and it wasn't up to Beth to look after her. But the five young women had been friends for so long that such mutual concern just came naturally to them.

She didn't have to ponder it for very long, because with a soft click, the door opened and Rose came in. She stopped short for a second when she saw that Beth was up; then she eased the door closed behind her.

"I hope I didn't wake you when I went out," Rose said. She wore her dressing gown and soft slippers on her feet, so Beth knew she hadn't been outside.

Beth shook her head and said, "This is the time I normally get up when I've got a stagecoach run. You're usually not awake this early, though. Is something wrong?"

"No, no." Rose started toward the bed. "I'm fine."

Beth didn't think she *sounded* fine, and although it was difficult to tell in the dim light, she thought Rose's face was pale and drawn. That was unusual, because Rose was the most robustly healthful one among them.

"If there's something going on, you can tell me. You know there's never been many secrets between the five of us."

"There's no secret," Rose insisted, but once again the words didn't strike Beth as being sincere. "I was just down the hall."

The Territorial House was fancy enough to have a convenience with running water on each floor, although there were also chamber pots in every room. Beth supposed that was where Rose had been, and she realized it would be indiscreet to pry any more than she already had.

She sat down on the edge of the bed to pull her boots on, but as she did, Rose suddenly took a step back toward the door, as if she was about to hurry out. Then, instead, she lunged for the other side of the bed and yanked the chamber pot out from under it. She fell to her knees and began to be violently sick.

Beth exclaimed in surprise and hurried around the bed to kneel beside Rose. She took hold of her friend's hair and held it back out of the way. After a couple of minutes, when Rose's spasms stopped and she could speak again, she gasped, "You . . . you don't need . . . to be in here. You can . . . go on about your business."

"Not with you this sick, I can't," Beth said. "What in the world, Rose?"

Before Rose could say anything, she began to heave again. Beth waited until the bout passed. When it did, Rose turned and sat down on the floor next to the bed. She leaned back against the mattress. She was breathing hard, and beads of sweat had popped out all over her face.

Beth stood up and went to the table on the other side of the room, where a basin and a pitcher of water sat. She poured water into the basin, got a cloth and soaked it, then went back to kneel beside Rose and wipe her face. Rose sighed.

"I'm all right," she said. Her voice was stronger now but still showed some strain.

"I don't think so," Beth said. "Not considering what you were doing just a couple of minutes ago. Is that why you left earlier? To go down the hall because you were sick?"

"Yeah. It came on me suddenly. I hope I didn't disturb you."

"No, of course not."

"And I'm sorry you had to be here for this—"

"Do you have any idea what caused it?" Beth asked. "Did you eat something you shouldn't have, or . . ." Her voice trailed off as her eyes widened. "Oh, no. Rose, have you been getting sick in the morning like this while I have been gone?"

Rose frowned but didn't answer, and she turned her head so she wouldn't meet Beth's intense gaze.

"You *have*, haven't you?" Beth went on. "Rose, are you . . . Is there any chance you could be . . ."

"All right, blast it!" Rose burst out. "Yes. I'm going to have a baby."

Beth's voice dropped to a whisper. "Steve's?"

"Who else?" Rose sounded angry now. "He's the only one. My first. First and only."

"Oh, honey. I didn't know that the two of you were . . ." Beth's eyes widened even more. "That scoundrel! That no-good, low-down—"

"Hold on. Don't start cussing him like you do those stagecoach teams. It's not Steve's fault. The whole thing was my idea to start with. Not . . . not to get in the family way, of course, but to do the other. . . . He tried to be a gentleman and convince me we shouldn't, in fact, but I wore him down."

Beth went back to wiping Rose's face. After a second, she sighed and said, "I don't suppose it matters now whose fault it was. The only really important thing is what he's going to do about it."

Two big tears rolled down Rose's cheeks, and she bent

forward and covered her face with her hands as she began to sob. Her back rose and fell raggedly.

The reaction startled an oath out of Beth. Maybe she *had* spent too much time yelling at horses recently. She tried to stay calm as she said, "Now what's wrong, Rose?"

"What . . . what Steve's going to do," she said between sobs. She started to hiccup. "He's going to . . . hic . . . leave! He says he . . . hic . . . doesn't want to see me anymore!"

Beth stared at her and said, "Why, that son of a—" She swallowed the rest of it, clenched her teeth, and went on, "You mean he's running away from his responsibility?"

Rose sniffled. "He said it . . . hic . . . it wasn't like that. Claimed he was gonna tell me . . . hic . . . all along that he was quitting his job and leaving these parts."

"Quitting the SJ? Why?"

Rose dragged the back of her hand across her nose. "He didn't say. He promised it wasn't because of me, but . . . I don't know if that's true. I didn't give him a chance . . . hic . . . to say anything before I blurted out my news."

Beth considered that and asked, "You think he just made it up on the spot when he found out that you're . . . in the family way?"

"I don't know. That's what I thought at first. But he swore he was telling me the truth . . . and Steve's never lied to me before."

"That you know of," Beth said. "He didn't change his mind about leaving after you told him?"

Rose shook her head. "No, but he . . . he looked so miserable. That's why I think . . . hic . . . he was telling the truth. I don't think he wants to go, but he can't help it."

"Men can always help it, if they want to bad enough,"

Beth snapped. She started to stand up. "I think I'm going to have to have a talk with Mr. Steve Hargett—"

"No!" Rose clutched her arm. "I'm not going to force him to do anything, and I don't want anybody else to, either. So you can't talk to him, and you can't tell anybody else. *Especially* not Bo and Scratch. You understand, Beth?"

Frowning in frustration, Beth said, "You can't keep this a secret forever. It's not physically possible."

"Maybe not, but nobody has to know right now. Maybe . . . maybe Steve will change his mind . . ."

"You really think he will?"

Rose took a deep breath. "I *hope* he will."

"And if he doesn't?"

Rose's chin came up and jutted out defiantly. "I suppose I'll just have to get along by myself."

"You can't! That would be . . . would be scandalous."

"A little scandal never killed anybody," Rose said.

"Maybe not," Beth said, but she wasn't convinced at all. She went on, "But no matter what happens, you won't be by yourself. You've always got the four of us. We'd never leave you on your own."

Rose caught hold of Beth's hand and squeezed it. "I know. Thank you." Her expression brightened. "Would you look at that? I think my hiccups stopped."

Beth wiped her face again, where the tears had left streaks. "Do you think you're over being sick?"

"For now I am." Rose smiled ruefully. "Whether it'll come back again tomorrow morning, I can't say. I hope it won't, but I won't be surprised if it does!"

"Then you're all right? For now?"

"Of course. And you've got a stagecoach run to make! You should go on. You don't want to be late, after you've been so good about keeping right to the schedule."

"Hang the schedule," Beth said.

"No, no," Rose urged her, "go ahead and take care of what you need to do. I'm going to get back in bed and rest a little while. Then I'll get up and get dressed."

"Are you sure?"

"Yes, absolutely." Rose took the cloth from Beth and wiped her eyes. She summoned up a smile. "I'm all right, see?"

Beth knew good and well that her friend *wasn't* all right, but there didn't seem to be anything she could do for Rose right now. And it was true that she was proud of how well she had kept to the stage line's schedule.

She came to her feet and said, "I can't make Mr. Mitchum have to find a replacement driver when the stage is supposed to pull out in less than two hours, but when I get back from El Paso, you and I are going to have a long talk about this, understand?"

"Whatever you say, but talking's not going to do any good."

"Between now and then, you should talk to Steve again."

Rose shook her head. "If his mind is made up, then it's made up. I'm sure as heck not going to go crawling to him on my knees and beg him to marry me. He'll either do the right thing . . . or he won't."

"He'd better," Beth muttered darkly. She blew out a breath and reached for her duster and hat.

Five minutes later, she reached the stagecoach station and found the coach sitting in front of the office with the team already hitched to it. She conducted her usual inspection of the horses, the harness, the wheels, the axles, and the leather thoroughbraces that ran underneath the coach.

The canvas cover on the boot was open so the passengers could place their bags in it when they arrived to board the stage.

Monte Jackson walked up while she was looking over everything. "Mornin'," he said. He looked closer at her and frowned. "Are you all right? You look a mite upset about something."

"I'm fine," she snapped. "Just ready to get this run started. The sooner we head for El Paso, the sooner we'll be back."

"I suppose so," he agreed. He took his turnip watch out of his pocket and opened it. "But it's still more'n an hour before we're due to leave. None of the passengers are here yet, and the express pouch isn't ready. I figured we'd go get something to eat."

He leaned his head toward the Red Top Café, where they usually had breakfast on mornings such as this. Beth realized he was right. The stage couldn't leave early just because she was upset about Rose's problem. She nodded and said, "Sure."

Once they were at the Red Top, sitting at one of the tables covered with a blue-checked cloth, they sipped coffee and waited for Gwendolyn Massey to bring them their plates of flapjacks, bacon, and eggs. Monte tried to make small talk, but, bless his heart, Beth thought, he just wasn't very good at it.

Finally, after realizing she hadn't heard a word he'd said for a while, she interrupted him.

"I'm sorry, Monte. I've got a lot on my mind this morning."

"Anything I can help you with?" he asked. He was

sincere, too, not just being polite. Although he *was* always polite, at least to her.

"No, there's nothing you can do," she told him. "I don't suppose there's anything *anybody* can do."

He looked mystified, but he didn't press her on it.

What she had just said wasn't true, Beth realized. She knew *exactly* who could do something about this problem. Rose wouldn't like it, but sometimes when a friend was in trouble, you couldn't allow such things to affect the decisions you made. You had to do what was best for them, because they might be too close to the situation to realize what that was.

With that thought in her mind, Beth abruptly shoved back her chair and got to her feet.

"Hey," Monte exclaimed, "where are you going? We haven't had our breakfast yet."

"I'm sorry, Monte," she said, "but I don't have time for that right now. There's something I have to do."

"But what about the stage?"

She had already started to turn away from the table. She said over her shoulder, "If I'm not back before it's time to leave, the blasted stage can just wait for me! And if Mitchum doesn't like that, he . . . he can go to blazes!"

Aware that the other diners in the café were staring at her, Beth ignored them and headed for the door. She was going to the marshal's office.

She had to talk to Bo and Scratch.

CHAPTER 15

B o was about to head to the Red Top for breakfast. Susan Hampshire likely wouldn't be working there this early, since she'd stayed late the night before, but it was still the best place in town for the morning meal, unless you were staying in the hotel to start with and wanted the ease of just going downstairs to the dining room.

Scratch sat at the desk in the marshal's office, sipping from a cup of the coffee he had just brewed on the pot-bellied stove. He said, "When you get done, I'll make the mornin' rounds and then have some breakfast myself."

"Sounds good," Bo said. He reached for the doorknob.

It turned before he could grasp it, and he stepped back as Beth Macy hurried into the office. She was dressed to take the stagecoach out, and that was what she was scheduled to do in another hour or so, Bo recalled.

"What's the hurry?" he asked. Beth looked upset, which was unusual. Normally, she was very calm and levelheaded, one of the results of her upbringing by a military father.

Without saying good morning or any other pleasantry, she asked, "Is Steve Hargett in town?"

"That cowboy from the SJ who's been courtin' Rose?" Scratch said. "I think I saw him yesterday evenin', but I don't know if he's still in town or if he rode back to the ranch last night."

"What do you want with Hargett?" Bo said. "Is Rose looking for him?"

"No. In fact, Rose doesn't know I'm here." Whatever had brought Beth into the office with such vehemence appeared to be wearing off a little. She looked uncomfortable now as she went on, "She'd be mad if she knew I came to see you. But I think it's important that the two of you know what's going on. Too important not to tell you about it."

Scratch put his hands on the desk and pushed himself to his feet.

"If somethin's goin' on," he said, "you're derned right we need to know about it. We're the law here in Silverhill, after all."

Beth shook her head and said, "This isn't really a legal matter. It's more that the two of you have looked out for us ever since Fort Worth, and you promised Mr. Keegan you'd help us with any problems we might have. You're sort of . . . well, like uncles to us, and we've gotten used to that."

"You're talking around whatever it is," Bo told her. "Maybe you'd better just tell us."

"All right." Beth drew in a deep breath but still hesitated, as if she couldn't figure out how to phrase what she had to say. Then, after a few long seconds, she blurted out, "Rose is going to have a baby."

That news jolted a profane exclamation out of Scratch. He immediately followed it with, "Beggin' your pardon,

Beth. I didn't mean to be so colorful. But I never expected to hear what you just said, neither."

Bo was as shocked as his old friend, but he took the revelation more stoically. He said, "I reckon Hargett must be the one responsible for that?"

"She says he is," Beth replied, "and I believe her. I don't think Rose would lie about something like that."

Bo frowned. "No, she's a truthful girl. Sometimes too truthful for her own good." He paused and thought. "How far along is she?"

Beth shook her head. "I don't know. She didn't say. But it can't be more than a month or so, I'd think. It's been only a couple of months since she and Steve started keeping company, and, well, she hinted that it was a while after that before they . . ." Her voice trailed off, and her face slowly turned red.

Bo held up a hand and said, "That's all right. We know what you mean."

Scratch said, "Dang it, I thought Rose had more sense than that."

"Having sense and being able to control your impulses and emotions aren't always the same thing," Bo pointed out. "And let's face it . . . this baby won't be the first one to come into the world a little quick-like after the wedding."

"That's just it," Beth said. "I don't think there's going to be a wedding. Steve told Rose last night that he's quitting his job at the ranch and leaving these parts."

Bo and Scratch both stiffened. Grim looks appeared on their faces.

"He told her that, did he?" Scratch said.

"Did he explain why?" Bo asked. "Was it after Rose told him she's expecting?"

Beth nodded. "That's what she told me. I kind of had to drag the details out of her, and she probably wouldn't have told me anything if she hadn't gotten sick while I was still in our hotel room. Sick like women get in the morning when they're . . . you know."

"Yeah," Bo said. He'd been married, and he and his wife had had children, so he was well aware of what it was like. "So after Rose told him, he made up some cockamamie story about quitting his job—"

"He swore to her he was already planning to tell her, and she believes him," Beth said. She shrugged. "I don't know if it's true. I wasn't there."

"It don't matter," Scratch declared. "Whether he made it up on the spot or there's some other reason behind it, he ain't gettin' away with it. What you just told us changes everything."

Beth looked a little apprehensive as she asked, "What are you going to do?"

"Have a talk with Steve," Bo said. "Not as lawmen, because like you said, this isn't really a legal matter."

"Well, there oughta be a law against that young whippersnapper runnin' off and abandonin' a gal like Rose after he's done got her in such a delicate condition," Scratch said.

"Maybe there should be, but there's not. We'll find him, though—"

"And read him from the book!" Scratch finished with an emphatic nod.

Bo said, "You go ahead and take the stagecoach out, like you're supposed to, Beth. With any luck, by the time you get back from El Paso, we'll have everything straightened out." He smiled. "You might even have a job as a bridesmaid at a wedding."

"I hope so," Beth said. "I'm pretty sure that's what Rose wants, but she's too proud to try to force Steve into it."

"Well, we ain't too proud," Scratch said as he turned toward the gun rack on the wall and reached for one of the shotguns stored there. "And we got us some mighty persuasive friends!"

"Still think we shoulda brought some Greeners along," Scratch groused as the Texans approached the Yancy Hotel. "There's nothin' like the double barrels of a shotgun starin' at an hombre to make him sit up and pay attention."

"I think we can make Hargett pay attention without shotguns." Bo paused. Then his voice hardened as he added, "But if a shotgun wedding is what it takes to make him stand up and do the right thing, I reckon we can oblige him."

Cowboys from the SJ and the other ranches in the area didn't stay in the Territorial House or even the less expensive Western Lodge. If they didn't pass out in some whore's crib or wind up snoring in an alley, they generally stayed at the Yancy, which was much cheaper, especially if you didn't mind sharing a bed with another cowpoke and maybe a few crawling varmints. If Steve Hargett was still in Silverhill, this was probably where they would find him.

The hotel was built of unpainted lumber and had a tarpaper roof. It looked like scores of buildings Bo and Scratch had seen in dozens of boomtowns and mining camps. They went up uneven stairs to a rickety porch and into a dimly lit lobby, made even more gloomy by the layer of grime on the lone window.

Tom Yancy, who owned the hotel and had named it after himself, was sweeping out the small lobby. He wouldn't get any new customers at this time of day. Most of the men

who had stayed here the night before soon would be stumbling out and wincing at the bright light of a new day, if they hadn't already departed.

Yancy, a small, wiry man with a face badly pocked by childhood illness, stopped sweeping, leaned on his broom, and said, "Morning, Marshal. Deputy. What brings you here? We didn't have any trouble last night."

"If there'd been trouble last night, we would've been here then," Scratch said. "We're here this mornin' because we're lookin' for somebody."

"Steve Hargett," Bo said. "Did he stay here? Is he here now?"

Yancy frowned. "Hargett," he repeated. "Lemme think . . . Rides for the SJ? One of Rance Plummer's crew?"

"That's right," Scratch said.

"All right, I know who you're talking about. But he didn't spend the night here. Are you sure he was even in town last night?"

Bo nodded and said, "He was in Silverhill, no doubt about that."

"Well, then, he either stayed somewhere else or rode half the night to get back to the ranch." The hotel man's shoulders rose and fell. "I don't have any earthly idea which."

"All right. Thanks, anyway," Bo said. He and Scratch turned to leave.

"Wait a minute," Yancy said. "When you came in here, you boys looked like you were fixing to cloud up and rain. Hargett must have done something mighty serious to rile up a couple of easygoing fellas like you. What'd he do? Rob a bank?"

"Worse," Scratch said. He opened his mouth to elabo-

rate, but Bo caught his eye and shook his head. They didn't need to be spreading Rose's private business all over town. They went out of the hotel, leaving a puzzled Tom Yancy behind them.

"You figure he's somewhere else in town?" Scratch asked.

"Only one way to find out," Bo said. "We can split up and check all the places he might be."

"That'll take a while, even if we do split up."

"Yeah, but if he rode back to the SJ, that's likely where he'll be. One of us can ride out there later if we need to."

"Unless he's already lit a shuck outta this part of the country," Scratch said. "We'd best get started lookin' for him, instead of standin' around jawin'."

Bo couldn't argue with that.

They rendezvoused at the marshal's office an hour later. They had checked every saloon, hotel, boardinghouse, and brothel in Silverhill. Steve Hargett wasn't at any of them. They had also made sure he wasn't sleeping in the hayloft at the livery stable or in any of the other sheds, barns, and alleys in town. That left the SJ Ranch as the only place to look.

Once that was clear to the Texans, Bo said, "Do you want to ride out there, or should I?"

"What do you think?" Scratch wanted to know.

"You're the marshal. It's your decision."

Scratch frowned at his old friend. "That's why you insisted that I be the marshal. You're just tryin' to make me think."

"Thinking is good for you," Bo said with a smile.

"Maybe so." Scratch pondered for a moment, then went on, "One of us needs to stay in town. I'll do that. You ride out to the SJ and see if Hargett's there. And in case you're wonderin' how come I decided it that way, I figure you stand a better chance of keepin' your temper with the boy than I do. I'd be liable to try to kick his hind end up around his ears."

"I don't guarantee I won't do the same thing," Bo said.

Scratch was right, though—Bo *was* the less impulsive of the pair. At least, that had usually been the case so far.

"You gonna take a shotgun with you?" Scratch asked.

"No, but I'll have my Winchester if I need it."

Bo went back to the livery stable, saddled his horse, and rode out of Silverhill, headed north toward the rolling hills that lay grayish green in the distance. He had never actually been to the SJ, but he had talked enough about the spread with Rance Plummer, the foreman, that he was confident he could find it without much trouble.

It was midday by the time Bo reached the hills. For a while as he approached, he had been able to see cattle grazing on some of the grassy slopes. He headed for the closest critters, and when he rode up to them, he saw the SJ brand on their hips. He was on the right range, just as he'd thought.

A short time later, he spotted a man on horseback. The other rider must have seen him, too. The man trotted his mount toward Bo and lifted a hand in greeting. It was easy to tell from his garb that he was a cowboy. He had a sheathed carbine strapped to his saddle but wasn't toting a handgun.

"Help you, mister?" he asked. "You're on the SJ spread, in case you didn't know."

"That's where I hoped I was," Bo said. "Reckon you could tell me where to find the headquarters? I need to talk to Rance Plummer."

He thought it best for the moment to keep his real object, which was to have a serious conversation with Steve Hargett, to himself.

"Sure," the cowhand began. "I can . . . Wait a minute. I know you. You're one of those lawmen from Silverhill."

Since Bo had his deputy's badge pinned to his shirt and it was easily visible, that wasn't a very difficult deduction. He said, "That's right, and you look a mite familiar, too."

The cowboy raised a hand, palm out, in defense. "Hold on. You've never arrested me. I never spent any time in jail in Silverhill."

"Never said you did, friend."

"Are you out here to arrest somebody?"

"Couldn't, even if I wanted to," Bo said. "I don't have any authority outside of town."

"Oh." The man rubbed his chin and frowned, in thought. "Well, I reckon that makes sense." He lifted his horse's reins. "Come on. I was about to ride back to the house myself. We can go there together."

"Obliged to you," Bo said with a nod. He could tell that the cowboy was mighty curious about the errand that had brought him out here, but the puncher didn't press for answers, and Bo didn't offer them.

Half an hour later, they rode over a hilltop and Bo saw the ranch headquarters spread out below. It consisted of a dozen buildings scattered around, including the foreman's house, which would double as the office; a long bunkhouse; the cook shack; a blacksmith shop; a couple of barns with attached corrals; a squatty, windowless smokehouse; and several smaller cottages, which provided living quarters for any married hands and their families. Everything appeared to be freshly whitewashed and in excellent repair, which came as no surprise to Bo since Rance Plummer ran things around here, and the foreman was a top hand.

"Do you know if the boss is here?" Bo asked his companion.

"Should be, but you don't never know for sure. Something could've happened to take Mr. Plummer off to some other part of the ranch."

Bo nodded in understanding. Running a big spread was an unpredictable job.

Rance Plummer answered Bo's knock on the front door of the main house. The foreman, a rangy, craggy-faced man with graying hair and a drooping mustache, grinned when he saw who the visitor was.

"Bo Creel!" he said. "Welcome to the SJ. What brings you all the way out here from town?"

"I'm looking for a member of your crew," Bo explained, figuring it was best to get right down to business. "Steve Hargett. Is he around here?"

"Steve?" Plummer repeated with a puzzled frown. "Yeah, he was here this mornin'. Looked a mite bleary eyed, like he didn't get much sleep last night, but that ain't my problem. I sent him out to check on some of the west range. We're fixin' to have a roundup of sorts and put together a good-sized bunch to sell off, and I've got the boys doin' preliminary sweeps so we'll know where to concentrate our efforts." His frown deepened. "If you don't mind me askin', what do you want with Steve? Is he in trouble with the law?"

"No, it's not a legal matter, and I don't have any jurisdiction out here, anyway. I just need to talk to him."

"Sure." Plummer stepped past Bo and called to the man who had ridden in with him, "Hey, Keller. Ride out to the west range and find Steve Hargett. Tell him to rattle his hocks back here."

The cowboy had been heading for the barn to put his horse up. He paused, gave Plummer a woebegone look, and said, "Aw, Rance, I was about to give this old boy a rest."

"I hope you're talkin' about your horse," Plummer said. "*He* deserves it. You can get yourself a fresh mount. Then go fetch Hargett for me."

"Sure thing, boss," the cowboy responded, then didn't bother trying to conceal the sigh that escaped from him as he walked away.

Plummer grinned. "You got to stay on these fellas, else they'll turn into lazybones. You want some coffee? Got plenty in the pot, inside."

"Sounds good," Bo said.

He could tell that Plummer was intensely curious about his business with Steve Hargett, but the foreman didn't prod him for explanations. Like most Westerners, Plummer didn't believe in prying into someone else's affairs without being invited. They just sat in the office, sipped coffee, and made small talk about how things were going on the ranch and in town.

"Funny thing," Plummer commented at one point, as a slight frown creased his weather-beaten forehead. "Sometimes I'd swear we've lost a few head lately, but other times that don't seem to be the case. I reckon we'll find out for sure when we make the big roundup next spring."

Bo leaned forward in his chair. "You think maybe you've got a rustling problem?"

"Could be," Plummer drawled. "But if we do, they just been pickin' at us, a few head here, a few head there. You're always gonna lose a little to predators, and we got catamounts roamin' these hills."

"If you need any help getting to the bottom of it, you know Scratch and I will be willing to pitch in."

"Yeah, I know, but you boys got your own rat killin' to do in Silverhill."

They heard a rataplan of hoofbeats outside. Bo figured the hand Plummer had sent to look for Hargett had returned with the young man. That hunch was confirmed a moment later, when a knock sounded on the door and the foreman opened it to reveal Hargett standing there.

"You wanted to see me, boss?" the young man asked as he stood there with his hat held respectfully in one hand. Then he glanced over Plummer's shoulder and spotted Bo standing up and turning toward him with a grim expression on his face.

Hargett gulped and looked like he wanted to bolt, but he stayed where he was, as stiff and motionless as if his boots had been nailed to the porch.

"Come on in, Steve," Plummer said as he stepped aside. "Deputy Creel's got somethin' to say to you."

CHAPTER 16

Because Beth Macy had shown up at the marshal's office with her unexpected and disturbing news about Rose before Bo and Scratch could really get started on their morning routine, neither of the Texans had had a chance to get breakfast.

They hadn't made the usual morning rounds, either, at least not formally, but the intensive search for Steve Hargett had effectively taken the place of that.

As for food, they had each grabbed a couple of pieces of jerky from the supply they kept in the office for emergencies and had gnawed on those while they were looking for Hargett. That wasn't much of a substitute for an actual meal, though, so by the time Bo had been gone for a while, on his way out to the SJ, Scratch found himself thinking about biscuits and gravy and a nice, thick slice of ham. Or maybe a fried steak. Jerky might fill a man's belly—for a little while—but it didn't do much for his soul.

Scratch resisted the temptation for as long as he could, almost a whole quarter of an hour, then locked up the office and headed for the Red Top.

As he walked, he glanced down the street toward the

stagecoach station. The coach was gone. Beth and Monte Jackson were well on their way to El Paso by now. Scratch hoped they wouldn't run into any trouble. He worried about Beth driving that stagecoach, even though he knew she was highly capable of taking care of herself. Also, she had a good shotgun guard in Monte Jackson, who seemed like a competent young fella.

It was hard to say just how competent he actually was, though, Scratch mused, because at least during the time he and Bo had been in these parts, the stagecoach hadn't been held up or jumped by Indians or anything like that. Monte's toughness may not have ever been tested. Just because a fella was big and looked like a hard-bitten hombre, that didn't mean he was.

With those thoughts going through his head, Scratch didn't notice Rose Winston until it was too late to avoid her. In fact, he almost ran into her as she emerged from the front doors of the Territorial House.

Scratch came to an abrupt stop, and so did she. Out of habit, he pinched the brim of his hat and nodded to her.

"Mornin', Rose," he said. "You look mighty nice."

That was true. She wore a long brown skirt and a dark green shirt with long sleeves and the button open at the collar to reveal the smooth, tanned skin of her throat. She smiled and said, "Hello, Scratch. Where are you headed?"

"Down to the Red Top. I missed my breakfast earlier and figured I might get a bite." He didn't explain why he hadn't had breakfast, but again being polite, he went on, "Would you like to join me?"

As soon as he saw the look that suddenly came over her face, he remembered what Beth had said, and realized he'd made a mistake. Rose shook her head weakly and said, "No, I don't think so, but thank you for asking me."

Just the thought of food had made her pale, but she didn't look like she was about to be sick again, and Scratch was grateful for that.

He realized that he had dropped his gaze and was staring at her belly. He jerked his eyes back up and hoped she hadn't noticed. He and Bo had agreed they wouldn't let on to Rose that they were aware of her condition. Eventually, they would have to, but until they'd had a showdown with Steve Hargett, there was no point in embarrassing her.

It was mighty hard not to think about that new life growing inside her, though.

Rose frowned and said, "What's wrong, Scratch? If you're upset because I said I didn't want anything to eat, I can—"

"No, no, that's fine," he assured her hastily. "Just got a lot on my mind this mornin'. You know, marshalin' stuff."

"All right," she said, nodding slowly. "If you're sure."

"Yep, I am. You just go on about whatever it is you were fixin' to do."

"All right." She started to drift along the boardwalk. "Be careful while you're doing your . . . marshaling."

"Sure will," he said with a smile and a nod. As he turned away from her and headed toward the café again, he blew out a silent but relieved breath.

Bo had told him about Susan Hampshire working at the Red Top, but she wasn't there this morning. Ed Massey and his wife, Gwendolyn, were the only ones working. They were always there because they owned the place.

The café wasn't busy, either, since it was past the time for the morning rush. A couple of tables had customers at them, but the stools along the counter were empty. Scratch sat on one of them and nodded to Massey, who stood behind the counter, with his cook's apron on, while he sipped from a cup of coffee.

"Morning, Marshal," the man greeted him. "What can I do you for?"

"How about a cup of that coffee?" Scratch said. "And a plate of biscuits and gravy? Got any ham left over from earlier? Or a steak?"

"I've got both."

"Well, all right," Scratch said. "I ain't one to turn my back on good fortune. Bring 'em on."

Massey set his cup aside and said, "Comin' right up." He headed for the swinging door to the kitchen.

Before he got there, the café's street door burst open and Hector Esperanza rushed in. He looked around frantically, spotted Scratch sitting at the counter, and exclaimed, "Marshal!"

Scratch had already turned halfway around on his stool, alerted by the liveryman's sudden entrance that trouble might be brewing. He asked, "What's wrong, Señor Esperanza?"

"Someone on the street said they saw you come in here. You have to come with me . . . down to my stable . . . It's terrible—"

"Hold on," Scratch said, breaking into the babble of words coming from Esperanza's mouth. "What's terrible?"

"The girl . . ." Esperanza's lips worked spasmodically under his thin mustache. "And all that blood!"

Scratch's mind instantly went back to Florence, the soiled dove who had worked at Lily's Place—the one who'd been murdered by someone who had carved her up with a knife. He and Bo had searched diligently for any clue to the identity of the man who'd committed that horrible crime, but they hadn't found anything. They had had to settle for hoping that the killer had moved on, no matter how unsatisfying that was.

Now, from what Hector Esperanza was saying, that hope might have been dashed.

Scratch looked back at Massey, who had paused with his hand on the swinging door, and said, "Sorry, Ed. Looks like that late breakfast is gonna have to wait."

Five minutes later, Scratch was glad that he hadn't gotten around to having that big breakfast. He wasn't squeamish by nature, but what he was looking at behind the livery stable might have made him lose everything he had eaten.

Hector Esperanza stood over by the corner of the building, not wanting to get too close. That was fine with Scratch. He had told the liveryman not to let anybody else back here. They had drawn some attention as they hurried along the street toward the stable, and Scratch didn't want the usual layabouts and lollygaggers cluttering things up and getting in his way.

Besides, the gruesome news would spread fast enough, anyway. No need to give it a head start.

He stood there looking at the pile of lumber behind the stable. Esperanza had explained that he intended to build another shed to store grain back here but hadn't gotten around to it yet. A while earlier, he had been inside, near the back of the building, and a loud buzzing had caught his attention. A man who worked around horse droppings all the time had to be used to the sound of flies, but this had struck Esperanza as coming from an unusually large swarm of them. He had gone around back, seen the flies clustered so thickly on and around the stacks of boards that they had turned them black, and figured an animal of some sort had crawled up in there and died. He had investigated, thinking that he would locate and remove the carcass.

Instead, after waving his arms to shoo the flies away and then moving a couple of boards, he had uncovered the head and torso of a young woman, who might have been pretty before someone cruelly took a razor-sharp blade to her.

As soon as he saw that, he had gone in hurried search of the law.

Esperanza had explained all that to Scratch while they were on their way. Scratch believed the liveryman—he had no reason not to. Esperanza was a respected citizen in Silverhill, a successful businessman, and one of the gents who had put up the money to hire a new marshal and deputy in the first place. A widower, he was always saying he wanted another pretty wife and a gaggle of kids.

None of which meant that he couldn't be a killer, too, but Scratch just didn't believe it. Esperanza was too smart to murder this girl and then try to hide her body behind his own business. And if he had, why would he pretend to discover it and go running to the law? Scratch supposed a killer who figured himself too clever to be caught might do such a thing, but again, that just didn't ring true for Esperanza.

Now, while the liveryman stood guard and kept the crowd back, Scratch moved closer and bent down to move some more boards. The girl's dress was dark brown with the blood that had soaked into it. A lot of that blood must have come from the gaping wound in her throat, but she'd been cut in other places, too, mostly on her trunk and legs. He could see where the blade had torn her dress. But there were also neat, precise vertical slashes on each cheek and a longer horizontal one on her forehead, above her open and staring but sightless eyes.

Scratch straightened and looked around, trying to get a better impression of the whole scene. He didn't believe the girl had been killed here. There would be more blood on the ground if that were the case. True, the sandy, thirsty soil could have soaked up a lot, but he still should be able to see some dried remnants.

If his guess was correct, that meant she had been killed somewhere else and then dragged here. The murderer had moved some of the boards to make room for her, had hidden the body, and had replaced the boards, making a slightly higher stack but not all that noticeable. The flies had given away the secret, but even if they hadn't, the smell would have before too much longer. The corpse was already starting to get pretty ripe.

So the killer hadn't intended for this to be a permanent hiding place. He'd just wanted to get the girl away from wherever he had butchered her and stash her out of sight so his crime wouldn't be discovered too soon. Pretty much the same thing had happened with the previous victim. Scratch had no doubt in his mind that the same man was responsible for both deaths.

He looked around for drag marks but didn't see any. Maybe the killer had *carried* the body back here. It was also possible, of course, that he had simply brushed away any marks his actions had left. Searching for footprints would be a waste of time. Folks wandered up and down this alley all the time, and there would be nothing to separate the killer's prints from the hundreds of others left behind.

"Señor Esperanza," he called to the stable owner.

"What is it, Marshal?"

Scratch gestured toward the partially uncovered corpse. "Do you know who this is?"

"Absolutely not," Esperanza replied with an emphatic shake of his head. "Why do you think I would? Because she was found behind my stable?"

The man sounded almost too defensive, but at the same time, Scratch knew how shaken up he was. Esperanza's attitude didn't have to mean anything suspicious. In fact, Scratch still couldn't make himself believe that the stableman had anything to do with this other than discovering the body.

"I just thought you might have seen her around."

"Oh." Esperanza calmed down a little. "Well, now that you mention it, I think maybe I have. It's hard to say with . . . well, you know . . . the way she looks now."

The previous victim had been a working girl. Maybe this one was, too. Scratch figured he would check with Miss Lily first—although after what had happened to Florence, it was unlikely any of her girls would have been careless enough to get in a position where this might happen—and then with the other madams and saloon owners. He looked again at the body, noted the lowcut dress the girl was wearing. It was the sort of garment that wouldn't be out of place in a saloon.

Clarence Appleyard, Silverhill's undertaker, was pretty good at preparing bodies for burial, too. Once he had the girl laid out and cleaned up, if Scratch hadn't discovered who she was by then, he could ask the townspeople for help in identifying her. They could go by the undertaking parlor and have a look.

For now, though, he had done all he could. The next step was to deal with the body itself, instead of trying to figure out who was responsible for crime.

"Why don't you go fetch Mr. Appleyard?" he said to Esperanza. "I'll stay here and keep an eye on things."

"No need," Esperanza replied. "I see Appleyard's wagon coming now. I suppose someone got word to him that his services were needed."

"Yeah, more than likely." Scratch knew how fast word traveled whenever anything important happened—especially something as lurid as this. So he wasn't surprised to hear that the undertaker was already on his way, but he was grateful for Appleyard's promptness.

And he would be even more grateful when Bo got back from the SJ Ranch and could take over handling most of the thinking again. Scratch could do that when he had to, but it was enough to make a fella's brain hurt.

CHAPTER 17

After a long moment while Steve Hargett stood on the front porch, the young cowboy took a deep breath and, with a visible effort, made his legs work and carry him into the house. He swallowed hard, nodded, and said, "Hello, Mr. Creel."

"Steve," Bo said.

Rance Plummer hadn't closed the door. He said, "I can give you boys some privacy if you want."

Bo shook his head. "That's not necessary, Rance. Since Steve works for you, you're probably going to want to hear this, too."

By inviting Plummer to stay, Bo felt a little like they were ganging up on Steve, but at the same time, he was too angry at the young man to care. Steve had good reason to look nervous. He was about to get the riot act read to him.

In fact, Bo thought he saw actual panic lurking in Steve's eyes. That seemed like an extreme reaction to what was going on here, but maybe Steve had a really strong aversion to the idea of getting married and settling down.

If that was true, he was just going to have to get over the feeling mighty quick-like.

"Steve, I reckon you have a pretty good idea why I'm here," Bo began, keeping his voice calm and level, even though he felt like yelling.

Steve didn't say anything, but he shook his head unconvincingly from side to side. He knew, all right.

"Scratch and I know what you've been doing," Bo went on. He played it straight with the boy because that was what he always did. "Rose told Beth, and Beth told us."

For a second after he heard that, Steve appeared to be totally thrown for a loop. He said, "Rose? But she doesn't—" Then he stopped short as understanding dawned in his eyes. It was like one fear replacing another, though, because again he looked like he wanted to stampede out of here, and devil take the hindmost.

Rance Plummer had closed the door. He stood with his hands tucked into the back pockets of his trousers as he frowned at Steve.

"What'n blazes have you been up to, boy?" he asked. "From the way the deputy looks and sounds, you're mixed up in some mighty serious business."

Steve opened and closed his mouth but couldn't come up with anything to say.

"It's serious, all right," Bo said. "About as serious as you can get. Steve here is going to be a father."

Plummer's bushy eyebrows rose in surprise. "A father? You mean . . . Blast it, Steve! After you won that horse race, when I said maybe you could ride back down to Silverhill and court that Rose gal, I meant doin' it proper and respectful!"

"I did, Rance," Steve said as he found his voice again. "I mean . . . I started to . . . I never figured on being too forward. But then Rose—"

"Careful there, son," Bo warned. "Best watch what you say."

Steve took a deep breath. His fingers clenched harder on his hat. "You're right, sir," he said. "It's my fault. Completely. I'm to blame, and nobody else."

"Derned right," Plummer snapped. "It's up to the fella to be responsible, always."

"Yes, sir." Steve looked down at the floor. His face was bright red with shame.

"But that's not the worst of it," Bo said.

"There's more?" Plummer looked and sounded shocked.

Bo nodded. "I'm afraid so. When Miss Winston told Steve that she was expecting, he said he was quitting his job and leaving this part of the country."

"What!" Plummer's bellow was almost loud enough to rattle the glass in the windows. "You mean to say that you're such a sorry son of a buck, you'd run out on a gal you got in the family way?"

Steve said, "That's not exactly how . . ." He looked utterly lost as his voice trailed off, as if he didn't have any idea what he ought to say or do next.

"I don't care how it was in your head," Bo said. "What's important is that you hurt Rose, and you've got to make it right. There's only one way to do that."

"Yeah," Plummer said. "There have been plenty of young'uns who've gotten in a hurry to get into this world after their folks got hitched. A birth bein' a month or two off don't raise any eyebrows except on busybodies who ain't got nothin' better to do, and nobody really cares about them. But any more than that and it starts lookin' mighty bad. Plumb scandalous, in fact." The foreman shook his head. "We ain't havin' that with anybody who rides for the SJ brand."

For the first time during this conversation, a trace of anger appeared on Steve's face. He said, "I hope you don't believe you've got a bunch of choirboys on that crew, boss!"

Plummer shook his head. "I'm not a fool, boy. I know plenty of 'em like to drink and gamble and cavort with immoral women. That's just bein' cowboys. They work hard nearly all the time, so when they get a chance to, they cut loose their wolf. But this ain't the same. Miss Rose ain't immoral. She's respectable."

"But I tell you, she—" Steve stopped short at the hard, dangerous glare Bo gave him. He took a breath, then went on, "I agree with you. Rose is respectable, and I'm mighty fond of her."

"I should hope so, considering what you've done," Bo said.

"But you fellas are acting like I need to marry her—"

"That's exactly what you need to do," Plummer said. "What you're *gonna* do."

"But I can't!" Steve protested.

"Why not?" Bo asked. His eyes narrowed. "Do you already have a wife somewhere else?"

"No! I mean . . . that'd be loco. I don't have a wife. I've never even come close to getting married."

"Until now."

To reinforce his words, Bo rested his hand on the butt of the holstered Colt on his hip. Plummer went even farther. He stalked over to the wall where a shotgun and several rifles hung on pegs, and took down the Greener. He broke it open, looked at the cartridges tucked into the barrels, and snapped the weapon closed again. Steve winced at the sharp sound, almost like it was the slamming of a cell door.

"You're forgetting one thing, both of you," he said.

"What's that?" Bo asked.

"What if Rose doesn't *want* to marry me?" Steve asked. "What if I ask her and she says no?"

Bo frowned. Steve was right; he hadn't considered that angle. He'd just assumed that any woman who found herself with a baby on the way and no husband would want to get married as quickly as possible, to the father if she could, but to some other willing male if that was necessary.

"She won't say no," Bo declared. "She must have strong feelings for you if she was willing to . . . well, if she went along with . . ." He stopped and raised his hand to point a finger at Steve. "Don't you say anything about it being her idea. I don't want to hear it."

Steve shrugged, which was infuriating, but Bo let it go for now.

"What it amounts to," Bo went on, "is that you're coming back to Silverhill with me. You're going to sit down with Rose, and the two of you are going to hash out this whole thing. And the end result of that conversation had better be an engagement, followed by a wedding a whole heap sooner rather than later. You say or do whatever it takes to make that happen."

"I tell you I can't," Steve said with pure misery in his voice.

"Then we'll be heatin' up the tar and catchin' a chicken," Plummer said. "And when that's done, you'll get off the SJ and never set foot on it again. If you do, all the boys will have orders to shoot on sight, just like they would with any other slinkin', worthless coyote. I'll be spreadin' the word to all the other ranches in these parts, too. Every hand'll be against you, son." Plummer shook his head. "I'd hate to be thought of that way."

"And that's assuming I don't borrow that shotgun from Rance right here and now," Bo added.

Despair warred with anger and regret on Steve's face, and bleak acceptance won. He nodded and said, "All right. I'll talk to Rose and ask her to marry me."

"You'll convince her to marry you," Bo said.

"Yes, sir. One way or another."

Bo nodded. "Now you're getting it."

"You want me to come to town with you today?"

"You don't think I'd leave you out here with the temptation to light a shuck, do you? I'm going to have my eye on you every step of the way."

"Fine. Is . . . is it all right if I go over to the bunkhouse for a few minutes before we leave? If I'm gonna be doing something as important as asking a girl to marry me, I'd like to put on a clean shirt."

Bo thought about it for a second and said, "All right. I'm coming with you, though."

"You don't have to do that. There's only one door. You can watch it."

"What about the windows?" Bo wanted to know. "Are they big enough to climb out of?"

Plummer said, "A scrawny young fella like Steve could probably make it through."

"That settles it, then," Bo said. "I'm not letting you out of my sight until you sit down with Rose."

"Fine," Steve said under his breath. He turned to leave the room.

Bo nodded to Plummer and said, "Thanks. I appreciate you backing me up, Rance."

"What else could I do?" the foreman asked. "I'm ashamed the boy's one of my riders."

"Everybody makes mistakes, I reckon," Bo said. "And by that, I'm talking about him, not you. But what counts, once somebody's made that mistake, is what they do about it."

They had stepped out onto the porch while they were talking. Plummer nodded toward Steve, who was walking toward the bunkhouse, and asked, "You reckon he's got it in him to do the right thing?"

"I hope so," Bo said as he started to follow Steve. "For Rose's sake. And for his."

Most of the SJ hands were still out on the range at this time of day, but Steve knew that Ben Wilcox had finagled the job of staying at headquarters today to mend some harnesses. Wilcox usually found a way to avoid the more strenuous tasks. If there was something he could do sitting down, out of the sun, he seized the opportunity.

With an attitude like that, Steve had thought more than once, it was no wonder the man had wound up being a rustler. But then he asked himself what his excuse was. . . .

Steve was hoping to find Wilcox in the bunkhouse, and sure enough, he was there, sitting on his bunk, with several leather harnesses spread out on the blanket in front of him. He was fiddling lazily with one of them when Steve came in.

Steve had to move fast. He knew Bo Creel wouldn't be far behind him. Wilcox looked up in surprise from the bunk as Steve strode toward him.

"What're you doin' here?" Wilcox asked. "You're supposed to be—"

"Shut up," Steve cut in, his voice low and urgent. "Listen."

As quickly as possible, he told Wilcox about the unexpected developments, spilling the whole thing in less than a minute. He spoke quietly enough that he hoped Bo wouldn't be able to understand if he reached the doorway way before Steve stopped talking.

He had to give Wilcox credit. The man might be as crooked as a broken-backed snake, but he was smart and cunning. He grasped the situation instantly, and when Steve finished his hurried recital and asked, "What should I do?" Wilcox had an answer ready.

"Marry the girl, you blasted fool," Wilcox said.

Steve was surprised. He said, "Marry her? You mean, you'll let me out of that other deal—"

"Not hardly." Wilcox glanced past Steve. "There's that deputy. If you're supposed to be gettin' a clean shirt, you'd better do it."

Steve stepped over to his bunk, which was only a few feet away. As he reached for his war bag, he glanced toward the door and saw that Bo had stopped there and had leaned a shoulder against the jamb. Evidently, Bo didn't intend to crowd him, just keep an eye on him and make sure he didn't take off for the tall and uncut.

"Now, you listen," Wilcox said, so quietly that only Steve could hear him well enough to make out the words. "You're still part of the deal. Getting married doesn't change that. But nobody's going to expect a fella who just got hitched to pull something crooked. That's why you've got to make it look good. Drag your feet some, but then marry her. This plays right into our hands."

Steve started peeling off his dirty, sweaty shirt. "I don't see how," he muttered.

"After the wedding, you go to Plummer and tell him you want more responsibility now that you're hitched. Ask him to put you in charge of the nighthawks ridin' herd on that bunch we're gatherin' next week."

Steve shot a glance at Wilcox. "You think he'd do that?"

"You ask him the right way, he will. And between now and then, you marry that girl and make everybody think you're the most respectable hombre ever to pull on boots. That way, you can get me and the other fellas on the crew with you." Wilcox chuckled. "This is gonna turn out to be a heck of a lot easier than I expected, thanks to you and that randy little girlfriend of yours."

Anger blazed up inside Steve at the crude way the other man had referred to Rose. He knew there was nothing he could do about it right now, so he swallowed it and started buttoning the clean shirt he had just pulled on.

The anger kindled a fire in his belly, though, and he told himself that someday he would make Ben Wilcox pay for that remark.

"Come on, Steve," Bo called from the doorway. "We're burning daylight."

"I'm ready." Steve reached for his hat, which he had hung on one of the posts at the end of the bunk while he was changing his shirt.

As he started toward the door, Wilcox called after him, "Good luck, kid."

Steve didn't look back.

As they walked toward their horses, Bo asked, "You told your pard back there what's going on?"

"Some of it."

"Seems to me you don't really need luck. You're fixing

to marry a fine girl and have a family with her, so I'd say your luck is already pretty good."

"Yeah," Steve said. The deputy was right in one way, he figured. He didn't need luck to get out of this mess he was in.

What he needed was a miracle.

CHAPTER 18

All the girls who worked at Lily's Place were accounted for, which came as no surprise to Scratch when he checked with the madam. Lily called them downstairs to be sure. This was pretty early in the day for soiled doves, so they stumbled and yawned as they assembled in the house's parlor. Their hair was rumpled from sleep. Most clutched dressing gowns around them, but a few stood there unashamedly in their unmentionables. Scratch, with his rough Texas chivalry, kept his eyes averted from their charms as much as was reasonable, considering that he was a lawman and had to maintain a certain degree of vigilance.

That scene was repeated with minor variations in Silverhill's other two houses of ill repute. Checking with the saloon owners proved more difficult, because many of the girls who worked in the various drinking establishments didn't actually live in those places, and if they weren't supposed to be at work yet, their bosses had no idea if something might have happened to them. Several of the men pointed Scratch in the direction of the boardinghouses where saloon girls stayed, but checking at those places didn't turn up anything, either.

At each stop, Scratch described the dead girl as best he could, but "brown hair and sort of pretty" fit a lot of gals. His frustration grew as his efforts continued to be futile. He was about to head for the undertaking parlor to find out when Clarence Appleyard would have the body ready for viewing when something else caught his attention.

A towering figure stepped out of Francis Dubonnet's store onto the high porch and paused there to look around. Scratch recognized Roscoe Sherman. He hadn't known the big miner was still in town.

A frown creased Scratch's forehead as he recalled one of the thoughts that had gone through his mind while he was looking around behind the stable. The killer could have *carried* the dead girl back there, if he was big and strong enough. That was another feasible explanation for the lack of drag marks.

Roscoe Sherman was big enough, no doubt about that, and recalling the way the miner had stopped that team of horses with one hand, Scratch knew that his strength must be enormous. Roscoe wouldn't have had any trouble toting the dead girl behind the livery stable.

Somehow, though, the idea of Roscoe using a knife to kill her struck Scratch as false. Roscoe could have just snapped her neck with no more effort than a normal man killing a chicken. Why would he need a blade?

Even with those doubts, Scratch felt like he ought to talk to Roscoe, at least.

The miner was still standing on the store's porch as Scratch approached. Roscoe's head swung slowly from side to side. A befuddled expression was visible through his bushy beard. He looked for all the world like a fella who had started to do something and then had forgotten what it was.

Scratch was old enough that the same thing had happened to him from time to time, so he could sympathize with Roscoe's confusion, although it wasn't age causing it in the miner's case. The big fella's brain was just a mite on the weak side, Scratch thought.

"Howdy, Roscoe," he called as he went up the steps. "What are you doin' still in town? I figured you would've ridden back out to the Minotaur yesterday."

Roscoe turned when Scratch called his name, and that caused the strong, gamy odor from his clothes and person to waft in the marshal's direction. Scratch tried not to wrinkle his nose in response.

"Hello, Marshal," the miner said. The words sounded like boulders rolling around inside his chest. His frown deepened. "What was it yuh just asked me? I don't recollect."

"I asked you how come you're still in town," Scratch said.

"Oh. Uh . . . lemme think. I rode in . . . yesterday afternoon, I reckon it was."

Scratch nodded. "Yeah, I know. Bo and I talked to you, remember?"

"Yuh did? Oh. All right. I reckon you must have. Sometimes I don't remember things too good. But Mr. Dubonnet . . ." Roscoe waved a huge hand vaguely toward the store's entrance. "He's puttin' together an order of supplies for me, and I'm gonna take it back to the mine today."

Scratch nodded and said, "I see. What'd you do last night?"

"Last night?"

"Yeah. Since you had to stay over and get those supplies this mornin'. Where'd you stay? How did you pass the time?"

Roscoe seemed to be thinking about the questions for a long moment before he said, "I rode back outta town a ways and spread my bedroll. Folks don't seem to like me stayin' around much. I hear 'em whisperin' and see the looks they give me. Then I rode in again this mornin' to get the things on the list the boss gave me. Mr. Dubonnet says he'll have 'em ready in a spell."

Scratch wondered if Roscoe's hesitation had been to give himself enough time to come up with a lie, or if it had just taken him several seconds to get his thoughts together enough to answer. The second possibility seemed more likely, but Scratch couldn't rule out the first one.

"Were you anywhere around the stable last night?" he asked quickly, thinking that he might catch Roscoe off guard by changing the subject.

"The stable? No, sir, Marshal. I kept my mule with me, and the pack mule I brung with me, too. Weren't no need to go to the stable."

He sounded sincere, and Scratch wasn't sure Roscoe was smart enough to put on an act. He tried one more question.

"Do you know a girl about yea tall, with brown hair, kind of pretty lookin'—" Scratch held out a hand to indicate the dead girl's height, but that was as far as he got before Roscoe began shaking his head emphatically.

"I don't know no girls," the big man said. "Don't want to know any. They scare me, the way they sorta flutter around, like they was butterflies or hummin'birds."

"You know Miss Cecilia," Scratch pointed out. "You told us to say hello to her for you."

"That's different," Roscoe said, glaring. "She ain't a girl. She's a lady. She ain't like that other sort, the ones who work in the saloons and laugh all the time, even when there ain't nothin' funny."

Scratch nodded and said, "I see what you mean." He had just about stopped being suspicious of Roscoe, but the miner's last answer rekindled some doubts. Somebody who felt that way about saloon girls might have gotten upset if one of them approached him on the street and suggested that Roscoe come with her back to her place, wherever it might be. However, the idea of the big man using a knife still just seemed wrong to Scratch.

Roscoe had one sheathed at his waist, though, under the buffalo coat. Scratch caught a glimpse of the weapon's bone handle.

"I got to go now," Roscoe said abruptly. Without waiting for Scratch to say anything else, he turned and shuffled toward the other end of the porch. Scratch might have some vague suspicions of the big man, but he didn't think he had enough reason to stop Roscoe from leaving.

He didn't have the chance to ponder that much, because at that moment someone called from behind him, "Marshal Morton!" He turned to see a stocky man in a flashy tweed suit hurriedly climbing the steps at that end of the porch.

The man was hatless and had a few strands of black hair combed across the large bald spot atop his head. His teeth were clenched on a short black cigar. Scratch recognized him as the owner of one of the saloons in town but couldn't come up with the man's name. He knew he hadn't talked to the fella in his questioning so far today, though.

"Marshal," the man continued as he came up to Scratch, "I'm Gerald Walsh. I own the Red Devil Saloon."

That confirmed Scratch's impression of why he recognized the man, and he recalled the name now, too. "Howdy, Mr. Walsh. What can I do for you?"

"My bartender told me you came around a while ago, asking about a girl."

Scratch's pulse quickened. Walsh hadn't been in the Red Devil when Scratch stopped by there, so he'd just talked to the bartender instead. And that hombre hadn't known a thing about any missing girl.

"That's right. You have a gal who works for you who hasn't shown up today? Brown hair, kind of pretty. Last night she was wearing a blue dress, cut a mite low in the front . . ."

Walsh puffed on the cigar, then took it out of his mouth. He held it tightly as he said, "That sounds like Julie Hobbs. She isn't supposed to be at work yet, so she could show up later, but . . . it sure sounds like her, Marshal." His fingers closed so hard on the cigar that it broke. "The girl you just described to me . . . She's the one Hector Esperanza found dead behind his stable this morning, isn't she?"

"Yeah, I'm afraid so." Scratch inclined his head in the direction of the undertaking parlor. "Why don't you come with me down to Appleyard's, and you can take a look at the gal?"

Walsh grimaced. "Are you ordering me to do that, Marshal? Because I don't mind saying, that's not my favorite kind of place to visit."

"I reckon everybody feels the same way about undertaking parlors, and it'd sure be helpful if we knew for sure who the poor young thing is. Or was."

Actually, Scratch had no idea if knowing the victim's identity would help locate the killer, but it wasn't going to hurt. And in a case such as this, that was just one of the things the law did, he supposed. Nobody needed to go to the grave anonymously.

Reluctantly, Gerald Walsh accompanied him to the undertaker's, which was also a carpentry shop, since the same skills went into building a cabinet as were required for hammering together a coffin. When they went in, Clarence Appleyard came out of the back room, wearing an apron and wiping his hands on a rag.

"Need to take a look at that newest customer of yours, Mr. Appleyard," Scratch said.

"Well, it's good that you didn't come before now," the man said. "I just got the deceased looking reasonably presentable. Give me a minute to put a sheet over her. I assume you just need to see the face?"

"Yeah." Scratch glanced over at Walsh, who looked a little sick, either from the smells that lingered in the room or apprehension at what he was about to see or both. Just looking at the wounds to the girl's throat and face was going to be bad enough.

A few moments later, Appleyard called them back to his workroom. The body lay on a table, with a sheet pulled up to its neck. The stitches where the undertaker had closed the gaping wound in the throat were barely visible. He had also sewed up the slashes in her cheeks and forehead, using fine thread and small, tight stitches. The girl's eyes were closed, and her hair was loose and fanned out around her head. Gerald Walsh stepped closer and stared down at her.

He swayed a little. Scratch put a hand on the saloon owner's shoulder to steady him.

"Is that her, Mr. Walsh? The girl who works for you?"

Walsh's Adam's apple bobbed up and down. "Yeah," he said hoarsely. He cleared his throat and went on, "Yeah, that's Julie Hobbs."

"Thanks. She was at your place last night?"

"That's right." Walsh reminded Scratch of a trapped animal as he looked around quickly. "Can we go outside to talk about it? This place is starting to get to me."

"Sure, I reckon." Scratch nodded to the undertaker. "We're obliged to you, Mr. Appleyard."

"Of course. I assume I continue preparing the body for burial?"

"You go ahead," Walsh said. "Whatever it costs, I'll pay it. She was a sweet girl. Never gave me a bit of trouble."

Scratch led the saloonkeeper back outside. Once they were on the street again, Walsh pulled a bandanna from his pocket and mopped his face.

"Sorry, Marshal," he said. "I was starting to get a little sick in there."

"I'm sorry you had to go through it. But we're still a lot better off than Miss Hobbs, ain't we?"

"Yeah. That poor girl."

"She worked at the Red Devil last night?" Scratch asked again.

Walsh nodded. He rubbed his chin, frowned, and said, "Yeah, but she wasn't there all the way until closing time, now that I think about it. She left early."

"How early? When was that?"

"I'm not sure . . . Maybe eight o'clock or so? Maybe a little later than that? She said she didn't feel well, and since we weren't busy, I told her just to go on home."

"Where did she live?"

"I'm not sure. She had a room somewhere." Walsh's

frown deepened. "I know what you may be thinking, Marshal, but I'm not one of those fellas who tries to take advantage of the girls who work for him. The Red Devil isn't a very fancy place, I'll admit that, but I treat my employees right. You can ask anybody who ever worked for me."

He might just do that, Scratch thought, but in the meantime, he said, "So Julie, she wasn't a workin' girl?"

"A whore?" Walsh shook his head. "I suppose I can't say for sure, one way or the other, because I don't have any idea what she did with her time outside the saloon. But the Red Devil is a place for men to drink and play cards, and that's it. Nothing else goes on in there."

From what Scratch remembered of his infrequent visits to the place, he knew Walsh was telling the truth. He thought about what the man had told him and then said, "So she left sometime between eight and nine and was headed home, but she never got there."

"You don't know that," Walsh pointed out. "Somebody could have been waiting for her there."

He was right. Scratch was going to have to keep looking until he found out where Julie Hobbs had lived.

Something else occurred to him, and he asked, "Do you know a fella named Roscoe Sherman?"

Walsh shook his head. "The name's not familiar."

"Great big fella. Wears a buffalo coat. He works at the Minotaur Mine. Smells kinda odiferous. Well, a lot odiferous."

Walsh's face lit up with recognition. "Oh, sure, I've seen him around. I reckon most of the folks in town have, one time or another. He's pretty hard to miss."

"Yeah, that's for sure. But he wasn't at your saloon last night?"

"No, sir. That I would remember, no doubt about it."

So there was still nothing to link Roscoe with the murder victim. And even though Scratch had narrowed down the time of the killing—sometime after eight o'clock the night before—that fact didn't help all that much. At this time of year, it was starting to get fairly dark by eight o'clock. Some people were still out and about, but a lot of folks had already had their supper and settled down at home for the evening. A good number of them had even turned in for the night by then.

Walsh broke into his thoughts by asking, "Do you need me for anything else, Marshal?"

"No, you can get back to your business. I appreciate you comin' and findin' me like you did, Mr. Walsh. You were mighty helpful."

"Does that mean you have some idea who might have done this terrible thing?"

"A lawman can't talk about that," Scratch replied, to cover up the fact that he *didn't* have any ideas.

But he wasn't through investigating, either. However, he still hadn't had much to eat today, and a man couldn't think properly when his stomach was gnawing at him. He sent Walsh on his way, then turned his own steps toward the café, hoping as he did so that his meal wouldn't get interrupted by news of a killing this time.

CHAPTER 19

Bo Creel and Steve Hargett got back to Silverhill late in the afternoon. It had been a long time since Bo had eaten those strips of jerky that morning, and his stomach was starting to think that his throat had been cut. He could have gotten something to eat at the SJ, but he hadn't wanted to take the time.

They hadn't talked much during the ride to town. Bo was still too angry with Steve to want to have a pleasant conversation with the young man, and Steve, not surprisingly, seemed pretty distracted.

He had every right to have a lot on his mind. He had to decide if he was going to do the right thing or ruin Rose's life—and his own to boot, because Bo didn't intend to let the boy just walk away from this. He knew Scratch would feel the same way.

When they started along the main street, Steve veered his horse toward the Territorial House, but Bo said, "Hold on there. Where do you think you're going?"

"To talk to Rose," Steve said as he reined in. "That's what you want me to do, isn't it?"

"Yeah, but I want to check in with Scratch first and see

if anything happened while I was gone, and I'm not just about to turn you loose to go see Rose on your own."

Steve's resentment sounded genuine as he said, "You're not even going to give us any privacy while I talk to her?"

"I didn't say that. But when you *do* talk to her, I want it to be someplace I can be sure you won't take off for the tall and uncut."

"That's not fair."

"You're the one who told her you couldn't marry her, because you were leaving these parts. I'm just taking you at your word."

Steve scowled and snapped, "You don't know the whole story." As soon as the words were out of his mouth, he looked like he wished he could call them back.

"Oh?" Bo said as he rested both hands on the saddle horn and leaned forward to ease aching muscles. "What else is there to it, then?"

"Nothin'," Steve muttered. He lowered his eyes and wouldn't meet Bo's gaze anymore.

Bo frowned. What else could there be to the story that he didn't already know? Everything seemed pretty straightforward to him.

Maybe he could puzzle that out as they went along. He leaned his head to the side and said, "Come on. You're going with me to the marshal's office."

"Blast it! You're not gonna lock me up and make me talk to Rose in a jail cell, are you?"

"I just told you that I want to check in with the marshal, didn't I? Now come on, and don't make me tell you again."

As they rode to the marshal's office, Bo became aware that some of the folks on the street and along the boardwalks were giving him strange looks, as if something had spooked them. That puzzled him, too, and he was mighty curious by the time he and Steve dismounted and tied their horses to the hitch rail in front of the office.

Scratch might not be here right now, but this was the best place to start looking for him. When Bo opened the door, he saw the silver-haired Texan sitting stiffly behind the desk, with a grim expression on his face. That confirmed the hunch Bo had gotten from the townspeople that something was wrong. It took quite a bit to knock Scratch out of his usual happy-go-lucky mood.

"I don't like that look," Bo said without any greeting.

"I'm mighty glad you're back, Bo," Scratch said. He put his hands flat on the desk and pushed himself to his feet, then reached for the badge pinned to his bib-front shirt. He took off the tin star and tossed it on the desk with a disgusted grimace. "I ain't fit to be the marshal. You need to pick that up and put it on."

Bo tried to contain his astonishment, but he couldn't stop himself from exclaiming, "What in blazes happened?"

"We've had another killin'," Scratch said. "And I ain't one bit closer to findin' out who done it than when I started lookin' into it."

"A killing?" Steve Hargett practically yelped. He had come into the office close enough behind Bo to have heard Scratch's statement. "Who got killed?"

"A girl—" Scratch began.

"No! He wouldn't," Steve interrupted, then shut up fast.

Bo turned sharply, caught hold of Steve's collar, and hauled the young man farther into the office. He kicked the door closed and stared hard at Steve as he demanded, "Do you know something about this?"

Steve held up his hands and said, "No, I swear it, Mr. Creel. This is the first I've heard of any killing. For a second I just thought maybe Rose or one of her friends had been hurt, and that idea threw me like a buckin' bronc. I couldn't think straight." He looked at Scratch. "Who was it?"

"Like I started to say, a girl named Julie Hobbs got herself killed sometime last night, after eight o'clock. That's all I've been able to find out."

"You know who she was and have at least a rough idea when the murder was committed," Bo pointed out. "I know you couldn't have found out about it until after I started for the SJ, so turning up that much information is pretty good for less than twelve hours. You need to pick up that badge and put it back on."

Scratch shook his head stubbornly. "I'm at the end of my rope. I ain't got any idea what to do next."

"Start by telling me everything you know," Bo said, then added, "And put that badge on!"

Scratch did so, although only with great reluctance. He spent the next fifteen minutes filling in his old friend on every detail he could remember. Bo listened closely for any clue he might catch that Scratch had overlooked, but when Scratch was finished, Bo had to admit that he was equally baffled.

"I was sure hopin' nothin' else like this would happen while we were in town," Scratch said dolefully. "But it has, and now we got to deal with it."

"I suppose everyone in Silverhill has heard about what happened by now."

"If they haven't, they ain't been payin' the least bit of attention. I've heard folks talkin' about it everywhere I've gone today, and I think I've set foot in every business in the whole danged town."

Steve Hargett cleared his throat and said, "You fellas seem to have your hands full right now." Bo and Scratch both turned to glare at him. Steve shut up in a hurry.

"Don't think we've forgotten about you," Bo said.

"Yeah, you still got to make things right with Rose," Scratch added. He looked at Bo. "I hope you done read him real good from the book."

"Chapter and verse," Bo said with a curt nod. "He understands what he's got to do."

"Hold on," Steve protested. "I didn't agree to do anything except talk to Rose."

"Well, when you have your conversation with her, both of you better come to the right conclusion." Bo pointed toward the door. "And there's no time like the present."

"But you've got a murder to investigate!"

"Marshal Morton has already covered everything I can think of, at least for now. I'd just as soon take care of any other distractions while we've got the chance . . . and that includes settling your little problem."

Scratch took down a shotgun from the rack and handed it to Bo, then took one for himself. The Texans checked the loads and snapped the weapons shut.

"March yourself on over to the hotel, youngster," Scratch ordered. "Might as well do this the right way. Me and Bo are gonna be right behind you."

Steve looked like he'd rather be anywhere else, but there was no arguing with two scatterguns, especially when they were in the hands of two determined Texans. He sighed, turned to the door, and went out.

Bo understood now why a nervous air seemed to hang over the town. People had started to relax when no more atrocities followed the death of the prostitute called Florence, but now folks were looking over their shoulders again, especially the women.

The sight of Silverhill's two lawmen marching someone down the street at shotgun point was pretty unsettling, too, even though it wasn't related to the two murders. The citizens didn't know that, though.

Bo wasn't surprised to see that four out of the five mail-order brides were sitting together in the hotel lobby. They were in the habit of relying on each other in times of trouble. Beth would be here, too, he knew, if she weren't off on that stagecoach run to El Paso.

Rose started up out of her chair when she saw Steve come in ahead of Bo and Scratch. Cecilia, who was sitting to her right, reached over and put a hand on her arm. Jean, to Rose's left, said quietly, "Don't go running to him, dear. If he has something to say, he can come to you."

Rose swallowed and sank back down in the armchair.

Other than the clerk behind the desk, the young women were the only people in the lobby at the moment. Bo caught the man's eye and leaned his head toward the entrance to the dining room. The clerk cleared his throat and strolled out from behind the desk. He vanished into the dining room.

Bo almost wished he could follow the man in there and get something to eat. But seeing that things were settled between Rose and Steve was much more important than his empty belly.

Steve looked back over his shoulder. Bo and Scratch weren't pointing the shotguns at him anymore, but they lifted the weapons a little. The sight of the barrels moving in his direction was plenty eloquent by itself. Steve took his hat off, held it in front of him, and stepped toward the four young women sitting along the wall, near the potted plants.

"Rose . . . Miss Winston," Steve began, "I'd sure admire to speak with you—"

Luella stood up, tilted her chin imperiously, and moved

smoothly between Steve and Rose. "Why do you think Rose would have anything to say to *you*?" she asked. "After what you did?"

Clearly, the others all knew about Rose's condition. Bo had guessed that from the grim, angry looks on their faces, but Luella's words confirmed it.

"I'm sorry," Steve said, "but I don't think that's any of your—"

Jean was on her feet, too, before the rest of the sentence could come out of his mouth. She said, "Don't you dare say that it's none of our business! We've known Rose a lot longer than you have, mister, and we love her. She's our dear friend, and if you've come to hurt her again, you can just turn around and march right out of here!"

"I'm not here to hurt Rose. I'd never hurt her on purpose—"

Cecilia interrupted him in a cool voice, saying, "Well, you did an excellent job of hurting her by accident, then."

Steve's fingers clenched on his hat. "Dadgummit," he burst out in obvious frustration, "can't I just talk to her? Can't you all just leave us alone for a few minutes?"

"That's probably the most sense you've made today, son," Bo said quietly.

Cecilia turned to Rose again and said, "It's up to you. Do you want to talk to him?"

"I don't know," Rose said with uncharacteristic uncertainty. That told Bo just how upset this whole situation had made her. Usually, she was ready to forge on no matter what, full speed ahead.

"Please, Rose," Steve said.

After a few seconds more, she nodded. "All right. We'll talk. Where?"

Scratch said, "Not up in your room, that's for dang sure."

"The two of you can step over there in that little alcove," Bo said, nodding toward the area that was partially screened by some of the potted plants. There were two chairs in it, as well as a small writing desk.

"That's fine," Rose said. She stood up, and with a proud dignity that was also uncommon in her boisterous nature, she walked to the alcove.

Steve glanced around at Bo and Scratch. Scratch motioned with the Greener he held. Steve followed Rose.

Bo said to the other mail-order brides, "You ladies might as well sit down. Those two should take as long as they need to hash this out."

"They certainly should," Cecilia said. She moved over to the chair where Rose had been sitting and patted the now-vacant one next to her. "You've had a long day in the saddle, Bo. Why don't you sit down and rest?"

"Yeah, go ahead," Scratch urged. "I'm gonna step over by the window, where I can keep an eye on the street."

Bo sat down next to Cecilia. Jean and Luella resumed their seats. Bo said quietly, "Scratch told me about the crime that was discovered today. I know it's mighty unlikely, but were any of you ladies acquainted with the poor girl who was the victim?"

Cecilia shook her head. "Actually, we talked about that very thing. None of us ever met her, as far as we can recall. But it's still a terrible thing."

"Yes, ma'am, it is. Did any of you happen to be out and about yesterday evening?"

"I was," Jean said. "I had dinner at Harbinson's with Dr. Chapman."

Scratch was listening from his post by the hotel's big

front window. He turned his head to ask, "Did you see anything unusual or suspicious on the street while you were walkin' to or from the restaurant?"

"No, not that I recall. We just had a pleasant dinner, and then Arliss walked me back here to the hotel."

"What time was that?" Bo asked.

Jean frowned slightly as she thought about the question, then answered, "About eight o'clock, I'd say."

Scratch had determined that Julie Hobbs left the Red Devil around eight, Bo recalled. He made a mental note that they needed to talk to Dr. Arliss Chapman. The physician was an observant sort. He might have seen something that would point them in the direction of the killer.

Even while discussing the murder with the young ladies, Bo kept one eye on the alcove where Rose and Steve were talking. They had sat down in the two chairs, rather stiffly, but as they carried on a low-voiced conversation, which none of the others could hear, Steve leaned closer to her and Rose didn't pull away. Bo didn't know if that was a good sign or not, but he thought it might be.

Then, abruptly, Steve was down on one knee, saying something earnestly, and Rose smiled and held out her hand to him. He didn't have a ring to slip on her finger, but he clasped her hand in both of his.

Bo wasn't the only one who saw that.

"Oh, my," Jean said.

"Did he just—" Luella said.

"I think he did," Cecilia said.

The three of them stood up, as did Bo, and Scratch turned away from the window. Rose and Steve came out of the alcove, with Steve still holding her hand. He had a bit of a wild-eyed look, as if he still might bolt without warning, but he managed to get a reasonably happy—if somewhat desperate—smile on his face.

"Well," Cecilia said, "do we get to plan a wedding?"

"You do!" Rose answered. "And soon, too."

Steve swallowed and said, "As soon as possible, if that's all right."

Scratch nodded solemnly, patted the barrels of the shotgun he held, and said, "You done made yourself a wise choice, son."

CHAPTER 20

Beth Macy took off her floppy-brimmed hat and slapped it against her leg to get some of the dust off it. With her other hand, she removed the pins from her blond hair and shook it out as it fell below her shoulders. That felt good, after having the hair tucked and pinned up under the hat all day.

She was standing by the right-hand coach door, facing toward the back. Monte Jackson came around the rear of the vehicle and stopped short.

"What's the matter?" Beth asked when she realized he was staring at her.

"Your hair . . ."

"Something wrong with it?" Beth lifted her hand and ran her fingers through it. Everything seemed all right, as far as she could tell.

"No, not at all. It just . . . I just . . ."

Him being tongue-tied like that was starting to annoy her. She said, "You've seen my hair before, you know."

"Yeah, but . . . with the sun shining on it like that, it looks kind of like . . . a halo."

Beth snorted and rolled her eyes. "If you're trying to be

poetic, Monte," she told him, "you might as well give it up, because it's not your strong suit."

And yet that had been sort of a nice thing to say, she realized. She wasn't looking for flattery from Monte Jackson, though. His job was to protect the coach, as well as its cargo and passengers, from road agents and hostile Indians. So far during Beth's tenure as driver on the El Paso run, that hadn't been necessary, because nobody had even attempted to bother them.

The stage was stopped at Ramsgate Station. Carl Anderson, who ran the place for the stage line, and his half-grown sons were changing the team. While they were hitching up fresh horses, the four passengers had gone inside the adobe station building, where Anderson's wife had coffee and pie ready for them, a snack to tide them over until they stopped for the night at Chullender Gorge, the station at the halfway point of the journey.

Frowning, Monte said, "I just thought I'd see if you were gonna have coffee and pie before we leave."

"Sure I am. Driving a stagecoach is hard work, you know. A jehu needs sustenance." Beth smiled, then grew serious. "I didn't mean to hurt your feelings, Monte."

He grunted and shook his head. "Didn't hurt my feelings none," he said. He jerked his head toward the building. "Come on. We'll let Carl and his boys finish up out here."

He turned and went inside. Beth followed, thinking that despite what he'd said, she actually had offended him. That was regrettable, but she wasn't going to worry too much about it. He would get over it.

Anyway, she didn't want anything distracting either of them from their jobs. Just because everything had gone smoothly so far, that didn't mean it would always be that way.

Half a mile away, atop one of the rocky ridges that snaked their way through this area, John Lee Kingery lowered the field glasses he'd been using to watch the stagecoach station. He'd had his hands cupped around the front of the lenses to make sure no rays from the lowering sun reflected off them. He didn't want the driver or the shotgun guard to spot a glint of light where it shouldn't be and realize that somebody was keeping an eye on them.

Shorthorn Nash knelt beside Kingery, who was stretched out on his belly, and said, "Do them passengers look well heeled enough to make it worthwhile stickin' 'em up, John Lee?"

"I believe so," Kingery replied. "And there's no way of knowing what might be in the express pouch. At any rate, we have little choice in the matter, seeing as how our funds are depleted and our future prospects are fraught with despair."

"You mean we're broke as all get-out and don't have nothin' better lined up?"

"That is exactly what I mean," Kingery said. He moved back away from the crest and stood up. He had taken his hat off when he started to spy on the stagecoach, and there was just enough breeze to stir the long dark brown hair that hung around his head.

He was a painfully thin man in a once fashionable and expensive but now shabby frock coat. His narrow mustache and pointed goatee made him look a little like John Wilkes Booth, and in fact, seeing a picture of that notorious assassin who shared a first name with him was what had prompted Kingery to grow the facial hair.

Someday people would know his name, too, he had told himself. He might not ever do anything as momentous as assassinating a president, but he could be a famous Western outlaw, like that fellow Jesse James.

He took his flat-brimmed black hat from Nash, who was holding it, and turned toward the horses. The other two members of his gang, the Kingery gang—he liked the sound of that—were holding the animals' reins.

Al Herbert wore gray-striped trousers, a dark gray vest, a light gray shirt, and a gray hat. His face was dour and colorless. People could take one look at him and five seconds later have no memory of ever seeing him, which made him a good man to send into a town for a look around.

Pancho Ninni was short and stocky, like Nash, and as undistinguished as Al Herbert. Kingery had promised his men that one of these days, not only would they be recognized, but they would also be feared. The trick would be to pull off the sort of robbery that made people sit up and take notice. Looting a bank, say, or stopping a train and blowing the door off the express car.

So far, Kingery and his men had held up half a dozen stores, raided a few isolated ranch houses, and robbed three stagecoaches. They hadn't gotten a lot of money from any of those jobs, but they had made enough to keep them going.

During that stretch, Kingery had shot and killed four men: two store clerks who had tried to fight back, a rancher who had done likewise rather than stand by and do nothing while his wife and teenage daughter were molested, and the shotgun guard on one of the stagecoaches. Al Herbert had told him of overhearing saloon talk that referred to Kingery as a bad man, and that pleased him no end.

They had hit a dry spell in recent weeks, though, and had drifted farther west in New Mexico Territory, with the hope of changing their luck. Maybe they had, because if what Kingery had seen a few minutes earlier wasn't a good omen, then he didn't know what was.

It wasn't every day one came across a stagecoach jehu who was also a beautiful blond young woman!

He didn't want to distract the others from the job at hand, though, so he decided not to say anything about that for now. There would be time enough for them to discover that enticing fact once they had successfully stopped the stagecoach and had the driver, guard, and passengers under their guns.

"All right, mount up, boys," he told them. "We want to get ahead of that coach and find a good place to stop it. With any luck, we'll be richer men by the time the sun goes down!"

A short time later, the coach pushed on from Ramsgate Station. As it rolled east, Monte Jackson watched the shadow it cast in front grow longer from the lowering sun. They would reach Chullender Gorge about the time the fiery red orb sank below the western horizon. There they would stop for the night.

The wide, hard-packed stage road ran straight as a string. A couple of miles east of the station, it went past a low mesa that sat fifty yards south of the trail, to the coach's right as it approached. On the other side, a little farther on, was a clump of low boulders interspersed with saguaro cactus.

Monte Jackson always kept a close eye on that mesa as the stagecoach rolled toward it, whether traveling east or west. The mesa wasn't very big, but it was large enough that men and horses could hide behind it. Monte had thought many times that it was a good place for an outlaw ambush.

For that reason, he sat stiff and straight on the seat today, holding the coach gun ready with his right thumb looped around one of the hammers. He could cock the weapon, bring it to his shoulder, and let loose with a load of buckshot in a little less than a second.

Beth had the team moving along at an easy pace. She knew they were on schedule and would reach the next station when they were supposed to, so she wasn't getting in any hurry.

As Monte watched the mesa, he said, "Might not hurt to whip those horses up a little."

Beth glanced over at him and asked, "Why? We're doing all right on our time."

"I don't know. I've just got a hunch."

He wasn't looking at her, because he didn't want to take his attention away from the mesa, but he heard her disdainful snort. He knew she didn't take him seriously, didn't even like him much. She put up with him because she had to if she was going to continue driving the coach, and she wanted to do that because of her love of adventure.

They had talked some—it would have been difficult *not* to, considering all the hours they spent sitting side by side as the coach rocked along—and he knew that her father had been some sort of war hero. Being a girl, she could never live up to that, but maybe this was her way of trying to do *something* to impress the old man.

He didn't know if that was true, of course. He had never

spent much time thinking about why folks did the things they did. He was more concerned with his own actions and was just trying to deal with life one day at a time. But even if he was right about Beth, that was no reason for her to be foolhardy and take chances with her life, not to mention the lives of the passengers and the stage line's property.

"I'd sure appreciate it if you'd do what I said," he told her.

"All right, all right," she answered. He couldn't see it, but he suspected she rolled her eyes. Then the whip snaked out and popped above the leaders, and Beth called out to the horses, urging them on to a faster pace. The coach's swaying became more pronounced.

Just in time, too, because they were about to pass the mesa. Monte lifted the shotgun a little and squinted at the formation, searching for any signs of movement around it. He didn't see anything yet, but that didn't mean there weren't owlhoots lurking around it. . . .

With a rolling rataplan of hoofbeats and the clatter of wheels, the stagecoach swept past the mesa. Monte lifted the shotgun higher and pressed the butt to his shoulder as he leveled the barrels. He turned on the seat to keep the weapon pointed toward the mesa.

Nothing happened. No outlaws charged out from hiding. Monte lowered the shotgun partway and was about to tell Beth she could slow down again when she suddenly cried out, "Son of a—" The pop of the whip obscured the last word.

Monte jerked around to face front again, swinging the coach gun with him as he did. He saw three men with bandannas tied around the lower halves of their faces running into the road and brandishing revolvers. One of them, a tall, thin hombre in a black hat and frock coat, had two guns and fired one of them in the air as he shouted, "Stop! Stop where you are! Stand and deliver!"

In the split second following that demand, Monte realized the would-be bandits must have been hidden in the rocks and cactus to the left of the trail. There wasn't enough cover there for horses, so he hadn't paid all that much attention to that side. The men's horses could be hidden somewhere else close by, though.

Maybe behind that mesa. That would make it a two-pronged ambush. Not a bad idea.

But it wouldn't work if Beth didn't stop, and she showed no signs of doing that. Instead, she continued popping the whip and leaning forward to shout at the team. The horses lunged ahead at a full gallop.

The outlaws weren't expecting that. They opened fire. It was difficult to be sure in the sudden noise and chaos, but Monte thought he heard the leader yell, "Don't shoot the driver! Don't shoot the driver!"

That was good for Beth but not for him, because it meant the men concentrated their fire in his direction. He sensed as much as heard the bullets whipping past his head. One of them came close enough that he would have sworn he felt its warm breath on his cheek.

Then he settled the shotgun's sights on a stocky figure in a Mexican sombrero and stroked one of the triggers. Flame gouted from the right-hand barrel. The outlaw jumped, stumbled, went down on the ground, and rolled. Monte couldn't tell if he'd hit the varmint or if the man had just leaped out of the way of the buckshot.

The leader must have realized that Beth wasn't going to stop or even slow down. He stood in the middle of the road for a second longer and triggered another shot in Monte's direction, then flung himself toward the edge of the trail. He fell, too, and had to roll frantically to get out of the path of the wheels.

Monte stood up, bracing his feet wide so the coach's jolting wouldn't throw him off, and loosed the other load of buckshot in the direction of the third outlaw. He spun around and pitched forward on his face, so Monte was pretty sure his shot had scored. He dropped back to a sitting position and broke the shotgun open. In a couple of seconds, he had shucked the empties and thumbed two fresh shells from the stash in his duster's pocket into the barrels.

The coach was completely past the bandits now. Monte twisted on the seat to look behind the vehicle. The cloud of dust the wheels kicked up made it hard to see, but he caught a glimpse of two figures climbing to their feet, the skinny leader and the hombre in the sombrero. The third man was still down.

Dust curling up from the south made Monte look in that direction. His guess about the outlaws' horses being hidden behind the mesa had been right. A fourth bandit rode hard toward his friends, leading the other three mounts.

Monte checked the three who had tried to stop the stage. The two who were already on their feet were helping the third man climb upright, so he wasn't dead, just wounded.

"Are they coming after us?" Beth shouted over the racket.

"They're fixing to!" Monte replied. He half stood and turned so that his knees rested on the seat as he faced backward. "Keep going! Don't slow down until you're sure they're not after us, no matter what happens!"

"What do you mean by—"

Beth didn't finish the question, or if she did, Monte didn't hear it. He had a fully loaded Winchester strapped to the brass railing that ran around the top of the coach, with the barrel pointed to the rear. He unfastened the buckles that held it down and replaced it with the shotgun. Then he lifted the Winchester, worked the lever to jack a cartridge into the chamber, and settled the rifle's butt against his shoulder as he leaned forward and rested his elbows on the roof.

One of the passengers shouted from inside the coach, "What's going on out there? Are we being robbed?"

"Keep your heads inside and stay down, folks!" Monte replied. "You'll be all right!"

That didn't really answer the man's questions, but Monte didn't have time to worry about that now. He peered through the dust, looking for signs of pursuit.

Those signs weren't long in coming. Three figures on horseback galloped into sight as they raced after the stage. The sun was low behind them, throwing them into silhouette and making a glittering canopy out of the millions of dust motes that swirled around them. Muzzle flashes spurted from gun barrels as the outlaws fired.

Monte figured the chances of them hitting anything were small. The range was long for a handgun, and the hurricane deck of a running horse was no place for accuracy. But flukes happened, and blind luck could be just as deadly as a marksman's eye.

He was being jolted around pretty good, too, but he pressed his cheek against the smooth wood of the Winchester's stock and tried to draw a bead on one of the outlaws. He squeezed the trigger, and the rifle kicked sharply against his shoulder as it cracked. He followed the first shot with three more, triggering them as quickly as he could work the Winchester's lever.

When he peered through the dust cloud again, he saw

only two riders giving chase. Whether he had knocked one of the varmints out of the saddle or if the third man had just given up, he didn't know, but either way the odds were better than they had been a few moments earlier.

Something spanged off the railing at the back of the coach's roof. Had to be a bullet, Monte knew. The bandits were getting the range. He cranked off three more swift shots, hoping to discourage them, if nothing else.

Then he yelled, "Yow!" as something snatched the hat right off his head.

"Monte!" Beth cried. She half turned toward him. "Are you hurt?"

"Keep driving!" he told her. "I'm all right!"

That last shot had come within a whisker of blowing out what brains he had. They were getting too close. He had eight rounds left in the Winchester, and he sprayed all of them along the road behind the coach, swinging the rifle's barrel from left to right and back again as he emptied it.

He couldn't see anything through the roiling dust now, nor could he hear any hoofbeats other than those coming from the team. He traded the Winchester for the shotgun again, and just as he did, a man on a lunging, straining mount suddenly appeared, almost drawing even with the coach. Monte twisted and half rolled against the railing as the gun in the man's fist exploded. One-handed, he thrust the shotgun out and fired both barrels. The recoil felt like it almost dislocated his shoulder, but he managed to hang on to the now empty scattergun.

The booming double report half deafened him. It echoed hollowly in his head, and everything else in the world was muffled. He heard a strange sound and realized after a moment that Beth was calling his name.

"Monte! Monte! You're hurt!"

Was he? He hadn't felt anything. He shifted the shotgun to his left hand and used his right to draw the holstered revolver at his waist, even though that arm and shoulder ached badly. He eared back the hammer and squinted through the dust, looking for one of the varmints to shoot at.

Nothing. He didn't see man or horse behind the coach now.

And Beth was slowing down.

"No!" he called to her. "Keep going!"

"The horses are played out! They can't!"

With all the danger and chaos and racket, his brain felt a little stunned. He forced himself to think and knew she was right. If the horses collapsed in their traces, the coach and its passengers would be sitting ducks. Assuming that any of the bandits were left alive, of course. But they couldn't take that chance, he decided. Better to slow down but keep moving.

"And you're hurt!" Beth added before he could say anything.

That was the second time she'd said that. Maybe he actually was wounded.

No sooner had that thought gone through his head than his left side started to hurt like blazes, high up under his arm. The pain made him gasp, but he didn't let it distract him from his main concern, which was making sure the outlaws weren't chasing them anymore.

The dust billowed and thinned as Beth brought the stagecoach to a rocking, swaying stop. Monte braced himself with his left hand, while the right gripped his Colt. Through narrowed eyes, he caught sight of several riders headed back west, toward the sun. Dust tails curled up from their flight. He couldn't tell if all four bandits were getting away or just the three who had pursued the coach.

He wondered if he had killed a man back there. If he had, it would be his first.

Beth clutched at him. During the chase, she had been as icy nerved as any jehu could be, but now he felt her trembling.

"Oh, Monte," she said. "How . . . how bad are you hurt?"

"Don't mind me," he told her. "You didn't get hit, did you?"

"I'm fine. But you're bleeding!"

That was true. He could feel the wet heat spreading down his side. He turned his head, thinking he'd see just how much blood was leaking out of him, but his head seemed to keep going, and that made the whole world spin crazily around him. Beth's arms around him, no matter how welcome their embrace might be, weren't enough to keep him tethered to the earth. He sailed off into a sea of blue that turned black as it swallowed him whole.

CHAPTER 21

Despite the somewhat hurried nature of the proceedings, Rose wouldn't hear of having the wedding until Beth was back in Silverhill for the ceremony. That meant waiting three days, but considering that the baby wouldn't come along for another six and a half to seven months, if everything went normally, that slight delay didn't matter.

Jean and Luella were really in their element when it came to planning a wedding, and Cecilia helped out quite a bit, too, by finding a gown at Silverhill's only dress shop that could be altered into a wedding dress. She appointed herself to supervise that process.

The ceremony itself would be a simple one in the local Baptist church and would be followed by a party in the town hall. Jean and Luella began making decorations for the celebration.

The citizens of Silverhill already intended to hold a social in honor of the mail-order brides, and the timing was such that the two things could be combined, although Jean, Luella, and Cecilia insisted that the real focus would be on Rose as the bride.

Everything came together with surprising speed, prompting Scratch to comment to Bo, "Them ladies can sure get a whole heap done when they put their minds to it. If I ever had to go to war and plan an attack on the enemy, I reckon I could do worse than to put them in charge of it."

"A wedding's not quite the same as an attack in a war," Bo pointed out dryly.

"No, I'd rather fight the war than get hitched, my own self."

They discussed locking up Steve Hargett in the jail, just to make sure he didn't try to run out on his responsibility, but he gave them his word that he wouldn't.

"We're pretty decent trackers, Bo and me," Scratch told him, patting the shotgun he held as he did so. The double-barreled Greener was never far from him these days. "We'd plumb hate to have to run you to ground, but I reckon we can do it if we have to."

"You won't have to," Steve assured the Texans. "I'm going to marry Rose. No two ways about it."

The upcoming wedding also served to take the townspeople's minds off the murder of Julie Hobbs, although it was safe to say that no one had completely forgotten about it. Since the preparations for the nuptials were in good hands, Bo and Scratch spent a couple of days combing the town and talking to everyone they could think of, searching for any clue, any indication of who might have committed that heinous crime. None of their efforts turned up a thing.

Bo talked to Dr. Arliss Chapman, who had been out and about that evening, after having dinner with Jean. Chapman told Bo he hadn't seen anything suspicious or unusual, then said, "I can tell you this much, though, Mr. Creel. I took a look at the body before Mr. Appleyard interred it, and whoever carried out the attack on Miss

Hobbs did so with a great deal of hatred. The ferocity of those wounds is a definite indicator of unfettered rage."

"The same thought occurred to me, Doctor," Bo said as he nodded slowly. "I can't understand how anybody could feel that way, but I think you're right whether it makes sense to me or not."

"Have you talked to the young lady's employer, her friends, and found out whether she had any enemies? Someone with whom she'd argued recently? A man?"

Bo shook his head again. "From what I can tell, everybody who knew her liked her."

"Well . . . not everyone. But it's possible that whoever killed her *didn't* have anything against her personally. She just happened to be there, a suitable substitute for whomever the killer's rage was truly directed at. There are depths to the human mind and heart that have never been explored. And like the ocean depths . . . there may be terrible, terrible things to be found there, lurking in absolute darkness."

After a couple of nights passed with no more killings, and no trouble of any kind, really, the apprehensive mood eased somewhat. When the day of the wedding dawned, folks were thinking about that and the party that would follow it. The stagecoach was due to arrive at four o'clock that afternoon. That would give Beth time to get ready. She was going to be surprised that she was in line to be one of Rose's four bridesmaids. The maid of honor, in fact, since she and Rose were closer to each other than to any of the others.

Bo was taking a turn around the town at mid-morning when he saw Cecilia step out onto the front porch of the Territorial House and look up and down the street.

He thought she might be looking for him or Scratch because something—or some*one*—was bothering her, and a moment later, when Hugh Craddock followed her out of the hotel, he took that as an indication that his hunch was right. He started in that direction.

Craddock was talking earnestly to Cecilia when Bo came within earshot. He heard the rancher say, "Stop being foolish."

Cecilia turned on him sharply and said, "You think I'm being foolish, do you?"

"Well, what would you call it?" Craddock wanted to know.

Cecilia looked coolly at him and said, "Mr. Sherman and I agreed that he would be my escort to the town social. He may not be aware that it's now going to be a wedding reception, as well, but I don't see how that will make any difference."

"That was two weeks ago! That dummy's not going to show up. He's not smart enough to remember anything for that long."

"I'm sure you're wrong," Cecilia shot back. "And even if you're not . . . even if the occasion has slipped Mr. Sherman's mind . . . I still owe it to him to proceed as if I expect him to be here. It's the only honorable thing to do."

"Honor!" Craddock snorted. "That's something a man has to worry about, not a woman."

Cecilia's eyes widened. "You don't believe that a woman has any honor of her own?"

"Well, sure, in some ways," Craddock said. "Like when it comes to, you know, chastity and virtue . . . her good name . . . things like that."

"But a woman's *word* means nothing?"

"To be honest, mostly, a woman will tell a fella what

she thinks he wants to hear, and it doesn't matter to her whether there's any truth to it as long as she gets what she wants."

Cecilia spotted Bo then and said, "Mr. Creel, would you be so kind as to let me borrow your shotgun for a moment?"

"Just what do you intend to do with it?" Bo asked, trying not to smile.

She turned a withering look on the rancher from Texas. "I see a varmint that needs shooting."

"I'm afraid I can't let you do that. I'd have to lock you up, and it'd plumb ruin the wedding."

Cecilia sighed. "I suppose you're right." She glared at Craddock. "But you're fortunate, sir, that I can't show you what a woman's honor means to her."

Craddock said, "I just figured you'd be reasonable about that big oaf—"

"You might as well give up, mister," Bo interrupted him. "You're not getting through to Miss Spaulding. Anyway, you're wrong about Roscoe."

Both of them turned their heads to look at him. Craddock said, "I am?" while Cecilia said, "He is?"

"Yep." Bo nodded toward the far end of town, where he had just spotted a massive figure slowly riding a mule along the street. "Here he comes now."

A look of apprehension flashed across Cecilia's face, but she suppressed it quickly and instead looked and sounded vindicated as she turned to Craddock and said, "See? I told you he wouldn't forget."

"You don't know that," Craddock answered in a surly tone. "Maybe he was coming to town today, anyway, and doesn't have any idea about tonight."

"We'll see." Cecilia went down the steps to the street

and started toward Roscoe, lifting her skirts slightly as she did so to protect them from the dust.

Craddock glared at Bo and asked, "Aren't you going to stop her?"

"Why would I do that?" Bo replied. "She's not breaking any law."

"You claim to care about her, and yet you'll stand by and let her make a fool of herself over that stinking ox?"

Bo's expression hardened. "Mister, I didn't like you when I first met you in Fort Worth, and you haven't done anything since then to make me feel different. Cecilia Spaulding is one of the smartest people I know. She's not just about to make a fool of herself over anything or anybody."

"Somebody as big and as dumb as Roscoe Sherman is dangerous," Craddock argued. "He probably doesn't know his own strength. He might hurt her without meaning to."

"I think you're wrong, but I'll be keeping an eye out for trouble. I always do, and tonight won't be any different."

Later, he would remember saying that—and would shake his head ruefully.

Roscoe reined in his mule and dismounted when he saw Cecilia Spaulding walking toward him with a friendly smile on her face. He didn't see expressions like that on the faces of many people whenever he came around. Mostly, they just frowned and looked like they smelled something bad and moved away from him.

Which was exactly what he wanted, of course. The less people had to do with him in general, the better. He had mentally kicked himself more than once because of the previous encounter with Cecilia.

Not because he'd pulled her out from in front of that team of horses, of course. He wouldn't have wanted to see her hurt, not for anything in the world.

But instead of lingering to talk to her, he should have ducked his head and gone on about his business right away, putting up the same surly façade that he did with most folks.

And he *sure* shouldn't have allowed himself to get roped into going to that town social with her. That was exactly the sort of thing he'd wanted to avoid when he came to this isolated region of New Mexico Territory.

However, once he had agreed to be her escort, he couldn't back out. Despite everything else that had happened, his word still meant something to him.

He dragged his hat off and held it in front of him as he nodded and said, "Howdy, ma'am."

Earlier, out at the mine, he had cleaned the hat as best he could, but there was only so much he could do with it. That was even more true of the shaggy buffalo coat, which made him look even bigger than he really was, so he hadn't even attempted to clean it up. He had left it in his tent instead and now wore a brown cloth coat over a tan shirt and gray trousers. All the garments were clean. He had washed them himself in a creek not far from the mine, pounding them with rocks to get the dirt out.

"You don't have to ma'am me, Roscoe," she said, still smiling. "My name is Cecilia."

"Well . . . I reckon I can call yuh that. Yuh look mighty nice, Miss Cecilia."

"Thank you, but this isn't what I'll be wearing this evening." She cocked her head a little to the side. "You seem . . . different."

"I told yuh I'd clean up a mite. I didn't forget."

"No, you didn't. And you, ah . . ." She hesitated, as if she wasn't quite sure how to broach the subject. Finally, she lowered her voice to a half whisper and asked, "Did you *bathe*?"

"Yes'm. I mean, Miss Cecilia. I was already at the crick, washin' these duds, so I climbed in my own self for a spell."

"And you trimmed your hair and beard."

"I hacked on 'em some with a huntin' knife," Roscoe admitted.

"You did a good job."

All of it was wrong, he thought. He should have let himself stay as filthy and smelly as he had been before, so Cecilia wouldn't want anything to do with him. If she was disgusted with him and sent him away, he could ride out of town with a clear conscience.

But then she smiled at him and lightly touched his forearm with her fingertips, and he felt like somebody had whacked him alongside the head with a plank. He wouldn't ever want to do anything to offend her, even if it did mean he might be putting himself in danger.

"You probably don't know about this," she went on, "but my friend Rose is getting married later today. The wedding is at six o'clock, and the social, which is now a celebration of the happy couple, as well, is at seven. You're welcome to attend the wedding if you'd like, or you can meet me at the church when it's over and walk with me to the town hall."

"Yuh don't think folks'd mind if I come to the weddin'?"

"I just invited you, so I don't care if they do or not."

"Then I'll be there, I reckon . . . but I'll stay in the back, so's not to bother anybody."

"All right. I have things to do, so I'll see you later?"

"Yes'm. I'll be at the church at six o'clock."

"Thank you." She started to turn away, then paused. "And, Roscoe . . . I'm glad you didn't forget."

He shook his head and said, "I don't believe I could ever forget you, Cecilia, even if I wanted to."

He winced inwardly. The emotions running riot inside him had made him forget momentarily to speak in the usual rumbling, semiliterate tones. But Cecilia didn't appear to have noticed. She just smiled and headed back to the hotel. Roscoe looked past her and saw that annoying rancher Craddock standing on the porch, along with Deputy Marshal Creel.

He wondered if Craddock was still pestering Cecilia and if he was going to have to take action to put a stop to that. He hoped that wasn't the case. Just being here in Silverhill today, cleaned up like he was, attending the wedding and the social with Cecilia, threatened to draw too much attention to him.

Logically, he knew that. But inside . . .

He was happier than he had been for a long time.

The Bonanzer Saloon was more crowded than usual this afternoon because cowboys from the spreads to the north and workers from the mines in the hills had come into town for the celebration. The two groups kept to themselves, congregating on opposite sides of the barroom. Some of the men had been involved in the big brawl a couple of weeks earlier, and they hadn't forgotten about it. Eventually, such stubborn grudges would erupt in fisticuffs again.

But not today. Nobody wanted to risk being thrown in jail and missing the social.

Three men stood at the bar, halfway between the two

factions and belonging to neither. They looked more like miners than cowboys in their sturdy work boots, thick canvas trousers, and woolen shirts, but they wore broad-brimmed hats and had gunbelts strapped around their hips. The one in the middle was a lean, lantern-jawed man with an air of leadership about him. A dark beard stubbled his cheeks. The other two bore a distinct resemblance to him, but they were shorter, stockier, and didn't seem to be hewn out of hardwood like he was.

The Bonanzer's batwings swung back to admit a man who entered in a hurry. He spotted the three standing at the bar, nursing beers, and came toward them.

"Del, he's here," the newcomer announced. "I seen him. Seen him with my own eyes when he rode into town!"

Del, the lean hombre in the middle, turned slowly, giving the impression of a man who never got worked up or in a hurry about anything. Dark eyes set in deep pits of gristle narrowed as he asked, "Are you sure about that, Ham?"

"Of course I'm sure," the man called Ham replied in an offended tone. "I ain't blind, and a fella would have to be to miss somebody like that!"

Ham resembled Del and the other two, as well. Given the relative closeness of their ages, they appeared to be brothers, although Ham and Del took after one side of the family and the remaining two more closely resembled the other side.

One of them leaned in and said, "Ham's right. That son of a buck's the size of a mountain. Can't be more'n one man in these parts who looks like that."

Del nodded slowly. "I'm just surprised he's making it this easy on us. We knew he might be in this part of the territory, but I didn't figure he'd fall right into our laps this way. Where'd he go, Ham?"

"He stopped and talked to some woman, and then he went toward the livery stable. Must've been plannin' to put up his mule."

"He didn't see you, did he?"

Ham shook his head. "No, sir. Soon as I spotted him, I stepped back in an alcove in front of a store and stayed there, watchin' him. I was ready to lean back outta sight if he looked toward me, but he never even glanced in my direction." He snickered. "He was too busy talkin' to that gal and moonin' over her."

"So Roscoe's got himself another girl, does he?" Del mused as he stroked his dark chin. His hand dropped to the walnut grips on the revolver on his hip. "Well, he's never going to be responsible for the death of another one, because I'm going to put that stinking snake in the ground, where he belongs."

Chapter 22

Bo and Scratch were on hand when the stagecoach rolled in that afternoon. It was on time, which they fully expected since Beth was at the reins, and she always stayed on schedule.

But although Beth was on the driver's seat, handling the team as the coach rolled along the street toward the station, Monte Jackson wasn't beside her. A burly gent Bo hadn't seen before was riding shotgun, with the butt of the Greener resting on the seat beside him and the twin barrels angled into the air.

"Who in blazes is that?" Scratch asked.

"Don't know. And where's Monte?"

"That's an even better question. I hope nothin' happened to him."

The best way to find out what they wanted to know was to wait right where they were. The stagecoach rolled up, and Beth brought the team to a smooth halt. She lifted a gauntleted hand in greeting and called, "Howdy, boys." She didn't look or sound much like the young woman they had met in Fort Worth months earlier, but to Western eyes, she was still quite appealing.

Beth set the brake lever, wrapped the reins around it, and dropped lithely to the ground. Her bulky companion climbed down from the coach in a more deliberate fashion. Beth nodded to him and said, "Bo, Scratch, this is Jack Neal. He's filling in for Monte for a while."

"Monte ain't dead?" Scratch asked.

"No, I'm not." The answer came from the coach door, which swung open to allow Monte Jackson to climb out. He was moving sort of gingerly, Bo noted.

"You're hurt," Bo said. "What happened? You take a tumble off the coach?"

Beth replied before Monte could, saying, "Not hardly! He got a bullet graze on his side when he shot it out with a gang of road agents. He's all bandaged up under that shirt."

"Holdup, eh?" Scratch said.

Beth grinned. "Attempted holdup. We weren't just about to go along with such a thing, though, were we, Monte?"

"Well, it wasn't exactly easy getting away from them," Monte said, "but we managed without anybody getting killed."

"None of us, anyway," Beth said. "I'm not sure about those blasted robbers. I know Monte winged a couple of them, at least."

"Where did this happen?" Bo wanted to know.

"A few miles on the other side of Ramsgate Station. I hustled us on to Chullender Gorge as fast as I could, since I knew Monte needed to be patched up."

Monte said, "I might've bled to death before we ever got there if Beth hadn't done some patching up of her own." He smiled at her. "I reckon I owe her my life."

She waved a hand. "Oh, don't make more out of it than

it really was. I just didn't want to lose a good shotgun guard, that's all." She glanced at Neal. "No offense, Jack."

"None taken," the man replied with a stolid grunt.

Beth glanced along the street, then said, "Here come Jean and Luella. They look like they're in a hurry and have something important to say." She turned to Bo and Scratch. "Is something wrong here in town?"

"Best let them tell you about it," Bo said. "I will say you got back just in time, though. You've got a busy evening ahead of you."

Beth began, "Blast it, Bo. You can't just not explain what—"

But then Jean and Luella got there and hugged her, despite the layer of trail dust on her clothes.

"We have such big news," Luella said.

"The best news," Jean said. "Well, maybe not the best, but under the circumstances—"

"Rose is getting married!" Luella blurted.

"Married?" Beth repeated, her voice rising into a surprised yelp.

That revelation led to several elated squeals and a babble of excited conversation. One minute Beth was a tough, dusty stagecoach jehu, but then the next she was giggling and pouring out questions to her friends.

"Come on to the hotel," Jean said as she took hold of Beth's arm. "We have a *ton* of work to do getting you ready and finishing all the preparations."

The three young women hurried toward the Territorial House. Monte watched them go and shook his head.

"It's a good thing that stagecoach doesn't have to go out again until tomorrow morning," he said. "I don't reckon

Beth is going to be thinking too much about teams and passengers and express shipments until then."

"Can't blame her," Bo said. "She's going to be the maid of honor."

"Really? Well, that's fine. Is everybody invited to the wedding?"

"The whole town, pretty much," Scratch said.

Monte nodded. "I'll be there, then. Reckon it'll be nice to see Beth in a dress again . . . although I've gotten used to how she looks when she's cussing those horses and popping the whip at them."

"You didn't figure she'd be able to handle the job at first, did you?" Bo said.

Monte smiled and said, "There's a lot about Beth Macy that I never figured."

Just about everyone in Silverhill turned out for the wedding. Businesses were closed, even most of the saloons, and citizens packed the Baptist church. The town had sort of adopted the five mail-order brides, and since Rose was the first of them to actually get married, interest was high.

Bo and Scratch were in a back room of the church with Steve Hargett and Rance Plummer, the foreman from the SJ, who was going to serve as the best man. The young cowboy didn't own a suit, but the Texans had talked Francis Dubonnet into donating one from the store.

Steve paced back and forth nervously, tugging at the collar of the white shirt he wore. It was buttoned up and had a tie snugged around it, which seemed to bother Steve quite a bit.

Scratch watched him for a few minutes, then patted the shotgun tucked over his left arm and said, "I'm glad we decided to bring along these Greeners. If I ever saw somebody who looks like he's ready to cut out for the high lonesome, it's you, boy."

"I'm not going anywhere," Steve said. "I gave my word I'd marry Rose, and I meant it." He pulled a bandanna out of his pocket and mopped his forehead with it. "But you've got to admit, this is a mighty big step for a fella to take. My life won't ever be the same after this."

"Most men regard that as a good thing," Rance said. "They figure their lives are gonna improve after they get hitched."

"Well, that's true," Scratch said, "but I reckon you can't blame the boy too much for feelin' like a long-tailed cat on a porch full of rockin' chairs. Gettin' hitched *is* a big deal. If I was doin' it, I might have the fantods, too."

Steve said, "No offense, but you're not helping, Marshal."

"I ain't tryin' to help. Just sayin' that you're right about everything bein' different from here on out. But you'll have a mighty fine gal by your side to help you out."

"Yeah," Steve muttered, but he didn't sound convinced or look happy about the situation. "Seriously, you don't need the shotguns."

"We'll keep them close by, just in case," Bo said.

A little later, they heard piano music start up in the church's sanctuary. "Time to go," Scratch said.

The four men filed out. Bo and Scratch were going to stand up with Steve, along with Rance.

Bo and Scratch placed the shotguns on a chair in the corner and joined Steve and Rance at the front of the church, forming a line angled out from the spot in front of the pulpit where the preacher was standing with a Bible in his hands. The pews were full, and people were standing in the back and along the side walls, in front of the stained-glass windows. Bo saw the crew from the SJ among them, looking uncharacteristically subdued as they got ready to watch one of their number take a wife.

Scratch leaned closer to Bo and whispered, "Maybe you should've offered to perform the ceremony. You could've, you know."

Bo shook his head. "My preaching and marrying days were a long time ago," he whispered back. Decades earlier, during the time he had been married, he had served as a lay minister in a small rural church, but any thoughts he might have had about following that call had ended with the death of his family. Since then, he hadn't even been inside churches all that often.

The lady at the piano wrapped up the sentimental song she'd been playing, let a dramatic pause go by, then launched into the "Wedding March." Everyone in the church who wasn't already standing got to their feet and turned toward the rear to watch the bridesmaids walk in, one by one, Cecilia first, followed by Luella, Jean, then Beth. Finally, Rose started up the aisle in the beautiful white gown that had been altered quickly to fit her.

Steve stiffened and drew a deep breath when he saw her. Bo said quietly to him, "Starting to think that maybe getting married isn't such a bad idea, after all?"

"I reckon I'm a pretty lucky hombre, at that," Steve said.

"You can say that again," Scratch told him. "You could be marryin' a shotgun."

Bo glanced over and shook his head. That was enough talk of shotguns for today.

Rose's chestnut hair was piled on top of her head in

an elaborate arrangement of curls. She carried a small bouquet of flowers. She wasn't far enough along to be showing yet, so the dress hugged the curves of her tall, athletic body. She was as lovely as any young woman Bo had ever seen, her beauty rivaled only by that of her close friends, who wore elegant blue gowns. She smiled as she walked slowly up the aisle to join Steve in front of the minister.

The ceremony moved along quickly and smoothly. When the preacher asked if anybody objected to this union, Bo and Scratch both turned their heads to look out over the crowd. The warning expressions on their faces made it clear that if anybody *did* have an objection, it had better be a darned good one.

No one spoke up.

Then the minister was saying that by the power vested in him by Almighty God, he pronounced Steven Fletcher Hargett and Rose Elizabeth Winston husband and wife, and the kissing of the bride commenced.

Cheers and applause came from the crowd when the kiss ended and Steve took Rose's arm to lead her back along the aisle, between the two packed sections of pews. The crowd in the back of the church parted to let them get to the doors, which Roscoe Sherman, who was standing closest to them, threw open so the happy couple could go outside and head for the town hall and the party awaiting them.

Up at the front of the church, Scratch nudged Bo with an elbow and asked, "You reckon we ought to take the shotguns to the party?"

"We shouldn't need them, since the wedding is over and done with," Bo said, "but I suppose it can't hurt."

The crowd flowed out of the church behind Steve and Rose. Bo and Scratch, along with Rance Plummer, stepped out a side door and walked past the building. The crusty old cowboy rubbed a knuckle against his right eye.

"Sure is bright out here," he said. "I'm ready for the sun to go down."

"Yeah, it is," Bo said dryly. "Bright enough to make a man's eyes water."

Rance scowled but didn't say anything else.

They took a shortcut through the alleys and reached the town hall ahead of Steve, Rose, and the crowd from the wedding. Bo and Scratch leaned the shotguns in a corner where they would be out of the way but handy if needed.

The musicians who would be providing tunes so folks could dance had hurried ahead, too, and were already tuning up their guitars and fiddles. A few of the ladies from the town were there, as well, and had punch and cakes ready.

Steve and Rose came into the cavernous building first, and everyone else followed them. A swell of talk and laughter filled the big room. This was probably the biggest moment in Silverhill's history so far—at least the biggest moment that didn't involve striking a rich new vein of ore in one of the mines.

Rance picked up a cup of punch from the table where the big crystal bowls were. He raised his voice over the hubbub in the room.

"As the best man and the boss of this young rapscallion here, I reckon it's my privilege to say a few words. Steve Hargett is a good hand and a fine young fella, although you won't catch me sayin' that any other time, 'cause it might give him a swelled head and he's still got work to do up at the SJ. But I'm mighty pleased and plumb proud of him today, because he's marryin' a mighty fine young lady in Miss Rose, and I know they're gonna be happy together for a long, long time." Rance lifted the cup high. "So I give you the bride and groom, folks! Here's to 'em!"

Quite a few people had crowded around and gotten cups of punch while Rance was talking. They raised their cups and echoed, "To the bride and groom!" Those who didn't have anything with which to toast settled for clapping and cheering and calling congratulations to the young couple.

When that had settled down enough that Bo could be heard, he stepped up and said, "I want to add my congratulations and best wishes to Steve and Rose, and I also want to say a word on behalf of four more of the finest young women it's been my pleasure to get to know. Folks, I give you Misses Cecilia Spaulding, Jean Parker, Beth Macy, and Luella Tolman!"

Cheers and whistles filled the room as the other four mail-order brides smiled and looked a little embarrassed by all the attention.

When that commotion died away, the fiddlers scraped their bows on the strings, and the guitar pickers plucked their instruments. Music filled the room, and many of the people began to dance, while others got cups of punch or drifted over to the edges of the hall to visit with each other.

In an open space in the center of the room, Steve and Rose danced together, and judging by the way they gazed into each other's eyes, at this moment they might as well have been the only two people in the world.

And that was as it should be, Bo thought with a faint smile on his face as he watched them.

Beside him, Scratch nodded toward where Cecilia

danced with Roscoe Sherman, and said quietly, "Do you believe how much that big hombre cleaned himself up? You wouldn't hardly know it was the same fella if he wasn't the tallest galoot in the room!"

"No, I was surprised, too," Bo agreed. "He put a lot of effort into it. I guess that means he really must have wanted to impress Cecilia."

"Craddock ain't impressed."

Bo followed Scratch's gaze and spotted the rancher from Texas standing by himself near one of the side walls. Craddock scowled in the direction of Cecilia and Roscoe.

"He's liable to cause a ruckus before the night's over," Scratch went on.

"He may try. I'm not sure how far he'll get with Roscoe, though. I wouldn't want to tangle with that fella."

"Me neither. It'd be like David goin' up against that Goliath hombre there in the Good Book."

"Yeah, but David won that fight," Bo pointed out. "I don't think Craddock would . . . unless he pulled a gun."

"And if he tries anything like that, we'll be there to stop him, and he'll sure regret it."

"Yeah, we'd better try to keep an eye on him," Bo agreed.

Thankfully, they didn't have to worry about jealousy swirling around any of the other young ladies who had become their special charges. Jean was dancing with Dr. Arliss Chapman, while Beth swept around the floor in Monte Jackson's arms. Monte was still moving sort of stiffly because of his injuries, but he was making a valiant attempt at being graceful.

Luella danced with a number of would-be suitors, including Hector Esperanza, who was a widower. Bo didn't figure Luella would have any real interest in Esperanza, who was twenty years older than her, but he was also a successful businessman, so it was hard to rule out anything.

While Bo was looking around, he spotted Susan Hampshire standing by herself. She looked lovely in a dark green gown, and Bo thought once again what a fool Hugh Craddock had been to cast her aside.

Just because Craddock was a fool, that didn't mean Bo had to be. He walked over to Susan.

"Hello, Bo," she greeted him with a smile. "It was a lovely wedding, don't you think?"

"Sure was," he agreed. "I hope everything works out for the two of them."

"Any reason to think it won't?" Susan asked.

"No, not at all." Bo changed the subject to the real reason he had come over. "Would you like to dance?"

"Why, I'd love to. Thank you."

Bo took her hand and slipped his other arm around her waist. They joined the couples moving around the floor in time to the sprightly tune coming from the musicians. He might have enjoyed a little slower dance—it wasn't easy to talk when they had to concentrate more on the steps—but honestly, it felt good just holding Susan and being this close to her. At his age, he sure wasn't looking to settle down, but he still enjoyed some pleasant female company now and then.

When the song ended, they applauded politely along with everyone else, and then Bo asked, "Would you like some punch?"

"That would be very nice."

He smiled and turned toward that side of the hall, but

he hadn't even taken a step toward the punch bowls when a cry of alarm sounded in the brief interval between songs. Surprised, angry shouts rang out. Bo jerked around toward the commotion and saw the crowd scattering, trying to get away from something near the doors.

A path opened up, and through it he saw four strangers who had just invaded the town hall with guns in their hands. One of them fired a deafening shot into the ceiling, and the lean, wolfish man in the lead shouted, "Everybody take it easy! We're just here to kill one snake! Get over here, Roscoe, and take what you got coming to you!"

CHAPTER 23

As soon as he heard the commotion, a feeling of fore-boding shot through Roscoe Sherman. For a long time, he had been expecting trouble to catch up to him. The frightened, angry shouts, the gunshot, and the harsh rasp of Del Kinney's voice told him that it finally had.

"Oh . . . my!" Cecilia gasped. "Roscoe, you're . . . hurting me!" To his horror, he realized his grip on her as they were dancing had tightened into a painful clutch. Instantly, he let go of her and stepped back.

Since he was taller than anyone else there, he could see over the heads of the crowd. He spotted Del and the other three Kinney brothers standing not far inside the town hall. Ham, the next-to-oldest brother, had a revolver in each hand. Smoke curled from the muzzle of the one in his left hand, so Roscoe knew he had fired the warning shot. Del and the two younger brothers, Emmett and Frank, sported just one gun apiece.

Idiots. To come marching into a gathering in a frontier town with so little firepower, only to start throwing shots around and giving orders?

The Kinney brothers were lucky nobody had filled

them full of lead yet. But they never had been renowned for their intelligence, Roscoe reminded himself. Only one person in that family had been smart, and she had been beautiful, too.

Mary . . . his late wife.

Mary, who had always been out of place in her family of ridge runners and thieves back in Missouri. Who had wanted to learn how to read, even though she was mostly grown, and hadn't been shy about asking the new schoolmaster, only recently arrived in the little mountain town, to teach her how.

She would have been more than willing for Roscoe Grant to teach her other things she didn't know, but he had been too much of a gentleman to give in to that temptation and take advantage of her. He had courted her properly and had never laid a finger on her—not with any lustful intent, anyway—until they were married.

The two years after that had been as close to heaven as Roscoe ever expected to get. Mary had learned how to read almost overnight, and within a couple of months, she was tackling the same volumes of poetry and fiction that had brought Roscoe so much pleasure over the years. Long evenings spent by the fireplace in their cabin, talking about Poe and Hawthorne and Melville and Shelley and Lord Byron. Longer nights, after the fire had burned down, in the big four-poster bed Roscoe had built after Mary agreed to be his wife. Roscoe was so big, and Mary was so petite, but despite that, they were a perfect match in every way.

Until she got with child.

There was no doctor in the little town, but there was a midwife, and she warned Roscoe and Mary that the birth might be troublesome, even dangerous. That worried

Roscoe, but Mary was excited and assured him that everything would be fine. He wanted to believe that. . . .

But when the time came, thirty hours of screaming agony produced only a dead wife and a dead son, despite the midwife's best efforts. A completely numb Roscoe buried both of them and then tried to force his brain to work so he could decide what to do with his life, worthless though it might be from that point on. There were some high cliffs nearby, in the mountains, and he seriously considered climbing to the top of one of them and throwing himself off. The only thing that prevented him from doing so was the sure knowledge that Mary wouldn't want that.

He didn't have long to brood about it. Mary's brothers—Del, Ham, Emmett, and Frank—showed up in the middle of the night, shot up his cabin, and then burned it down. Somehow the bullets didn't find Roscoe, and when he burst out of the inferno with his clothes ablaze, he grabbed one of the brothers—to this day, he wasn't sure which one—dragged the man off his horse, and used him as a battering ram to knock two more out of their saddles. In terrible pain from the burns he'd suffered, he charged off into the woods, with bullets clipping through the brush around him, and disappeared into the night.

He knew the Kinney brothers were crazy, especially Del. They wouldn't stop looking for him until they had settled the score with him for what they considered his killing of their sister. It was a matter of family honor.

So Roscoe left, heading west. There was nothing in Missouri to keep him there. The burns had left him with distinctive scars on his face, so he grew his beard long and thick to cover them. Letting his hair get shaggy changed his appearance, too. For a long time, as he drifted through Arkansas and Indian Territory and then Texas, he didn't talk to anyone unless he had to, and that dulled his mind to the point that he spoke coarsely, like a man who had never read a book in his life. Like a man who *couldn't* read a book . . .

In a fit of uncharacteristic whimsy, he started using the name of another Union general from the war instead of the name he'd been born with. He kept the name Roscoe, though. It was all he had left of the man he had been before.

Keeping himself clean became too much trouble, and the resulting stench had the added benefit of making people avoid him, which was easier than him avoiding them. He became this new person—filthy, illiterate Roscoe—with surprising ease. Roscoe Grant was the one mourning the wife and child he had lost. Roscoe was just a big, dumb brute, and nobody wanted anything to do with him.

That was fitting, he decided. And it would help him avoid being tracked down by the vengeful Kinney brothers. The only things he couldn't change were his towering height and his massive build. He couldn't do anything about those. He just hoped Del and the others never found him. He wasn't afraid of them, but he'd been through enough trouble in his life.

Working at the Minotaur Mine, in this isolated region of New Mexico Territory, seemed to be the best pursuit he had found so far. The menial, mind-numbing labor was just what he needed. A man who was exhausted didn't have the energy to think as much.

But over time, stubborn sections of his brain began to complain. They didn't want to waste away from disuse. So, he began ordering books, ostensibly for the mine owner, W.J.M. Carling, but actually for himself. He read them in secret. When he could, he read them aloud to Mary, just as he had back there in the mountains, on those winter evenings when the wind blew and the sleet ticked against the windowpanes and the logs crackled in the fireplace. Haunted by the past, caring little what the future might bring, still, it was a life, of sorts.

Then he saw Cecilia Spaulding on Silverhill's main street and acted without thinking, and that second of weakness, of giving in to a totally unexpected impulse, had led to this moment now, when hate from the past loomed up and threatened these innocent people, including one he had come to care for. . . .

With all those thoughts and memories rushing through his head in less time than it took to blink an eye, he thrust out a tree trunk–like arm, moved Cecilia behind him, and stepped forward.

"Put those guns away, boys!" he boomed. "I'm right here. And if you hurt any of these folks, you'll regret it."

Instead of holstering their guns, Del and the other Kinney brothers snapped the weapons up and leveled them at Roscoe. He halfway expected a barrage of bullets to smash into him, but they didn't fire.

Ominous clicking sounds came from behind him. Roscoe glanced over his shoulder and saw Bo Creel and Scratch Morton standing there holding shotguns. The hammers were drawn back. That was what Roscoe had heard.

"Roscoe, drop to the floor, out of the line of fire," Bo said quietly without changing his grim expression.

"We'll take care of these fellas," Scratch added. "Varmints think they can come in here and bust up a weddin' celebration. Buckshot's what they got comin'!"

Roscoe lifted both hands, held one out toward the Kinneys, while the other made an imploring motion toward Bo and Scratch.

"Please, everyone, just hold your fire," he said. The crowd in the hall had split in two, with folks pressing back against the walls on the sides and leaving an open space in the middle, a space where Roscoe now stood between guns. "I don't want anybody to get hurt."

"It's too late for that," Del called. "You got a killin' coming for what you did to our poor sister. She's lying cold in the grave because of you, mister!"

That accusation made gasps come from some of the women in the crowd, and men muttered angrily. From behind the giant, Cecilia asked, "What's he talking about, Roscoe?"

Without taking his eyes off Del and the others, he said, "Those fellows used to be my brothers-in-law. I was married to their sister."

"And she's . . . dead?"

"Yes. And they blame me for it." Roscoe's mouth tightened into a grim line. "And not without some justification, I might add."

He was so upset by the unexpected, untimely appearance of the Kinney brothers that he wasn't giving any thought to how he spoke. He answered Cecilia's questions in his normal voice.

She certainly noticed, though. She said, "Listen to the way you talk. You've been lying to me . . . to everyone around here."

The hurt, angry tone in her voice finally made him look around at her. He said, "It's not like that—"

"It's exactly like that," Cecilia interrupted. "You've been letting everyone believe that you are this filthy, smelly, illiterate oaf, when actually you're an educated man, aren't you, Roscoe?"

A hush had fallen over the entire room, so her words were clear to everyone there.

Del Kinney let out a harsh laugh and said, "Educated? Why, ma'am, that fella right there was the schoolteacher in our little town. And he used that to take advantage of our poor sister!"

Roscoe's head snapped back around. "That's a lie! I never took advantage of Mary. We were in love—"

"You bewitched her with all them fancy words you were always spewin' at her!" Del cried. "A simple country girl like her never had a chance with a sly devil like you."

Roscoe blew out a frustrated breath. "This is insane," he muttered. "I was as devastated as you were when she died. More devastated, because she was my wife, and I lost our child at the same time. But it was just a tragedy, something that no one could have done anything to prevent—"

Ham spoke up for the first time since the brothers had stormed into the town hall, yelling, "You coulda prevented it! You coulda stayed away from her! She didn't go to your school. You didn't have any right messin' with her."

Scratch eased forward with the shotgun still leveled in his hands. He said, "Speakin' of rights, you boys don't have any right to come bustin' in here and wave guns around and ruin a special day for folks who happen to mean somethin' to me. So you'd best holster 'em and get outta Silverhill right now, or—"

"No." The interruption came from an unexpected source: Roscoe Sherman. He motioned for the Texans to stay back, then walked slowly toward the Kinney brothers with his hands held out in front of him.

"I don't want anybody here hurt," he went on. "If you feel like you have to kill me to set things right, then we can at least go outside before you start shooting, so none of these people will be in danger."

"No!" Cecilia exclaimed. "Roscoe, you can't just go with these lunatics."

He looked back at her. "Maybe that's exactly what I *should* do. When I . . . when I lost Mary . . . my wife . . . and our son . . . I thought about ending my own life. I thought about it a great deal. I've been running away from that, and maybe I shouldn't have. Maybe a man can never escape his fate." He turned back to Del and the others. "I'm ready. Let's go."

Bo said, "Just hold it right there." He had moved up to the left, while Scratch had gone to the right, and now they both had good angles around Roscoe if they had to open fire on the Kinney brothers. But there were still too many other people in here who would be in danger if gunplay erupted. "It's our job to keep the peace here in Silverhill. We're not going to let these hombres just march you out of here and gun you down, no matter what grudge they believe they have against you."

"You'll never stop them," Roscoe said. "They're determined to have their revenge . . ." His voice trailed off. Something had occurred to him, and he thought it was worth a try. "Del, listen to me. I have an idea how we can settle this."

Del frowned. "Is this some sorta trick?" he demanded. "You know how it's gonna be settled . . . with lead!"

"How about fists instead?" Roscoe suggested.

"What're you talkin' about?"

"Let's go outside. I'll fight all four of you at once. You can give me a good thrashing. You can beat me to death if you're capable of it."

Emmett Kinney said, "Don't listen to him, Del. I seen

him fight six men one time, out in front of the general store back home, and he done whipped 'em all."

"Yeah, I remember you tellin' me about that." Del glared at Roscoe. "No deal! Not when we already got the drop on you!"

Scratch said, "You boys know that if you shoot Roscoe, Bo and me are gonna open up on you with these scatterguns half a second later. Four loads of buckshot will scatter you all over creation!"

Frank Kinney swallowed hard and said, "That lawdog's got a point, Del. We can kill Roscoe, but then they'll kill us."

"Not if we kill them first," Del growled. "We just gotta be fast enough to do it."

"But then we'd be outlaws," Emmett argued. "We'd be on the run for the rest of our lives, and star packers from here to yonder'd be gunnin' for us."

Del gave them a disgusted glance. "You two always was the weak sisters in the family! Ham and me, we know what's got to be done, don't we, boy?"

Ham looked uncomfortable as he said, "Maybe it woulda been better if we'd waited and jumped Roscoe outside of town, where nobody could interfere. I don't like the idea of goin' up against shotguns, and those two old pelicans look like they know how to use 'em—"

"Old pelicans, are we?" Scratch said as he raised his Greener's barrels a little higher.

"You, too, Ham? You've turned yellow?" Del said. He grimaced and lowered his Colt, shoved the revolver back in its holster. "All right, then. Blast it! Have it your way. We'll take Roscoe up on his idea." He faced Roscoe again. "We'll go outside and settle this, if you ain't too yellow to face us all."

"I'm the one who suggested it, remember?" Roscoe said.

Del pointed a jutting finger at him. "You may have whipped those six fellas back home, but you ain't ever tangled with the Kinney brothers! We're gonna stomp you into such a deep hole, you won't never climb out!"

"Let's get on with it, then," Roscoe said with a bleak nod.

Cecilia came up beside him and put a hand on his arm. "Those men are still going to try to kill you," she said.

He looked at her, summoned up a faint smile. "I know. Not that long ago, I wouldn't have minded so much if they did."

He left her there to ponder the implications of what he had just said, as he followed Del, Ham, Emmett, and Frank out into the twilight settling over Silverhill's main street.

CHAPTER 24

Scratch looked over at Bo and asked, "Are we gonna let them do this?"

"As long as there are no guns involved, I don't see that we have a good excuse for stepping in and stopping it," Bo replied with a shrug. "Fellas have a right to settle a grudge with their fists. That's pretty much accepted out here."

Cecilia hurried over to them with an anxious look on her face. She said, "You have to do something about this."

"We were just talking about that," Bo told her. "There's nothing we can do as long as none of them break the law."

"What about disturbing the peace?" Jean suggested. She, Luella, and Beth had come up behind Cecilia and looked almost as worried. "Surely having a brawl in the middle of the street qualifies!"

Scratch rubbed his chin and frowned. "Reckon you've got a point there. And I reckon we could lock up those fellas for what they've already done, namely, bustin' in here and firin' off a gun and threatenin' folks." He nodded emphatically. "That's disturbin' the peace if I ever seen it!"

Bo had to agree with him. But he also saw Roscoe's side of it. The big man didn't want that threat from the past hanging over him from now on. He wanted it settled, one way or the other. That wouldn't happen if the strangers were locked up. A few days' sentence—or even a month—wouldn't change anything. They would still hate Roscoe.

But that would give him time to run, Bo mused. To hide from his enemies. The question was, Would he do that?

Bo had a hunch he wouldn't. He had heard the weariness in the man's voice, seen it in the dejected slump of his massive shoulders.

Roscoe just wanted his troubles over with.

Bo could understand that. Roscoe's words about losing his wife and child had struck a painful chord in Bo. Although he didn't know the details in Roscoe's case, he'd heard enough to know that he had gone through a similar tragedy. During that awful time in his own life, Bo had questioned God and fate and anything else he could think of to rage against.

But he'd had his good friend Scratch to help him get through the ordeal, and he had come out the other side with his heart and soul and mind intact. The painful memories would always be there, but so would the good ones, and in time they came to be what he thought of first when his family came to mind.

From the sound of it, Roscoe hadn't had anyone like that to stand by him. Even worse, he'd had his wife's brothers blaming him for what had happened, and that had to have taken a toll on him, as well.

Those thoughts went through Bo's mind as Scratch started toward the doors. Already, some of the crowd had followed Roscoe and the other men out of the town hall. A fight always drew plenty of spectators. Like a wedding or a social, it was something to break the monotony of frontier life.

Bo put a hand on his old friend's arm to stop him.

"Arresting those men won't settle anything," he said. "We can put a stop to it for the time being, but that won't change the situation. They'll still be out for revenge."

Scratch grimaced and said, "You're right. In the end, it's best that a fella stomp his own snakes, ain't it?"

Cecilia stared at the Texans in disbelief. "You mean you're just going to let them fight? Someone's liable to be killed!"

"It may come to that," Bo said. "But this is the way Roscoe wants it."

Cecilia let out an exasperated exclamation. She turned and hurried toward the entrance. Maybe she intended to try to talk some sense into Roscoe's head. That wouldn't do her any good, Bo thought. The time had passed for reason and logic. Roscoe and the Kinney brothers were running on raw emotion now.

As Bo and Scratch headed out, too, they passed Rose and Steve. Rose looked angry as she said, "This is my wedding day those idiots are ruining."

"We're still married, no matter what other folks do," Steve told her. "To my way of thinking, that's all that really matters."

The words appeared to mollify Rose a little, but Bo didn't blame her for being upset.

Roscoe and the Kinney brothers had walked out into the middle of the street, where they would have plenty of room. The crowd spread out around them on all sides. Folks stepped out of the way as Bo and Scratch strode through the press of people, still toting their shotguns. They came to the edge of the open area around the would-be combatants.

Roscoe had taken off his coat. He stood with his hands at his sides, not yet clenched into fists.

The brothers still wore their guns. As they advanced slowly toward Roscoe, Scratch called, "Hold it right there! Before this ball gets started, you boys shuck those irons. I don't want you bein' tempted to slap leather if things don't go to suit you."

The lean, lantern-jawed brother called Del objected. "We said it was gonna be a fair fight, him against us. Kinneys don't go back on their word."

"Then you can figure we're just helpin' you keep that word," Scratch said. He motioned with the shotgun. "Get those gunbelts off now, or march on down to the jail and take 'em off there. Your choice."

With surly reluctance, the Kinney brothers untied their holsters, unbuckled their gunbelts, and removed them. Bo told one of the bystanders to collect the weapons. The townie did so although he was visibly nervous about performing the task and scurried out of the way once he had all the gunbelts draped over his arm. Bo told him to take them to the marshal's office.

Everybody was out of the hall now, even Rose and Steve, who stood on the porch with Cecilia, Jean, Beth, and Luella. Monte Jackson stood behind Beth, and Dr. Arliss Chapman had a hand on Jean's shoulder. Steve put his arm around Rose.

Del Kinney glared at Bo and Scratch and said, "All right, you've got your fair fight, no guns. But that don't mean we won't kill this varmint. He's got it comin'."

"This fight was his idea," Scratch said. "I reckon he knew what he might be lettin' himself in for." He took a deep breath. "It goes against the grain, I'm tellin' you, but as long as it's fist against fist, we won't step in. You've got *my* word on that."

Bo glanced at the town-hall porch. Cecilia had caught her bottom lip between her teeth and was worrying it. She was angry with Roscoe for deceiving her, but she appeared to be genuinely concerned about him, too. Clearly, some feelings had sprung up between them, even in the short time they had been acquainted.

Now that they were disarmed, the Kinney brothers began closing in on Roscoe again. They spread out so that they could attack from different directions.

"This still don't hardly seem fair," Scratch muttered to Bo, "even if Roscoe *is* as big as two of them varmints put together."

"Like you said, it was his idea."

The brother called Ham made the first move, launching himself toward Roscoe and swinging a wild, looping punch. Roscoe threw up his left arm and blocked the blow, then grabbed Ham's shirtfront with his right hand. He swung Ham into the path of the two younger, stockier brothers as they charged him, and Ham was powerless to stop himself from colliding with them. All three got their legs tangled up and went down in a sprawling heap in the dusty street.

That was enough of a distraction to let Del get close. His height allowed him to reach Roscoe's jaw with a fist, even though Roscoe was still a head taller than him. The blow made a sound like an ax biting into a tree trunk when it landed.

Bo could tell that the punch was powerful enough to put most men down and out, but it barely budged Roscoe's head, just twisted it a little to the side. Roscoe put a hand in the middle of Del's chest and shoved. Del flew backward, arms windmilling, and wound up skidding through the dirt on his butt.

By now, the other three brothers had scrambled back to their feet. Ham darted behind Roscoe and leaped on his back. He wrapped both arms around Roscoe's neck, and his legs around the big man's waist, and yelled to Emmett and Frank, "I got him! I got him! I'll hold him, and you boys wallop him!"

The other two tried to close in, but before they could, Roscoe reached up, grabbed hold of Ham's arms, and bent forward at the waist. He heaved, and Ham's grip came loose. Ham cried out in alarm as he wound up flying through the air over Roscoe's head. For the second time in this fracas, he crashed into Emmett and Frank, bowling them off their feet like the ball in a game of ninepins.

Roscoe swung around toward Del, who was trying to get up. Roscoe waited, obviously unwilling to hit a man who was down. Del must have realized that a hamlike fist was waiting for him as soon as he reached his feet, because he didn't go that far. Instead, he launched himself in a diving tackle at Roscoe's knees.

Roscoe outweighed Del by quite a bit, but Del was no lightweight, and he caught Roscoe perfectly to jerk his legs out from under him. Roscoe went down like a tree toppling. That brought a surprised gasp from the crowd, because until now Roscoe had been handling the Kinney brothers with ease and seemed invincible.

The impact of landing knocked the breath out of Roscoe. He lay there, apparently unable to move, while Del pushed himself up and leaped atop him, driving a knee at his groin. Roscoe twisted his hips at the last minute and took the knee on his thigh, rather than allowing Del to land what might have been a crippling blow.

Del wasn't through, by any means. He clubbed his hands together and smashed them down in the middle of Roscoe's face. Blood spurted from Roscoe's nose. Del's hands rose and swept down again and again as he battered Roscoe's face.

Roscoe wasn't going to just lie there and let Del hammer him into submission. His right hand shot up suddenly and closed around Del's throat. That brought Del's attack to an abrupt halt. Watching, Bo thought that Roscoe might try to choke Del to death then and there, but instead, he flung Del to the side, like a child tossing away a toy he was bored with.

As Del rolled away, unable to stop himself, Roscoe turned on his side and then pushed himself to hands and knees. He shook his head, causing crimson drops to fly from his bleeding nose. He surged to his feet and dragged the back of a hand across his nose, smearing the blood even more. His eyes were already starting to swell from the blows Del had landed.

But Roscoe was on his feet, and none of the Kinney brothers were. Ham, Frank, and Emmett were still trying to recover, moaning and muttering as they thrashed feebly on the ground. Del had come to a stop on his belly and lay there, with his breath rasping in his throat. None of them appeared to be a threat anymore. The fight was over, Bo thought.

But Del's rage and hate gave him the strength to lever himself up off the ground, and as he turned toward Roscoe again, he reached underneath his shirt. He was going for a hideout gun, Bo realized.

Del was fast. The little pistol seemed to appear in his hand as if by magic. Flame spurted from the muzzle as he thrust it at Roscoe and fired. Roscoe grunted and took a step back.

Bo was already moving as soon as he saw what Del was doing, but he couldn't stop the man from getting that first shot off. Also, Bo had to hesitate because there were too many people beyond Del in the line of fire. He couldn't just cut loose with the shotgun.

Instead, Bo had to lunge to the side and palm out his Colt. As he brought the revolver up, he saw that he had changed the angle on the crowd enough to risk a shot. Hard on the heels of the spiteful crack from Del's hideout gun, Bo's Colt blasted and slammed a slug into Del's right shoulder, shattering it.

Del screamed as the impact twisted him halfway around. The little pistol flew from his fingers and thudded onto the dirt a few yards away. Del caught himself but fell to his knees as he clutched at his wounded shoulder with his left hand.

Some of the bystanders had been shouting in excitement, but the shocking roar of gunfire caused silence to fall over the street, except for the echoes that went rolling away.

"Del!" Ham cried into that shocked hush. He leaped to his feet and rushed to his brother's side. He knelt, took hold of Del, and eased him to the ground so that he was lying down. Ham looked up and yelled, "He needs a doctor!"

Arliss Chapman was already on his way, having left Jean on the town-hall porch. He knelt on Del's other side and said, "I'm a doctor. I've sent someone for my medical bag. Do you have a bandanna?"

"What?" Ham struggled to understand what Chapman had asked him. "Yeah, I reckon—"

"Get it out, fold it into a square, and press it against the wound. Firmly, you understand, but not too hard. We don't know yet how much damage was done in there, and we don't want to make it worse."

Scratch kept his shotgun on Emmett and Frank Kinney, just in case they wanted to try something, but both of them still seemed stunned. They sat up but didn't get to their feet, just stared toward Del and Ham instead.

Bo turned to Roscoe Roscoe. He knew Del's shot had struck the giant. Roscoe was still standing. He had his left hand wrapped around his right upper arm.

Cecilia reached him before Bo did. "Roscoe," she said, "how bad are you hit?"

Roscoe lifted his hand from his arm, revealing a small bloodstain on his shirtsleeve. "Not that bad, I don't think," he said. "I believe his bullet just nicked me."

"But you *are* wounded."

"Well, yes, I am."

"Then you need a doctor." Cecilia started to turn away from him. "I'll get Dr. Chapman—"

"Cecilia," Roscoe said. "I'm not hurt that bad, really. The doctor is tending to Del. Let him do what he can over there, and then he can see about me."

"That man tried to kill you!"

"Yes, well, he believes I deserve it. At times I've thought the same thing. But I don't wish that on him."

By now the sun was down, and night was about to fall. Bo said, "Roscoe, why don't you go over to the hotel? It wouldn't hurt for you to sit down. Anytime somebody's losing blood, they're liable to pass out. Cecilia, go with him and make sure he's all right."

"Yes," she said, nodding. "Yes, of course." She turned to Roscoe. "Bo's right. You need to sit down. Come on."

"You're not still mad at me?" he asked.

THE SHOTGUN WEDDING   237

"I didn't say that! But . . . that can wait."

Roscoe started to let her lead him toward the Territorial House, but then he stopped short and said, "Wait a minute." He turned toward the town hall and said, "Mr. and Mrs. Hargett, my sincere apologies that my troubles intruded on your special day and evening. I wish you both every happiness in your marriage."

"Thank you," Rose said, a little stiffly. Then she shrugged and added, "Doesn't seem like it was really your fault, so we'll just chalk it up to bad luck."

Roscoe smiled. "I appreciate that, ma'am." Then he walked off toward the hotel, towering over Cecilia as she kept a hand on his uninjured arm and paced along beside him. With his long legs, she had to hurry to keep up, even though he was walking slowly.

The crowd was starting to break up, now that the fight was over. Most people went back in the town hall. Just because trouble had broken out, that didn't mean the social was canceled. Westerners were accustomed to picking up where they'd left off, once the fists or the bullets stopped flying.

Bo saw Rance Plummer and said to the foreman, "Rance, would you mind going into the town hall and getting a lantern? I figure Doc Chapman could use some better light while he's working on that hombre."

Plummer nodded and said, "Be right back."

Scratch told Frank and Emmett, "Get up and go over there where your brothers are. I want all of you varmints in the same place, so I can keep an eye on you easier."

With an air of dejection, the two men climbed to their feet and shuffled over to join Del and Ham. Ham was holding the folded bandanna on Del's bullet-shattered shoulder to slow down the bleeding. In the next few minutes, the bystander Chapman had sent to fetch his medical bag returned with it, and Rance Plummer walked up with a lantern, which he held so that its light washed over the wounded man.

Del appeared to have recovered a bit from the shock of being shot. His face had a little color in it again as he said, "Patch me up, Doc, so I can get back to settling accounts with that snake Grant."

"You mean Roscoe Sherman?" Bo asked as he stood back a little with the others to give Chapman room to work.

Ham glanced up and said, "His real name's Grant. Reckon he thought it was funny, calling himself Sherman."

"He won't think it's funny when I put a bullet in him," Del snapped.

"You won't be puttin' a bullet in anybody," Scratch said. "Tryin' to ventilate Roscoe like you did is attempted murder. You're gonna be spending the next few years in territorial prison, old son."

CHAPTER 25

Del stared at him in horror. "You can't mean that! He had it comin'!"

"We were willing to let you boys fight it out with fists," Bo said, "but guns make it a different matter. Dozens of witnesses saw what you did, Kinney. I don't reckon it'll be a very long trial."

Del looked at his brothers. "Ham . . . Emmett . . . Frank . . . You've got to do something."

"Like what?" Emmett asked with a surprising amount of bitterness in his voice. "We already followed you halfway across the country because you were crazy mad at Roscoe. You didn't care what it took . . . You didn't even care if you got the rest of us killed . . . as long as you got your revenge on him."

"That's true, Del," Frank added. "We didn't even want to come with you. You made us."

Del started to curse, then gasped in pain as Dr. Chapman probed his shoulder. When he could talk again, he said, "I knew I couldn't count on you two. But you, Ham . . . you're with me, ain't you?"

"You heard the lawmen, Del," Ham said heavily.

"You're goin' to prison. I reckon it's time for the rest of us to go home."

"No! You can't mean that, Ham. You wouldn't abandon your brother!"

"I'll stay around long enough to make sure you don't die from bein' shot," Ham said. "But after that, it's time the rest of us got back home. We have families of our own, Del. Have you forgotten that?"

Del turned his head and wouldn't look at his brothers anymore. "Just get away from me, all of you," he said through clenched teeth. "If that's the way you feel, I don't want you around anymore. Don't stay on my account."

"All right," Emmett said. "We won't."

Frank nodded. "As far as I'm concerned, we can get our horses and start now."

"You boys go on," Ham told them. "I'll catch up to you later."

Scratch said, "None of you are leavin'. Not just yet."

"You're lockin' us up, too?" Emmett asked. "You said it was all right for us to fight with Roscoe!"

"We're not lockin' you up, but I don't want you to leave town right away. Just stay here for a spell." Scratch looked over at Plummer. "Rance, how'd you feel about bein' temporarily deputized?"

"That'd be a first for me," Plummer replied with a grin, "but I reckon it's all right."

"Then keep an eye on these fellas while Bo and me go tend to another errand."

Dr. Chapman looked up and said, "I'm going to need to move this man to my office. There's nothing else I can do for him here."

"That's fine," Scratch said. "Rance'll go with you, just

to make sure there's no trouble. And I reckon you can get the hombre's brothers to tote him for you."

"I'll see to it," Plummer promised.

Scratch motioned to Bo and started toward the hotel. As they walked, Bo asked, "What's going on up in that head of yours, Scratch?"

"As loco as that varmint Del is, I know what grief can do to a man. I've seen it with my own eyes." Scratch gave Bo a meaningful look. "So I'm thinkin' maybe it might be better if, instead of sendin' him to the pen, we let him go on back home with his brothers, as long as he promises never to bother Roscoe again or even set foot in these parts."

"You really think we could trust him, even if he did promise that?"

"That's what I want to talk to Roscoe about," Scratch said. "Del claimed that he's a man of his word. We'll see what Roscoe thinks about that." Scratch paused, then added, "I want to make sure he ain't hurt worse'n what he said, too, before we decide for sure what to do with Del."

They reached the Territorial House and stepped up onto the porch. When they went into the lobby, they immediately saw Roscoe sitting in one of the chairs by the potted plants, with Cecilia in another chair pulled up close to his, leaning forward and clasping one of his hands in both of hers.

A bloodstained piece of cloth was tied around Roscoe's upper right arm. When Bo looked closer at it, he could tell that the cloth had been torn off a petticoat. He had a pretty good idea whose petticoat had provided the makeshift bandage.

Cecilia looked at them and said peevishly, "Where's that doctor? Roscoe needs medical attention."

"He'll be along directly," Scratch told her. "He's havin'

Del Kinney moved down to his house right now. I expect he'll be done patchin' up Del pretty soon."

Roscoe said, "Del's not going to die, is he?"

"Probably not," Bo said. "You almost sound like you're worried about him."

"Well . . . I guess I am. I won't lie to you. I never got along all that well with the Kinney brothers even while my wife was still alive, but I don't want them to come to any real harm."

"That's one reason we came to talk to you," Scratch said. "So we can decide what to do about those varmints. First, though, just how bad are you actually hurt?"

"We don't know," Cecilia said, "because the doctor hasn't examined him yet!"

"I'm fine," Roscoe said, using his free hand to pat Cecilia's hands. "The bullet just nicked me. It hurts some, sure, but I can still use that arm, and the wound just needs to be cleaned. It might require a couple of stitches, but that's all."

Stubbornly, Cecilia said, "No matter how badly Roscoe is hurt, that man still tried to kill him. Everyone on the street saw that. I expect you to arrest him and charge him with attempted murder, Marshal."

"That's just what I was thinkin' about doin'," Scratch admitted. "That was my first impulse, for dang sure. But I've been ponderin' on it, and I wonder if it wouldn't be better to let Del and his brothers just go home, as long as we've got their word they won't come back and cause any more trouble."

Cecilia stared at him and asked, "You'd actually believe men like that?"

Scratch didn't answer her directly. Instead, he said, "How about it, Roscoe? If Del gave you his word, would he keep it?"

Roscoe frowned as he thought about the question. After a long moment, he replied, "I believe he would. They may be disreputable and considered shady characters back where they come from, but I never really knew any of them to lie, even Del. If he said he would do something, he generally did it." A hollow laugh came from Roscoe. "Like he said he would come after me and seek revenge. He certainly did that. He broke his promise not to use a gun, too, but that was in the heat of the moment."

Cecilia shook her head. "I don't like it," she said. "You can't trust those men. And it's a simple fact that they broke the law. They need to answer for that, don't they?"

"Well, technically speakin', I reckon you're right, Miss Cecilia," Scratch said. "But Bo and me, we've accidental-like found ourselves on the wrong side of the law and needin' a break now and then."

"You never tried to kill an innocent man, did you?"

Bo said, "She's got you there, partner."

"No, I like the idea," Roscoe said. "There may not have been any mercy in Del's heart, but that doesn't mean I can't have some in mine." He looked directly at Bo and Scratch. "I won't press charges against Del and his brothers, and I ask that you extend them leniency in return for their promise to leave these parts and never return."

Scratch nodded. "That's what we'll do, then. But if they ever show their faces around here again, all bets are off."

"Agreed."

Cecilia still looked upset about the arrangement, but she didn't argue. It probably wouldn't do her any good, Bo thought. Roscoe seemed like the sort of man who didn't change his mind easily once it was made up. He was just as stubborn as . . . well, as she was.

Whether or not that might make them a good match remained to be seen.

Just then, Hugh Craddock threw the hotel's front doors open and strode into the lobby. When he spotted the little group on the other side, by the potted plants, he hurried over and exclaimed, "Cecilia! Are you all right?"

"Of course I am," she said, sounding annoyed. "I wasn't the one being attacked."

"You can see, though, that I was right. You never should have been around this ignorant ox. He's the sort that just attracts trouble wherever he goes."

"Sounds like you weren't payin' attention, mister," Scratch drawled. "Roscoe ain't really what you'd call ignorant. Fact is, he was a schoolteacher."

"So he lied about his past," Craddock said, waving off Scratch's words. "Just another indication that he's not to be trusted."

Bo said, "Did you want something, Craddock? Or did you just come in here to harass folks?"

Craddock ignored that. He held out a hand and said, "Cecilia, will you come with me back to the social? Let these so-called lawmen handle this ugly situation. There's no need for you to be involved with it."

"Mr. Sherman is my escort for the evening," she replied coolly. "Nothing about that has changed. And as such, I'm going to remain at his side."

"Then you're a fool," Craddock snapped.

A rumbling sound came from Roscoe's chest. He leaned forward, as if he was about to get to his feet.

"Take it easy," Bo advised him. "You're injured, remember?"

"I'm not hurt so badly that I can't defend Miss Spaulding's honor," Roscoe said. "I'll never be hurt that badly, as long as I'm drawing breath!"

Cecilia said, "I appreciate that gallantry, but it's not

necessary." She let go of Roscoe's hand and rose to face the rancher from Texas. "Mr. Craddock, I'll thank you to leave me alone. Never speak to me or even approach me again."

Craddock's eyes narrowed as he glared at her. "You know," he said, "I'm awful thickheaded—"

"Nobody's gonna argue with you about that," Scratch said.

"But I can get things through my skull eventually," Craddock went on, as if Scratch hadn't spoken. "I'm done trying to make you see reason. I won't bother you again, Miss Spaulding."

"I certainly hope you mean that," she said with a defiant lift of her chin.

Craddock turned on his heel and stalked out of the hotel lobby. As the door slammed behind him, Scratch said, "I don't reckon any of us are sorry to see that fella go."

The door opened again almost immediately, but this time it was Dr. Arliss Chapman who came in.

"How's Del?" Roscoe asked right away as the doctor briskly crossed the lobby, medical bag in hand.

"He's in no danger of dying, at least at the moment," Chapman replied. "I got the bleeding stopped and stabilized his arm and shoulder as much as possible. There's nothing I can do about the damage to the bones, however. I doubt that he'll have much range of motion in that arm once it's healed." Chapman looked at Bo. "He'll almost certainly never be able to use it to attempt to shoot someone again."

"Things like that happen when you try to shoot somebody," Bo said. He wasn't going to lose any sleep over what had happened to Del Kinney. Hate had driven the man halfway across the country, and in the end, his own lust for violence had caught up with him.

"Well, I've given him something to help him rest, and Mr. Plummer is standing guard over him," Chapman said. "Now, if you'll excuse me, Miss Cecilia, I'll take a look at Roscoe's arm."

"Of course, Doctor," Cecilia said as she stood up and surrendered her chair to the medico. Chapman unwrapped the makeshift bandage and had Roscoe take his shirt off.

The thick slabs of muscle on Roscoe's arms, shoulders, and chest were even more impressive when they were bared. He looked rather embarrassed, though, and after a glance at the wound told Bo that Roscoe was right about it being minor, he suggested, "Why don't the rest of us go on back over to the town hall? I reckon the dancing's probably started back up again."

"I should stay here with Roscoe—" Cecilia began.

"No, that's not necessary," Roscoe said. "Dr. Chapman can tend to this, and then I'll join you over there."

Chapman opened his medical bag and said, "Yes, it won't take long. You were fortunate, Roscoe. You should recover fully from this wound in a fairly short time."

"It's about time I had some good luck," Roscoe said, then glanced at Cecilia and added, "And it sure appears that it's taken a turn for the better."

CHAPTER 26

The wedding of Rose Winston and Steve Hargett, the party that followed the ceremony, and the trouble that broke out at that celebration were the talk of Silverhill and the surrounding vicinity for the next few days, but then folks' attention drifted on to other things, as it usually did.

Rose and Steve made arrangements to move into one of the cabins for married hands at the SJ Ranch. It was hard for Rose to leave her friends in Silverhill, and when they said their goodbyes, a lot of crying and hugging went on.

But they had all known that sooner or later they would go their separate ways. After all, they had come west to get married. Rose was just the first of them to accomplish that goal.

Steve figured he would need to rent a buggy or a buckboard to take his new bride out to the ranch, but Rose wouldn't hear of that.

"I can ride a horse just as good as you," she insisted. "And I'm used to being in the saddle for long hours. I've taken a lot of rides around Silverhill." A smile brightened her face. "You think Mr. Plummer would let me go to work

as a cowboy? I'll bet I could make—what do you call it?—
a top hand!"

The other mail-order brides were still standing on the
porch of the Territorial House, where this conversation
took place. "Rose!" Jean exclaimed, looking horrified.
"You can't go galloping around the range, chasing cows.
You're in . . . you're in . . ." Her voice dropped to a whisper.
"A delicate condition."

Rose laughed and said, "I'm not all that delicate just
yet."

"Maybe not," Steve said, "but I don't reckon it'd be a
good idea. I can ask the doctor about that, if you want."

Jean said, "If you don't, I'll ask Arliss myself!"

Rose shook her head. "No, that's not necessary. I'll
behave myself, I suppose."

Her tone made it clear that she might not care that much
for behaving, though.

Not that long after coming to Silverhill, Rose had
bought her own horse from Hector Esperanza at the
livery stable, so she had her own mount for the ride to
the SJ. Rance Plummer rented a packhorse to carry all
her belongings—the foreman said that was his wedding
present to the couple—and they traveled back to the
ranch with Plummer and the rest of the hands who had
come to town for the wedding.

The cowboys probably gave Steve plenty of hoorawing
about being an old married man whenever Rose wasn't
around, but they were awkwardly, stiffly polite to her, as
Western men invariably were with respectable women.
They would get used to her, she thought. They didn't need
to treat her like she was some sort of delicate flower or
china doll.

The cook at the SJ was a stocky, mostly bald-headed

old-timer known as Powderkeg, because of his tendency to blow up without much warning. He hadn't attended the wedding but had stayed at the ranch with a skeleton crew of hands chosen by drawing straws.

Powderkeg seemed to view Rose's arrival as a fresh intrusion. Three other hands were married, and no doubt he had "welcomed" their wives with the same lack of enthusiasm. When they reached the ranch and Rance Plummer introduced Rose to the cook, Powderkeg informed her in no uncertain terms that she wasn't to poke her nose into his cook shack and try to take over.

"You don't have to worry about that, Mr. Powderkeg," she told him. "I don't intend to interfere with anything you do. I've never been a very good cook."

"Oh," he said, evidently disappointed because he hadn't gotten an argument out of her. Then, with a belligerent scowl on his face, he asked, "What *are* you good for?"

"I can ride and shoot," Rose informed him coolly. "I'll bet with a little practice, I'll be a pretty good hand with a lasso, too." She paused. "And, of course, I'm going to have a baby, so I reckon you can draw your own conclusions from that."

Powderkeg's mouth opened and closed a couple of times as he gawped at her in surprise. A bright red flush started in his jowls and climbed steadily up his face to the top of his bald head. The cowboys who were gathered in front of the ranchhouse porch, where this conversation was taking place, struggled mightily not to burst out in gales of laughter at Powerkeg's discomfiture. Most of them couldn't hold back grins. They liked seeing the cantankerous old-timer get as good as he gave.

Smiling, Steve put a hand on Rose's arm and said,

"Come on. I'll show you the cabin. We've got some moving in to do."

"That's fine." Rose smiled sweetly at the cook. "I'll see you later, Mr. Powderkeg."

He just stood there, still unable to find his voice, as they walked away.

Things settled down fairly quickly. He would enjoy married life more than he ever dreamed possible, Steve thought more than once—

If it weren't for the looming disaster hanging right over his head.

He was out on the range a few days later when he saw a rider coming toward him. The man didn't have to get very close before Steve recognized him. He knew Ben Wilcox by the way he sat the saddle.

Not only that, Steve had been expecting Wilcox to corner him somewhere where they could talk in private.

For a second, he wanted to yank his horse around and gallop away. But it wouldn't do any good. Wilcox would just chase him down or find another opportunity. Angering the rustler by trying to avoid him wouldn't accomplish anything.

Steve reined in and waited. Wilcox rode up and thumbed back his hat as he brought his mount to a halt.

"Howdy, Steve," he said with a grin. "I've been hopin' we'd get a chance to have a little talk."

"Well, here we both are," Steve replied. "Say what you've got to say."

"No need to be proddy about it. In case you haven't noticed, I've been trying to make you a rich man."

"I wouldn't call what we've made so far being rich."

"That's because we haven't gotten to the big payoff yet." Wilcox's smile disappeared. "But we're about to, and the other boys and I want to make sure you're not going to do anything to mess that up for us."

"I've told you all along that I'm not going to give you away," Steve said. "I may not like it, because I hate like fire to be disloyal to Rance, but you can trust me. I just want out of it. You don't need me anymore."

Steve despised the wheedling tone he heard in his own voice. For the hundredth time or more, he wished he had told Wilcox to go to blazes back when the rustler had followed him into that barbershop in Silverhill.

"Now, Steve," Wilcox said, "don't you remember what we worked out? You're going to ask Plummer to put you in charge of nighthawking that herd, and then you're going to pick me and the rest of the boys to fill out the crew. It's the simplest plan anybody ever came up with. Shoot, we'll be halfway to the border with those cows before anybody even knows we're gone!"

"I'll be halfway to the border," Steve grated, "but my wife will be here."

"You can send for her later," Wilcox replied with a dismissive wave. "Or maybe you'll get down there below the border, find yourself a nice, friendly señorita, and decide you weren't cut out to be a married man in the first place."

Steve's lips drew back from his teeth as he leaned forward slightly in the saddle. His right hand swung a few inches toward the butt of his gun.

Wilcox stiffened and said, "You don't want to do that, Steve. You're not fast enough."

"We don't know that."

"If you want to risk makin' that new bride of yours a widow so soon, you go right ahead," Wilcox invited. "Be a lot easier for all concerned if you don't, but we'll muddle through without you if we have to."

Slowly, Steve forced himself to relax. He moved his hand away from his gun and muttered, "Take it easy."

"That's good advice for you to follow. You need to remember that Mrs. Hargett is living right here on the ranch now, where she's mighty easy to find if anybody was to need to."

"Are you threatening her?" Steve asked tightly.

"Just giving you some good advice, like I said."

Steve didn't say anything, but the sigh he heaved and the defeated slump of his shoulders told Wilcox everything he needed to know.

The rustler's grin reappeared as he said, "That's more like it. Now, we're gonna start gathering that herd tomorrow. Shouldn't take more than a week to put it together. You go ahead and start workin' on Plummer. Put the idea in his head of making you the top nighthawk. Be subtle about it, though. We don't want to tip him off."

Steve nodded. "I understand."

"Good boy. I always knew you were a smart hombre. You'll see, it's all gonna work out just fine."

Steve didn't believe that for a second, but there didn't seem to be a blasted thing he could do about it.

One week later . . .

"Here," Rose said as she pressed a paper-wrapped bundle into Steve's hands. They were standing just inside the door of their cabin. "Some biscuits left over from supper tonight. I managed to talk Powderkeg into letting me take a few."

"You didn't have to do that," he told her.

"You're liable to get hungry before morning. Also, I'm sure it gets a little boring just riding around and around a cattle herd all night, so having something to gnaw on will give you something to do." Rose laughed. "And Powderkeg's biscuits sometimes take a little gnawing, that's for sure."

"You're mighty sweet," he said. He bent over—not much, because she was almost as tall as he was—and brushed his lips over her forehead.

That was all he'd intended to do, but suddenly he found himself putting his arms around her and drawing her tightly against him. His lips found hers in an urgent kiss. Rose seemed surprised at first, but it didn't take long for her to respond. She wrapped her arms around Steve's neck and returned the kiss with equal enthusiasm.

"Well," she said when the kiss ended, "I didn't expect that much of a reaction just for some ol' biscuits. But I'm not complaining, mind you."

He hugged her again, clutching her with a desperation that he tried but failed to suppress. He had to stop, he told himself, otherwise she might realize something was wrong. He couldn't keep hugging her with the intensity of a man who never expected to see his wife again.

He managed to put a smile on his face as he said, "I'm just happy to be married, I reckon."

"I'm glad." With a mock solemn look, Rose went on, "Bo and Scratch told me about how you needed some double-barreled convincing, you know."

"It wasn't really a shotgun wedding," he said defensively. "Not really."

"I wouldn't care if it was. We're together now, and that's all that matters."

He had to clamp his jaws together hard to keep from

groaning in despair. She didn't intend to, but she was sure making this more difficult.

He put his hands on her shoulders to get some space between them and said, "I got to get going."

"Steve, I have an idea. Why don't I come along and ride nighthawk with you?"

His eyes widened. He never would have expected her to suggest that, but once he thought about it, he realized that it was perfectly logical—from her point of view. She was a good rider, she was a newlywed and wanted to spend time with her husband, and the idea probably sounded adventurous to her. . . .

He swallowed and shook his head. "No, you can't do that," he said. "Uh, Rance would never allow it."

"I'm sure he would. Mr. Plummer seems like a very reasonable man. And since he put you in charge of guarding the herd at night, don't you have the right to decide who'll handle the chore with you?"

"No," he said flatly. "I'm sorry. You can't."

"But, Steve—"

"I have to go." He turned and walked out the door while he still could. If he didn't leave now, he might not be able to go through with this at all.

And then Rose would be in danger. When this was all over and they were together again—if they were ever together again—she would just have to understand that he'd done what he did in order to protect her. He wasn't sure what Ben Wilcox was capable of—and he didn't want to find out.

"Fine," she called after him, but she didn't sound like she thought it was fine at all. In fact, she sounded hopping mad. She would get over it, though, and, anyway, there was worse to come. She just didn't know it yet.

His horse was saddled and waiting for him. He put his foot in the stirrup and swung up. He didn't look back as he rode away into the late afternoon.

Because he didn't trust himself to. If he did, if he saw her standing there in the doorway . . .

Steve kept moving, his eyes grimly turned ahead.

CHAPTER 27

The herd's bed-ground was about three miles from the SJ ranch house. The plan was to drive the cattle about eighty miles east to the nearest railroad stop, where they would be loaded on cars and shipped north to Cheyenne and eventually on to the stockyards in Chicago.

If Ben Wilcox's plan came to fruition, though, those cows would never make that drive and would wind up below the border in Mexico instead.

The sun was down and shadows were gathering by the time Steve reached the herd. Rance Plummer rode out to meet him, cantering easily through the dusk.

"The critters seem to be settled down for the night already," the foreman said as he waved a big hand toward the dark mass of cattle. "And the sky's clear as a bell, so I ain't expectin' any storms to come along and spook 'em. You ought to have a nice, easy night, Steve."

"I hope so," Steve said. He had to make an effort to keep his voice sounding normal and relaxed. Rance was pretty sharp. Steve didn't want him to notice the strain he was under.

Rance went on, "I'm obliged to you for volunteerin' to

take care of things like this, son. I always knew you had the makin's of a top hand, and I figured the responsibility of bein' married might get you to take on more responsibility around the ranch, too." He rested both hands on the saddle horn and leaned forward. "You know, I can see a day when you might be runnin' things for the bosses around here, instead of me."

Steve said, "Oh, no, not for a long time yet."

"Might be sooner'n you think," Rance drawled. "I ain't exactly no spring chicken anymore. I'm startin' to spend more and more time thinkin' about how nice it'd be to just sit for a spell and take life easy."

"I can't imagine you doing that, boss."

"Well, we'll see." Rance lifted his reins. "The herd's in your hands now, Steve, but if you need me durin' the night, don't hesitate to send one of the boys to fetch me."

Steve managed to nod. Blast it, why was Rance making this so hard for him? Steve hadn't wanted to betray the foreman to start with, and the faith Rance placed in him just made things worse.

Then he thought about Rose and the vague threats Wilcox had made against her, and he knew he had no choice. His first loyalty was to the woman he loved.

Since the bed-ground was relatively close to the ranch headquarters, Powderkeg hadn't brought a chuck wagon out here. However, the men who had been riding night-hawk since the gather began had built a small campfire on a low bluff overlooking the herd, so they could boil a pot of coffee and keep it warm during the night.

Steve headed for that orange glow, which was already visible as night fell and the stars began to wink into view in the darkening sky.

Several men were hunkered around the little fire,

drinking their last cups of coffee before their shifts began. Another man stood nearby, holding their horses.

Ben Wilcox looked up from the fire and grinned. "Evening, Steve," he said. "Light down and have a cup while you've got the chance." He paused and then added meaningfully, "It's going to be a long night."

Several of the other men chuckled. Steve looked around at them to make sure they were all part of the scheme Wilcox had put together. Wilcox had warned him not to include any of the other ranch hands in the crew that would be riding nighthawk tonight. Any witnesses would have to be "dealt with," as Wilcox had put it, and Steve knew exactly what he had meant by that.

Steve got his tin cup out of his saddlebag and poured himself a cup of coffee. He stood there and took a couple of sips, then said, "We'll go and relieve the boys who are riding herd in just a few minutes."

"And then we'll make our move once it's good and dark, but before the moon comes up, just in case there's anybody around to get curious," Wilcox said. "We'll rendezvous on the northeast side of the herd when I give the signal. That'll be three hoots of the owl. We'll get those cows moving west for a few miles before we swing south. That'll let us go around Silverhill." His commanding tone made it clear who was actually in charge here. "We'll be pushing the herd pretty hard. I want to put plenty of distance between us and the SJ before morning."

"We all understand what we're doing," Steve said, not bothering to keep his voice civil.

Wilcox didn't seem to take offense at the curt tone. He was probably thinking about how much money he was going to make from this night's dishonest work. He just said, "It never hurts to be sure." He dashed the grounds in his cup into the fire. "Let's go."

Steve gulped down the rest of the hot brew in his cup. He mounted up along with the others and rode down the slope to the wide flat that was serving as the herd's bed-ground.

The group of rustlers spread out to find the cowboys who were watching the herd and relieve them so they could back to headquarters and have supper. Within fifteen minutes, the changeover was complete, and the only men riding slowly around the herd, keeping the cattle quiet and calm, were the members of Ben Wilcox's gang.

And that included him, too, Steve thought bitterly. He was just as much an outlaw and a rustler as any of them. His son or daughter would have to grow up with an owlhoot for a father. The thought put a tight band around his chest, and he couldn't seem to loosen it no matter what he did.

The last glow of sunset faded from the western sky. Stygian darkness lay over the vast landscape. The light from millions of stars relieved the gloom a little, but not like the moon would when it rose in another hour or so.

Minutes dragged by. If he had to do this, Steve told himself, he wanted to go ahead and get it over with. The longer he had to think about what he was doing, the more miserable he would be. The hard work of driving the cattle through the night would be a welcome distraction.

He listened intently for Wilcox's signal, but instead, he suddenly heard something he wasn't expecting: hoofbeats approaching from the wrong direction. Stiffening in alarm, Steve swung his horse around and peered through the darkness, trying to spot whoever was riding toward him.

He hoped it wasn't Rance Plummer, coming back to the herd for some reason.

The newcomer wasn't the foreman. The shock of recognition that went through Steve was even worse when he heard Rose call softly, "Steve! Steve, where are you?"

He bit back a curse and heeled his horse into hurried motion toward the sound of her voice. It was bad enough that she had followed him out here, but as figures on horseback loomed up out of the night, he realized that she wasn't alone. Someone was with her.

"Rose!" he answered "Rose, what are you doing out here?" The two riders came up to him and reined in. A familiar gravelly voice rasped, "Hargett, this gal you married is the stubbornest dang filly I ever run into! When I seen her saddlin' her pony and asked her what she was doin', she said she was gonna ride out here and surprise you by keepin' you company all night! Wouldn't listen to reason when I told her it was a plumb foolish notion!"

"Powderkeg," Steve said hollowly. "Is that you?"

A disgusted snort came from the old cook. "Well, who else would it be?" His irritated tone softened a little as he went on, "When I couldn't talk any sense into her head, I figured I'd better ride along with her, just to make sure she was safe." The stocky figure leaned forward in the saddle and gazed out across the dark mass of cattle. "To tell yuh the truth, I don't really mind all that much. I used to be a cowboy myself, you know, 'fore I got too stove up to do it anymore. Rode many a turn as nighthawk. Why, I bet I can still warble a tune—"

Steve brought his horse closer to Rose's and interrupted the old-timer by saying, "Rose, you need to ride back to headquarters right now. You can't be out here." He continued listening with one ear for Wilcox's signal. "It's not safe for you to be traipsing around at night like this."

"I don't see why not," she said. "Everybody tells me the Indians haven't caused any problems in this area recently, and I brought along a carbine, just in case I ran into any trouble." She patted the stock of the rifle, which stuck up from a saddle boot. "But Powderkeg insisted that he was coming with me."

"Blast it, what about the baby?" Steve's tone was harsher than he intended, but he was consumed with worry now. He had to get Rose and Powderkeg out of here before Wilcox put his plan into action. He couldn't stop thinking about how Wilcox had said that any witnesses would be "dealt with."

"Honestly, the baby is fine," Rose responded, sounding a little exasperated herself now. "You've got to stop wrapping me up in tissue paper, Steve. Women have been having babies for thousands of years now without having to be pampered constantly—"

Steve heard another horse close by. Dread welled up inside him. He nudged his horse against Rose's and said, "You've got to go, now!"

"Steve, stop acting so crazy!" she said as her horse shied and she tightened the reins. "We'll just take a couple of turns around the herd with you, and then we'll go back, all right? You don't have to—"

Another rider came out of the shadows. Ben Wilcox reined in and said sharply, "Steve, what's going on here?"

"Nothing," Steve said. "Rose just came to visit—"

"Wilcox, is that you?" Powderkeg said.

"Yeah. I'm riding nighthawk," Wilcox replied. He sounded tense but under control. Steve was glad the rustler hadn't just drawn his gun and started shooting as soon as he realized someone else was here. There was still a chance he could ease Rose and Powderkeg away from the herd without any trouble, Steve told himself.

"Hargett, I thought Rance put you in charge of this crew," Powderkeg said.

"That's right. He did—"

"Then why in tarnation did you pick Wilcox for it? I never trusted this ranihan. Always seems like he's skulkin' around, up to no good. If I'd been foreman, I'd've run him off a long time ago, but Rance has got hisself too much of a generous nature—"

"Why don't you stop flappin' your jaws, you obnoxious old pelican?" Wilcox cut in. "Nobody asked your opinion."

"Obnoxious old pelican, is it!" Powderkeg practically howled. "Why, for two cents, I'd—"

Wilcox lost his temper then. He lunged his horse next to Powderkeg's mount, yanked his gun from its holster, and lashed out with it. The barrel thudded against Powderkeg's head and shut him up. The old-timer toppled out of the saddle and crashed to the ground as Rose cried out in surprise.

"What did you *do*?" she shouted at Wilcox. "What's wrong with you?"

Wilcox jerked his horse around. Steve spurred his mount forward to put himself between Wilcox and Rose. He would take a bullet for her if he had to.

"Rose, get out of here!" he barked. "Ride for the ranch!"

"Don't move, gal!" Wilcox shouted at her. He leveled the gun at Steve and pulled back the hammer. "I'll shoot this stupid husband of yours if you do."

"Go, Rose!" Steve yelled. "Forget about me!"

"No!" she cried as she fought again to bring her skittish mount under control. "What's going on here?"

"Your husband's fixin' to be a rich man, once we get this herd below the border into Mexico," Wilcox said in a gloating tone. "That is, if he doesn't do anything foolish."

Steve groaned. Now that Wilcox had admitted they were rustlers, Rose was in even more danger. He didn't think he could survive a shoot-out with Wilcox, especially when the rustler already had his gun in his hand, but maybe he could get off a shot or two and give Rose a chance to escape. . . .

He had just started to make a desperate stab for his gun when something smashed into his head from the side. He hadn't heard a shot, but he had heard men say that you never heard the shot that killed you. Although, how anybody would know a thing like that, he couldn't say.

That crazy thought whirled through his head as he felt himself falling; then the ground came up and smashed him in the face. He lay there, vaguely aware that he wasn't dead yet. Then Rose screamed, and the shrill sound dispelled some of the fog that threatened to overwhelm him. He forced his muscles to work and pushed himself up from the ground.

Then a booted foot slammed into his side and rolled him, gasping, onto his back.

Wilcox said, "Grab that girl! Don't let her get away!"

Knowing that Rose was in danger almost gave Steve the strength he needed to get to his feet, but then Wilcox kicked him again. He couldn't do anything except curl up around the pain that filled him.

"Well, this went to Hades in a hurry," Wilcox muttered. Steve's vision was blurry, but he was able to make out Wilcox hunkering in front of him. "Don't worry. We're not gonna hurt that little wife of yours. This actually isn't that bad of a break. We've got ourselves a nice hostage, in case anybody comes after us and does happen to catch up."

Breathing hard, Steve struggled into a half-sitting position, propped up on one hand. He saw Rose struggling a few yards away in the grip of one of the rustlers, who had an arm around her waist and his other hand clamped over her mouth. Steve's other hand trembled as he lifted it to his head and found a wet, sticky lump above his ear.

"That was a broken branch that hit you and not a bullet, in case you're wondering," Wilcox went on. "Tarver was comin' to meet me when he saw the four of us on horseback and realized something was wrong. So he slipped up on foot until he figured it out, then walloped you and knocked you out of the saddle. Count yourself lucky, Steve. He could've shot you."

Steve's voice echoed oddly inside his head as he said, "Let . . . her . . . go. You don't need . . . to keep Rose—"

"Like I said, she'll be a nice hostage." Wilcox's teeth were visible in the starlight as he grinned. "Mighty nice to have around, I'd say. But we'll be gentlemen . . . as long as you cooperate and hold up your end of the bargain, Steve."

"Why don't you just . . . go ahead and shoot me?"

"Shoot you?" Wilcox laughed. "Why can't you get it through your thick head that I like you, kid? You remind me of me, when I was young."

The very thought of that made Steve sick. Or maybe it was getting walloped in the head that sickened him.

"Anyway," Wilcox continued, "I figure you'll be the hardest-workin' cowhand anybody ever did see, since you know your wife's safety is riding on it. We'll get some good use out of you, and then, once we're below the border, where the law can't touch us anymore, we'll cut you loose if that's what you want. Both of you."

Steve didn't believe that for a second. Once they were in Mexico, Wilcox wouldn't have any more reason to keep him alive. The man would kill him as soon as he got the chance. More than likely, that had been Wilcox's intention all along.

Now, with Rose as his prisoner, the rustler would have even more reason to get rid of Steve. A beautiful young woman like her would be worth good money below the border.

"All right, we're wasting time." Wilcox straightened to his feet, and Steve realized that the rest of the rustlers were gathered around them. Wilcox must have summoned them with the hoot owl signal, but Steve had been too groggy to hear it. "Tie the girl's hands behind her back and put her on her horse. Stick a gag in her mouth, too. She could yell her head off out here without anybody hearing, but all that racket would get on my nerves after a while."

"What about Hargett?" one of the other men asked roughly. "Do we tie him, too?"

Wilcox chuckled. "No need to do that," he said. "Steve's gonna be only too happy to do whatever we tell him. Isn't that right, Steve?"

Steve muttered a curse.

"I said, isn't that right, Steve?" Wilcox's words lashed at him.

"Yeah," he grated as he fought his way to his feet. Dizziness almost made him fall down again, and then he felt like he was going to retch. He fought to suppress both of those things.

Somebody brought his horse to him. He leaned against the animal and held on to the stirrup to steady himself.

"You didn't have to do this," he said to Wilcox. "I was gonna go along with you. All you had to do was let me convince Rose and Powderkeg to go back to the ranch."

"I know," Wilcox said, "but I got too blasted tired of listening to that old man work his mouth. He's always ridin' somebody about something, and he's not even that good of a cook!"

The rustlers had lashed Rose's wrists together behind her back, and now a couple of them struggled to get a gag in her mouth. One of them jerked his hand back, yelled a curse, and said, "She bit me!"

"She's a feisty one, all right," Wilcox said. He had holstered his gun, but now he drew it again and pressed the barrel against the back of Steve's head. "She'll cooperate now, I'll bet."

Rose glared murderously—Steve could tell that even in the darkness—but she stood there and let the men gag her, then lift her into the saddle.

Wilcox took the gun away from Steve's head but didn't pouch the iron. "That's the way it's going to work from here on out," he said. "Both of you are gonna do as you're told, or the other one will suffer for it. Got that?"

"We understand," Steve said. His voice shook with anger and despair.

"Mount up, then."

Steve looked around for his hat, found it, and picked it up, being careful not to fall down as he leaned over. He stuffed the hat in his saddlebags. His head hurt too much to wear it right now. Then he got his foot in the stirrup and hauled himself onto the horse's back.

Wilcox mounted, as well, and so did the others. Wilcox said, "I reckon we're ready to start pushin' these cattle on their way to Mexico. There's just one more thing to take care of first."

He reined his horse over next to a dark shape sprawled on the ground. Steve realized it was the still-unconscious Powderkeg.

"I think I busted the old varmint's skull when I hit him," Wilcox said, "but just in case . . ."

He aimed the gun in his hand at the cook.

"Ben, wait a minute," one of the other men said. "A shot's liable to spook those cows. We don't want to start this off with a stampede if we don't have to."

"Yeah, you're right about that," Wilcox said. He lifted the gun, hesitated a second longer, and then slid it back into leather. "We'll just do it another way."

He backed his horse off, and Steve suddenly realized what Wilcox was about to do. He could only watch in horror as Wilcox goaded his mount into a run and then galloped right over Powderkeg, the horse's steel-shod hooves smashing the old-timer into the ground. Wilcox hauled back on the reins, wheeled his horse, and laughed.

"He won't be goin' anywhere after that. Come on, boys. We're headed for Mexico!"

CHAPTER 28

Rance Plummer slept in the main house at night. In addition to the foreman's living quarters, the big dining room and the ranch office were located in the house, which was a single-story frame structure built of whitewashed lumber freighted in at considerable expense in this region, where trees were few and far between.

After spending years living in bunkhouses as a regular working cowhand, Rance wasn't that fond of being separated from the rest of the crew, but he had found that it was necessary if he was going to maintain discipline.

He was asleep when something nagged at his senses enough to disturb him. Unsure what it might be—indeed, not completely sure he hadn't dreamed or imagined it—he lay there in the darkness, frowning as he listened intently.

Then he heard it again, drifting in through the window: the soft clopping sound of a horse's hooves as the animal moved back and forth. It had a jerky rhythm, stopping and starting, as if the horse were moving around aimlessly. That thought made alarm bells start to ring in Rance's head.

Normally, the ranch headquarters was quiet at this

time of night, except for the snoring coming from the bunkhouse. No horse should have been out there. Rance sat up in bed, reached over, and closed his hand around the butt of the holstered Colt lying on the little table beside the bed. He swung his bare feet to the floor.

Wearing just his long underwear, he carried the gun to the window and peered out into the night as he used the Colt's barrel to part the curtains.

This window overlooked the area to the east side of the house. He didn't see anything moving, but he could still hear the horse. It snorted and snuffled uncertainly. The sound came from the front of the house, so Rance headed in that direction.

He knew better than to just open the front door and step out onto the porch. Fellas that careless had a habit of getting bushwhacked and shot full of holes.

He didn't light a lantern, either. No sense in making himself a target.

Instead, he reached out with his left hand, found the knob in the darkness, and flung the door back at the same time he was taking a swift step to his right. He pressed his back to the wall beside the door. The thick planks of which the house was built would stop most bullets.

No guns went off, but he heard the horse outside blowing. Then a whisper came, so soft he wasn't sure it was even a voice at first.

"R-Rance . . ."

That harsh, gravelly tone could belong to only one man Rance knew of. He said, "Powderkeg?"

"H-help . . ."

He had no doubt that this was the squatty cook pleading for help from the porch, but this could still be a trick or a trap of some sort. Somebody could be forcing Powderkeg to lure him out of the house.

Despite that, Rance and Powderkeg were old friends, and he knew he couldn't just stand here in the dark and do nothing while Powderkeg seemed to be suffering.

With the gun held level in front of him, Rance stepped quickly around the doorjamb onto the porch. He swung the Colt from side to side as he searched for any threat. From the corner of his eye, he saw the dark, unmoving shape lying on the porch. A groan came from it.

A saddled horse paced back and forth nervously in front of the house, not going very far each time before it stepped on the dangling reins, then stopped, backed, and turned around. Powderkeg must have ridden up on the horse, Rance thought, but what the cook was doing out on the range at this time of night, he had no idea.

He didn't know what was wrong with Powderkeg, either, but the old-timer seemed to be hurt. He had made it as far as the porch before collapsing.

Rance didn't see anything else moving. The ranch head-quarters was dark and quiet, just like it was supposed to be. He lowered the gun and said, "Hang on, Powderkeg." He couldn't tell if the cook heard him.

After stepping back just inside the door, the foreman placed the Colt on a small table and felt around for the oil lamp that was kept there, along with a box of matches. He found both and snapped a lucifer to life with his thumb-nail. Lifting the lamp's chimney, he held the tiny flame to the wick, and after a second, yellow light welled up as it caught.

Rance replaced the chimney, picked up the lamp with his left hand, and took the Colt in his right again. He stepped out onto the porch and held the lamp so its flickering yellow glow washed over the figure at his feet.

What he saw jolted a curse out of his mouth. Powderkeg lay there on his side, his face covered with blood and his eyes closed. More bloodstains darkened his clothes in places.

For a second, Rance believed that the old-timer had died, but then he heard air bubbling through what looked like a broken nose. Powderkeg's eyes were swollen shut, and bruises and scratches covered his face, along with the blood. One arm was twisted at an unnatural angle. He looked like a gang had attacked him brutally with clubs and beaten him nearly to death.

Rance knelt and set the lamp on the porch a couple of feet away. He rested his left hand lightly on the cook's shoulder and said, "Powderkeg! Powderkeg, can you hear me?"

Powderkeg stirred slightly. His eyes didn't open, but his bloody lips moved. "Rus . . . rustlers," he breathed. Even as badly hurt as he was, he was able to follow that word with a few colorful profanities. Then he struggled to form a more coherent response and said, "Stole . . . herd . . . took Hargett . . . and the girl . . ."

Rance leaned closer and said urgently, "The girl? You mean Rose? The girl Steve married?"

"R-Rose . . . yeah . . . They . . . took her . . ."

Rance felt like he'd been punched in the gut. It was bad enough that rustlers had gotten away with the herd, if that was actually what Powderkeg was trying to tell him. The fact that they'd kidnapped Rose and, evidently, Steve, too, was even worse. He had no idea at first what Rose had been doing at the bed-ground, but once he thought about it for a second, riding out there to be with her new husband seemed exactly like the sort of impulsive thing she would do.

He could get the details later, assuming Powderkeg pulled through, but right now there was one more thing he needed to know. He asked, "Who did this to you, Powderkeg? Did you recognize any of the rustlers?"

"Who . . . done . . . it?" Powderkeg's voice strengthened. Despite the injuries, a note of fury tinged his words as he said, "Wilcox! That blasted . . . Ben Wilcox . . . and the rest of . . . the nighthawk . . . crew . . ."

A long sigh came from him, and again, Rance thought the old-timer had crossed the divide. Powderkeg continued breathing, though. He had just fallen into an exhausted, battered stupor.

Rance straightened to his feet and moved quickly onto the porch steps. He pointed the gun in the air and triggered three fast shots, the rangeland's universal signal for trouble. In a matter of seconds, the hands began boiling out of the bunkhouse, all of them in various stages of undress but all carrying guns, too.

"Over here!" Rance bellowed across the ranch yard. "We got a man hurt!"

The crew charged across to the house. Rance barked words, telling them as efficiently as possible what had happened and then issuing orders. Several of the men carefully lifted Powderkeg's unconscious form to carry the cook into the house and put him in Rance's bed.

"Take it easy with him," Rance snapped. "We don't know how bad he's hurt, but it ain't good, that's for sure. He looks like he could be all busted up inside."

Other men rushed to the barn and the adjoining corral to saddle some horses. The sooner they got on the trail of the rustlers, the better.

Rance went on, "I want a man on a fast horse to head for Silverhill, too. Get the doc and bring him back out here. Powderkeg's liable to need him. And tell those Texans what's happened!"

"You mean Creel and Morton, Rance?" a man asked. "Yeah, they're lawmen, but they don't have any jurisdiction outside of town."

"Jurisdiction be hanged!" Rance said. "Rose is in trouble, and I don't want to be the one who didn't tell 'em about it. I know those old boys, and they'll want to be right in the thick of it, with hell in their holsters!"

Bo and Scratch took turns sleeping on the cot in the marshal's office, and tonight it was Bo's turn. Scratch was in his room at the hotel, having made night rounds, checked with Bo at the office to make sure nothing had come up, and then turned in.

No prisoners were locked up in the cell block. Since it was the middle of the week, not many cowboys or miners were in town, and the ones who were hadn't raised enough of a ruckus in the saloons to get themselves locked up. Bo lay on the cot, in a light sleep, part of his senses alert for any signs of trouble, as always.

He came awake instantly and fully when somebody pounded on the locked office door and shouted, "Marshal! Are you in there, Marshal?"

Bo had been lying down long enough for his muscles to stiffen some. At his age, that couldn't be avoided. But he still got to his feet pretty spryly and moved through the door of the small back room where the cot was located. He had taken off his boots, coat, and string tie, as well as his gunbelt, but other than that he was fully dressed.

As he passed the desk on his way to the door, he picked up the loaded shotgun he had left there. He didn't need any light to do that. The inside of the office was completely familiar to him by now, even in the dark.

A lamp burned in a holder attached to the wall outside the door, its flame turned low so that the oil in it would last all night. That way folks in town could always find their way to the marshal's office if they needed help. Bo leaned close to the window and parted the curtain enough to look out. In the lamp's flickering glow, he recognized one of the hands from the SJ Ranch. He couldn't recall the man's name but was certain of his identity.

The cowboy hammered on the door again with his fist and called, "Marshal!"

Bo turned the key in the lock, twisted the latch, and pulled the door open. He thrust the shotgun's twin barrels at the man and said, "Quit making so much noise! The marshal's not here right now, but I am. What's wrong?"

The cowboy gulped as he stared at the Greener's muzzles. When he found his voice again, he blurted, "Rance sent me to fetch you! Rustlers stole that herd we gathered, and they run off with Steve Hargett and Miss Rose, too!"

That news was such a shock to Bo, he almost didn't hear it when the puncher added, "They almost done for ol' Powderkeg, the cook, too. He's hurt powerful bad and needs the doc."

Bo's thoughts were whirling, but he forced them to settle down. This wasn't the first time in his life that trouble had come calling unexpectedly, not by a long shot, and he knew how important it was to keep a cool head.

"You know where Dr. Chapman's house is?"

"Yeah, I think so," the SJ hand replied.

"You go on down there and roust him out. Tell him

what's happened and stay with him while he gets ready to go. Then you can lead him back to the ranch. Scratch and I will probably be headed that way ourselves by then. I'm going to wake him now, as soon as I get my boots and hat and gun."

"Thanks, Deputy."

The man started to turn away, but Bo stopped him with a question.

"I reckon Rance took some men and went after the rustlers?"

"Yes, sir. I rode out just before they did."

The SJ crew would have a good start, then, but not as good as the rustlers. Bo and Scratch would have to hurry to catch up to any of them—but that was exactly what Bo intended to do.

The question of jurisdiction flitted briefly through Bo's mind, and then he completely dismissed it. He and Scratch would be going after those kidnapping, wide-looping varmints not as the marshal and deputy marshal of Silverhill, but as Texans with a score to settle.

And in that case, jurisdiction didn't mean a blasted thing.

CHAPTER 29

Traveling at night was always risky, especially when a fella wasn't really familiar with the country. He might ride off into a ravine that he didn't see until it was too late or run afoul of some other danger lurking in the darkness.

But Bo and Scratch had to run that risk, because Rose's life might well hang in the balance. Both Texans still felt like the young ladies they had escorted to Silverhill were their responsibility.

It was well after midnight and still dark when they neared the SJ. Their instincts had done a good job of guiding them. Locating the ranch headquarters wasn't difficult, since the main house and the bunkhouse both had lights burning in them, and those yellow glows were visible for a long distance.

A scrawny, birdlike old-timer carrying a Winchester came out of the main house to greet them. Bo recognized him as the head wrangler, Asa.

"Boys, I'm glad to see you," Asa said when he realized who they were and lowered the rifle. "Where's Rich?"

"Who's that?" Scratch asked.

"The fella who rode to fetch help from town."

"He's coming along behind us with the doctor," Bo said. "How's Powderkeg?"

"Still alive. He's a stubborn old coot. He's restin' in Rance's bed."

Scratch asked, "Has he said anything else about what happened?"

"Nope." Asa sighed. "Fact of the matter is, he ain't woke up again. I reckon that's a bad sign, but there ain't nothin' we can do except wait for the sawbones to get here, and keep our hopes up."

"There are a couple of other things you can do," Bo said. "Pick out some fresh horses for us, and point us in the direction Rance went chasing after those rustlers." He thought for a second. "Four horses, so we can switch back and forth and make better time that way."

"By gum, I can do that, all right!" Asa said. "Come on. I'll cut some good mounts outta the remuda."

As Bo and Scratch were switching their saddles to the new mounts, Scratch asked, "How many men did Rance leave here at headquarters with you?"

"Four, and they weren't happy about bein' left out, let me tell you. Ever'body wanted to go chasin' after them no-good wide-loopers."

Bo tightened his cinch and said, "Stay alert. Not likely you'll have any more trouble tonight, but you never know."

Asa told them how to find the bed-ground from which the herd had been stolen. Once there, they would be able to follow the trail of the rustled cattle. A herd of that size left enough of a mark to be visible even by moonlight, and that silvery orb still rode fairly high in the western sky.

With that, Bo and Scratch swung up and rode away from the ranch headquarters.

On the way out here, they hadn't talked much about the danger Rose was in. Neither of them had wanted to think about that, and they certainly hadn't wanted to let their worst fears creep into their minds.

Scratch hadn't been able to keep his worry contained, though. He'd said, "What do you reckon Rose was even doin' out yonder with the herd at night?"

"I don't know," Bo had said. "Riding nighthawk with Steve?"

Scratch rubbed his chin and nodded slowly. "That does sound just like somethin' she'd do, don't it? Sorta romantic and sorta adventurous at the same time."

"She generally doesn't waste much time thinking about a thing before she jumps right in," Bo said.

He hoped that in this case, that impulsive nature wasn't going to get Rose killed.

By the time the eastern sky was turning red and gold with the approach of dawn, Steve could tell how uncomfortable Rose was. Not just scared, but also in pain and miserable. She had talked about how she was used to spending long hours in the saddle, but she had never ridden all night before, and at a fairly brisk pace, too, because Ben Wilcox wanted to put as much distance as he could between the rustled herd and the SJ Ranch.

Steve's dizziness had gone away while they were riding during the night, but his head still ached from being hit with a branch by the rustler called Tarver. He was glad when Wilcox finally called a halt, not just for himself but mostly for Rose's sake. He said to Wilcox, "Can I help Rose down? She can't rest any while she's still in the saddle."

"Sure," Wilcox said with that easy, meaningless grin. He probably thought he was being generous to his captives, and they ought to be grateful to him for any small kindness he showed them.

Steve wished he could show Wilcox just how grateful he was. He'd show it with a .45 slug right through the rustler's cruel, larcenous brain. . . .

He shoved that thought out of his head and dismounted. He had been leading Rose's horse; that was the job Wilcox had given him. He moved quickly to her side and reached up to her.

"Just take your feet out of the stirrups and slide down into my arms," he told her. "I'll catch you."

Rose nodded. The sky was light enough now that he could see the trust in her eyes. A trust that he had betrayed by getting mixed up with these rustlers in the first place.

He helped her down, and as soon as her feet were on the ground, she leaned against him. He felt her trembling from exhaustion and couldn't stop himself from putting his arms around her in an attempt to comfort her.

"Don't try anything, Steve," Wilcox warned. He had swung down from the saddle, too.

"I'm not going to try anything," Steve said. "I've got more sense than that although you couldn't prove it by some of the decisions I've made in the past."

"You mean deciding to throw in with us and get some of the payoff you've got coming to you for all the hard work you gave Plummer and the SJ? Is that what you're talking about, Steve?"

He didn't respond, just tightened his embrace around Rose. Her trembling eased a little as he held her.

After a minute, he said to Wilcox, "Is it all right if I take this gag off of her? We're a long way from anywhere she could yell for help."

That was true. The rustlers had turned the herd south during the night and had swung wide around Silverhill. The lights of the settlement hadn't even been visible in the distance. In this stretch, all the way on down into Mexico, there wasn't much of anything. Maybe an isolated farm here and there, where a peon and his family tried to scratch a living out of the poor soil, but that was all.

"Sure. Go ahead," Wilcox said, again being magnanimous.

Steve lifted his hands to the knot in the bandanna that was tied behind Rose's head. He fumbled a little but then worked it loose and took the gag out of her mouth. She panted and tried to form words, but he told her, "Wait just a minute. I'll get you something to drink."

He had a canteen on his saddle. His horse was close, so he was able to just reach over, snag the canteen, and pull the cork out with his teeth while he kept his other arm around Rose. He held the canteen to her lips and tipped it up. She swallowed the lukewarm water greedily.

"That's enough," he told her after a moment, as he lowered the canteen. "You don't want to drink too much and make yourself sick."

She licked her lips and said in a husky voice, "Steve . . ."

"Go ahead and cuss me out, if you want to," he said. "I deserve it. I've been downright stupid."

"There's only one person here . . . who deserves a good cussing . . ."

She turned her head to glare at Ben Wilcox.

He just laughed and said, "Go ahead and untie the lady's hands, too, Steve. I expect her arms are pretty tired and sore from being pulled back behind her like that. When we start movin' again, though, I want them tied to the saddle horn. And between now and then, if she does anything foolish, like making a grab for a gun, I won't be responsible for what happens. Neither of you will like it, though."

Steve looked her in the eye and said, "Rose, you can't try anything. Wilcox won't hesitate to kill both of us if we give him any trouble."

Anger burned in her gaze. "So we just let him get away with this?"

"For now," Steve told her quietly, hoping she would understand. "Turn around and I'll see if I can untie your hands."

She did, and after a few minutes of struggle, he managed to loosen the bonds enough for her to slip out of them. She groaned in relief as she brought her arms in front of her. Then she reached around his neck, and he hugged her again.

"Steve," she whispered in his ear, "I hurt so bad, it feels like my legs and my . . . rear end . . . are on fire. I don't know if I can ride again."

"I don't figure Wilcox's gonna give us any choice. But I'll see if I can get him to let us rest here as long as possible."

Without the rustlers pushing them along, the cattle had stopped and were grazing on the sparse grass that grew in these parts. It wasn't enough to support a herd for very long, but for now, it had the cows satisfied. As long as nothing happened to spook them, they weren't going to wander off.

That allowed the rustlers to rest their horses, as well as build a small fire from greasewood branches to boil a pot of coffee. They wouldn't be stopped here long enough to cook any breakfast, Wilcox announced, so for the time being, they would have to make do with gulping down cups of coffee and gnawing jerky once they were back in the saddle.

Rose was grateful for the coffee, judging by the way she clutched the cup Steve brought to her. The strong black brew brought some color back into her face. Steve saw the fury smoldering in her eyes and worried that she wouldn't be able to keep it contained.

"As soon as we get a chance, we'll slip away from them," he told her, quietly enough that none of the others could overhear. "If they're over the border, or even close to it, they won't bother coming after us. They'll be out of the reach of the law in Mexico, so there won't be anything we can do to hurt them."

"You really think so?" she asked, keeping the words equally quiet.

"Sure," he said easily, although he wasn't convinced of what he had just told her. Wilcox might be so furious that he would come after them, anyway, and there was still the matter of how much he'd be able to sell Rose for, once they were south of the border. Some of those Mexican brothel owners would pay a small fortune for a young, pretty gringo gal like Rose, even one who was with child.

So there was a chance that getting away wouldn't be as simple as Steve made it sound, but they were going to try, anyway. They had no choice. The only things waiting for them south of the border were a bullet in the head for Steve and a short, brutal life of shame and degradation for Rose.

Steve got himself a cup of coffee, too. There was no place to sit down, but Rose wasn't really interested in sitting down. It felt good to her just to stand up for a while, Steve knew.

All too soon, Wilcox kicked dirt over the fire's embers

and ordered, "Everybody mount up. It's time we rattle our hocks outta here." He looked at Steve. "I'm glad Mrs. Hargett has been reasonable about all this, but I want her hands tied to that saddle horn, anyway."

"Is that really necessary?" Rose asked. "My wrists are sore, and it'll be so much more comfortable if they're not tied again. I give you my word, I won't try to escape or cause you any trouble, Mr. Wilcox."

The meek, pleading tone in her voice worried Steve. He knew it wasn't genuine, and Wilcox probably did, too.

But he smiled and said, "Well, I'm glad to hear you say that, ma'am. You believe I should trust you, is that it?"

"Yes," Rose said, nodding. "You can trust me."

"I reckon maybe I can." Wilcox reached over to his horse, pulled the Winchester from its saddle scabbard, and worked the rifle's lever to throw a cartridge into the firing chamber. "You know why I can trust you? Because I'm gonna be ridin' right behind that husband of yours, and if you try anything . . . if you let that horse even twitch in a way I don't like . . . I'm gonna put a forty-four-forty round right through his head and splatter his brains all over the place. You understand what I'm sayin' to you, Mrs. Hargett?"

Rose had turned pale at Wilcox's seemingly calm, quiet words. Steve felt a little washed out himself. Rose jerked her head in a nod and said, "I understand."

"Good." Wilcox mounted, still holding the Winchester, and raised his voice to call to the other rustlers, "Move out! We've got cattle to take to Mexico!"

CHAPTER 30

Bo and Scratch caught up to Rance Plummer and the other hands from the SJ not long after the sun came up. They had ridden hard all night, switching horses every couple of hours.

Even doing that, their mounts were pretty worn out, and Bo knew they would have to give the horses some real rest soon, no matter how much the delay would chafe at him and Scratch. If they did otherwise, they risked being set afoot, which might wind up being a death sentence for Rose.

When they spotted the group of riders in front of them, however, they kept going, and within minutes they recognized Rance and the other SJ punchers. The men must have noticed the two Texans coming up behind them, because they reined in and waited for Bo and Scratch to catch up.

"You boys must've really been foggin' it," Rance greeted them as they rode up and reined in. "We had a good lead on you, and we ain't been dawdlin'."

Bo nodded toward the two extra horses trailing behind

them on a lead rope and said, "Your wrangler Asa was kind enough to provide good mounts for us."

"Yeah, we hurried because we didn't want you boys havin' all the fun," Scratch added. Then the silver-haired Texan grew somber as he went on, "How far ahead of us are the varmints?"

"A couple of hours, I'd say," Rance replied as he nodded toward the wide trail of hoofprints left by the stolen herd. "Maybe three hours. If we push on, we ought to close in on 'em by sometime this afternoon." The foreman's mouth hardened into a grim line. "How was Powderkeg doin' when you were at the ranch?"

"He was still alive," Bo said. "Dr. Chapman should have been on his way out from Silverhill by then, but we didn't wait around for him. Sorry I can't tell you any more than that, Rance."

"Powderkeg's a tough old coot. If anybody can pull through, he's the one to do it."

"He wasn't able to tell you what happened to him?" Bo asked.

"Not exactly. He just said that Ben Wilcox and the rest of the nighthawkin' crew stole the herd, and they took Steve Hargett and Miss Rose with 'em."

"Was Hargett in on the rustling?" Bo asked sharply.

"I'd hate to think that he was, but I plumb just don't know."

Rance told his men to go ahead and dismount. Their horses needed rest, too. They knew they could catch up to the rustlers before the day was over, so they didn't feel quite as much urgency now.

A thought nagged at Bo's brain, and he said to Rance, "Will they be across the border in Mexico by the time we close in on them?"

"I don't know, but I don't reckon there's a man among us who's gonna worry about a line on a map," Rance replied. "And you fellas are town lawmen, so you're already a long way outside o' your bailiwick."

"Oh, we ain't worried about that," Scratch said. "We're proper Texans, after all. We go where we need to go and do what needs doin'."

Bo said, "I just wondered if we'd be liable to encounter any *Rurales*. They're not much better than outlaws themselves—"

Scratch snorted. "They *ain't* any better'n outlaws. We've had enough run-ins with 'em to know that."

"They might try to steal those cattle for themselves. That would complicate things," Bo said.

"Whatever we need to do, we'll do it," Rance Plummer said. Then he shrugged. "Whoever we need to fight, we'll fight 'em. But it'd be simpler if we didn't run into any of those Rurale varmints, that's for sure."

They rested the horses for half an hour. The time grated on everyone's nerves, but with the rising of the sun, they had been able to see the tracks they were following well enough to get an idea of how far behind they were. Knowing they could catch up to the rustlers before the day was over made accepting the wait easier.

Bo and Scratch switched horses again. When the group set out, they rode in the lead with Rance Plummer.

Down here along the border, it was always hot except for a brief interval during the winter. As the sun rose higher in the sky, the temperature climbed with it. After a while, the hot, dry air seemed to leach all the moisture out of a man.

Water holes and creeks were few and far between, too,

especially out on the flats. Small ranges of grayish-green mountains lay around the men, miles away in several different directions. Water could be found easier in those mountains, but even there it would be scarce.

"They can't be pushin' those cows very hard through country like this," Rance mused as he rode with Bo and Scratch. "Wouldn't surprise me none if we come in sight of 'em by midday."

"The problem is, if we can see them, they can see us, too," Bo said.

Scratch pointed out, "We ain't raisin' near as much dust as that herd of cows will. We'll have some warnin' before we come up too close on 'em."

Bo rubbed his chin and frowned in thought. "I'm wondering if we couldn't get in front of them somehow."

"We could, but maybe not all of us ought to," Rance suggested. "We already got 'em outnumbered. If we were to split up and catch 'em between us, they wouldn't have a chance. We could wipe out the whole bunch."

Scratch said, "Hold on there. What about Rose and Steve?"

"They'd be in danger if a bunch of bullets started flyin' around," Rance admitted.

"What about this plan?" Bo said. "You take some of the men, get ahead of the bunch, and set up an ambush. Blow a couple of them out of the saddle, and the rest will stop. That's when Scratch and I will hit them from behind and try to get Steve and Rose to safety."

"Like cuttin' a couple of cows out of a herd," Scratch said. "Could happen."

"And as soon as they're clear," Bo went on, "the men

who are with us can go ahead and close in, and we'll clean up that pack of wolves."

"I think you've got the right idea," Rance said. "We can start figurin' exactly how to go about it once we've spotted their dust ahead of us."

Scratch took off his hat, sleeved sweat from his forehead, and said, "Can't happen soon enough to suit me."

The sun was directly overhead when the pursuers came close enough to the haze in the air ahead of them for it to coalesce into a cloud of dust. The sight gave the riders new energy, although it didn't do anything for their weary horses.

"That's got to be them," Rance exclaimed. "Wouldn't be any other bunch that big out here in the middle o' nowhere."

Bo agreed. They pushed on, slowly but steadily closing in on the dust.

When they were close enough to make out the dark mass of cattle moving against the tan and brown landscape, as well as the tiny figures of men on horseback pushing the herd southward, Rance called a halt.

"We can't risk gettin' any closer," he said. "Some of those varmints may be keepin' an eye on their back trail. Time for us to split up."

Bo asked, "Have you been down in these parts much? Maybe know of a good place to ambush them?"

Rance rasped a thumbnail along his beard-stubbled jawline and said, "Matter of fact, I do. There's a humpbacked ridge about five miles south of here. Folks call it Camelback Mountain, but it ain't really a mountain or hardly even a hill. But it's big enough that the herd'll have to swing around it, either east or west, and if I'm up on the ridge with a few of these eagle-eyed young bravos, we can plunk a couple of them rustlers and bring those cows to a standstill."

"It'll take you a while to get in position, though," Scratch said. "How much time you reckon we'd best allow?"

Rance thought again, then said, "Give us two hours. Can the two of you get closer without bein' spotted?"

"We'll be there, right behind them," Bo promised. "The men you leave with us can hang back half a mile or so."

Scratch said, "When the shootin' starts, Bo and me will hustle in and see if we can get Rose and Steve outta harm's way. The rest of the fellas will be close enough to hear the shots, and they can charge, too. They should come a-shootin'."

"What if you haven't been able to get those young folks clear?" Rance asked.

"We'll have a few minutes to do that before the attack from the rear starts," Bo said. "That'll just have to be long enough."

Rance looked at the Texans for a moment and then nodded. The plan wasn't perfect—but no plan ever was, except maybe in hindsight.

Rance picked out the men he wanted to take with him as he circled the herd and got into position in front. Then he lifted a hand in farewell and said, "Good luck," to Bo and Scratch.

They would need it, Bo thought.

And so would Rose and Steve.

Sweat plastered Rose's shirt to her body. Under other circumstances, Steve might have appreciated that, but the heat also reddened her face and made her look absolutely miserable. His heart went out to her.

He was pretty much worn down to a nub himself. The cattle were starting to look gaunt, and so were the men and horses pushing them along.

Steve wondered if they had crossed the border into Mexico by now. It seemed like they should have, but he was no expert on such things. He had never been through this particular area before and didn't know the landmarks— what few of those there were.

One such landmark was right in front of them, however. A ridge jutted up from the flats, maybe a hundred feet tall at its highest and no more than five hundred yards wide.

Steve and Rose and Ben Wilcox were riding on the herd's right flank. Wilcox hipped around in the saddle and waved to the rustlers riding drag, signaling them that the cattle should angle to the west and go around the ridge on that side. He thrust his rifle into the air above his head with one hand and swung it back and forth to catch the attention of the men on the other flank. They would have to push the herd in this direction.

"Are we ever going to stop again?" Rose croaked. Steve could tell that her throat was so dry, she had trouble forming the words.

Steve looked around at Wilcox and asked, "How about it, Ben? We've been riding all morning with only one break. Look at the sun. It's time we were nooning for a while."

"After we get around this ridge," Wilcox snapped. The heat and the long ride had caused his usual mock-jovial mood to evaporate. "I don't like the way it's just sittin' there, like an animal getting ready to spring."

Steve didn't see that at all. The ridge was just a long

mound of rock and dirt. But if Wilcox was bound and determined to get past it before they stopped, Steve hoped it wouldn't take very long to do so.

"I'm going to give Rose a drink from my canteen," he said. "No! Water's hard to come by in these parts. We may need it later."

"But she's parched, blast it."

"I can . . . speak for myself," Rose husked. "I'm . . . all right. Save your . . . water, Steve."

He would have argued with both of them, but he knew it wouldn't do any good, especially where Rose was concerned. She was as stubborn as

A distant crack interrupted Steve's thoughts. He frowned, realizing that it sounded like a rifle shot, and no sooner had that thought occurred to him than he heard another one.

He looked toward the front of the herd and saw a horse running loose, spooked and riderless. Not far away, the second of the two rustlers riding ahead of the herd toppled out of his saddle. Both men were down, and Steve spotted what might be a thread of powder smoke curling from the top of the ridge.

"Ambush!" Wilcox shouted. "This is your doing, Hargett!"

The boss rustler was wrong about that. Steve had no idea what was going on. But that didn't matter. As he reined in and swung his horse around, he saw Wilcox jerk the Winchester toward him, obviously about to blow him out of the saddle.

CHAPTER 31

Before Wilcox could pull the trigger, Rose rammed her heels into her horse's flanks, making the animal lunge toward the rustler's mount. Wilcox's horse shied just as he fired. The bullet flew wide, somewhere out over the vast flats.

Steve acted instantly. He charged Wilcox, too, and came at him from a slightly different angle. Wilcox was trying to get his horse under control again and at the same time swing the Winchester's barrel toward Steve. He wasn't able to do that before Steve kicked his feet out of the stirrups and left the saddle in a diving tackle that drove Wilcox off the back of his horse.

Both men crashed to the ground. The impact jolted the rifle out of Wilcox's hand. The spooked horses capered around the two men and almost stepped on them several times. Steve rolled out of the way of the flashing hooves and hoped one or both of the horses would trample Wilcox.

No such luck. Wilcox rolled clear, too, and came up clawing at the holstered revolver on his hip. Steve had no idea who had ambushed the rustlers from the top of that ridge up ahead, but he was sure that Ben Wilcox intended to kill him, no matter what else was going on.

But instead of aiming the Colt at Steve when he cleared leather, Wilcox whirled toward Rose. Her horse was dancing around, too, and she had her hands full not being pitched off. Steve realized that Wilcox intended to shoot her first, right in front of him.

"No!" Steve shouted as he threw himself forward and sprang off his feet in a leap that carried him in front of Wilcox just as the Colt boomed and flame spurted from its muzzle.

Steve felt the hammerblow of a slug against his body and spun in midair. He slammed to the ground on his face and couldn't move. But as more shots blasted, he forced his head up and blinked rapidly as he gazed through sweat and dust.

A bloody spectacle met his eyes. Ben Wilcox danced backward jitteringly, gun still in hand but sagging now as bloodstains bloomed on his shirtfront like crimson flowers. He must have been hit at least half a dozen times.

As the rolling gun thunder came to an end, the Colt slipped from the rustler's fingers and thudded to the ground at his feet. He swayed there for a second; then his knees buckled. He crumpled to the ground and lay in a heap, which shuddered for a couple of seconds before becoming motionless.

Then hoofbeats pounded close by, and suddenly, Rose was with him, on her knees beside him. Her strong hands took hold of him, rolled him over, pulled him up against her.

"Steve!" she wailed. "Steve!"

"Rose . . . ," he said. "Are you . . . all right?"

"I'm fine, but you're shot!"

"Don't . . . care." His eyelids started to droop. "Long as you're . . . all right . . ."

"Steve! Don't you die, blast it! Don't you *dare* go and die!"

More hoofbeats, then a deep, familiar voice said, "Let me take a look at him, Rose . . . I don't think he's hurt too bad. He should be all right."

Steve forced his eyes open more and looked up through the midday glare. It eased as a shadow fell over him. Bo Creel smiled down at him and went on, "Hang on, son. We'll get you patched up as soon as things settle down."

Another familiar voice said, "Looks like the rest of the SJ crew don't need our help, Bo. They're cleanin' up on those low-down wide-loopers."

That was Scratch Morton, Steve realized. No surprise. Bo and Scratch were never far apart. And they had a habit of showing up at just the right moment, too.

Vaguely, he became aware that guns were still popping, but that fire dwindled. While Bo was pulling Steve's shirt up and examining the wound, another rider came up and said, "We got 'em all, 'cept for Wilcox, and I can see you fellas done for him. How bad is Steve hit?"

"The bullet chewed a chunk out of him, but I don't think it hit anything vital," Bo said. "If anybody's got a flask of whiskey in his saddlebags, I can clean the wound and get a bandage on it. Then Dr. Chapman can do a better job of tending to it when we get back to the ranch."

Rance Plummer chuckled. "Just so happens I got a flask with me. Never go anywhere without one. Strictly for medicinal purposes, you understand."

"They do come in handy sometimes," Scratch agreed.

Rance dismounted, handed the flask to Bo, and then hunkered on his heels a few feet away.

"How about you, ma'am?" he asked Rose. "Are you hurt?"

"Just my dignity," she said, and even in his condition, with pain filling his body, that made Steve laugh. He knew that by her *dignity*, she meant her sore rear end, but he wouldn't embarrass her by saying that.

Instead, he grew sober and said to the foreman, "Rance, I . . . I got to tell you something—"

"No, you don't, boy," Rance interrupted him. "You sure as blazes don't have to tell me a blamed thing. Plenty of time for talkin' later, now that we got the two of you young folks back safe and sound. Relatively speakin'."

"But the herd—"

"The herd's safe, too. You don't have to worry about that. Kinda scattered, because they spooked from all the shootin', but it won't take long for us to round them up again."

"But . . . all the other stock . . . the spread already lost . . ."

"Ranches are always losin' a few head," Rance said firmly. "Now, you just lay there and let Bo tend to you while that pretty wife o' yours comforts you. And that's an order. You *do* still ride for the SJ, don't you?"

Steve's heart slugged in his chest. He had to swallow hard before he was able to say, "Yeah, I . . . I reckon I do."

"Then you'll do what your boss tells you."

Steve nodded weakly. Then he winced and his breath hissed between his teeth as he felt the fiery bite of the whiskey Bo was trickling into the bullet hole. Rose's arms tightened around him.

"You'll be all right," she whispered.

For the first time in a while, he was starting to think that maybe he would be.

* * *

Steve and Rose were riding up ahead, stirrup to stirrup, close enough that Rose could reach over and steady Steve if he started to sway in the saddle.

Bo, Scratch, and Rance Plummer ambled along about twenty yards behind them, and trailing out behind *them* were the rustled cattle and the SJ punchers who were taking them back to the ranch.

In the very back, a drag rider had a lead rope fastened to his saddle horn, and attached to that rope were eight more horses, all of them carrying corpses roped facedown over their saddles. The SJ had had a couple of men wounded in the battle with the rustlers, but none of them had been killed. Wilcox and all his men had been wiped out.

As they rode, Scratch said quietly, "You know that boy was fixin' to tell you he was in the rustlin' with Wilcox, don't you, Rance?"

"I figured as much," the foreman admitted. "But I've had time to think on it, and I don't believe he ever would've thrown in with the varmints if Wilcox hadn't threatened Rose. I don't know for sure that's what happened, but it's the sort of thing Wilcox would've done." Rance shook his head ruefully. "I should have run him off a long time ago . . . but he was a decent hand, when he wasn't busy bein' a no-good skunk."

Bo said, "If that's what happened, you can't blame a man for wanting to protect his wife, no matter what. Especially a newlywed like Steve."

"I don't blame him. We got the herd back, and the cows they got away with earlier are long gone, so there's nothin' we can do about them. It's a loss, but not a big enough one that it'll hurt the ranch in the long run, and the fellas responsible for it have already got what's comin' to 'em." Rance shrugged. "So I don't see what good it'd do to press things any farther."

Bo nodded toward Steve and Rose riding ahead of them and said, "That youngster's going to punish himself for a good long while, I imagine."

"And that's punishment enough," Rance declared. "I don't reckon I'll ever have to worry about him strayin' from the straight and narrow again." A smile appeared on the foreman's craggy face. "Like I told him, I can see the day comin' when he'll be runnin' things on the SJ. Nothin's happened to change that, far as I'm concerned."

Scratch said, "He's lucky to have a good friend like you, Rance."

"Just doin' what's best for the spread." Rance frowned. "Speakin' of which . . . I'll be glad when we get back, so we can find out how Powderkeg's doin'."

"He'll be laid up for a good long time," Dr. Arliss Chapman said as he stood on the ranch-house porch with Bo, Scratch, and Rance. "He has a concussion from the blow to the head, three broken ribs, and a dislocated shoulder, which I've put back in place. There may be some internal injuries, as well, from that horse trampling him, but he's just going to have to be watched closely for any signs of that. All in all, I'm guardedly optimistic that he'll recover, but at his age, it's entirely possible that he'll never be the same again. He certainly won't be able to work for months, at the very least."

Rance shook his head and said, "That don't matter. I can always find another cook. Powderkeg'll always have a place on the SJ, whether he can work or not. This is his home now."

"Well, it's good that he has someone to look after him," Chapman said with a smile.

"How about Steve?" Bo asked.

"Ah, my other patient. You did a fine job of cleaning and bandaging the wounds, Deputy Creel. Both entry and exit wounds were clean, and I believe the bullet missed the young man's lungs. He'll need some time to recuperate, too, but he should be up and around fairly quickly. He has an excellent nurse, which helps matters . . . although Mrs. Hargett did suggest that she could take his place riding the range until he's back on his feet again."

Scratch laughed and said, "That sounds like an idea Rose'd come up with, all right."

"I told her it would be better, medically speaking, for both her and her husband—and their child—if she abandoned that notion," Chapman went on.

"I'll keep an eye on her and make sure she don't get carried away," Rance promised. He stuck out his hand. "Thanks, Doctor. We're much obliged to you."

"Just doing my job," Chapman said crisply. "And speaking of which, I had better get back to Silverhill, just in case there's anyone there who requires my services." He paused, then added dryly, "From what I've heard, it never stays peaceful for too long in these frontier towns."

"Seems to be that way wherever Bo and me go," Scratch agreed.

Chapter 32

The big Concord coach rocked along the stage road between Silverhill and El Paso, heading east. Beth Macy handled the reins with practiced ease.

If she were forced to admit it, she felt better now that Monte Jackson had recovered from his injury and was back beside her on the driver's seat, with the coach gun across his lap. Jack Neal had filled in just fine as the guard while Monte was recuperating, and the stagecoach hadn't run into any trouble during that time, but Beth was just more confident with Monte around. She had come to realize that she liked him—liked him a lot, in fact—but she would have to be forced to admit *that*, too.

Especially since she had seen the same sort of affection and admiration in his eyes when he looked at her. They worked well together, getting the stage safely back and forth to and from El Paso, and Beth wasn't sure what would happen if the two of them allowed any sort of romance to spring up between them. It might cause a problem, and she didn't want that.

"What're you thinking?" Monte asked over the hoofbeats and the rattle of the coach.

"Oh, nothing," Beth answered, maybe a little too quickly. She didn't want to talk about what was really on her mind, so she said, "I would have liked to go along when Bo and Scratch went after those rustlers who kidnapped Rose."

"I don't think Mr. Creel and Mr. Morton would have let you do that."

She snorted. "And how would they have stopped me? One thing about me, when somebody I care about is in trouble, I don't let anything stand in the way of me helping them."

"Actually, I can believe that," Monte said, nodding. "I don't think I'd want you on my trail if you had a grudge against me." She was about to say that he didn't have to worry about that.

She would never hold a grudge against him. But she caught herself in time. *No need to be* too *nice to him*, she told herself. It might give him a swelled head.

And she still had to work with him, after all.

Al Herbert slid back down into the gully and reported, "I can see the dust cloud from the coach. It's about a mile away, I'd say, but moving at a pretty good clip."

John Lee Kingery nodded and turned to the other three men. "Mount up," he ordered curtly. "We're not going to let them get away from us this time."

"We didn't let that coach get away from us the first time," Walt Hammerling said.

His brother Cress dug an elbow into Walt's side and giggled like a little girl. "We weren't even along on that job!" he announced gleefully.

Kingery's teeth ground together. Cress Hammerling

was a brain-addled idiot, but his brother Walt was tough, a good man in a pinch. The problem was that Walt had promised their dying mother he would look after Cress, so when you got Walt, you got his simpleton brother, too.

But Kingery supposed the two of them put together were about the equal of Pancho Reyes, who was dead now. Badly wounded the last time they had tried to hold up this stagecoach, Pancho had begged to be taken back to his village below the border so he could see his wife and children again and be laid to rest in the little cemetery behind the mission. Kingery had agreed, thinking that Pancho wouldn't last through the night, but the bandido had clung stubbornly to life, and they'd had no choice but to take him home, as Kingery had promised.

Even after they got there, Pancho hadn't died rightaway. He had rallied and looked like he might recover, but then he'd developed a fever and expired. Kingery hadn't wanted to continue with only three men in the gang, so he and Shorthorn Nash and Al Herbert had swung over to El Paso and had found the Hammerling brothers in a cantina that catered to the owlhoot trade. Walt and Cress weren't the type to operate alone. They needed a leader.

El Paso was also where they had recruited Earl Hockaday as the sixth member of the gang. Earl was sullen and hard to get along with, but few men were better at handling explosives, from blasting powder to dynamite to nitroglycerin.

He was the one who had dug the hole in the stage road, eased the bundle of dynamite down into it so that just the ends were sticking up, and run the fuse to a clump of chaparral not far off the road. Earl lay in that chaparral now, just waiting for the right moment to light the fuse. He had timed it all out and had planted a little stick at the edge of the road, where he could see it through a pair of field glasses, so he knew to strike the match as soon as the coach passed it.

Kingery swung up into the saddle. All the other men were already mounted. The gully was deep enough that they couldn't be seen from the stage road fifty yards away, but they couldn't see the stagecoach, either.

Kingery heard the pounding hoofbeats as the team approached, though. He listened intently, and when he judged that the coach had gone past, he waved to the others and called, "Now!"

The five riders lunged up a place where the side of the gully had collapsed, forming a slope gentle enough for the horses. They charged out into the open. Sure enough, the stagecoach had just gone past their position and was rocking along the road at a normal pace.

That would soon change, because with shouts coming from their throats, Kingery and his men galloped after it, drew their guns, and opened fire.

Beth and Monte both jerked around on the seat when they heard the volley of gunshots behind them. The dust boiling up from the coach's wheels made it difficult to see back there, but through gaps in the billowing cloud, Beth caught glimpses of several men on horseback pounding after them. It was impossible to say how many.

She saw the muzzle flashes from their guns, as well. It looked to her like the pursuers were still out of handgun range, but it wouldn't take them long to close in.

Well, she was going to make it more difficult for them, she thought as she yelled, "*Hyaaahhh*!" and popped the whip above the horses' heads. The team surged forward. The coach's rocking and bouncing became more pronounced.

"You think it's the same bunch as before?" she shouted to Monte as she let the horses run.

"Don't know!" He twisted around even more on the seat and lifted the shotgun to his shoulder. "Don't care! If they get close enough, I'll blast them, whoever they are!"

Beth didn't waste any more effort looking back. That was Monte's job. Hers was to handle the team, and she had her hands full doing that.

She continued popping the whip and tried to figure out how far they were from Ramsgate Station. If she could keep the coach ahead of the road agents until they reached the station, she thought, it was likely they would abandon their holdup attempt. The station was thick walled and built to be defended, originally from Indians, but bandits could be held off from inside there, too.

She heard frightened shouts coming from the passengers inside the coach but ignored them. Only two people were riding the stage today, both salesmen. They wouldn't have much to steal, but she had noticed when Monte was loading the express pouch that it seemed heavy. Whether with coins or gold or silver, it didn't matter; it was likely the robbers would make a reasonably good haul if they got their hands on it.

"Something funny about this!" Monte said. "They're not closing in! Even with the team running flat out like they are, those owlhoots ought to be able to close the gap—"

He didn't get any further before the road exploded in front of them. Beth cried out involuntarily as the ground heaved up and a ball of flame erupted for a second, before a thick cloud of dust swallowed it. The horses didn't care about the whip anymore. Terrified by the blast, they tried to stop short, but the coach had too much momentum for that. It crashed into the team. A couple of the horses screamed in agony. Beth was thrown forward into a maelstrom of flailing hooves, choking dust, and pelting clods of dirt.

She didn't know what had happened to Monte or the coach. She was stunned, and only her own momentum kept her rolling across the ground. Blind luck carried her away from the panic-stricken horses and kept her safe for the moment.

She came to a stop on her stomach and lay there, with her head ringing, as she gasped for air and seemed to swallow only dust. Coughing racked her body. She couldn't see anything and didn't know what was going on, but she heard some loud noises, which she gradually realized were gunshots.

Then there was a louder boom, and Beth knew it came from Monte's shotgun. Another volley of revolver shots followed that thunderous report, then an ominous silence.

She lifted her head, pawed her hair out of her eyes, and blinked enough of the dust away to see that the coach had tipped over and slid to a stop on its side. The team was still hitched to it. The leaders were up and seemed to be all right, but they were so spooked, they might hurt themselves trying to get away.

Several men on horseback galloped up to the coach as one of the passengers threw open the door on the side that was now turned up, and tried to clamber out. The drummer had his head and shoulders out but hadn't gotten clear before a robber in a long coat thrust a gun at him and pulled the trigger. Beth gasped in horror as the shot made the passenger's head jerk back. Blood sprayed from the back of his skull. He dropped out of sight.

That was cold-blooded murder, and Beth knew she might be next. Without thinking about what she was doing, she scrambled backward on hands and knees and then dropped flat again as thick mesquite chaparral closed in around her.

The butt of her revolver dug into her belly, reminding her that she was armed and had a responsibility to protect the stagecoach. It might be too late for the passengers, at least one of them, but there was still the express pouch.

She had another, even better reason for wanting to open fire on them. The silence that had followed the exchange of shots between Monte and the outlaws told her there was a good chance they had killed him.

Something twisted painfully inside her at that thought.

She reached underneath her, hauled the long-barreled gun out of its holster, and gripped it in both hands as she started to push it out in front of her and pull back the hammer.

A hand came over her shoulder, grasped the revolver's cylinder, and pushed it back down.

"Don't," Monte Jackson whispered in her ear as he stretched out on his belly beside her.

She jerked her head toward him. His hat was gone, and blood trickled from cuts on his cheek and forehead.

"I thought you were dead!" she said. "I heard the shotgun go off, and then there was all this other shooting—"

"The dust was too thick," Monte said. "They couldn't see me. They shot at the muzzle flash, but I was already moving. I used the horses for cover and got around on this side of the coach. Then I spotted this chaparral and headed for it. I don't believe they know where we are."

"They'll come after us and find us," Beth said grimly. "They killed at least one of the passengers, for no good reason. Just shot him dead."

"That's the kind of skunks they are," Monte said. "We'll lie low here. I've still got my Greener, and both barrels are loaded again. If they come after us, we'll make it hot for 'em."

"We have to stop them from robbing the coach!"

"With odds of six against two, we wouldn't be stopping them. We'd just be getting them to kill us before they took that express pouch, anyway." Monte shook his head. "No, we'll fight if they come after us and give us no choice, but if they're more interested in the loot and are willing to ride off with it, I say we let them." He paused, and there was an odd catch in his words as he added, "I don't want you getting hurt."

He left the rest of it unsaid, but she heard the concern in his voice and knew what it meant. She knew because of the tearing, grinding pang of loss she had experienced when she thought the outlaws had killed him. They had gone from hostility to grudging respect to being friends to . . . something else.

They would never get to explore what that something else might be if they got themselves shot to pieces.

"All right," she said softly. "We'll wait for them to come looking for us. But if they do—"

"If they do," Monte said, "then, by grab, I want to do this first!"

He reached over, put a hand behind her head, and leaned in to kiss her, hard.

and took out the pouch. He hefted it and called something to his companions that made them laugh.

Then the man inside the coach pulled himself out of it. Something shiny dangled from one hand. *Watches taken off the bodies of the two drummers*, Beth thought. He tossed them to one of the mounted men, then followed with what appeared to be money clips.

One of the men kept turning his head and staring around at the landscape. Beth wondered if he was looking for any sign of her and Monte. They had to realize that the driver and shotgun guard had gotten away but were afoot and had to be somewhere nearby.

If they felt like it, they could have themselves a nice little hunting party.

On the other hand, they also knew that Monte was armed with a shotgun, and most jehus carried a handgun, so there would be a certain amount of risk if they went looking. And they already had the loot they were after. . . .

Some loud words were exchanged. Not really angry, just debating. Then the outlaw in the long coat, who seemed to be the leader, waved his arm and said something, and everybody mounted up. The leader headed north at a fast pace, and the others trailed behind him. Their departure raised a cloud of dust, which dwindled in the hot breeze.

After a moment, Beth asked in a hushed voice, "You think they're really gone?"

"We'd better wait a little bit to make sure," Monte said. Minutes dragged past. Finally, Monte said, "You stay here. I'll go take a look."

"We should both go," Beth said. "I work for the stage line, too."

"Yeah, but I'm the guard." A bitter edge crept into his

CHAPTER 33

Despite her grudging acknowledgment of the feelings that had developed between them, Beth wasn't expecting Monte to do that. The hungry, urgent pressure of his lips on hers kindled a fire within her, though, even under these extraordinarily bad circumstances. She put a hand on his arm and clutched it hard.

When he broke the kiss and pulled back a little, he said, "I'm sorry. That was way too forward—"

"Hush," she said. She glanced toward the robbers. They were still gathered around the overturned stagecoach, all six of them. Since they weren't looking in the direction of the chaparral, Beth risked taking the time for another kiss, one that she initiated. Monte responded fervently.

When they broke apart again, she said, "When this is all over, you and me are going to have to have a talk, mister."

"Yeah, I think so, too," he agreed. "But right now we need to keep an eye on those varmints."

One of the outlaws climbed into the coach, lowering himself through the open door on what was now the top instead of the side. While he was doing that, the man in the long coat pried open the express box under the driver's seat voice. "I'm the one who's supposed to keep things like this from happening."

"How were you going to stop it? They blew up the road!"

"Well, that's true," Monte admitted. "I sure wasn't expecting that." He pushed himself to his hands and knees. "Anyway, stay here until I've taken a look around."

Beth still didn't like it, but she could tell it wasn't going to do any good to argue with him. She watched intently, holding the revolver in both hands again, as he crawled out of the chaparral and stalked toward the coach with the shotgun held level in front of him.

He walked all the way around the overturned vehicle and then pulled himself up to stare down into it for a few seconds before letting himself drop back to the ground. Something about his demeanor told Beth that neither of the traveling salesmen had survived.

Monte made another circuit and then waved for Beth to join him. He stood beside the two leaders, rubbing the horses' noses and talking quietly to them in an attempt to get them to calm down.

As Beth walked up, he told her, "Neither of those drummers made it."

"I'm not surprised. I saw one of them get shot in the head."

"Looked like the other one broke his neck in the crash, when the coach went over," Monte said. He sighed. "I hate losing passengers worse than I do losing the express pouch."

"So do I," Beth said. She nodded toward the horses. "That's one more reason to cut these fellas loose, mount up, and go after the sons of—"

"Hold on a minute," Monte interrupted her. "You're not going after anybody."

"What are you talking about? We can't just let them get away with this . . . this atrocity!"

"We're not going to, but if we chase after them now, the odds are still going to be six against two. That's still not going to work."

"So six to one is better? That's what it'll be if you go after them by yourself."

"Not if you ride to Silverhill and bring help," Monte said. "Bo and Scratch can get a posse together and ride out here. I'll trail the outlaws and make sure to leave enough sign that they can follow. I won't try to jump that bunch by myself, but maybe I can track them to wherever they're holed up, and then the posse can deal with them."

Beth frowned and said, "Well . . . that might work. But it's still going to be dangerous for you."

"That comes with the job," Monte said, shrugging. "Besides, I reckon I've got a score to settle with those varmints." His voice hardened. "They could've killed you when that dynamite, or whatever it was, blew up."

"And they could've shot you," she pointed out. "They certainly tried hard enough."

He smiled. "Yeah, they came plenty close. But close doesn't count."

"Why don't we both ride back to Silverhill to get help?" she suggested. "I'm sure Bo and Scratch can track those outlaws . . ." Her voice trailed off when Monte shook his head.

"I don't want to risk them getting away. Like I said, I can leave sign so that the posse won't have any trouble following."

Beth tried to come up with an argument for that but couldn't. She frowned and said, "You promise you won't try to capture them all by yourself?"

"I'm not a fool," Monte said. He put a hand on Beth's arm. "Especially not now that—"

"We'll talk about that later," she said. "Right now we need to cut these horses loose from their harness before they get skittish again."

"I'm sorry you'll have to ride bareback. You can manage that, can't you?"

Beth snorted. "You just hide and watch, mister!"

In the week since they had gotten back from helping recover the rustled SJ herd and rescuing Rose and Steve, Bo and Scratch had been pleased that things were quiet in Silverhill. This afternoon they were sitting on the benches in front of the Territorial House and looking out at the street, which was almost deserted in the sun-splashed heat.

"I've been thinkin' about those poor gals," Scratch said.

"Which poor gals would those be?" Bo asked.

"The ones who got killed. That soiled dove Florence and Julie Hobbs, who worked at the Red Devil."

Bo nodded and said, "I know who you're talking about. And I haven't forgotten what happened to them."

"Neither have I," Scratch said, "but we ain't one bit closer to findin' out who was responsible for it, are we?"

"We've questioned just about everybody in town," Bo replied with a sigh. "I don't know what else we can do."

"Since the killer ain't struck again, it's temptin' to think that he moved on."

"We thought that before, didn't we?"

"Yeah," Scratch said, "and that's what's got me worried. Folks are startin' to forget about him. They ain't bein' as careful as they were for a while. When I make my evenin' rounds, I see ladies out and about more often than I did a few weeks ago."

"Nobody should have to shut themselves up in their homes out of fear," Bo said.

"Nope, they sure shouldn't. I just wish we'd caught the varmint, that's all."

"So do I."

After a minute of companionable silence, Scratch asked, "How are things goin' with Miss Hampshire?"

"Susan? We're still friendly."

"Friendly?" Scratch repeated. "Or more'n that?"

Some men might consider that prying, but Bo and Scratch had been friends for so long, there was nothing they couldn't say to each other. Bo considered the question.

"I'd say we're friends . . . but lately, I've gotten the feeling she might be ready for it to be more than that."

"And what do you think?" Scratch asked pointedly.

Bo pondered that for a moment, too, before saying, "A couple of mornings ago, early, when it was still cool, I smelled a little something in the air."

"The scent of somewhere that ain't here?"

"Maybe," Bo said.

Scratch nodded slowly. "I know the feelin'. I've caught a whiff of that a time or two lately myself."

"Rose is settled in with Steve, Cecilia is spending a lot of time with that big galoot Roscoe, and Beth likes her job with the stage line . . . and Monte Jackson."

"Monte's a good hombre," Scratch said.

"He is," Bo agreed. "Jean's keeping company with Dr. Chapman. Luella's the only one who doesn't have a regular suitor, and there are plenty of fellas around who'd like to court her. It's just a matter of her settling on one of them."

"So what you're sayin' is, our job here is just about done."

"It's getting there," Bo agreed. He thought of something and added, "That blasted Hugh Craddock is still hanging around town. He must have a mighty good ramrod on that spread of his back in Texas, to be gone so long from it."

Scratch laughed. "When he finally does go home, he'll be lucky if they didn't steal him blind while he was off gallivantin' in New Mexico Territory! With some of the trouble he's caused, I'd almost say it'd serve him right."

"Can't argue with you there, partner." Bo had just expressed that sentiment when he sat forward and frowned. "You hear those hoofbeats? Sounds like somebody's coming fast."

"That usually means trouble," Scratch said as he stood up.

He and Bo went to the railing along the front of the hotel porch, rested their hands on it, and leaned forward to peer along the street, toward the eastern end of town, where the swift rataplan of hoofbeats drew closer. The Texans both spotted the tail of dust that curled up and marked the location of the galloping rider.

A startled oath escaped from Scratch. "That looks like Beth!"

"It sure does," Bo said as he headed for the porch steps. There was a time when he would have just vaulted over the railing, but his bones wouldn't take a jolt like that anymore.

Beth swept along the street, riding astride and bareback on one of the horses from the stagecoach team that had left Silverhill a few hours earlier. She wasn't wearing a hat, and her blond hair was loose and streaming behind her.

She didn't start to slow the horse until Bo and Scratch stepped out into the street and raised hands to hail her.

Beth hauled back on reins that appeared to have been rigged out of pieces cut from the team's harness. The horse came to a stumbling, skidding halt. Beth threw a leg over its back and dropped to the ground before the animal had stopped moving completely.

She was breathing hard and seemed a little unsteady on her feet. Bo took hold of her arm to brace her and said, "Beth, what's wrong? Where's the stagecoach? And Monte?"

"Outlaws!" she gasped. "Hit the stage . . . this side of Ramsgate Station! Blew up the road! Wrecked the stage. Killed the passengers. Monte . . . Monte went after them . . . sent me to . . . fetch help."

"And that's what you're gonna get," Scratch declared. "We'll get a posse together and light a shuck after those thievin', murderin' varmints!"

"Are you all right?" Bo asked the young woman. "Were you hurt?"

Beth shook her head. She already seemed to be recovering from the hard ride into town. "I'm fine," she said, "but you've got to go find Monte. There were six of those outlaws, and no matter what he promised me, I'm afraid he might try to tackle them on his own!"

CHAPTER 34

One thing Monte Jackson had never told anybody was that he didn't like horses. Actually, what he didn't like was *riding* horses. He wasn't scared of them and was all right being around them, so the stagecoach teams didn't bother him, but something about climbing on the back of one of the critters and galloping around had always rubbed him the wrong way. He didn't know the reason for it, but he accepted that he felt that way.

Riding bareback was even worse, but he didn't have any choice in the matter. It wasn't like the outlaws had left him a saddle.

He had gotten a good look at the way the robbers had gone as they rode away from the wrecked stagecoach, so he started in the same direction. The sandy ground was soft enough that the horses left hoofprints, but Monte knew there might be some rocky stretches up ahead, too. He would have to work harder there to follow the trail.

As he rode, he used the folding knife he took from his pocket to cut small strips off his bandanna. He tied these strips to branches of stunted mesquite trees, greasewood bushes, and other bits of brush that he found. Where there wasn't any vegetation, he found a rock and used it to weight down one of the pieces of cloth. He left a marker every three or four hundred yards. The bandanna was bright blue, so he figured the sharp-eyed Texans wouldn't have much trouble spotting the sign.

The trail gradually meandered off toward the north-west. One of the scattered ranges of small mountains that dotted the region lay in that direction. Monte wondered if the outlaws had their hideout in those mountains. The rugged-looking peaks appeared to be only a few miles away, but he knew how deceptive distances could be out here. It was probably at least ten miles to the mountains.

Even so, he figured his quarry would reach the peaks by nightfall if they kept going. Then maybe if they believed themselves to be safe from pursuit, they would build a fire, and he could use it to locate them.

Would they believe they were safe, though, since they knew they had left the driver and shotgun guard alive behind them? It was possible they thought they had killed him when they burned all that powder at him, but they hadn't even looked for Beth and didn't know what had happened to her.

Were they really that confident in their ability to get away?

"I still say we should've hunted down that driver and guard," Earl Hockaday groused as the six men rode toward the mountains. They were called the San Cristobals, John Lee Kingery thought as he tried to ignore Hockaday's complaints. Not that the name of the mountains really mattered. The only important thing about them was that they were rugged enough to provide a number of good hiding places. Kingery and the men who had been with him for a while had holed up there in the past.

Walt Hammerling said, "Yeah, I don't much cotton to leaving loose ends like that. They can make things come unraveled."

Kingery couldn't suppress the icy comment that came to his lips. "Yes, perhaps, if you're a member of a ladies' sewing circle. But I was under the impression that you were a *man*, Walt."

Hammerling muttered a curse under his breath. Kingery knew the man was glaring at him. He could feel it. But he didn't turn around to acknowledge the insubordination any further.

"You know what the rooster says, Walt?" Hammerling's brother Cress asked. "Cock-a-doodle-doo! Ain't that funny? Cock a doodle-doo!"

"Shut up, Cress."

"But I was just talkin' about a rooster—"

"Shut up."

Kingery waited for the boy to start sniffling. If he did, Kingery knew it would be difficult not to turn in the saddle and fire a bullet through the half-wit's brain. It might even be a mercy to put him out of his feeble-minded misery.

Cress just rode along in sullen silence, though, so Kingery didn't have to shoot him. Yet.

Shorthorn Nash brought his horse alongside Kingery's and said quietly, "Hockaday's like a burr under the saddle, but he might have a point, John Lee. It wouldn't have taken long to look for those two, and then we could've put 'em out of the way."

"And in looking for them, we might have ridden right into an ambush. I don't like having shotguns fired at me." Kingery waved a slender hand. "Anyway, I'm relatively certain I gave that guard a fatal wound when we exchanged fire. I saw him stagger. He was hit hard."

"With all that dust flyin' around, it's hard to be sure just what you saw," Nash argued. "I didn't see much of anything clear, that's for sure."

"Well, I did," Kingery snapped.

Nash persisted. "You killed the drummer, and it just seems like it woulda made sense to wipe the slate clean—"

"I killed that drummer because he was trying to pull a hideout gun as he climbed out of the coach. He gave me no choice."

"All right, John Lee. If you say so."

Kingery had half convinced himself that the business about the hideout gun was true, but he knew that he had shot the drummer because he had seen the man's dough face and the cow-like eyes staring at him in terror, and had seemed to him that such a pathetic existence had no real reason to continue.

Besides, it had felt so good to pull the trigger and watch a man's life end. There was nothing else like it in the world.

On the other hand, Kingery had no desire to be on the receiving end of such "kindness," so it had seemed to him that it was best to get out of there while they had the chance. Besides, they had the express pouch, and when he'd broken the seal on it and looked inside, he had seen why it was so heavy: it was full of gold double eagles. He didn't know whom the money had belonged to or where it was supposed to go, but it was his now, all his.

Except for the shares going to his men, of course.

He estimated that there might be as much as ten thousand dollars in the pouch. That would keep him in luxury for a long time. Perhaps he should give some thought to slipping away from the others and taking *all* the money. . . .

"Somebody behind us," Al Herbert announced.

Herbert had been dropping back from time to time to check their back trail. Now it appeared that his diligence had been rewarded. He went on, "I spotted one rider about half a mile back."

"Could be some driftin' cowhand," Walt Hammerling suggested.

Herbert shook his head. "I don't think so. This fella is moving at a pretty fast pace in the same direction we are, like he has some purpose in mind."

"Such as trailing us," Kingery said coldly. He reined to a stop, and the others followed suit. Kingery looked around and then pointed to a sandy hummock with a few clumps of stubborn grass growing from it. "Al, you and Walt hide behind there and wait for this fellow, whoever he is."

"And then blow him out of the saddle?" Hammerling said.

Kingery narrowed his eyes, in thought. He shook his head.

"No shooting, if possible. The man might be an advance scout for a larger party, and they might hear shots. I want to know who he is, one way or the other. Take him prisoner and bring him to the hideout in the canyon."

Earl Hockaday said, "Probably either the guard or the driver from the stagecoach."

Hockaday was getting on his nerves, Kingery thought. He wouldn't abandon the entire group, he decided. Nash and Herbert didn't deserve such treachery. When he got a chance, he would kill Hockaday and Cress. That meant he would have to kill Walt, too, which was unfortunate, but that was how things went sometimes. You had to take the bad with the good.

And splitting the loot from this robbery three ways instead of six was definitely good.

"Whoever it is," Kingery said in response to Hockaday's annoying comment, "take him prisoner and bring him to camp, so we can question him. Do you understand, Al?"

Herbert nodded and said in his unflappable way, "Sure, John Lee."

As he and Hammerling turned their horses to ride toward the hummock, Cress wailed, "I'm going with Walt!"

Hammerling turned and motioned him back. "No, you ride along with the others, Cress—"

"I won't! I'm stayin' with you!"

Hockaday said, "I can't take any more of that caterwauling. *I'll* stay and help Herbert grab whoever it is back there. Is that all right?"

Kingery had been about to order the same thing, but he didn't like Hockaday stealing his thunder like that. Still, he didn't want to waste time arguing, and what did one more reason to kill Hockaday matter, anyway?

"That's fine," he said. "Be careful, Al."

"Sure," Herbert said again. He clucked to his horse and heeled it into motion. Hockaday followed him toward the hummock.

The others started riding toward the mountains again.

Cress grinned and said, "Cock-a-doodle-doo!"

Monte's hunch was right. The trail crossed several rocky flats, where he couldn't see the hoofprints anymore, and he wasn't exactly what anybody would call an expert tracker. When he reached softer ground on the other side of the flats, he had to ride back and forth until he found the tracks again, and that cost him some time.

Even with that, though, he felt like he was closing the gap between him and his quarry. He watched closely ahead of him. He didn't want to ride right up on top of them.

His senses remained alert, but despite his intentions, his thoughts drifted. These days, whenever that happened, they drifted toward Beth Macy.

When she'd first suggested that she take over as the driver on the El Paso run, he had thought it was the craziest thing he'd ever heard. Sure, maybe there had been other female drivers here and there, but as far as he was concerned, that was no job for a woman. He'd even thought about quitting the line, although he hadn't actually given it any serious consideration. He liked being a shotgun guard.

Now he couldn't imagine making the trip to and from El Paso without Beth by his side. She had turned out to be a fine driver, and she was coolheaded when trouble broke out. Smart as all get-out, too, and shoot, all anybody had to do was look at her to see how beautiful she was.

He wasn't certain when it had happened, but he had no doubt that he was in love with her. That was why, when they'd possibly been facing death, he had kissed her. For all he knew, she'd slap his face, but instead, she had kissed him back. Part of him figured that he could die a happy man now. . . .

But he didn't want to die. He wanted to live—with Beth.

Nothing improper had ever happened between them. When they spent the night at a stage station, it was in separate rooms. Monte spent probably more time than he should, though, thinking about how it would be after they were married. Assuming, of course, that she said yes when he got around to asking her.

He wanted to propose, but at the same time, the idea worried him. What would happen to the friendship and camaraderie they had developed during all those hours and miles of rocking along on the coach? Would she want to continue driving? Well, of course she would, Monte told himself. Beth was strong willed, and marriage wasn't likely to change that. But eventually, some young'uns would come along, and things would change after that. They were bound to, and nothing anybody could do would stop it.

It was a lot to think about, all right, and Monte was sunk so deep in his pondering, he wasn't watching as well as he should have been. He didn't see the men who came riding out from behind the hummock he had just passed until they were practically on top of him.

He tried to twist in the saddle and swing the shotgun up and around, but the two hard-faced hombres already had their guns drawn and leveled at him. The muzzles stared at him like a pair of deadly black eyes.

"Drop it, mister," one of the men ordered. He was dour, pale faced, with a dark stubble of beard. The hard, flat menace in his voice told Monte that he'd better cooperate.

It pained him to do so, but he tossed the coach gun on the ground.

"I say we just go ahead and shoot him," the second man suggested. "We can tell Kingery he put up a fight and we didn't have a choice."

"And bring a posse down on our heads that much faster?" The sour-faced, colorless gent shook his head. "No. We're going to follow orders." He looked over the gun barrel at Monte. "Unless you give us trouble, and then we *will* risk shooting you."

"No trouble," Monte promised. He forced himself not

to glance back in the direction he had come from. He didn't want to do anything to tip off his captors that he had been leaving a trail for others to follow—and right now a couple of wily old Texans named Bo and Scratch represented his best hope of making it back to Beth alive.

CHAPTER 35

"I'm coming with you."

Scratch shook his head in response to Beth's declaration and said, "No, you ain't."

"I don't see how you think you're going to stop me."

"I'm the marshal—"

"Here in town you are," she interrupted him. "Outside of town, you're just another old codger."

Scratch's eyes widened. He drew in a deep breath and pressed a hand to his chest, as if she had wounded him deeply.

"Old codger, is it?" he said. "Why, you sassy little thing! I oughta turn you over my knee—"

"Let's all just settle down," Bo said. He worked the lever of the Winchester he held to throw a cartridge into the firing chamber, then thumbed another round through the loading gate before sliding the rifle into the sheath attached to his horse's saddle.

Eleven men, including the two Texans, had gathered in front of the marshal's office. Scratch had deputized the others who had volunteered to go along in pursuit of the outlaws who had held up the stage. Hector Esperanza was a member of the posse, along with a young man who worked for him at the livery stable. Three more townies had joined in, and luckily, they weren't drunks or lay-abouts. Three miners who happened to be in town, plus a lone cowboy, filled out the posse.

They were just about ready to leave when Beth strode up, leading a saddled horse. She had found another hat somewhere and had tucked her hair up under it. Other than that, she had on the same outfit she wore to drive the stage, including the gunbelt with the holstered Colt.

"Monte's out there somewhere, chasing those thieves and killers, and I'm not going to just sit around here and wait to find out what's happened to him." Her chin lifted defiantly. "If you won't let me come with you, I'll just follow along by myself."

"She'll do it, too," Cecilia said from the boardwalk, where she, Jean, and Luella had come up. "We tried to talk her out of it, but there's no reasoning with her."

Scratch rubbed his chin and frowned. "Maybe what I ought to do is lock you up. Then you couldn't chase after nobody."

"You wouldn't!" Beth exclaimed.

"I'm mighty tempted." Scratch heaved a sigh. "But I won't. I reckon I understand why you want to come along. You feel a heap of loyalty to Monte, and you're mad those varmints robbed the stage and killed the passengers. I can't blame you one bit for feelin' that way, and if you were a fella, I wouldn't have a problem with you bein' part of the posse." His frown deepened. "Maybe that ain't fair. I'm mighty tempted to say I don't care whether it is or not. But . . . even though it goes against my better judgment . . . I reckon you can come along, with the understandin' that if there's any gunplay, you'll stay well back away from it."

"Of course," Beth said without hesitation.

Bo didn't fully believe she was sincere about that, but locking her in one of the jail cells probably *was* the only way to stop her from accompanying them. Neither he nor Scratch wanted to do that.

Besides, even if they did, more than likely, Beth would talk one of her friends into turning her loose, and then she'd be on her own, trying to catch up to them. At least this way, they could keep an eye on her and try to make sure she was safe.

The same thoughts must have gone through Scratch's mind. The silver-haired Texan jerked his head toward the horse Beth was leading and said, "Mount up, then. We're burnin' daylight."

The two outlaws kept Monte at gunpoint as they rode into the mountains. With them watching him like hawks, he couldn't leave any more markers, so he just had to hope that Bo and Scratch would still be able to follow the trail.

Their route twisted and turned through the creases between the peaks and finally went through a narrow passage between two towering slabs of rock that seemed to lean in ominously. They had to travel single file through it.

At the other end of that hundred-yard-long slash in the earth was a sandy-bottomed canyon with a spring-fed pool at one end. An ancient stone cabin with a collapsed roof stood not far from the spring. Some old prospector must have built it, Monte thought, interested in spite of his dangerous predicament.

Now the canyon served as the hideout for the gang of stagecoach robbers. They had a fire going, and Monte smelled coffee and bacon. His stomach clenched. It had been a long time since he'd eaten anything.

Maybe they would feed him before they killed him, he thought wryly.

A tall, lean man in a long coat strode out to meet them. He had long hair and a pointed beard and looked like pictures of the Devil that Monte had seen. He smiled and said, "I see you caught him."

"That's what you told us to do," the pale, dour-faced outlaw said.

The leader looked up at Monte and said, "You're the shotgun guard from the stagecoach."

Monte didn't see as how that deserved a response.

"But you're not wounded," the man went on. "I would have sworn I winged you."

This time Monte shook his head and said, "Afraid not."

"Well, get down off that horse. How close behind you is the posse?"

"There's not any posse," Monte said as he slid down from the horse's bare back. "Just me."

The leader shook his head slowly. "Don't lie to me," he warned. "The only reason I told my friends not to kill you is that I want you to answer my questions. If I believe you're not being truthful with me, I have no reason to keep you alive. Now, how many men are after us?"

"There aren't any," Monte said. "I told you, it's just me."

"I find that very hard to believe—"

Monte allowed the anger that had built up inside him to come out as he said, "You'd better believe it! You and your bunch killed the best friend I've ever had!"

That was a half-truth. Beth *was* the best friend he'd ever had, but she wasn't dead. Still, she easily could have been killed in the attack, and Monte let the fury he felt at that thought fuel his words as he went on, "The driver died in that wreck, and so did one of the passengers. And you killed the other one in cold blood! I saw it with my own eyes. You're nothing but low-down, murderous skunks! Of course I came after you. I'm gonna kill all of you and even the score!"

All the outlaws were looking at him now, even the young one with the vacant expression of a half-wit on his face. Anger glittered coldly in the leader's eyes, but then he suddenly laughed.

"Such righteous outrage!" he said. "You're going to deliver justice to all of us, are you? One man against six?"

"You'll get what's comin' to you," Monte growled. If not from him, then from Bo and Scratch, he thought, but he kept that to himself.

A short, stocky outlaw built like a bull came over to the leader and said, "Even if he's tellin' the truth as far as he knows it, John Lee, there could still be a posse after us. When the coach didn't show up at Ramsgate on time, they might've sent somebody out to check on it. They'll find the wreck and probably run right to the law in Silverhill."

"There's only a town marshal there," the leader said.

"That won't stop 'em from comin' after us. The town relies on the stagecoach for mail and passenger service and suchlike."

"What are you getting at, Shorthorn?"

The outlaw nodded toward Monte and said, "It might be a good idea to keep this hombre alive, for a while, anyway. I don't expect a posse to find us up in here, but if they did, we could use this fella as a bargainin' chip."

The leader stroked his pointed beard. "Perhaps. We don't have to kill him right away, at any rate. But I don't

want to take a chance on him causing any trouble, either."
The man looked past Monte and jerked his head in a nod.
"Al, make sure he doesn't cause trouble."

Monte realized what that signal meant and tried to spin
around, but he was too late. The pale-faced outlaw reversed
his gun and struck with the butt, slamming it against
Monte's head. Monte's knees gave out as pain exploded
through his brain. He felt himself falling but was out cold
by the time he hit the ground.

Scratch held up a hand in a signal to stop. He looked
over at Bo and said, "Somethin' odd goin' on here."

It was late afternoon, several hours after the posse left
Silverhill. They had picked up the trail leading north from
the wrecked stagecoach without any trouble. Beth had
seen the outlaws ride off in that direction, just as Monte
had. And they hadn't been following that trail for very long
when Bo had spotted a tiny bit of bright blue cloth tied to
a greasewood branch.

"That looks like it's from Monte's bandanna," Beth had
said excitedly. "He said he would leave signs for us to
follow."

"I reckon that's what this is, then," Scratch had agreed.
"That'll let us move a little faster. Let's see if we can find
the next one."

Since then they had been following the bits of blue
cloth, which had come in very handy when the trail
crossed rocky areas, where the outlaws' horses hadn't left
any prints. Experienced trackers that they were, Bo and
Scratch almost certainly would have been able to pick up
the trail again, but it would have taken more time.

And none of them knew how much time they had to spare.

Now Scratch hipped around in the saddle and looked back along the way they had come. "We ain't found any more of those markers for a while," he said. "Monte'd been leavin' 'em every three or four hundred yards, and I reckon it's been twice that far since we come across one."

"Maybe he ran out of bandanna," Beth said.

Bo shook his head. "Doubtful. And if he had, I expect he'd have used something else." He looked at Scratch. "You're thinking what I'm thinking."

"If he stopped plantin' 'em, he did it for a reason," Scratch said. "Like somebody *made* him stop."

Bo reined his mount around. "Let's go back and take a closer look."

Scratch nodded and told the rest of the posse, "You boys stay here. We don't want to mess up any tracks worse'n we might have already."

"What about me?" Beth asked.

"Stay with the others," Bo told her. She looked like she didn't care for that command, but she didn't argue.

Bo and Scratch rode slowly back along the trail. After a few minutes, Scratch reined in and said, "This is about the spot where he should've left a marker. We'll go ahead on foot from here."

They dismounted and led their horses. Walking slowly, with their keen gazes sweeping from side to side, they had covered another hundred yards when Bo stopped abruptly, pointed to the right, and said, "Over there."

They approached cautiously and hunkered on their heels to study the marks on the ground Bo had spotted. After a few moments, Bo said, "There were three horses milling around here. Monte's and two more, which came out from behind that hummock over there." He nodded toward the small, grassy height.

"They were layin' for him," Scratch agreed. "How come they didn't just bushwhack him and kill him while they had the chance?"

"I don't know, but if they had, they would have left his body here." Bo looked around. "Even if they took it with them for some reason, I don't see any blood."

"So he's still alive," Scratch said.

"We have reason to hope so, anyway." Bo swept a hand toward the tracks again. "But the three horses left here together, so he's almost certainly a prisoner."

"We'll just have to follow the trail they left."

Bo nodded and straightened. He waved for Beth and the rest of the posse to come back and join them. Beth reached them first, with an anxious expression on her face.

"What did you find?"

"Looks like a couple of the outlaws grabbed him," Bo said. "They're headed a little more northwesterly now."

"But we can follow their trail," Scratch added. "They ain't gettin' away from us. Don't worry about that."

"But if he's their prisoner, there's no telling when they might decide to kill him," Beth said. Her voice showed the strain she was under.

"No, there's not," Bo admitted. "But they decided to capture him instead of just ambushing him, so they had something else in mind. There's no reason for us to give up."

"I'm not giving up," Beth said. "But if they hurt Monte, I'll hunt them to the ends of the earth."

Bo believed her, and he thought to himself that he sure wouldn't want to have a vengeful Beth Macy on *his* trail.

CHAPTER 36

Shadows had gathered with the approach of dusk, and in the rugged outcroppings and upthrusts at the edge of the mountains, some areas were almost as dark as night already.

Because of that, Bo, Scratch, Beth, Hector Esperanza, and the rest of the posse had to make their way slowly, which led to a growing sense of frustration.

Beth gave vent to some of that frustration when she said, "Pretty soon we're not going to be able to see the tracks. How do we follow them then?"

"We can't," Bo said. "If we go on much longer, we'll lose the trail, and even worse, we might stumble onto that bunch in the dark. We outnumber them, unless there are more in the gang than you saw, but in a wild shoot-out like that, there'd be a big risk of Monte being hit."

"To say nothin' of the rest of us," Scratch added. Then he sat straighter in his saddle. "Wait a minute." He sniffed the air. "Bo, you smell that?"

Bo took a deep breath and nodded. "Wood smoke. That's a campfire if I ever smelled one. They're here, all right."

"And close by," Beth said. "We have to find them!"

"We will," Bo told her. "Keep your voice down. Sounds carry in this maze."

"You reckon we can follow our noses?" Scratch asked.

"I think so. Beth, you and Señor Esperanza and the other fellas stay here while Scratch and I do some scouting around."

"No, I'm coming with you," Beth insisted.

"Can you be quiet and do what you're told?" Bo said.

"Of course."

Scratch grunted to show that he doubted that, but Bo didn't trust Beth not to sneak away from the others and try to follow them, anyway. He said, "All right, but just remember . . . Monte's life may well be riding on us."

They dismounted and led their horses, so they wouldn't make as much noise, as they wound through the rugged country, and the rest of the posse quickly fell out of sight behind them.

As the smell of smoke grew stronger, Bo whispered, "Better leave the horses here and go ahead on foot."

They weighted the reins down with rocks so the horses wouldn't wander off, then moved slowly and quietly along a twisting path, deep between upthrusts of rock so high that the fading blue sky was only a thin line far above them.

They stopped short when an eerie moaning sound came from somewhere close by. Beth whispered, "What's that?" Bo could tell that she was trying not to sound scared, but she didn't quite succeed.

Scratch pointed. "Look yonder. See that opening up ahead? A breeze has come up, and it's makin' that noise when it blows through there."

Beth leaned forward, squinted, and said, "Is that a cave?"

"No, the rocks don't quite come together above it," Bo

explained. "So it's not actually a cave or a tunnel, but it almost might as well be."

Scratch sniffed the air again. "And I think the smoke we've been smellin' is comin' through there, too. Which means the outlaw camp is on the other end, wherever that is."

"Then we can find it," Beth said with excitement in her voice now.

Bo shook his head. "No, they're bound to have at least one guard posted in there. They'd be fools not to."

"And as narrow as that passage is, I reckon one fella could hold it against an army," Scratch added. "We go waltzin' through there, and we'll just get ourselves killed, which sure won't do Monte no good."

"Then what *are* we going to do?" Beth asked, sounding exasperated again.

Bo looked up at the heights looming above them and asked, "You have any mountain goat blood in you?"

The fading light made climbing difficult, and having Beth along caused Bo and Scratch to set a more deliberate pace, as well. Bo took the lead, searched out the best routes, and worked his way higher and higher, while at the same time trying to stay within sight of the narrow opening at the top of that cleft. Following it would be easier, but without knowing where—or even if—sentries were posted below, they couldn't risk it.

It took them half an hour to cover a hundred yards of distance on flat ground. When they had done that, though, in the last of the light from the lingering glow on the western horizon, they were able to see the top of the canyon that opened up not far away.

"Stay here," Bo breathed to his companions. "I'll take a look."

He edged forward, dropped to hands and knees, and finally onto his belly as he approached the brink. He was careful not to knock any rocks over the edge and into the canyon. That would alert the men down there that someone was up here.

The smell of wood smoke was strong now. Bo took off his hat and looked over the edge, which dropped off sharply to the canyon floor fifty feet below. He saw the campfire's leaping flames in front of what looked like an old, abandoned stone shack. Several men were gathered around the fire, and off to the side, near a small pool of water that had to be spring fed, half a dozen horses were picketed.

Bo's jaw tightened when he saw a shape sprawled on the ground at the edge of the circle of light cast by the campfire. He recognized Monte Jackson, and he knew from the awkward way Monte was lying that his hands had been tied behind his back. It looked like his feet were tied, too.

Well, that was a good sign, Bo told himself. If Monte was dead, the outlaws wouldn't have bothered tying him up. As Bo watched for a few moments longer, he saw Monte move slightly, trying to ease what had to be an uncomfortable position, and that was more confirmation that he was alive.

Bo counted four men around the fire. That left two unaccounted for. It was possible both might be guarding the narrow passage that led into the canyon.

Armed with that knowledge, he backed away from the edge and rejoined Scratch and Beth. They pulled back even farther so they could talk quietly without being overheard.

Bo told them what he had seen, and Scratch said, "Sounds to me like if we bring our Winchesters up here, we could get all four of those varmints before they'd be able to put up much of a fight."

"Maybe," Bo agreed, "but what worries me is that Monte's lying there, trussed up and helpless, and one of them might decide to put a bullet in him first thing if any shooting started."

Beth said, "We can't risk that. Is there any way to get Monte loose *before* you ambush them?"

Bo thought about it for a moment, then said, "We'd have to wait until they were all asleep, then get down there and cut those ropes. The canyon wall is steep, but I reckon a man could climb down it if he was careful."

"Without makin' enough racket to wake up that bunch?" Scratch asked.

"He'd have to be *real* careful," Bo said.

Beth said, "I can do it."

Both Texans turned their heads to look at her. "What?" Scratch said.

"I can do it. Climb down there and cut Monte loose. It can't be either of you who do it, because you have to be up here with your rifles. Let me go down instead."

"Not hardly!" Scratch told her. "That's too dangerous."

"Not really. You'd be covering me. If something did happen to warn the outlaws, you'd be able to open fire on them. The risk would still be greater for Monte that way, and me, too, I suppose, but I really believe it's worth a try."

Bo turned the plan over in his mind, considering the various angles. He had the same instinctive reaction as Scratch. He didn't want Beth taking that risk.

Yet what she'd suggested made sense in a lot of ways. He said, "As long as that passage into the canyon is guarded, the posse can't get through there without losing several men. I don't like the idea of any of our men riding right into certain death."

"Neither do I," Scratch said. "But if guns start to poppin' back here, there's a good chance they'll come a-runnin' to get in on the fight. Then our boys can charge through that cut and hit any of the varmints who are left from behind."

Bo nodded. "There are risks all around, but that sounds like it might be our best chance to round them up without losing anybody on our side."

"And by round 'em up, you mean ventilate the skunks, don't you?"

"That's probably what it's going to take. I don't expect any of them to surrender, do you?"

"Not likely," Scratch said. "I'll head back to where we left the other fellas and explain the plan to them, then fetch our rifles up here. You two can keep an eye on things down there. I should be back in an hour or so."

He cat-footed off into the darkness. Beth sat down on a rock and sighed.

"Is it all right if I go over there to the edge and look at him?" she asked.

"Can you do it without making any racket?" Bo asked.

"I'll be very careful. I . . . I just want to see for myself that he's all right."

"I'm sure he's pretty uncomfortable, but it didn't look like he'd been hurt." Bo thought about it, then told her, "Go ahead."

Beth followed the example he had set earlier, crawling and then stretching out on her belly for the last few feet.

She took off her hat and eased her head forward so she could peer over the brink.

Bo sat down and propped his back against a rock to rest for a spell before things started to get hectic. He was tired from the long ride, and the climb up here had been wearying, as well. Maybe he ought to give some consideration to the feelings for him that Susan Hampshire had been displaying. He was too old for her, of course, but if she didn't care about that, he couldn't get too worked up about it, either.

But what he had told Scratch earlier in the day was the truth. Those old restless feelings had started cropping up lately. No matter how pretty and sweet Susan was, he wasn't sure she could ever compete with the lure of far places. True, he and Scratch had been just about everywhere west of the Mississippi, north of the Rio Grande, and south of the Great White North . . . but there had to be *some* place they hadn't seen yet.

Beth broke into his reverie by scooting back from the canyon's edge, standing up, and quickly but quietly coming over to him.

"Bo," she said, "I think there's about to be trouble down there."

CHAPTER 37

He stood up and went back over to the canyon's edge with her. They knelt close to the brink, still being careful not to dislodge any rocks or clumps of dirt.

The four outlaws below might not have noticed even if they had, because the men were standing around Monte Jackson, clearly trying to intimidate him. Bo and Beth were close enough to hear what the leader was saying.

"We've given you plenty of chances to talk," the man said in a menacing tone.

"And I've told you the truth," Monte snapped. "There's no posse. I followed you by myself."

The leader drew his gun. "There's no point in keeping you alive any longer, then."

Beth tensed at Bo's side and whispered urgently, "Stop him!"

Bo wouldn't have any trouble shooting the outlaw with a rifle, but the range was a little far for a handgun. He could make the shot, but he wasn't sure he could down the others in time to save Monte's life.

Instead of drawing his Colt, he reached down, picked up a fist-sized rock, and heaved it toward the canyon's entrance as hard as he could. A distraction might be more useful right now than gunfire.

The rock landed and bounced, and the resulting clatter made all four outlaws spin around. They leveled their weapons in the direction of the sound and crouched tensely, ready to open fire.

"What was that?" one of them said.

"Cock-a-doodle-doo!" another added, surprisingly. He watched the one who had just spoken and imitated his every move.

The leader said, "Shorthorn, you and Walt go check it out. It could be that a rock just got overbalanced and fell from up on the rim, but I want to be sure. And keep an eye out above you. Someone could be lurking up there!"

"Yeah, we will," a short, stocky owlhoot said. "Come on, Walt."

"Me too!" cried the young man who had crowed like a rooster a moment earlier. He wasn't right in the head, Bo realized. That didn't make him any less dangerous as long as he had a gun in his hand. In fact, it would make him even more unpredictable than the others.

"All right. Go ahead," the leader said disgustedly. "I'll stay here with the prisoner."

As the other three moved off into the darkness away from the fire, Bo leaned over to Beth and said, "We can't wait for Scratch. We'll both go down there and see if we can't get the drop on that boss outlaw who stayed with Monte. With him as a prisoner, maybe we can hold off the others."

She nodded. Even in the gloom, he could tell that she was nervous, but her desire to save Monte's life helped her overcome her fear.

"I'll go first," Bo whispered. "But before we do that . . ."

He picked up another rock, stood up, and heaved it in the direction the three outlaws had gone. The men would be on edge, he knew, and just as he expected, when the rock hit the ground and made a racket, the outlaws yelled in alarm and started shooting, firing blindly. Tongues of flame licked out in the blackness as their guns roared again and again.

Bo was already moving by then. He lowered himself over the edge and let himself slide a short distance down the steep slope before catching himself. Dirt trickled down around him as Beth started descending above him. The canyon wall wasn't sheer. Bo was able to slide down it but had to be careful, stopping and starting to keep himself from losing control and starting to tumble head over heels.

When the shots erupted, the leader of the outlaws had run out to the edge of the firelight. "What's going on out there?" he shouted to his companions as the shooting died away, except for the echoes that filled the canyon. "What do you see?"

"We heard somebody!" the answer came. "Couldn't tell who it was!"

"Cock-a-doodle-do!" the young outlaw warbled, only to be rapidly shushed by one of the other men.

All that noise going on covered up the small sounds Bo and Beth were making in their hurried descent. They reached the canyon floor in less than two minutes.

"Cut Monte loose," Bo told Beth as they passed the old, abandoned stone shack. "I'll see if I can grab that hombre in the long coat."

Beth pulled the knife she had brought along from a sheath at her waist and headed for Monte. He saw her coming, and his eyes got wide with surprise in the firelight. The outlaw was still looking down the canyon toward the entrance and didn't appear to hear Bo cat-footing toward him with gun drawn.

Bo intended to hit him with the Colt and knock him out, but some instinct honed by life on the owlhoot trail must have warned the man. He whirled around just as Bo struck. Bo landed only a glancing blow to the head with the gun. It knocked the outlaw's hat flying but didn't put him down and out.

Instead, the man's gun roared so close that Bo felt the sting of burning powder grains against his cheek. The bullet whipped past his ear, though, and smacked harmlessly into the canyon wall. Bo fired at close range, too, and the shot flung the outlaw backward, away from him.

The other men were headed back this way, shouting curses and questions. Bo jerked his head around and saw that Beth had succeeded in freeing Monte's feet.

"Take cover in those ruins!" he called to them. He knew there was no way they could climb back out of the canyon without the stagecoach robbers picking them off as they went up the wall. The old shack was the only chance they had.

He looked back at the man he had shot, expecting to see him still down, but the hombre was on his feet again and was running toward the horses. He snapped a shot at Bo as he ran. That slug ripped past Bo's head, so close he seemed to feel the heat of it.

He triggered twice as he made a run for the old shack, too. The roof had collapsed, and the walls had partially crumbled away but were still standing for the most part. A bullet struck one of the rocks at the edge of the door and sprayed dust and stone chips as Bo dived through the opening.

As he rolled over, he saw that Beth and Monte had reached the shelter ahead of him. Beth was busy cutting the ropes off Monte's wrists.

"What in blazes are you doing here?" he exclaimed as he stared at her. "You're gonna get yourself killed!"

"What about you?" she shot back at him. "You didn't think I was going to let those outlaws kill you, did you?"

Awkwardly, because his arms were probably half numb, he put them around Beth and drew her to him. She embraced him, as well, and they stood there in the shadows of the old shack, clinging to each other.

Bo knelt at what was left of a window, risked a glance outside, and didn't see anything to shoot at. He drew back as guns blasted, and heard several bullets thud into the thick old walls.

The ruins provided pretty good cover, but there was nowhere for them to go. They were trapped in here, at least until help arrived.

But Scratch, Esperanza, and the rest of the posse were bound to have heard all the shots and would know that something had gone wrong. Bo knew he could count on Scratch to come a-runnin', drawn irresistibly by the sound of trouble.

Beth and Monte were kissing now, Bo saw when he glanced in their direction, which came as no surprise. From what he had seen, the two of them had been denying their feelings for each other for a while now, and once danger had forced those feelings out into the open, there was no holding them back. Bo smiled slightly as he gave them some privacy by devoting his attention to the task of thumbing fresh cartridges into his Colt's cylinder.

He filled every chamber this time, instead of leaving an empty for the hammer to rest on, as he usually did. He was liable to need a full wheel.

His two companions started talking in low voices. Bo wasn't trying to listen, but he couldn't help but overhear when Monte said, "I wish we'd gotten a chance to get married. If we're not gonna make it out of this fix . . . if we're going to die here . . . it should have been as husband and wife."

Beth laughed. "That's the worst proposal I've ever heard."

"Well, it wasn't really a . . ." Monte took a deep breath. "But why not? We can at least be betrothed. Will you marry me, Elizabeth Macy?"

"Yes," she whispered. "Yes, I will."

Monte kissed her again.

Bo glanced out the window and spotted one of the outlaws darting from rock to rock, trying to get closer to the old shack. He threw a shot at the man, who dived for cover as the bullet kicked up dirt at his feet. Bo shook his head in disgust because he'd missed the shot.

Then, remembering what Scratch had said to him at Rose and Steve's wedding, he told the young couple, "I'll do you one better."

"What?" Beth asked.

"I'm sorry for eavesdropping, but I heard you two talking about being engaged. If you want to get married right here and now, I can do that for you."

Beth and Monte both stared at him in the faint light

reflected into the shack from the campfire. "You can?" Monte said.

Bo nodded solemnly. "I was a Baptist minister for a while, a long, long time ago. I don't have any legal standing with the Territory of New Mexico, but I remember how the ceremony goes . . . and I reckon I've got as much standing with the Good Lord as I ever did. I can join the two of you together, and then you can make if official when we get back to Silverhill. And if we don't get back . . ."

"We'll be married in the eyes of the Lord, anyway," Monte said. He looked at Beth. "What do you think?"

She didn't have to consider the question for very long. She nodded and said, "I'd like that very much. Should we come over there?"

"No!" Bo held up a hand to stop them before they could start. The outlaws weren't pouring in a barrage of shots like they had been a few minutes earlier, but the canyon still rang with regular gunfire, and slugs pounded into the shack's walls. "Just stay where you are."

"Gunshots don't make much of a wedding march, and I don't have a pretty dress or a bouquet, and we don't have rings . . ." Beth took Monte's hands in hers. "But I'm ready if you are."

"I sure am," he told her.

Bo nodded, searched his memory for the words, and launched into at least an approximation of the wedding ceremony he remembered from his preaching days.

"Do you, Monte, take Beth to be your wife, for better or worse, for richer or poorer, in sickness and in health, from this day forward for the rest of your life, until death do you part?"

"I do," Monte declared.

"Do you, Beth, take Monte to be your husband, for better or worse, for richer or poorer, in sickness and in health, from this day forward for the rest of your life, until death do you part?"

"I do," she said.

"Then, in the eyes of the Lord and by the power He's invested in me, I pronounce you man and wife." Bo tried not to duck as a bullet whistled fairly close overhead. "You may kiss the bride."

Then, while Monte was busy doing that, Bo stuck his gun over the crumbling windowsill again and blasted a couple of shots toward the muzzle flashes he had spotted.

He ducked back down, but as he did so, he glanced up through the opening and saw a spurt of orange muzzle flame where he hadn't expected to—about halfway up the canyon wall, a hundred yards toward the entrance. The sharp crack of a rifle sounded at the same time, followed instantly by the deadly whine of a ricochet close by.

"Get down!" Bo shouted at Beth and Monte after he realized one of the outlaws had climbed up there and now had an angle where he could fire down *into* the shack, where the fallen roof had been.

More shots followed as the rifleman cranked off several rounds and filled the shack with screaming, bouncing slugs. Beth cried out in fear as she and Monte sat against the front wall, huddled together. Bo pressed himself against the wall on the other side of the door, filled the Colt again from the loops on his shell belt, then thrust the weapon around the edge of the window opening and emptied it, sending all six shots in the rifleman's direction.

At this range, though, it would be just the blindest of blind luck if he hit the man. The best he could realistically hope for was to come close enough to slow down the assault momentarily, and even that was pretty unlikely.

Then he heard boot soles slapping on the ground outside and knew the other outlaws were rushing the shack. Hastily, he reloaded, hoping he could at least put up a fight as they stormed the place.

Drumming hoofbeats sounded, a swift rataplan that drew closer as it came up the canyon. Bo heard shouts of alarm; then gun thunder pealed and echoed from the surrounding walls. He raised up enough to glance through the window, caught a glimpse of a limp figure tumbling down the slope from the area where the rifleman had been concealed. Bo could think of only one explanation for that.

Scratch and the rest of the posse had arrived!

Bo went to the ground and rolled into the doorway on his belly. From there he looked out across the fire and saw men rushing around and shooting wildly. Other men, members of the posse from Silverhill, rode among them, guns geysering smoke and flame. Bo knew the bloody melee would last only moments, since the stagecoach robbers were outnumbered and afoot, while their enemies were mounted.

The boss outlaw, the man in the long coat, hadn't given up on killing the three people in the ruins. His left arm was limp, and that sleeve of his coat was dark with blood where Bo had winged him earlier, but he charged the old shack, anyway, triggering shots as he attacked.

From the ground, Bo fired at an upward angle and saw the man's head jerk back as the slug caught him between the eyes. Momentum made him run a couple more steps before he pitched forward and landed face-first in the fire. He didn't move as the flames ate into his clothing and flesh, mute testimony that Bo's shot had killed him instantly.

Bo looked over at Beth and Monte. "Are you two all right?" he asked. His ears were ringing so much from the gunfire that his voice sounded funny to him.

He could hear well enough to understand Monte when the shotgun guard said, "We're not hit. Are we? Are you hurt, Beth?"

"I'm fine," she assured him. "Just scared out of my wits."

"No need to be scared now," Bo told her as he pushed himself to his feet and watched Scratch riding slowly toward the shack. The silver-haired Texan held one of his long-barreled Remingtons, ready to fire, but there didn't seem to be any more targets. Outlaw carcasses lay scattered around the little canyon.

"Bo!" Scratch called when he caught sight of his old friend. He swung a leg over his horse's back and dropped to the ground. "Are you ventilated?"

"Nope," Bo replied. "My ears may ring for a week, though."

Scratch came up to him and slapped him exuberantly on the arm. "We got all six of the varmints," he reported. "Well, five of 'em, anyway. Looks like you did for this last one."

He nodded toward the fire and wrinkled his nose at the pungent smell of burning flesh. A couple of the posse members rode up, and following Scratch's orders, they grasped the outlaw's ankles and pulled his body out of the flames.

Beth and Monte came out of the ruins with their arms around each other, and Scratch greeted them enthusiastically when he found out they were all right, too.

"I was still with the fellas when we heard the shootin' break out," he said. "I figured you'd gotten a jump on things, for some reason, so instead of climbin' up and around like we did before, I decided it'd be best to come at the trouble head-on."

"Did you run into any guards in that passage?" Bo asked.

Scratch shook his head. "No. I reckon they'd already rushed back here to see what all the commotion was. The way through was free and clear. So the plan sorta worked like it was supposed to. Just not quite."

"We have some more news," Beth said. "Monte and I are married!"

Scratch stared at her. "Married?" he repeated. "How in tarnation did you manage to get—" He broke off and looked at Bo. "Went back to your old preachin' ways, did you?"

"It's probably not legal," Bo said.

"Feels legal to me," Monte said. "I'm not sure I could feel any more married than I do right now."

"But just in case," Beth said, "we can have the justice of the peace in Silverhill marry us again."

Monte grinned. "As long as that means I get to kiss the bride again, I won't argue!"

Chapter 38

Clarence Appleyard had driven out to the site of the wrecked stagecoach and retrieved the bodies of the two salesmen killed in the holdup. The men were laid to rest in Silverhill's cemetery, since there was no practical way of transporting the bodies back to the men's homes in St. Louis and Little Rock, Arkansas. As marshal, Scratch wrote letters—with considerable help from Bo—to the families of both men, advising them of their sad demise and expressing condolences.

The stage line was forced to suspend the El Paso run temporarily, while Henry Mitchum, the manager of the local office, got word of the incident to his boss in El Paso, who then had to arrange for a replacement coach and another driver and guard pair to bring the vehicle to Silverhill. Those two would continue in their jobs for the next couple of runs, giving Beth and Monte a chance to have a brief honeymoon once the justice of the peace made their union official as far as New Mexico Territory was concerned.

With yet another violent uproar behind them, Bo and Scratch hoped that tranquility would reign in Silverhill for a while. Neither of them actually *quite* believed that would happen—but they hoped for it, anyway.

Bo was in the Red Top Café, enjoying a bowl of Ed Massey's chicken and dumplings, when Hugh Craddock came into the eatery. Just the sight of the rancher from Texas made Bo frown. Nine times out of ten, Craddock was looking for trouble, or at least it seemed that way to Bo.

This evening, however, the usual arrogant sneer was missing from Craddock's face. In fact, he looked tired and dispirited more than anything else. He came over to the counter, where there was an empty stool to Bo's left, and said, "Mind if I sit down?"

"It's a free country," Bo said, which wasn't really an answer but was as close to one as he felt like giving to Craddock.

"I was looking for you, Creel," the man said as he settled himself on the stool. "Thought I might find you in here."

"I eat supper here most evenings."

"Yeah, I've noticed."

Bo frowned slightly. Craddock seemed to mean something by that comment.

Gwendolyn Massey, who was working behind the counter, came over to see if Craddock wanted anything. He ordered coffee, then went on to Bo, "I've noticed a lot of things, like how the two of you seem to be mighty friendly."

Bo frowned in confusion. "Me and Mrs. Massey? I don't think you could say—"

"No, I'm talking about you and Miss Hampshire."

The mention of Susan's name made Bo turn his head to

look at her. She was on the other side of the room, talking to a couple who were eating in one of the booths along the far wall. Susan laughed in a friendly fashion at something the woman had said.

"The lady and I are friends," Bo admitted. "Anything wrong with that?"

Craddock shook his head glumly. "No, I suppose not. The only thing wrong is that I'm a blasted fool."

"What in blazes are you talking about, Craddock?"

"I've been taking some of my meals here, too, and I've gotten to know Susan. It took a while, since she was so mad at me . . . and with good cause, I might add. She has a forgiving personality, though, and I suppose it wouldn't let her stay angry."

Bo stared at the rancher for a long moment, then said, "Wait just a minute. Are you trying to tell me that you've gotten fond of Susan?"

Some of the familiar haughty pride flashed in Craddock's eyes. "If you're going to make sport of me—"

"I'm not, I swear," Bo said quickly. "I'm just surprised, that's all."

Mrs. Massey arrived then with a saucer and a cup of coffee and set them in front of Craddock, who thanked her politely. Craddock took a sip of coffee while the woman drifted back to the other end of the counter.

"I had it in my head that I wanted a certain kind of woman," Craddock went on quietly.

"A young, pretty one," Bo said.

Craddock shrugged. "That kept me from seeing how nice Susan is, and how smart and good-hearted and strong, too. That's why I said I was a blasted fool."

Bo sipped his own coffee and smiled. "A downright jackass, in fact."

Craddock's jaw tightened, but he said, "I deserve that. Anyway, I give up, Creel. Even if I wanted to court her now, I'd be wasting my time. You've won. She talks more about you than anything else."

This was mighty interesting, Bo mused. He and Scratch had been talking about how they were starting to feel fiddle-footed again, but one thing that had stopped him from thinking seriously about leaving Silverhill was the knowledge that it might hurt Susan. In the long run, he knew that day was coming, but he wanted to postpone it as long as he could.

Now, if Craddock was serious about his feelings for her, that might soften the blow if Bo left.

"So that's why I'm going back to Texas," Craddock said as he rested his hands on the counter's edge, as if he were about to stand up. "There's nothing left here for me. I threw away any chance I had with Susan, and Cecilia only has eyes for that big oaf Roscoe—" He stopped himself. "I'm sorry. I know Roscoe Sherman isn't the half-wit he pretended to be. Even though it pains me to say it, he's actually a pretty decent hombre. Better suited to Cecilia than I am. So I might as well go home and find out if I have a ranch left."

Bo was about to tell the man not to get in any hurry to leave Silverhill, but before he could, somebody came up behind him and tapped him on the shoulder.

It wasn't a threatening tap, by any stretch of the imagination, so Bo looked around unhurriedly and didn't reach for his gun. The man who stood there was familiar. Small, slightly built, and fair haired, the man wore a shabby suit and clutched an old cap in front of him.

"Something wrong, Milo?" Bo asked him.

Milo Mullaney worked as a swamper at the Silver King Saloon, and he was fond of taking some of his wages in trade. Once or twice a week, Bo or Scratch found him passed out in an alley and had to haul him in to sleep it off in one of the cells. He wasn't a troublesome drunk, though, and even when thoroughly snockered, he was still mild and unassuming.

"Deputy Creel," he said, "I've got somethin' eatin' at me."

Craddock snorted and said, "Some sort of vermin?"

Bo glared at Craddock for a second and then said, "What is it, Milo? Are you sick?" The little swamper seemed a mite more pale than usual.

Milo shook his head, though, and said, "I heard a fella whistlin' just now. You know that song about the beautiful dreamer? What's it called?"

"'Beautiful Dreamer,'" Bo said. "That's the name of it."

"Oh. Yeah, that makes sense, I guess. Well, I was sittin' on a crate in the alley there by Mr. Dubonnet's store, and I heard a fella whistlin' that song. I looked up, and I seen him go by on the boardwalk. It was Doc Chapman."

"All right," Bo said with a nod. "So the doctor likes Stephen Foster songs. I don't see why that would bother you, Milo."

"But he was with a lady. A pretty blond lady."

Milo seemed to be struggling to keep his thoughts together. Bo figured he hadn't been sitting on that crate in the alley by himself. He'd had a companion—in a bottle of Who-Hit-John.

"Dr. Chapman keeps company with Miss Parker," Bo said. "I'm sure she's the one you saw."

"Yeah, I . . . I think that's right. One of those mail-order brides who came here with you and the marshal. I knew that, and that's why I came lookin' for you. That and the 'Beautiful Dreamer' song."

Bo shook his head. "I don't understand any of this, Milo. Why does it bother you?"

Overcome by emotion, Milo reached up and plucked at Bo's sleeve. "Because it ain't the first time I heard somebody whistlin' it." His voice shook from more than drink. "I heard it twice before . . . when I was . . . when I was sittin' in an alley . . . and a fella came along, whistlin' that tune and . . . and it's hard for me to remember things, you know, but I remember those nights because of . . . because of what happened . . ."

Alarm bells started to ring in the back of Bo's brain. He wasn't sure what had set them off, but he reached out, clasped a hand on Milo's shoulder to steady him, and asked, "What happened those other nights when you heard somebody whistling 'Beautiful Dreamer'?"

"Them girls got killed!" The words were almost a sob as they came out of Milo's mouth. "Them girls who got cut up so bad. I swear it's true, Deputy. I swear I ain't makin' it up. I'm afraid it's gonna happen again!"

From the stool beside Bo, Craddock said, "This little drunk is loco, Creel. He imagines he hears somebody whistling a tune, and he thinks it means a girl's going to be killed? That's crazy!"

Bo's pulse had begun to hammer in his skull. He tried to remember if he or Scratch had ever questioned Milo Mullaney after the other murders. He was pretty sure he hadn't, and he didn't believe Scratch had ever mentioned doing so, either. A gent like Milo was sort of invisible. . . .

Which was all the more reason they should have talked to him, Bo realized now. Nobody ever paid any attention to Milo. But that didn't mean he didn't see things that went on in town.

"You're sure it was Dr. Chapman you heard?"

Milo swallowed hard and bobbed his head up and down.

"And Jean Parker was with him?"

"Yes, sir, she was. They was headed toward the doc's house."

Craddock was probably right. The very idea probably *was* crazy. A song didn't mean anything, and the word of a drunk meant even less.

But Bo didn't even grab his hat before he left the Red Top at a run.

"My, you're certainly in a good mood tonight," Jean said as she and Dr. Arliss Chapman went through the gate in the picket fence in front of the doctor's house.

"I'm always in a good mood when I'm in your company, my dear," Chapman said. He closed the gate behind them and took Jean's arm again.

"That's a sweet thing to say, but you seem in even higher spirits than usual. You were whistling that lovely tune just now. I don't believe I've ever heard you whistle before."

"I'm moved to do so only every now and then." They went up onto the porch, and Chapman opened the door to the house. "It's called 'Beautiful Dreamer.' One of Mr. Stephen Foster's songs."

"I know. I've heard it played and sung many times."

Chapman ushered her into the parlor. "My mother used to play it on the piano. It was her favorite. It came to be my favorite, too, I suppose. I'll admit, I've been feeling a bit nostalgic today." He went over to a sideboard where a bottle and some glasses sat. "May I pour you a bit of sherry?"

Jean smiled and said, "I suppose that would be all right."

This was the first time she had been in the doctor's house. It felt positively scandalous, being alone with him like this, and having a drink with him made it even more so. But she would be careful not to let the drink go to her head, and even though she might allow him a *few* more liberties than usual, she would put a stop to it, firmly, if she thought things were about to go too far.

Arliss Chapman was a gentleman. She knew he would never do anything she didn't want him to.

She took the glass of sherry he offered her, and sipped the sweet liquor. He had a drink, too, and he gestured with it as he said, "Shall we sit on the divan?"

"That would be very nice."

They sat down, close but not indecently so, and Jean said, "You know, you've never really spoken much about your childhood. I believe just now may have been the first time you've even mentioned your mother."

"Well . . . not all the memories are good ones."

"Oh, I'm sorry," she said when she saw a brief flash of pain in his eyes. "I didn't mean to—"

"No, that's all right, quite all right," he said, smiling. "She passed away when I was young. Fourteen years old."

"I'm so sorry. That must have been dreadfully hard for you and your father and your brothers and sisters."

He shook his head. "I had no brothers or sisters. I was

an only child. And my father . . ." A slow, dismissive wave of the hand. "My father was barely a presence in that house. A ghost almost. He was wounded, you see, when he served in the war against Mexico, and when I look back at the situation with the medical knowledge I now possess, I can see that he was probably addicted to laudanum. That rendered him . . . less than a man."

"How terrible. I . . . I had no idea your past was so tragic, Arliss."

He set his glass aside on a small table and said, "Please, don't feel sorry for me, Jean. I appreciate your sympathy, but it's not necessary. I've made a decent life for myself, you see. A very decent life."

"You have indeed. You're a well-respected physician . . ."

He nodded. "Yes, yes."

"And quite a gentleman."

"Thank you. And of course I do have some good memories from my past, such as that song. I can see her now . . ." A wistful note came into his voice. "Sitting at the piano in the parlor, playing that tune, her fingers moving so deftly on the keys. She would call me over to sit next to her as she played . . . I adored watching her. She was so beautiful right there beside me, her neck so long and slender and delicate . . . like yours, my dear . . ." His hand strayed to her neck, caressed it. Jean closed her eyes as a thrill of passion went through her. He was so tragic, yet so romantic. . . .

"And then she," Chapman whispered as he leaned closer to her. "Then she—"

He couldn't seem to finish, but Jean didn't care. She felt the warmth of his breath on her cheek and wished he would just go ahead and kiss her.

Instead, the softly stroking fingers closed suddenly. Closed tight with a strength that took her totally by surprise. She would have gasped, but she couldn't. His grip completely closed off her windpipe.

Her eyes flew open. His face was right in front of hers, but instead of gazing at her with affection, his eyes burned with some other emotion and seemed not even to see her. His features twisted into lines that were positively demonic. Jean's heart began pounding madly as he closed his other hand around her neck and leaned closer so his weight pinned her to the divan. Instinctively, she began trying to fight back, but he didn't seem to feel her fists as she pounded them against his back and shoulders. Her pulse hammered deafeningly inside her head. Red and black curtains began to close in over her vision.

She didn't hear the front door being kicked open, but she heard the familiar voice of Bo Creel shout, "Chapman!"

Jean fell back against the cushion when Chapman let go of her and whirled toward the door. Her eyesight was still blurry, but she could see well enough to know what was going on when Chapman's hand dipped into his coat and came out clutching something shiny and sharp looking. It was a scalpel, she realized as he rushed at Bo, slashing with the medical instrument.

Bo jerked back and yelled, "Stop it! Drop that, you fool!" Instead, Chapman lunged at the Texan again, filthy obscenities spewing from his twisted lips as he did so. Bo's gun came up, and flame spurted from the muzzle, a fiery tongue so long, it seemed to touch the front of the doctor's vest. The bullet drove Chapman backward, and when his stumbling feet tangled with a throw rug on the floor, he fell and landed on the divan, next to Jean. She stared in horror at him as he pawed at his chest, where blood welled through the smoking hole in his vest. His mouth opened and closed, and incoherent sounds came out.

Then his wide, staring eyes glazed over, and his bloody hands—those hands that had been trying to choke the life out of her mere moments earlier—fell limply to his sides.

Jean felt her eyes start to roll up in their sockets as she fainted, and that was the last thing she was aware of.

CHAPTER 39

"There's no doubt in my mind that Chapman was responsible for what happened to Julie Hobbs and Florence, too," Bo said. He and Scratch were standing on the front porch of the doctor's house. "I don't reckon we'd ever be able to prove it, though. But we know for a fact he was trying to kill Jean. I saw that with my own eyes."

"And he came at you with that scalpel and tried to carve you up," Scratch said. "Any way you look at it, Bo, you did the right thing by shootin' him. The *only* thing you could've done."

Bo nodded slowly and said, "Yeah, I don't reckon I'll lose any sleep over it."

"Wish we could've figured it out in time to save Julie. We didn't have any clue that we had a hydrophobia skunk in town before he killed that Florence gal. You have any idea *why* he done it?"

"From what Jean was able to tell me after she came around, it probably had something to do with his mother. Evidently, she died when he was a boy." Bo frowned. "You know, I sort of wonder if maybe he killed *her*, too. But again, that's something we'll never know for sure."

"But we know he won't ever hurt nobody again, and that's what matters."

"I suppose so." Bo shook his head. "You know, as a doctor, he helped a lot of folks, too. I'm not saying that balances things out, not hardly, but they say there's good and bad in just about everybody, and I don't know if there was ever a better example of that than Dr. Arliss Chapman."

Cecilia came to the door behind them and said, "Jean seems to be feeling a little better, but she's still very weak and shaky. Do you think we could get a buggy or something to take her back to the hotel?"

"Sure," Scratch said. "Doc Chapman's buggy is right out back, beside the shed where he keeps his buggy horse." He frowned. "Kept his buggy horse, I reckon I should say. And it ain't hardly his buggy no more, either."

"I'm not sure how good an idea *that* is," Cecilia said with a frown. "Jean's gone for rides with him in that buggy. I think it might remind her too much of him. It's bad enough that she's resting in his parlor, in the very room where he tried to murder her."

"And where he died," Bo added. "We understand, Cecilia. We'll go down to Esperanza's Livery Stable. I'm pretty sure Señor Esperanza has a buggy or two he rents out to folks."

Cecilia nodded. She, Luella, and Beth had come down to the doctor's house to be with Jean and to comfort her as soon as they found out what had happened. Bo was glad they had. He was sure Jean would feel even worse without her friends around her. It was bad enough that she had almost been killed by a man she had trusted—a man she might have even been falling in love with.

Cecilia went back inside and closed the door. Bo and

Scratch went down the steps and started along the walk toward the gate.

"It's a good thing Clarence Appleyard was able to get here as quick as he did and haul off the body before Jean woke up," Scratch said. "It'd have been a terrible thing for her to wake up with that mangy varmint's carcass still layin' right there beside her. Good, too, that he didn't bleed all over the place. You done a good job, Bo, shootin' him in the heart like that."

"I was just trying to put him down like the mad dog he was, before he could hurt Jean or me," Bo said. "If I hadn't killed him, though, we could have questioned him and maybe found out why he did the things he did."

"I can tell you why. Because he was evil. Maybe not bad up one way and down the other, like you was just sayin' about folks bein' a mixture, but there was a heap more bad than good in that one, if you ask me."

Bo couldn't argue with that.

As they reached the gate and opened it, Susan Hampshire walked up, carrying a tray with a cloth over it. Bo and Scratch both took their hats off as they nodded to her.

"What are you doing here?" Bo asked.

Susan smiled. "Aren't you glad to see me, Bo, even under the circumstances?"

"I'm always glad to see you, and the circumstances could've been a whole lot worse. Silverhill's lost a doctor, but Jean didn't lose her life."

"And thank goodness for that," Susan said. "Anyway, I have a little bowl of hot stew and some bread. When the word got around town about what happened, Ed Massey thought Jean might need it to give her some strength right now."

Bo cast a dubious glance toward the tray. "I'm not sure she has much of an appetite . . ."

"Honestly, I thought the same thing, but Ed insisted. He thinks there's nothing that some good home cooking won't fix."

Scratch said, "And I reckon most of the time, he's right about that. But if Jean don't want it, maybe one of the other ladies would."

"I'll just take it in, anyway, if one of you gentlemen will hold the gate for me . . ."

"Of course," Bo said, moving quickly to do so. As Susan moved past him, he caught the pleasant scent of her, a clean, fresh blend of lilac water, clean hair, and her own indefinable scent. The appetizing aromas of stew and fresh-baked bread just added to the appeal.

Bo watched her go up the walk and climb the steps to the porch as he slowly closed the gate. She was a mighty fine woman, he thought. Any man would be a fool to pass up a chance to be with her.

Hugh Craddock wasn't the only blasted fool in the world, he told himself. He had been following the lure of far trails for so long, though. . . .

"Sometimes a fella's got some mighty hard choices facin' him," Scratch said shrewdly. "And no matter what he does, he's always gonna wonder how things would've gone if he'd taken the other trail. That's just the way life is."

"You're right," Bo said. "I can always count on you for a bit of homespun philosophy when I need it, old friend." He slapped Scratch on the shoulder. "Let's go fetch that buggy, so Jean can get back to the hotel and get some real rest."

They headed for the livery stable, never glancing toward

a couple of sombrero-wearing figures ambling along the other side of the street.

"Honestly, I'm all right," Jean told her friends as they hovered around her. They had helped her over to an armchair near the fireplace so she wouldn't have to sit on the divan where Arliss Chapman had died—and where he had tried to choke her to death.

Cecilia sat on one of the chair's arms and stroked Jean's forehead with soft fingertips as she said, "The last time you tried to stand up, you almost fainted again. As soon as Bo and Scratch get back with that buggy, we'll help you out to it and take you back to the hotel. You need to stretch out in your own bed and get some rest."

"I'm really not tired," Jean insisted. "I just feel so . . . *stupid*."

Luella and Beth, who stood nearby, exclaimed in unison, "No!" Beth went on, "You're not the least bit stupid, honey. I don't know why in the world you'd say that."

"I allowed myself to be taken in by that man. That awful man. Just because he . . . he sounded so educated . . . and cultured . . ."

"But he actually was both of those things," Luella said. "He really was a doctor, so he had to be educated. And he knew all kinds of things about art and music and literature."

"And he was a murderer," Jean insisted. She sighed. "But I guess those things don't have to be mutually exclusive, do they?"

The front door opened, and Susan Hampshire came in, carrying a tray with a cloth draped over it. The smell of food suddenly filled the room. Susan smiled and said,

"I hope I'm not intruding, but Mr. Massey at the café sent this down here in hopes that it would help."

Jean shook her head. "I don't see how I could eat anything. The way I feel right now, I'm not sure I'll ever have an appetite again."

"Of course you will," Cecilia told her. "But right now might not be the time . . ."

"It smells really good," Beth said.

Jean waved a hand. "If any of you want it, just go ahead. It won't bother me."

Susan said, "I'll just put the tray here," as she placed it on the sideboard where Chapman had gotten the glasses of sherry. She turned back to the others and said, "I could go in the kitchen and make some coffee, if that would help."

"How about that?" Cecilia asked Jean. "A cup of coffee?"

"Maybe," Jean said. "Perhaps with some of that sherry in it."

Beth looked at the sideboard and said, "There's a bottle of bourbon there, too. That might be even better."

Jean just summoned up a weak smile.

"I'll be right back," Susan said. She looked around, clearly searching for the kitchen, since she had never been in this house before, but it wasn't so large that she had any trouble finding what she was looking for. She disappeared through a door.

"I think it may be time for me to go back to Four Corners," Jean said. "I don't mind admitting that this . . . adventure . . . hasn't exactly turned out the way I hoped it would. Rose is married to that young cowboy, and, Beth, you've found the love of your life in Monte Jackson. Cecilia, you're being courted by that giant miner, who seems, well, wonderful in a rough-hewn way."

Luella said with a smile, "You left me out. I haven't found anyone yet."

"Not for lack of trying on the part of nearly every eligible bachelor in Silverhill!" Jean exclaimed. "You'll settle on one of them sooner or later. But there's no one here for me."

"You haven't really given it a chance yet," Beth argued. "There are a lot of men in Silverhill—"

"And how many of them will want anything to do with a woman foolish enough to get involved with a murderer? To . . . to fall for a man who . . ." Emotion forced Jean's voice to trail off.

"It's not like you married him or anything," Luella said.

"But I might have," Jean insisted. "In fact, there's no telling what I might have let him do tonight . . . if he hadn't tried to kill me."

Cecilia leaned closer and said firmly, "Just don't think about that anymore. Put it all out of your mind. And the *last* thing you want to do when you've been through such a terrible ordeal is to make any important decisions. For tonight, just don't think about any of it."

Jean sighed and said, "I'll try." She looked around at her friends. "And thank you all so much for . . . for being here for me. I know you're just trying to help."

"Of course we are," Cecilia said. "We're your friends, after all."

The door into the hall that led to the kitchen swung open then, and the four mail-order brides turned their heads to look in that direction, expecting to see Susan Hampshire coming back, even though it seemed like the older woman hadn't had enough time to brew any coffee.

Susan stepped into the parlor, all right—but she wasn't alone. A man was with her, prodding her forward. He had his left hand on her left shoulder as he stood behind her, and his right hand held a gun so that its barrel dug into her side.

They all stared in shock at this slender newcomer, who wore tight trousers with decorative stitching down the sides, a short embroidered charro jacket over a white shirt, and a gray steeple-crowned sombrero.

However, the face that peered out from under the sombrero's brim didn't match the Mexican garb. It was tanned lightly but belonged to a gringo, rather than a native from south of the border. He had light brown hair and a neatly trimmed mustache of the same shade.

Most incongruously of all, a pair of rimless pince-nez spectacles perched on his nose and were attached to a ribbon tied to a button on his jacket. Intense blue eyes peered through the glasses.

All four of the young women recognized him, but it was Luella who blurted out his name first.

"Philip Armbruster!"

"That's right, my dear," Philip Armbruster, once a journalist for the *New York World*, currently the leader of a band of Mexican bandits and revolutionaries, said as he smiled. "You probably believed I was never coming back for you. But I'm here now, and you're coming with me." He looked around at the others. "You're all coming with me."

CHAPTER 40

Philip Armbruster had never expected to land in his current situation. In fact, when his editor at the *World* had given him the job of going to Mexico to interview the revolutionary leader Jaime Mendoza and possibly even travel with Mendoza's army for a time, Armbruster had believed that he might not ever come back alive. They were always having wars and revolutions and slaughtering people in Mexico, and he had been convinced he would be one of the hapless victims of that habitual violence—if he was even able to locate Mendoza.

Instead, once he had actually got to Mexico, after traveling south across the border from El Paso, not only had he found Mendoza, but the man had taken a liking to him and had taken him under his wing, too. Armbruster had joined Mendoza's "army," which, as it turned out, was more of ragtag gang of bandidos. True, Mendoza always insisted that he planned to use the loot he accumulated to help him overthrow the government in Mexico City, but Armbruster soon realized the great leader was really just interested in the loot itself—and the tequila and the giggling, hot-blooded señoritas it could buy.

Mendoza had it in his head that once the revolution was over and he was the supreme ruler of Mexico, Armbruster would write a book about his exploits that would make him an international sensation. Any such book would have to be mostly fiction, Armbruster knew, but if it meant preserving his life, he was up to the task.

Then Mendoza got himself killed in a raid on the mining town of Silverhill, across the border in New Mexico Territory, and leadership of the band fell to his second-in-command, Guadalupe Sanchez. Sanchez was an amiable man and plenty tough when he needed to be, but he was no strategist. He looked to Armbruster for advice, and as the months passed, it came to be accepted among the bandidos that the real jefe was the gringo from New York.

Armbruster might have been able to get away from them and go back to New York, but they made it clear they wanted him to stay. He had never really been looked up to before, had never known any sort of power, and even though his followers were just a motley crew of bandits, he enjoyed leading them. He toyed with the idea of putting together a *real* revolution—but so far, all they had managed to do was hold up a few banks and trains.

Still, that was as much as Jaime Mendoza had ever been able to accomplish.

There was one more reason Armbruster didn't try to slip away and return to his old, boring life.

Luella Tolman.

Armbruster had first seen her when she and the other mail-order brides were on their way to Silverhill, when Mendoza's gang went after the wagon in which they were traveling. Mendoza had fallen in love with Luella at first sight and had decided that he was going to marry her.

What he hadn't known was that Philip Armbruster had felt the same way about the sultry, exotically beautiful young woman. Ever since the battle in Silverhill during which Mendoza was killed and Armbruster wounded, the young former journalist had planned to come back here sooner or later and claim Luella as his own. From time to time, he and his men had ridden up here, across the border, and one of the bandits had slipped into town to spy on Luella, to make sure she was still in Silverhill and not married.

Not that it would have mattered all that much if she had been married. He would just steal her away from her husband, Armbruster had thought, and she would realize from the sheer romantic daring of such a deed how much he loved her.

Now he stood there in the parlor of the doctor's house, gazing at Luella's shocked but lovely face, and thought that although he wasn't sure what had happened here tonight, it was a stroke of luck for him and his men. Not only would Luella come with him to be his bride, but there were four other ladies here, as well, three of the mail-order brides and one older but still attractive woman. Guadalupe Sanchez could marry one of them, and the others would make excellent wives for three more of his men.

There would be no mistreatment of these women, Armbruster vowed to himself. They would be coddled, pampered, and courted. If any man laid a finger on them improperly, he would shoot the offender himself.

He had gotten quite good with a gun, actually, fast on the draw and, as long as he was wearing his spectacles, deadly accurate with his aim.

He didn't like threatening the older woman like this, but he had to make sure none of them screamed or tried to

fight or raised any commotion. Those two old Texans—
who could fight like the devil, despite their age—hadn't
been gone long, and there was no telling when or if they
might come back.

The four young women stared at him in shock. Cecilia
Spaulding found her voice first and exclaimed, "You're
insane!"

Armbruster shook his head and said, "Not at all. Luella
knows how I feel about her. She knows I could never stay
away from her forever."

"What are you talking about?" Luella said. "The last
time I saw you, you were wounded. I thought you died,
like the rest of those . . . those bandits!"

"My love for you gave me strength." Armbruster winced
inwardly at the mawkishness of that statement. As a writer,
he should have been able to come up with something better
to let her know how he felt, but putting words on a page
was a lot easier than dealing with real life and all its messy
emotions.

Sanchez came out of the kitchen behind him. "We
should go, jefe," the burly bandit said. "The men have
brought the horses up."

"I know, there's not much time." Armbruster tried to
look fierce as he glared at the women. "Come along. You
won't be harmed. You have my word on that."

Beth Macy said, "What good is the word of a man who's
thrown in with a bunch of bandits?"

Armbruster stiffened, drew himself up taller. "My word
is my bond," he declared. "And if you don't come with
me . . . you'll regret the consequences of that decision.
I can promise you *that*, too."

That was a vague enough threat to be believable, he

hoped, but the women still didn't budge, just sat there staring at him in a mixture of horror and anger.

Armbruster frowned in frustration and said, "All right, Guadalupe. We'll tie and gag them and carry them out. Fetch some of the men, so we can accomplish this quickly—"

"Wait," Cecilia said. "We'll come with you."

"We will?" Luella said.

Cecilia nodded. "Yes. We don't want them to hurt anyone, so it's best that we cooperate."

"Good!" Armbruster said. "I was hoping that you'd all be reasonable about this."

Sanchez leaned closer to him and said, "Señor Felipe, is it not likely that as soon as they are outside, they will all scream their heads off?"

"Oh," Armbruster said. "Oh, yes, I suppose that is possible." How could he be so foolish? He, who had successfully planned a number of daring raids? It must be being so close to Luella that was flustering him, he told himself. He went on, "I'm sorry, ladies, but we'll have to gag you, anyway—"

Cecilia opened her mouth to scream.

Sanchez barked an order in Spanish and leaped forward to clamp his hand over Cecilia's mouth before she could get the cry out. Several more members of the gang, who had been waiting in the hallway, rushed into the parlor and grabbed the other women, stifling their attempts to scream, as well. Armbruster hung on tight to the older woman and dug the gun barrel into her side. He slipped his other hand up and covered her mouth.

"Please, don't fight," he said in her ear. "It won't end well."

He felt her shoulders slump in despair.

For the next few minutes, the parlor in the doctor's house was a whirlwind of frantic activity punctuated by the rustle of clothing and grunts of effort. Since the men were gagging their prisoners, anyway, it just made sense to go ahead and tie them up, as well, so Armbruster issued that command. He didn't let go of the older woman until Sanchez had knotted a gag behind her head.

Then he stepped back, looked around, and said, "I'm sorry about this, ladies. I genuinely am. I maintain my pledge, though, that none of you will be harmed, and once we're well away from Silverhill, I'll see to it that you're untied, and we'll get rid of those gags. I want this to be a pleasant journey for you."

All five captives just glared daggers at him when he said that. He was a little hurt because they had no reason to think that he was lying to them, but he knew that soon they would see his intentions were good.

He motioned for his men to escort the prisoners out. Sanchez picked up the older woman, slung her over his shoulder like a bag of grain, and carried her that way. Since that was the easiest, the other men followed his lead, except for the one who started to pick up Luella. Armbruster moved in quickly to stop that before it could happen.

He took Luella's arm and said, "You'll come with me, my dear, and ride double with me, too. We have a great deal to talk about."

She looked at him like she wanted to kill him, but she didn't struggle as he led her out of the house. She must have realized by now that it wouldn't do any good. There were too many of the bandits.

Within minutes, they were mounted up and riding away slowly, so as not to make too much noise. But when they were about half a mile from the settlement's edge,

Armbruster heeled his horse into a trot, and the others trailed out behind him as they all picked up speed.

A million stars glittered in the deep black sky overhead. The wind, fragrant with the scent of sage, blew in Armbruster's face and pushed the brim of his sombrero up. He had a powerful horse underneath him, and his arm was around the most beautiful young woman he had ever seen, as he galloped south through the night, toward the border.

It was glorious!

CHAPTER 41

Armbruster kept his word. Once they were well away from Silverhill, the outlaws removed the gags from the prisoners. None of the young women wasted any breath screaming. It was the middle of the night, and they were miles from the settlement. Miles from anywhere, actually. No one was around to hear them.

For a while, Luella rode in silence in front of Philip Armbruster. She was still too stunned by the sudden turn of events, so soon after the attempt on Jean's life, and to be honest, too frightened by what had happened even to form a fully coherent thought.

But as time passed and the miles fell behind them, the anger smoldering inside Luella erupted into a full-fledged blaze. She tamped it down, though, knowing that she couldn't afford to lose control.

Instead, she thought about everything Armbruster had said, as well as the careful way he was holding her on the horse's back, in front of him, firmly enough that she was in no danger of falling—or jumping—off, yet gently enough that he wasn't hurting her. He seemed to be trying to be careful about *where* he held her, too, so she wouldn't think he was pawing her.

He really did believe that sneaking into Silverhill and stealing away with her and the other women was some sort of grand romantic gesture, she realized. He had filled his head with his own nonsense and had started to believe it.

She turned her head slightly and said, "Philip?"

"Yes, my dear?" he answered immediately, leaning his own head forward so that she felt his breath against her cheek.

"You don't *really* want to do this," Luella said. "I know what kind of man you are, and you can't honestly believe that kidnapping us is the right thing to do."

"I'm not kidnapping you!" he objected.

"What would you call it, then? You made us come with you against our will. You tied and gagged us. You've put us at the mercy of these bandits—"

"Wait just a minute," he interrupted her. "They're bandits, yes, but they're also decent men. Circumstances have forced them to take desperate measures to battle for their homes and families against the oppressive regime in Mexico City. All they really want to do is overthrow *el presidente* Díaz and restore honor and justice to their homeland."

Again, he sounded like he believed what he was saying. Perhaps some of the men who rode with him believed those same things. But from what Luella had seen of them, they all struck her as bandidos, more interested in loot than anything else.

Well, loot . . . and women . . .

"What you need to do," she said, "is take us back to Silverhill and turn us loose. We won't raise the alarm. We'll give you and your men a chance to get away. But you can't take us to your hideout, or wherever you have in mind, Philip. If you think we'll all come to love you and your men, you're wrong."

"I hate to argue, but you're the one who's wrong, Luella. Once you really get to know me, once your friends get to know my men, you'll understand. You're a great treasure, all of you. We'd never do anything to harm you."

She lost her temper for a second and blurted out, "This isn't *Ivanhoe*, blast it! You're not some knight in shining armor, and we're not cringing maidens waiting for you to carry us off! You need to put a stop to this right now!" Hoping perhaps to mollify him a little and make him more likely to be persuaded, she added, "If you actually do the right thing, it might make me change my opinion of you. I already know that you're a strong leader, or else these men wouldn't follow you. If you could demonstrate that you're a kind man, as well . . ."

"But to do that, we'd have to take you back?"

"Yes," she said. "You would."

He didn't say anything, and for a moment, she dared to hope that she had gotten through to him. It was open to question whether the bandits would obey him if he ordered them to turn around and ride back to Silverhill, but convincing Armbruster was a place to start, anyway.

Unfortunately, he said, "I'll have to think about this, but I promise you, I'll consider everything you've said, Luella. By morning, we'll be at the village where we've been staying. Once we get there, you and I can talk some more."

She bit back the groan that tried to well up in her throat. He was still determined to take the prisoners over the border into Mexico. She had a horrible feeling that once they were across the border, they would never return.

* * *

They rode all night, and by the time the eastern sky was turning pink and gold, all five captives had dozed off as they rode in front of their captors. Luella didn't rouse until she sensed the horse slowing its pace beneath her.

The group was going through a gap in a small ridge. Below, at the base of a long, gentle slope, was a shallow watercourse with a tiny stream twisting through the wide bed. The width of that bed testified as to what a raging monster the stream turned into once or twice a year, during flash floods.

On the other side of the creek lay the village, which consisted of a single street with adobe buildings scattered haphazardly along both sides. At the far end of the street was an old mission with a bell tower. Along the creek in both directions were the small fields that the villagers cultivated. Even with the creek to provide water, it was doubtful that anyone here did more than scratch a meager living out of the sandy, rocky soil.

"San Benito," Philip Armbruster said quietly. "Some of my men have families here."

"It looks very nice," Luella lied. Her throat was dry, and she had to force the words out. "When we get there . . . can we have something to eat and drink?"

"Of course. It won't be fancy, but it will be good, simple fare. And the coffee . . . the coffee the señoras brew here is magnificent."

They reached the creek, went down a path into the dusty creek bed, crossed it, with the horses' hooves splashing in the little creek, then climbed the far bank. The village was fifty yards away.

"That's strange," Armbruster murmured.

"What is?" Luella asked, interested in spite of her fatigue and discomfort.

"I know it's early, but usually there are a few people moving around by now. I thought someone would have seen us and come out to greet us. We've been benefactors to this village." Armbruster paused, then added, "There should at least be some dogs barking at us."

His puzzlement was contagious. Luella felt it, too, but as they rode along the deserted street between apparently empty buildings, the feeling turned into fear. Armbruster had said this was strange, but it was more than that. It was *wrong*. . . .

With no warning other than that eerie emptiness and silence, guns suddenly roared from both sides of the street, and men cried out in pain. Armbruster yanked his horse to a stop and hauled the animal around. Luella gasped when she saw some of the bandits toppling from their saddles as blood gushed from the wounds they had received.

"Watch out for the women!" a powerful voice bellowed from somewhere nearby. "Spare the women!"

Luella realized the shots had targeted the dozen or so men riding toward the back of the group, the ones who didn't have a prisoner riding double with them. About half of those bandits were down, some sprawled motionless, other thrashing around in their death throes. The ones who hadn't been blasted off their horses scattered wildly, spurring their mounts and clawing out guns to return the fire in a frenzied, confused volley.

"Take cover!" Armbruster shouted to the men nearest him. "Head for the stable!"

He whirled his horse again and jabbed his heels into

the animal's flanks to send it leaping ahead. Sanchez and the other men riding double with the prisoners pounded after him. Armbruster's grip was tight around Luella's waist now, holding her firmly against him. He guided the horse with his knees as he drew his gun and fired at something Luella couldn't see. The heavy reports slammed against her ears and made her wince.

The gunshots weren't any louder than her own pulse thundering inside her head, though. She and the other mail-order brides had been in dangerous situations before, but this mad dash through the village, with guns going off all around them and bullets whining through the air, was the most terrifying thing she had ever experienced.

Then, as Armbruster's horse approached a big adobe barn, the stable's double doors flew open, and men rushed out, brandishing long, heavy machetes. They wore crude uniforms consisting of loose gray trousers, shirts, and crossed bandoliers around their torsos. Gray steeple-crowned sombreros were on their heads. They swarmed among the bandits, chopping and stabbing with those terrible knives. Horses screamed and went down, with blood spurting from severed throats.

Men died, as well. Luella saw one man's head fly into the air as a machete lopped it off the shoulders where it had rested only a second earlier. It was an unspeakable horror that made her sick to her stomach.

The bandits weren't the only ones being killed, though. Some of the gray-uniformed men fell, driven off their feet by bullets as Armbruster's men blasted away from horseback. But the bandidos were outnumbered and continued to fall. Jean and Cecilia and Susan Hampshire screamed as soldiers jerked them out of the arms of dying bandits.

Luella looked for Beth, saw that she had gotten away

from the man with whom she had been riding, and that somewhere she had gotten her hands on a pistol. She leveled it and pulled the trigger, and one of the soldiers flew backward. As much as they hated and feared the bandits, these new attackers seemed even more ruthless and dangerous.

Armbruster's horse twisted and reared. He fought to keep the mount under control, while at the same time firing the revolver in his other hand. But with all that going on, he couldn't maintain his hold on Luella. She slipped out of his grasp and fell to the street, where she landed with such an impact that it knocked the breath out of her and left her lying there, stunned and unable to move. Horses capered around her, their steel-shod hooves narrowly missing her.

Beth darted in among the animals, bent and grasped Luella's arm, and hauled her to her feet. "Let's get out of here," Beth cried. Then Luella screamed when she saw one of the men loom up behind her friend, with a machete raised for a killing stroke.

The machete flashed down, but at the last second the man reversed it so that he struck Beth in the head with the handle instead of the blade. The blow knocked her forward. She slumped to the ground, senseless.

A few yards away, Armbruster's horse fell to the side, riddled with bullets. The former journalist kicked his feet out of the stirrups and jumped to safety, but as he rolled through the dust and came back up on his feet, one of the gray-clad men slammed a rifle butt into the back of his head. Armbruster went down again, out cold this time.

That left Luella standing alone in the middle of the rapidly dwindling melee. This ambush had been brutally successful. All the members of Armbruster's group were down, either dead, dying, or unconscious. Beth had been knocked out, as well, and Cecilia, Jean, and Susan struggled futilely against the soldiers who held them.

Luella knelt next to Beth and rolled her onto her back. Beth's eyes were closed, but her chest rose and fell in a regular rhythm. Luella pulled her up, cradling Beth's head in her lap.

The shooting had stopped, but silence had not returned to San Benito. Now the early morning air was filled with groans and soft curses in Spanish from wounded men, as well as the pitiful whimpers of dying horses. Luella heard all that but kept her eyes on Beth's face and didn't look up until she heard footsteps approaching her.

She raised her head. The man was nothing but a silhouette at first against the dawn sky behind him, but then he walked past the two women in the middle of the now bloody street and turned so that the rosy light fell on his face. It was a cruel face, lean and hard, all flat planes broken by a hawk-like nose, a thin-lipped mouth topped by an equally thin line of mustache, and black eyes that glittered with menace, even as the mouth twisted in a ghastly semblance of a smile. He wore the same crude uniform as the other men, except that he didn't have crossed bandoliers around his chest and a crimson sash was tied around his waist.

"*Buenos días, señorita,*" he said, then continued in English. "My name is *Capitán* Norberto Rivera, and you are all my guests."

CHAPTER 42

Scratch hunkered next to a pile of horse droppings, picked up a piece of it, and rubbed it between his fingers. As he wiped his hand in the sandy dirt to clean it, he looked up at Bo and said, "I reckon they're not more than an hour ahead of us. We've done a good job of closin' in on 'em."

Bo turned his head to look at the group of riders not far away and said, "We've worn out men and horses, too. But I haven't heard anybody complaining about it or asking us to stop and rest for a while."

Scratch straightened from his study of the droppings. "That's a good thing," he said, "because I ain't in any mood to slow down."

"We'd better do that, though," Bo said as he stood there holding the reins of his horse and Scratch's mount. "We can put up with being tired, but it won't do those ladies any good if we ride these horses into the ground."

Scratch frowned but didn't argue. He knew his old friend was right.

"We're still on the trail, aren't we?" Hugh Craddock called from horseback.

"Yeah," Bo replied, "but we're going to stop here for a while and let the horses rest."

"We can't stop," Monte Jackson objected. "We have to keep going."

"I don't want Cecilia in the hands of those savages for one second longer than necessary," Roscoe Sherman rumbled. "Of course, the same is true for the other ladies."

Craddock, Monte, and Roscoe had insisted on coming along with the posse, which numbered eighteen men besides them, some of whom had been part of the group that had tracked down the stagecoach robbers. With Cecilia and Beth among the captives, it was no surprise that Roscoe and Monte were here. And when Craddock had heard about Susan Hampshire being kidnapped, he wasn't going to be denied his place in the posse, either. He had developed feelings for her, despite his earlier behavior toward her, which he now regretted.

"We won't stop for long," Bo assured them. "But the horses need a little rest and water, and I reckon all of us could do with that, too."

With some grumbling but a few sighs of relief, as well, the men swung down from their saddles. They poured water from their canteens into their hats and let the horses drink before they swigged some of the lukewarm water themselves.

The previous night, when Bo and Scratch had returned to Dr. Arliss Chapman's house with the buggy to take Jean to the hotel, they had known immediately that something was very wrong. The house was empty, and there were signs of a struggle in the parlor, where they had left the women—an overturned chair, a table shoved out of place, throw rugs crumpled on the floor. When they hurriedly searched the house, they discovered the rear door standing wide open. Scratch carried a lamp outside, where they found the tracks of numerous horses in back of the house. Some of the prints were deep enough to indicate that the animals probably were carrying double.

The only explanation they could come up with was that the women had been kidnapped, and when they discovered that the tracks led south toward Mexico, that seemed to confirm it.

The Texans didn't waste any time spreading the word, and they didn't even have to put out the call for a posse. Men began showing up at the marshal's office right away, packing iron and leading horses. Monte Jackson, who hadn't fully recovered from the wound he'd received in the stagecoach robbery, was well enough that Bo knew it would be a waste of time trying to convince him to stay behind. Roscoe Sherman, who had been spending more and more time in Silverhill as his relationship with Cecilia grew stronger, was on hand, too. And then Hugh Craddock showed up, insisting that he was going to accompany the posse, as well. Bo and Scratch weren't going to turn down that offer, despite the trouble they'd had with him in the past, since Craddock was a fellow Texan and a good fighting man.

The group they were following was large enough that they didn't have any problem picking up the trail and sticking with it. Almost as straight as an arrow, the tracks led toward the border. Evidently, the kidnappers intended to seek refuge in Mexico.

"Who do you reckon done it?" Scratch asked while they were riding.

"I've been pondering that very question," Bo replied. "The only thing I can think of is that some of Mendoza's men got away after that last ruckus we had with them. We never did find the body of that Armbruster fella, either."

"That four-eyed little weasel from New York? You don't think he'd be behind something like this, do you, Bo?"

"I don't know what to think. I suppose it could be some other group of bandidos, but if that is true, why didn't they try to rob the bank or any of the stores? Why just grab those five ladies and ride off with them?" Bo rubbed his chin as he frowned in thought. "It's almost like they came here just to take the ladies prisoner."

"Maybe that's a good thing," Scratch said. "Maybe it means they won't hurt 'em."

"We can sure hope," Bo said.

Now, as the men and horses rested, Roscoe Sherman came over to Bo and Scratch and asked, "Have we crossed the border into Mexico yet?"

"I ain't sure, but there's a good chance of it," Scratch responded. "Why? Does it make a difference to you which country we're in, Roscoe?"

The massive shoulders rose and fell. "No. I was just curious, that's all."

Hugh Craddock had walked up in time to hear the conversation. He said, "I don't give a hang about borders. We're getting those ladies back if we have to chase them all the way to South America."

"Even to Tierra del Fuego," Roscoe muttered.

Craddock nodded emphatically. "I don't know where that is, but I'll go that far if I have to."

Bo knew that the region Roscoe had referred to was at the very southern tip of South America, but he also knew that the chase wouldn't last anywhere near that long. They were close enough behind the kidnappers that they ought to catch up before the day was over. Possibly even sooner if their quarry stopped somewhere. Bo thought there was a chance they had headed for one of the villages scattered through this border country. Bandits usually had a place they could hole up where there was food and drink and women.

Of course, they had women *with* them now—but Bo didn't want to think too much about that.

When he and Scratch agreed that enough time had passed, they told the other men to mount up. They started following the tracks south again, moving at a fairly fast pace, but not so fast that they risked losing the trail.

This was empty country through which they traveled. Long semiarid stretches broken up by small bands of rolling hills, sandstone spires, and rocky ridges. They were approaching one of those ridges when Bo spotted a thin gray thread of almost invisible smoke climbing into the sky on the other side.

He lifted a hand in a signal to stop and reined in at the same moment Scratch did likewise.

"You see it, too, eh?" the silver-haired Texan asked.

"That's smoke from a chimney," Bo said. "Must be one of those villages we expected to find. I suppose it could be some lone farmer's jacal, but most of them don't have chimneys."

"One way to find out." Scratch pointed at a gap in the ridge ahead of them. "You and me can go up yonder and take a look. The rest of the fellas ought to stay here until we know what we're dealin' with."

Bo nodded in agreement.

Scratch passed along the orders. Not surprisingly, Roscoe, Monte, and Craddock objected and wanted to accompany Bo and Scratch on the scouting mission.

"It's possible that the fellas we're after are keepin' an

eye on that gap," Scratch said. "If a whole bunch of us go crowdin' in there, they're liable to spot us. Better if Bo and me just sorta Injun our way up yonder. We've done things like that before, a heap of times."

The three men grudgingly agreed. Bo and Scratch left their horses with the other men and went ahead on foot, taking their Winchesters with them. They didn't expect to need the rifles, but it was always better to be ready for trouble.

As they approached the gap, they split up, angling wide to each side of the opening. Then they edged in until they could take off their hats and risk a look.

The village they expected to see was about half a mile away, on the other side of a wide creek bed, which probably had only a small trickle of water in it at this time of year, especially as dry as the weather had been recently. The place looked like any number of other small Mexican villages the Texans had visited. There was nothing special about it.

Other than the bodies lying sprawled in the street, between the lines of adobe buildings.

"What in the Sam Hill!" Scratch exclaimed quietly. He called across the gap to Bo, "Looks like there's been a massacre down there."

Bo had brought a spyglass with him, having taken it out of his saddlebags and stuck it in his pocket before he and Scratch left the others. He pulled it out now, extended it, and peered through the glass, being careful not to let the sun reflect off the lens.

"They look to me like bandits," he reported after a moment. "I can tell by the way they're dressed that they're not the farmers who live here."

"You think it's the bunch that carried off the girls?"

"Might be," Bo said. As he moved the field of view around, he went on, "I don't understand—"

"What is it?" Scratch asked when Bo stopped short.

Bo's eye narrowed. He had just spotted a man lounging inside the open double doors of what looked like a stable. He recognized the uniform and sombrero the man wore.

"Rurales," he said. "I see one in the stable." He shifted the glass. "And there's another one ambling from one building to another. Doesn't look like he's in a hurry or worried about anything." Bo watched the man for a moment. "He's headed for the mission. I think maybe he's the captain. He's got a sash around his waist, and he's wearing a gunbelt, too. The hombre in the barn is just carrying a rifle."

"Rurales," Scratch repeated, practically spitting the word. "As if we didn't have enough trouble."

"Yeah," Bo said as he continued looking around the village through the telescope.

He and Scratch had run into the Mexican "rural police" several times during their long, adventurous career as drifters. Some of the Rurales were honest and tried to do the job they were supposed to, keeping the people who lived here in these northern regions of Mexico safe from the depredations of bandits and Indians.

Most of them, however, were as crooked as a dog's hind leg and, if anything, were worse than the threats they were supposed to police. From the looks of the slaughter that had taken place here, there was a good chance this bunch fell into that category.

"You see any of the villagers?" Scratch asked.

"Nope. They could all be hiding in their homes."

"Yeah, and those varmints could've murdered 'em

all, too, just to make it easier for them to ambush those bandidos."

Bo studied the village for a few minutes longer. His jaw tightened when he saw the bodies of several dogs lying here and there. He had no doubt that the Rurales had gunned them down wantonly, for sport if nothing else. That was the sort of cruel devils they were.

Bo moved the glass back to the mission, at the far end of the settlement. The man he had taken to be the commander of this troop was no longer in sight, but as Bo watched, the heavy wooden entrance door swung open and another Rurale stepped out. Bo tried to look past the man into the shadowy interior. He glimpsed several splashes of bright color before the door closed behind the man who was leaving.

"I think the girls are in the mission," he told Scratch. "I saw something that might have been their dresses. I might be mistaken, though."

"I doubt it," Scratch said. "I was already thinking that was the most likely place for the Rurales to be holdin' 'em. It's the biggest place in town, and that's where I'd have my headquarters if I was the boss of that bunch."

Bo nodded slowly. "I suspect you're right. But we're going to have to find out, and we can't do it right away. It's too open all around the village. They're bound to have guards posted. They'll spot us if we try to slip up on them, even if we're careful."

Scratch muttered a curse under his breath. "You mean we're gonna have to wait until after dark?"

"I'm afraid so. We can take some of the men and make it down to that creek bed—there's enough cover over here for us for that—but we'll have to wait there until night falls to make it the rest of the way."

"I can think of some fellas who ain't gonna like that."

"So can I," Bo said, "but they're just going to have to put up with it. Once it's dark, you and I and maybe a couple of others can try to reach that mission and take care of the Rurales who are guarding the prisoners. Then the rest of our group can attack, including the ones we'll leave up here with the horses."

"Sounds like a good plan," Scratch agreed. "When they do that, we can leave the fellas we take with us to watch over the gals while you and me hit the Rurales from behind."

Bo smiled. "That's just what I was thinking."

"But it's gonna be a long wait . . . especially for those ladies. I hope they ain't bein' mistreated."

"So do I," Bo said. "If they are, those blasted Rurales are going to be sorry they were ever born."

CHAPTER 43

Philip Armbruster's head ached abominably from the blow that had knocked him out, but at least he was still alive. That was more than he could say for any of his other men, except Guadalupe Sanchez, who had been wounded several times but was still breathing as he lay stretched out and unconscious on one of the pews in the mission. Armbruster sat at the end of the same pew.

The bodies of the other men in the band had been left in the street, in the hot sun, and were out there bloating, blackened by the thousands of flies swarming on them. Eventually, the buzzards that had to be circling overhead by now might grow bold enough to come down and start picking at them.

In a way, Armbruster wished that he had died with his men. That would have been the just and honorable thing to do. But it would have left the women with no one to help them—not that there was much of anything he could do right now. Four of Captain Norberto Rivera's men were guarding the prisoners, and Rivera had told them that if either of the two surviving bandits tried anything, to go ahead and kill them. He wanted the women alive, of course, but Armbruster and Sanchez meant nothing. Armbruster was surprised Rivera hadn't just killed them out of hand.

That was probably because of the sadistic streak Rivera possessed. When the prisoners were brought in here, Rivera had boasted to the women about how he had been on the trail of the bandidos for weeks.

"There was never any doubt that sooner or later I would catch them and deal with them like the vermin they are," the captain had bragged. He had spat in the direction of Armbruster and Sanchez.

The white-haired little priest, Friar Robusto, had scurried up to Rivera and said, "Please, *Capitán*, do not show such disrespect in the house of the Lord."

For a second, Rivera had drawn back his hand and had looked like he was about to strike the priest, but then he'd lowered his arm and said, "Have a care, Padre. I am in command here. I give the orders."

"Only one is truly in command of our lives—" Friar Robusto stopped short. Rivera probably wouldn't hurt him, because of the problems it might cause with his men, some of whom could be religious, despite being Rurale scum. But the officer *could* take out his anger on the prisoners, and Friar Robusto didn't want that.

That was what Armbruster believed went through the little priest's mind at that moment. He couldn't be sure. But the priest withdrew to the front of the sanctuary and stood there uncomfortably, frowning and muttering. Praying, perhaps.

If Armbruster were a praying man, that was what he would be doing at this moment.

Rivera barked some low-voiced orders at one of the

guards. The man hurried out of the mission, on whatever errand Rivera had given him. The captain turned toward the prisoners, who all sat together on a pew.

"You," he said as he pointed at Luella. "Come here."

Armbruster stiffened in alarm. He didn't want Rivera bothering any of the ladies, especially Luella. Without thinking about it, he started to stand up.

One of the Rurale guards standing nearby moved his rifle so that the muzzle stared right at Armbruster. In Spanish, the man told him to sit down. For a second, Armbruster considered disregarding the order, but then he saw the anticipation in the guard's eyes. The man wanted to blow a hole in him.

No need to give him an excuse to do that, Armbruster decided. Not yet, anyway.

He settled back onto the pew.

Luella didn't answer Rivera's summons. She lifted her chin defiantly and said, "What do you want now? Haven't you caused enough harm already? Did you murder everyone in this village?"

"No one who lives here was murdered," Rivera snapped. He shrugged. "A few spoke up against us and had to be killed, but that is a matter of enforcing the law, not murder. Most are huddled in their pathetic little huts. They will not be harmed as long as they continue to cooperate." Rivera hooked his thumbs in his gunbelt and swaggered closer to the prisoners. "As for what I want . . . I want to speak with you, señorita."

"I couldn't possibly be interested in anything you have to say."

"We shall see about that." Rivera turned and crooked a

finger at Friar Robusto. The priest hesitated but came over to him with obvious reluctance.

Rivera pointed at Luella again and said, "I like this one. She is beautiful, and she has spirit. She will be my wife, and you will perform the ceremony, Padre."

That brought gasps of surprise and outrage from not only Luella but the other women, as well. Armbruster let out a curse, something he hardly ever did.

Friar Robusto shook his head. "I cannot join two people in holy wedlock if one of them objects, as I suspect the young señorita does."

"I most certainly do object!" Luella said as her anger forced her to her feet. "I would never marry you!"

"I believe you will," Rivera said, clearly undisturbed by her outburst. He drew the pistol from the holster on his hip.

"Go ahead and shoot me!" Luella challenged him. "I prefer a bullet to you!"

Rivera shook his head. "No, I will not shoot you, señorita. But I will walk over there and shoot that wounded man in the head." He nodded toward Sanchez. "Then, if you still refuse, I will shoot the gringo. If neither of *them* matter to you . . . well, you have four friends there, do you not? I feel certain that by the time I reach the last of them, you will have changed your mind. Too late for the others, though."

Luella looked over at Armbruster. He shook his head and said, "Don't worry about me, Miss Tolman. I wouldn't want to live with myself if I knew that a threat to me forced you to give in to this monster's demands."

Rivera swung the pistol toward him and said, "If you really want to go first, gringo . . ."

In that moment, Armbruster believed he was about to die. He tensed his muscles, ready to throw himself at the guard and try to wrestle the man's rifle away from him. He wasn't going to just sit there and allow Rivera to execute him. He would rather leave this world on his feet, fighting—something the meek little man he had once been never would have considered.

But Luella cried out, "Stop!" then said in a strained voice, "Don't kill him, Captain. I . . . I will consider your . . . proposal."

Rivera shook his head. "It is not a proposal. It is me telling you what you will do." He glanced at the priest. "And you, Padre."

"N-no," Friar Robusto answered in a quaver, which was a little stronger when he added, "I will not."

"Then my men will go through the village and kill every third man they find. Continue to be stubborn, and three such sweeps will wipe out every man in San Benito. After that, the women and children."

Luella sneered at him and said, "Why not just take me, if that's what you want? It's not like anybody can stop you. Why do you insist that there has to be a wedding?"

Rivera pressed his free hand to his chest. "You think me a dishonorable, immoral man? I am many things, señorita, and have done things that would make a normal man blanch and call on *el Señor Dios* for aid and comfort, but I would not force a respectable woman to submit to me against her will."

She stared at him for a moment before she said, "I think you actually believe that."

"*Sí*, of course I do."

She drew in a long breath and let it out in a sigh. Armbruster realized what she was about to do and cried, "Luella, no!"

Rivera snapped at the guard, "If he opens his mouth again, shoot him."

"It's all right, Philip," she said, and even under these horrible circumstances, a little shiver of pleasure went through him at hearing her say his name. "I refuse to be responsible for any harm coming to you or anyone else." She looked at Rivera. "I will marry you."

He laughed and said, "Of course you will. Was there ever any doubt?" He looked at the priest. "And you, Padre, will do your part?"

Friar Robusto sighed even more dispiritedly than Luella. "You leave me no choice, if I am to protect those of my flock."

"That's right, Padre."

"But *el Señor Dios* will know that this union is false! And may He strike me dead for trying to sanctify such an unholy match!"

"If He does not strike you dead, I will, should you fail to cooperate," Rivera said with a smirk. He holstered his pistol and then held out that hand to Luella. "Come. Soon you will be my wife. Then there will be a feast, if such a thing is even possible in a squalid little village such as this, and I will find the finest house for us to spend our wedding night together."

"What about my friends?" Luella asked.

"They will not be harmed," Rivera said, but everyone inside the church heard the insincerity in his voice. Sooner or later, the other prisoners would be turned over to the Rurales. That might well be Luella's fate, too, once Rivera grew tired of her.

And as for him and Sanchez, Armbruster thought, a bullet in the head waited for each of them . . . if they were lucky. Rivera might decide to get more creative than that, though. After all, he had to keep his men's morale up, and what better way to do that than by torturing a gringo? A lot of the Rurales had some Yaqui Indian blood running in their veins, and torturing their enemies was considered great sport by the Yaquis.

Rivera clapped his hands, rubbed them together, and grinned. "Come! There is a wedding to plan."

Scratch had been right, all the way around. Monte Jackson, Roscoe Roscoe, and Hugh Craddock weren't happy about being told they had to wait until nightfall to rescue the prisoners. Neither were the other members of the posse, but they didn't have the same emotional stake in the matter as those three. Monte, Roscoe, and Craddock were mollified a little when Bo and Scratch agreed to take them along on the foray into the village.

And it was a mighty long day for all concerned, as Scratch had also predicted. More than half the posse withdrew about a mile to a clump of boulders so they would not only be out of sight but also would have a little bit of shade in the heat of the day.

They took the horses belonging to Bo, Scratch, Monte, Roscoe, and Craddock with them. Those five went on foot to the gap in the ridge, where Bo and Scratch filled in the other three men on what they had seen and deduced.

"We're going down there," Bo said as he pointed to the mostly empty creek bed. "There are enough rocks and brush on this slope to give us some cover while we work our way down. You'll need to be mighty careful, though, especially you, Roscoe."

"Because I'm so big?" the miner asked.

"Ain't no way around it," Scratch said. "You're a mite noticeable."

"I understand," Roscoe said, nodding. "I'll stay low and out of sight as much as I can."

"Once we get there," Bo went on, "the banks of that creek bed are high enough to keep us from being seen from the village. As long as none of the Rurales wander out there to the creek, we'll be all right."

"What if one of them does?" Craddock asked.

"Then we'll deal with him," Scratch said. "Just have to be quiet about it."

The others nodded in understanding.

Bo said, "We're pretty sure the prisoners are being held in the old mission at the other end of town. Once it's dark enough, we'll skirt around, get there, and take a look to be certain, then jump the guards and put them out of action. By that time, the rest of the posse will be up here at the gap, mounted and waiting for the signal to gallop in there and take the fight to the Rurales. You three will stay in the mission and keep it and the ladies secure while Scratch and I go lend a hand to the other boys."

"The three of us are younger," Craddock said. "We ought to get in on the fight and leave you two with the prisoners."

"No, we'll do it the way Bo said," Scratch told him. "That ain't open for negotiation."

Craddock muttered a little more but didn't persist in his argument. Led by Bo and Scratch, the men began their stealthy descent of the ridge. Silently, Bo pointed out the best routes for them to follow that would take advantage of the natural cover. They might still be noticed if one of the Rurales happened to look too closely up here, but Bo believed the chances of that were slim.

He listened for shouts of alarm but didn't hear any. One by one, they reached the mostly dry creek bed, slid down the bank into it, and then trotted across the sandy, grass-tufted bottom to the other side. When they were all together again, they sat under a slight overhang, which provided a small amount of shade, and settled in for the long wait. Under the circumstances, no one dared to talk, so there was nothing to do but sit and doze and listen for the sounds of anyone approaching their position.

Finally, the sun dropped toward the western horizon, and once it actually fell below the curve of the earth, night closed in with the abruptness that was common in this part of the world. Bo whispered, "Come on," and led the others to a spot where they could climb out without much trouble.

From there they trotted quietly across the sandy ground, circling well around the village. Most of the buildings were dark, but the church at the far end of the street was brightly lit. The door was open, so that a yellow glow spilled out into the night.

The five men reached the old mission and pressed their backs to the thick adobe wall on one side. A window was nearby. Bo edged toward it, took his hat off, and leaned over to peer through the glass.

He wasn't expecting the sight that met his eyes. Some of the pews had been pushed back to make room for a table that had been brought in from somewhere. The table had platters of food and jugs of wine on it. This wasn't a sumptuous feast, because there wasn't enough food in the village for that, but even so, enough was spread out to feed the dozen or so Rurales seated at the table.

The men weren't alone. The five women were there, too, each of them seated between Rurales, as if they were guests, not prisoners, and the captain sat at the middle of the table, in a position of honor, with Luella beside him. He poured wine from a jug into a glass and got to his feet, then lifted the glass toward Luella, as if proposing a toast.

Which, as it turned out, was exactly what he was doing. With a big grin on his face, he spoke in a loud, ringing voice as he said, "To my beautiful bride!"

CHAPTER 44

That was a shock to Bo, but he tried to shove his surprise aside and keep his brain working. Judging by the look on Luella's face, she hadn't married the officer willingly. The other women didn't appear to be the least bit happy about the situation, either.

Philip Armbruster sat on one of the pews that had been shoved back, along with a burly man, who was probably a member of the same gang of bandidos. Bo had speculated earlier that the former journalist might still be alive, and there he was, in the flesh. He and his wounded companion were prisoners, though, with a rifle-toting Rurale standing guard over them.

Bo pulled back from the window and rejoined the others. Whispering, he told them, "We're going to have to change our plan." He explained what he had seen and went on, "There are too many of them in there for us to just charge in and free the prisoners. We need to lure some of the Rurales out of the church."

Scratch said, "They're bound to have their horses in that stable up the street. We didn't see 'em anywhere else. How about if a couple of us get in there, take care of the guards, and then stampede the horses? With the door of the church open like it is, those varmints are bound to hear the commotion, and most of 'em will run out to see what's goin' on."

"Then we can deal with whoever's left," Bo said, nodding slowly. "Sounds like it ought to work. So we'll need to split up again. Craddock, you'll come with me to the stable."

He wanted Scratch to be here to take charge of the effort to free the prisoners.

"I'd rather stay here, where I can help Susan," Craddock said.

"You'll be helping her by doing what I told you," Bo snapped. "Come on." To Scratch, he added, "Give us a few minutes. You'll know when to make your move."

"Darned straight I will," the silver-haired Texan said.

Craddock didn't put up any more argument as he slipped away into the shadows with Bo. They made their way quietly toward the back of the stable.

When they got there, though, Craddock whispered, "I've changed my mind, Creel. If we all get out of this alive, I'm not going to just step aside and let you have Susan. I'm going to tell her I was wrong, throw myself on her mercy, and try to win her back."

"You do that," Bo said, a lot more concerned at the moment with rescuing the prisoners rather than with matters of the heart. In fact, his heart was set on ventilating a few of those blasted Rurales. They were brutal, ruthless killers, not deserving of any mercy.

Bo drew his Colt and stood beside the small door in the stable's rear wall. He reached over and scratched on the wood with the gun barrel. The sound was persistent enough to draw the attention of any guard standing inside the building, near the door.

After a minute or so, somebody took the bait. The door swung open, and a Rurale stepped halfway out, with his rifle held ready. He turned his head from side to side as he peered around curiously.

He wasn't prepared for the speed with which Bo struck. Bo clamped his left hand around the man's throat and jerked him all the way through the door, then used the Colt's barrel to sweep his sombrero from his head. Bo reversed the gun as he lifted it. The butt crunched down on the Rurale's skull. He went limp, and Bo let him slump to the ground.

The whole thing hadn't taken more than two or three heartbeats.

"I thought we wanted to raise a racket," Craddock whispered.

"Not until we know what we're dealing with inside," Bo told him.

They slipped into the stable, where a small candle burned in a holder sitting on a barrel near the open double doors at the entrance. Two more Rurales were sitting on crates, rolling dice on another crate, which served them as a table.

One of those men suddenly stared at the candle flame, which had begun bending toward the rear of the stable because the back door was open. The man grabbed his rifle, which was leaning on the wall next to him, and leaped to his feet.

Bo shot him in the chest just as the Rurale's eyes started to widen in surprise. The bullet knocked him into the doorway. Almost faster than the eye could follow, Bo swung the Colt to the left and triggered a second shot. This one caught the other Rurale in the throat as he started to his feet. He went over backward, with his arms windmilling, as blood fountained from the wound.

Bo dashed to the nearest stall and yanked open the gate. The horse inside, spooked by the shots, lunged out and started toward the entrance. Bo yelled, "Hyaah! Hyaaah!" to keep it going as he opened another stall.

On the other side of the center aisle, Craddock was turning those horses loose, as well. They charged out of the stalls and stampeded after the others. Bo fired a shot into the ceiling to stir the animals up even more. Panic stricken, they bolted out of the stable, trampling the body of the Rurale who had fallen at the entrance, and ran wildly up the street.

Guns in hand, Bo and Craddock followed the horses out of the stable. Someone shouted angrily to Bo's right. He wheeled in that direction and saw two Rurales running toward him. The men stopped to bring their rifles to their shoulders and try to draw a bead on him, but Bo didn't give them a chance. He fired twice before either of the Rurales could get a shot off. The first slug plowed deep into the guts of the man on the left, while the second punched a red-rimmed hole in the other man's forehead and then exploded out the back of his skull in a grisly spray of blood, bone, and brain matter.

That left Bo with only one round in the Colt. He ducked into the shadows next to a building and dumped the empties, then thumbed fresh cartridges into the cylinder. A few yards away, Hugh Craddock knelt behind a water trough and fired at several Rurales who had appeared on the other side of the street.

Bo joined in that exchange of shots for a moment, then glanced toward the old mission at the far end of the street.

Just as he had hoped, uniformed men were pouring out of the old adobe structure and hurrying in this direction.

That meant it was time for Scratch, Monte, and Roscoe to make their move.

Scratch had already located the rear door into the mission. When he heard the shots coming from the stable, he knew Bo and Craddock had started the ball. He motioned toward the door and said quietly to Roscoe, "It's your deal, amigo."

"Stand back," Roscoe said. Then he launched himself against the door, lowering his shoulder as he drove powerfully into it.

Wood splintered and cracked, and the door flew open. Roscoe stumbled a little going through the opening he had made, but he caught his balance quickly. Scratch and Monte were right behind him.

Scratch had a Remington in each fist, and the long-barreled guns spoke in unison, spitting flame and death as he scythed bullets through a trio of Rurales taken by surprise.

Monte had brought his coach gun with him. It thundered and belched fire and flung another Rurale backward against a wall. The man hung there for a second, eyes wide and staring, in shock and pain, then slid down to a sitting position, leaving a wide bloody smear on the adobe.

Roscoe didn't bother with a gun. He grabbed two men by the neck and smashed their heads together, leaving their skulls so misshapen that there was no doubt the impact was fatal.

As far as Scratch could see, that accounted for all the Rurales who'd remained inside the mission. The captain and the other men had hurried out to see what all the shooting was about.

The five young women were still at the table, looking shocked and frightened but unharmed. Scratch wanted to make sure of that, so as the echoes of gun thunder died away, he told Monte and Roscoe, "Go check on the ladies. Make sure none of 'em are hurt."

While they were doing that, Scratch hurried toward the pew where Philip Armbruster and the burly bandit sat. Both men were tied hand and foot, Scratch saw, and the Mexican's clothes were bloodstained in several places from wounds he had suffered. In his shape, he didn't look like he could be any danger to anybody.

"Morton!" Armbruster exclaimed, showing that he remembered Scratch, too. "Cut me loose!"

"After what you done, stealin' those ladies from Silverhill, why in blazes would I do that?" Scratch asked.

"Because I have a score to settle with that Captain Rivera! He's a mad dog! He needs to be put down!"

"Some folks might say the same about you, mister."

Armbruster took a deep breath. "I give you my word I'll surrender. I'll go back to Silverhill with you, and you can do whatever you want with me. Just let me go after Rivera!"

Something about the man's words sounded honest to Scratch. He knew what it was like to have such a powerful hate for a fella that it overrode everything else. Seemed like Armbruster couldn't have known Rivera long enough to cultivate such a hate—but Scratch didn't know what all had happened here today.

Acting on impulse, Scratch pouched his left-hand iron and drew his knife from its sheath. The razor-sharp blade made short work of the ropes around Armbruster's wrists and ankles.

"If this is some sort of trick, you'll be mighty sorry," he warned the former journalist.

"No trick," Armbruster promised. As he stood up shakily and rubbed feeling back into his hands, he glanced toward the women and asked, "Is Luella all right?"

"Appeared to be. Don't worry. We'll take care of the ladies." Armbruster nodded, picked up a rifle that a dead Rurale had dropped, and ran out of the mission, toward the sounds of battle.

Bo and Craddock had the element of surprise on their side, but that wasn't enough to offset the overwhelming odds against them. Craddock had pulled back to join Bo in the alley, and they used the corners of the buildings on both sides for cover as they tried to hold off the attacks coming from both right and left. They wouldn't be able to stop the Rurales for much longer, Bo knew, so if the rest of the posse didn't get here in a hurry, it might be too late.

Then, over the ragged blasts of gunfire, he heard a steadier sound—hoofbeats pounding along the street as riders galloped into the village. More shots rang out. Bo risked a look and saw that the men from Silverhill were charging into the fight. Colt flame stabbed through the darkness. Some of the Rurales who had been throwing lead at the alley toppled off their feet as bullets ripped through them. Others tossed their rifles aside, thrust their arms high in the air, and cried out, begging for mercy.

The battle wasn't over, but the tide definitely had turned!

As Armbruster left the old mission and trotted along the street, he checked the rifle he had picked up to make sure it was loaded. He would have preferred a Winchester instead of this single-shot weapon, but when he pulled back the bolt, he saw there was a cartridge in the chamber. He pushed it closed again.

He would just have to make that one shot count, he told himself.

He was looking for Captain Norberto Rivera and didn't really care about the other men. Up ahead, shots crisscrossed the street, and the night was bright with spurts of muzzle flame. At the northern end of the settlement, riders suddenly appeared to join the fight. The rest of the posse from Silverhill, he guessed. If Morton was here, so was Creel, and those Texans would have brought help with them.

None of that mattered. He just wanted a showdown with Rivera.

The Rurale captain hadn't actually molested Luella, but only because he hadn't gotten around to it yet. He had been too busy showing off with the wedding and then the so-called feast afterward. The ceremony had taken place, though, and that was enough. Rivera was married to Luella.

And if Armbruster had his way, very soon now she would be a widow. . . .

He spotted the officer's colorful sash first. Rivera stood in front of a building, watching the battle going on up by the stable. He wasn't getting in on the fighting himself, which told Armbruster that for all his bullying and blustering, Rivera was actually a coward. That came as no surprise.

Armbruster lifted a hand and settled his spectacles more firmly on his nose. One lens was cracked slightly, but he couldn't do anything about that except hope that it wouldn't throw off his aim. He took a deep breath and held the rifle ready without actually lifting it to his shoulder.

Then he called, "Rivera!"

The Rurale captain spun around. Rivera's eyes widened when he saw Armbruster. He clawed at the revolver on his hip. Coward he might be, but he was smart enough to know that he had no choice except to fight.

He should have just gone ahead and shot Rivera in the back, Armbruster realized as the man's gun came up with astonishing speed. There wouldn't have been anything grand, glorious, or romantic about that, but it would have been highly practical.

As it was, Rivera got off the first shot, and as Armbruster pressed the rifle's butt against his shoulder, he felt the shock of the bullet striking him. He stayed on his feet, settled the rifle's sights on Rivera's chest, and pulled the trigger. The rifle kicked hard against his shoulder, and Rivera took a step backward as the slug smashed all the way through him. The gun in his hand sagged as he looked down at the blood welling from the hole in his chest.

Then he dropped the gun and dropped straight down into a lifeless heap.

Armbruster swayed but managed to use the now-empty rifle as a crutch and prop himself up. He hobbled over to Rivera, looked down into the glassy eyes to assure himself that the Rurale captain actually was dead, and then turned to start back toward the mission. He wanted to see for himself that Luella was all right.

He made it ten halting steps before he passed out and fell on his face.

CHAPTER 45

The residents of San Benito were so grateful to the men from north of the border for liberating them from the iron fist of the Rurales that they would have been happy to have the posse stay in the village for a while. But Bo and Scratch knew they needed to get back to Silverhill, and the ladies were all anxious to return to what they now considered their home.

So the next morning, everyone mounted up for the ride back—including the prisoner. Philip Armbruster's left shoulder was heavily bandaged, and that arm rested in a sling. He was pale, but insisted he was well enough to travel.

"I gave you my word," he had told Bo and Scratch earlier that morning. "I intend to face justice for my crimes, just as I promised. And when I'm done with that . . . well, my dearest hope is that Miss Tolman might consent to have me pay her a visit."

"You mean you expect that gal to wait for you, even after you kidnapped her?" Scratch had asked.

"I expect nothing. I only hope."

"Well, you hang on to that, son," Bo said. "I figure you'll spend only a few years behind bars. You were in on some robberies, but if you're telling the truth, you didn't kill anybody and weren't responsible for any killings."

"That is indeed the truth," Armbruster said. "But I'll have my day in court and face whatever is coming to me." He had paused then, before adding, "And I really do appreciate the mercy you're showing to Guadalupe."

"When you get right down to it," Scratch said, "we ain't got a bit of jurisdiction down here, so we sure ain't got the right to haul Sanchez back across the border. Besides, he's so shot up, he's gonna be unfit to travel for a long spell, and he claims since he's the only one left outta Mendoza's old band, he's gonna settle down here and try farmin'." Scratch shrugged. "I don't suppose it'll hurt anything to give him that chance."

"Speaking of jurisdiction," Bo said, "I suspect the Mexican authorities will regard *us* as criminals for coming down here and ventilating all those Rurales, so we'd best be getting back across the border."

With that in mind, the group set out for Silverhill, and neither Bo nor Scratch looked back. If they didn't return to Mexico for a long time—or ever—it would suit both of them just fine.

Three months later . . .

With everything else that had been going on during that wild time in Silverhill, no one had paid much attention to the fact that construction on the railroad spur line came closer with every passing day.

By now the station had been built, and the final rails hammered into place. A viewing platform had been erected, where the leaders of the community would stand to welcome the arrival of the first train, which was due within the hour. A large crowd had gathered to watch the locomotive roll in, and a brass band was tuning up rather raucously.

Bo and Scratch stood nearby, leaning against a hitch-rack as they kept an eye on the crowd. Everybody was in such a good mood that they didn't expect any trouble today, but as always, it was best to be prepared.

"You know, I never expected to be here this long, let alone wearin' badges the whole time," Scratch mused. "Figured we would've lit a shuck a long time ago."

"We could have," Bo said, "but it would have meant letting Cyrus down."

They had received another letter from Cyrus Keegan, asking them to stay on in Silverhill for the time being, if they were agreeable to that. The generous bank draft he had enclosed with the letter had convinced them to be agreeable. He had another job he wanted them to do, Keegan had promised. It was just a matter of waiting until everything was set up.

So in spite of their restless nature, the Texans had remained in Silverhill, and the town council—official now, and led by Francis Dubonnet, who had been elected mayor—had insisted that they continue on in their jobs as lawmen.

Luckily, things had stayed peaceful. The death of Arliss Chapman meant that the string of brutal murders had come to an end, too. The rustling threat in the area was over, at least until some other bunch of wideloopers drifted in. The stagecoach hadn't encountered any more road agents.

With the arrival of the railroad, though, the need for the stagecoach line would dwindle away, and Monte Jackson would have to find some other line of work.

Beth had already given up her job as jehu, since bouncing around on a stagecoach seat all day probably wouldn't be very good for the baby they were expecting.

Rose was still in the family way, too, which was obvious from her swollen belly as she stood with Steve in the crowd waiting to celebrate the train's arrival. Rance Plummer and quite a few members of the SJ crew had ridden down for the fandango.

Rance had told Bo and Scratch that he intended to pass along his job as foreman to Steve within the next year or so, but he didn't want to burden the young cowboy with the added responsibilities until Steve had had the chance to enjoy being a new papa for a while.

Cecilia and Roscoe were on hand, too, Roscoe towering over the folks around him, as usual. Their wedding was set for the next week, and she had asked Bo and Scratch both to walk her up the aisle.

They'd agreed, of course.

Staying on in Silverhill had been a little easier for Bo than it might have been otherwise, because Susan Hampshire had gone back to Texas with Hugh Craddock to become his wife. Bo missed her at times, but deep down he was happy for her—and relieved that she had been won over by Craddock's renewed courting. He truly wasn't ready to settle down.

Evidently, neither was Luella Tolman, because she was still skillfully fending off a number of would-be suitors. Bo wasn't sure why she'd do that, unless she actually was waiting for Philip Armbruster, who had been sentenced to two years in the territorial prison. Bo and Scratch had talked to him briefly after his trial, and he'd said that if Silverhill didn't have a newspaper by the time he got out, he might try his hand at such an enterprise.

The Texans had wished him luck, and had meant it. He wasn't a bad sort when you got to know him. A mite on the pompous side, and his head was in the clouds too much, full of all sorts of grandiose notions, but as Scratch had put it, "I reckon you sort of have to be like that if you're gonna be one of them writer fellas, because they all seem to be that way!"

Even Jean Parker was still in town. She had planned to return to Four Corners, Iowa, but before she did, a young minister had come to town to start a church, and Jean had befriended him. Bo had a hunch that sooner or later it would turn into more than friendship.

Bo couldn't help but mull over all of that as he and Scratch waited for the train. More and more, it seemed to him like their work here was done. His feet were getting downright itchy again, and although he had been able to put aside the feeling for a while, he thought that once Cecilia's wedding was over, there really wouldn't be anything holding them here anymore, other than their promise to Cyrus Keegan. And if he didn't come through pretty soon with what he'd hinted at . . .

The band launched into a tune and tried to make up for any lack of talent with sheer enthusiasm. To a certain extent, they succeeded. When they finished, several dignitaries, including W. J. M. Carling, Albert Hopkins, and Mayor Dubonnet, got up and made speeches.

The distant moan of a train whistle made Scratch lean over and say quietly, "I'm glad to hear that. Maybe it'll put an end to all the speechifyin'."

"Maybe it will for a little while," Bo said, "but where there are politicians, there'll always be speeches."

Scratch just nodded in doleful agreement.

Cheers, whistles, and applause welled up along with the

band music to blend with the rumble of the engine, the clatter of drivers, the hiss of steam, and the squeal of brakes as the train pulled in and came to a stop. The platforms at the back of several cars were draped in bunting, and when Scratch saw that, he groaned.

"More politicians and muckety-mucks from the railroad, I expect."

"More than likely," Bo said. Then something caught his eye, and he nodded toward a car farther back. "But look there!"

"By grab!" Scratch exclaimed. "That's Cyrus!"

Indeed, Cyrus Keegan, small, portly, mostly bald, and definitely dignified, came down the steps from the car and onto the station platform. He turned and extended a hand to an attractive, well-dressed woman who followed him.

Then another woman and another and another—until a dozen ladies were clustered around him, filling the air with the sea of feathers attached to their stylish hats.

"Gentlemen!" Keegan exclaimed in his high-pitched voice as he saw Bo and Scratch approaching. "It's so good to see you again!"

"Howdy, Cyrus," Bo said. He pinched his hat brim to the women. "Ladies."

"What in tarnation are you doin' here, Cyrus?" Scratch asked. "We didn't expect you." He looked at the women, who were all smiling in what seemed to be anticipation. "And we sure didn't expect you to be in such admirable company."

"These ladies are all clients of mine," Keegan explained with an expansive gesture. "From the letters you've sent me, I know that this area is still full of mining men and cattlemen who are in dire need of matrimonial assistance, and I intend to fulfill that need!"

Scratch's bushy eyebrows climbed his forehead. "You mean you're gonna marry off all these gals to the fellas around here?"

"That is the plan, yes."

Bo frowned and said, "I hope you're not expecting us to give you a hand with that. We're not exactly match-makers, although we've taken on the chore now and then. Reluctantly."

"As in the case of Miss Winston and Mr. Hargett, yes, I recall. Or Mr. and Mrs. Hargett, I should say." Keegan waved a hand again. "No, no. Rest easy on that count, Bo. I do have a job for you and Scratch, but it won't involve pouring tea and sending invitations and planning wed-dings. No, indeed." He clenched a pudgy fist and punched the air. "But I expect that there *will* be the potential for excitement. Danger, perhaps, and a trek through a wild, untamed wilderness!"

"Quit spoutin' words and just spit it out," Scratch said.

"What do you have in mind?" Bo said.

A brilliant smile spread across Keegan's cherubic face. "Have you boys ever been to . . . *Alaska*?"

*Smoke is back! Keep reading for a special excerpt
of the all new Mountain Man adventure!*

National Bestselling Authors
WILLIAM W. JOHNSTONE
and J. A. JOHNSTONE

TEXAS KILL OF THE MOUNTAIN MAN

*Bestselling western authors William W. Johnstone and
J. A. Johnstone take their best-known sharpshooter,
Smoke Jensen, deep into the heart of Texas, where
justice comes from the barrel of a gun . . .*

Smoke Jensen has met some down-and-dirty murdering
prairie scum over the years. But this time it's personal and
it's bloody—and going to get bloodier. First, they stole
fifty of the hundred horses Smoke delivered to his old
friend Big Jim Conyers in Tarrant County, Texas. Then
they stole two thousand cattle from Big Jim—and killed
him just for the fun of it. Now they're going to pay . . .

The leader of this unholy band of devils is Delbert
Catron—but everyone calls him The Professor. Whatever
he's called, he leads the most ruthless gang of vicious,
kill-crazy desperadoes this side of the border. Hellbent
on avenging his friend's murder, nothing will stop
Smoke Jensen from hunting these killers down.

And celebrating their funerals . . .

Look for **TEXAS KILL OF THE MOUNTAIN MAN,**
on sale now.

The Jensen Family
First Family of the American Frontier

Smoke Jensen—*The Mountain Man*
The youngest of three children and orphaned as a young boy, Smoke Jensen is considered one of the fastest draws in the West. His quest to tame the lawless West has become the stuff of legend. Smoke owns the Sugarloaf Ranch in Colorado. Married to Sally Jensen, father to Denise ("Denny") and Louis.

Preacher—*The First Mountain Man*
Though not a blood relative, grizzled frontiersman Preacher became a father figure to the young Smoke Jensen, teaching him how to survive in the brutal, often deadly Rocky Mountains. Fought the battles that forged his destiny. Armed with a long gun, Preacher is as fierce as the land itself.

Matt Jensen—*The Last Mountain Man*
Orphaned but taken in by Smoke Jensen, Matt Jensen has become like a younger brother to Smoke and even took the Jensen name. And like Smoke, Matt has carved out his destiny on the American frontier. He lives by the gun and surrenders to no man.

Luke Jensen—*Bounty Hunter*
Mountain Man Smoke Jensen's long-lost brother Luke Jensen is scarred by war and a dead shot—the right qualities to be a bounty hunter. And he's cunning, and fierce enough, to bring down the deadliest outlaws of his day.

Ace Jensen and Chance Jensen—*Those Jensen Boys!*
Smoke Jensen's long-lost nephews, Ace and Chance, are a pair of young-gun twins as reckless and wild as the frontier itself . . . Their father is Luke Jensen, thought killed in the Civil War. Their uncle Smoke Jensen is one of the fiercest gunfighters the West has ever known. It's no surprise that the inseparable Ace and Chance Jensen have a knack for taking risks—even if they have to blast their way out of them.

CHAPTER 1

Laramie County, Wyoming Territory

E mma was hanging up her wash when she saw a rider approaching. At first she felt a sense of joy, thinking perhaps her husband was returning from his trip, but as that rider came closer, her joy turned to dread.

"My husband isn't here," she said, when her unwelcome visitor rode right up to her and dismounted.

"That's good, because I didn't come to see him. I came to see you."

"What do you want, Marvin?"

"You know what I want, Emma. I want you. I've always wanted you. Come with me now. We can start a new life somewhere else, just you and me."

"No, Marvin. I made my choice a long time ago."

"How can I convince you that you made the wrong choice?"

"You can't convince me. I didn't make the wrong choice."

"All right, then, at least invite me in for a cup of coffee. I've come a long way today, and you owe me that much."

"What do you mean, I owe you? Why would I owe you anything?"

"Let's just say it's for the memory of the way it once was between us."

"There was never anything *real* between us, Marvin," Emma said. "Except in your imagination."

"But I thought we were *enga*— Well, at least let me leave with some dignity. A cup of coffee together? Would that hurt?"

"All right," Emma replied with a resigned sigh. "One cup of coffee, then I want you to please leave." She nodded toward the clothes basket, which was half-filled with just-washed items she had not yet hung up to dry. "I need to finish hanging out my clothes."

Minutes later, Marvin followed Emma into the house. As soon as the door was closed behind them, he grabbed her, then turned her around, and even as she was fighting him, he forced a kiss on her. "You want me, you know you do."

"No, no, go away. Leave me alone!" Emma slapped him.

Marvin smiled at her, but the malevolent smile was without warmth. "All right, bitch. As you said, you have made your choice." He pulled out his pistol and brought it down on her head.

She dropped to the floor and he fell upon her, ripping off her clothes and having his way with her. She regained consciousness in the middle of his attack and tried to fight him off, but he was too strong for her.

When he was through, he stood and looked down at her naked and bruised body. "If I can't have you, he can't, either." Marvin pulled his pistol and shot her in the stomach, then left her moaning on the floor behind him.

The clothes on the line were flapping in the wind as he rode away.

Three months later

Smoke Jensen sat on the top rail of the corral looking at the horses that had just been brought in. These were five of the one hundred horses he had just sold. The contract not only called for the delivery of one hundred horses, it also specified that the horses be saddle broken.

Four of the horses had been broken, but so far, three riders had been unable to break the fifth. His ranch hand was about to try.

"Cal, there's no need for you to break your neck trying to ride that horse," Smoke said. "Turn him loose. We'll just keep him as a stud for breeding. We can replace him with another."

"Now, Smoke, if you order me to do that I will," Cal replied. "But I'd like to give it a try. I don't like to think that a horse can get the better of me."

"Ha!" Pearlie said. "If you ask me, that horse already has the better of you. Why, I wouldn't doubt but that he could beat you at checkers."

"We'll see," Cal said as, without any preliminaries, he swung into the saddle.

The reaction of the horse was instantaneous and violent. The horse leaped straight up with all four legs leaving the ground. Coming down on four stiff legs jarred Cal, but it didn't dislodge him from the saddle. On the next move, however, the horse kicked his back legs into the air so that his back formed about a sixty-degree angle pointing to the ground. The maneuver caused Cal to be tossed forward over the horse's head, where he wound up lying on his backside.

"Cal! Are you all right?" Smoke shouted. Jumping down from the fence, he hurried over to the young man who had become more like a son than an employee. "Are you hurt anywhere? Is anything broken?"

"Nah, I'm all right," Cal said as Smoke and Pearlie helped him to his feet. Cal put his hands, gingerly, to his backside. "I'll tell you this, though. I don't think that horse is going to let anyone ride him."

"That's because he hasn't had anybody who knows what they're doing try it yet," Pearlie said.

"Are you telling me that you can ride him?" Cal asked.

Pearlie smiled. "You just watch."

The horse was tethered by a long rope to a pylon in the middle of the paddock. The idea was to let the horse run in concentric circles, the circles decreasing as the rope wound itself up on the pylon.

Pearlie mounted the horse but he, too, was thrown from the saddle perhaps even more quickly than Cal had been.

"I'll tell you what," a sheepish Pearlie said as he regained his feet. "That horse just pure dee doesn't want anyone to ride him."

"It's not worth someone getting a broken neck," Smoke said. "Turn him loose and bring in a replacement."

"All right, Punch. It looks like you're going to get your way," Pearlie said as he began removing the saddle. "Out you go."

"Punch?" Cal said.

Pearlie nodded. "He punched three others out of the saddle before he took us on," Pearlie said. "Can you think of a better name?"

"He's Smoke's horse," Cal said. "It's up to Smoke to name him."

"Punch it is," Smoke said.

"Are you going to try and ride him, Smoke?" Cal asked.

Smoke chuckled. "No, and I'm not likely to try and stick my hand up a bear's butt, either. I told you. We've got enough horses to meet the contract, so we don't need this one."

"Which just goes to show how smart you are and how dumb we are," Pearlie said.

"I'm going to check with Herman and see how he's doing," Smoke said, turning away from the others to complete his task.

"I hate confessing that the horse beat me."

Smoke heard Cal's remark as he headed toward the tool-shed that was being remodeled by Herman Nelson.

As he approached, Smoke heard sawing and knew Herman was gainfully occupied. Behind only Pearlie and Cal, Herman was the most dependable of all his permanent hands. One thing Smoke particularly appreciated was how efficiently Herman took over the ranch and ran it during the many times Smoke, Sally, Pearlie, and Cal were away.

When Herman saw Smoke approaching, he stopped sawing. "Hello, boss. Is there anyone left that's crazy enough to try and ride that horse?"

"Did you try?" Smoke asked.

Herman laughed. "Oh, yes, I have to admit that I was the first one dumb enough to get throwed by 'im. 'N I'm tellin' you right now, even if you ask me to, I don't plan to try again."

"I'm not going to ask anyone else to try," Smoke said. "I don't want to take a chance on anyone getting his neck broken. How are you coming in here?"

"I need some angle iron for the shelves, and I'll have this place looking like some grand mansion somewhere," Herman said proudly.

"How many do you need?"

"Three per shelf, four shelves, so I'll need twelve."

"All right. I'll make a run into town," Smoke said.

"Great, I would love to go into town," Sally said enthusiastically in response to Smoke's announcement of his plans a few minutes later. "I have so many errands to run."

"I was just going to run into town and come right back. I hadn't really planned on you—" Smoke stopped in midsentence.

"You hadn't planned on me what?" Sally challenged.

"Uh, I had no idea you would be willing to go into town with me. What a pleasant surprise this is. I'll be happy to have you go into town with me."

"Oh, Smoke, you say the sweetest things to me," she teased. "I can be ready right away."

Kansas and Pacific Railroad Depot, Big Rock, Colorado

Roy J. Clemmons and Sue Martin were two of the six passengers who stepped down from the train. They stood out from the others—four men were wearing jeans and cotton shirts. Clemmons was wearing a black suit with a red vest over a white, collared shirt with a black string tie. His dark hair was perfectly coiffured, and his moustache, which didn't extend beyond each end of his lips, was well-trimmed.

Sue stood out, not only because she was an exceptionally pretty woman with bright red hair, but also because of what she was wearing. The provocative V-neck of her dress was low enough to show the tops of her breasts.

"Our train doesn't leave for six more hours," Clemmons said. "There is plenty of time for us to earn a coin or two."

As they walked away from the depot, they paid no attention to the two riders, man and woman, just coming into town on Jensen Pike, the road that came in from the west.

"I'll go on down to Earl Cook's place," Smoke said. "You can do whatever it is that you have to do.

"It shouldn't take me too long," Sally said. "If you don't mind, I'll just go on back home when I'm done."

"I may be a little later," Smoke said.

"Tell Louis I said hello."

"What makes you think I'll be going to Longmont's?"

"I don't know. What makes me think the sun will set in the west tonight?" Sally replied with a little laugh.

CHAPTER 2

S moke Jensen was in Longmont's Saloon sitting at Louis Longmont's special table with Louis.

"What are you doing in town at this time of day, anyway, Smoke? Is there not enough to keep you busy out at Sugarloaf?" Although Louis Longmont was a longtime resident of Big Rock, he still spoke with the lilt of a French accent.

"We're gathering some horses to take down to Texas, but Pearlie and Cal seem to have things well in hand," Smoke answered. "Who's your new girl?"

"What are you talking about? I don't have a new girl."

"That one," Smoke said, pointing to an attractive young red-haired woman who was setting drinks before the card players. Though what she was wearing was as provocative as what was worn by any of the other bar girls, even Smoke could tell that her dress was more expensively made.

He recognized only two of the players.

"Oh, *non, monsieur*. She isn't working for me. She came in with the man in the suit. But you have changed the subject. What brought you to town in the middle of the day?"

"Sally had some things to do, so I volunteered to come with her, to help out."

Louis chuckled. "*Oui,* one can easily see that you are being a big help."

"I *am* being a big help. Sally said I would be most helpful just by staying out of her way."

"You could have stayed out of the way by staying out at the ranch."

"That's true," Smoke agreed. He held up his beer. "But then I couldn't be sitting here talking with you. Anyway, I had to take care of something down at Earl's."

"What did you need done at the blacksmith shop?"

"Nothing major. I just needed some braces made for a few shelves I want to put up in the machine shop."

Their conversation was interrupted by a woman's scream. They looked toward the source and saw that someone had grabbed the red-haired woman who had been the subject of Smoke's earlier observation. The woman's assailant had his arm around her neck. He was holding his pistol to her head, but he was yelling at the well-dressed man sitting at a card table.

"You've been cheatin', mister! You've been cheatin' from the moment I sat down here. And this woman has been helpin' you."

"What are you talking about? I haven't done anything!" the woman said, her voice breaking with fear.

"Don't give me none o' that, lady. Do you think I don't know how you've been sneakin' around behind all of us, givin' him signals 'n such on what cards we was holdin'? Now all of you, get up and leave the money on the table. We've been cheated out of a lot of money, and I plan to get back my share of what he stole."

Smoke stood up and walked toward the table while

aiming his pistol at the man holding the woman hostage. Because everyone's attention was on the scene playing out before them, neither they, nor the man with the gun, saw Smoke until he was within ten feet of the table. When the man did see Smoke, he jerked around, still holding his gun to the woman's head.

"Stop right there, mister!" he called out, angrily. "What is it you think you're about to do?"

"I'm not real sure, but it could be that I'm about to kill you," Smoke said, his voice flat and completely emotionless.

"What do you mean, you're about to kill me? Are you blind? Don't you see that I have a gun pointed toward this woman's head?"

"Now that you mention it, I have noticed that. By the way, you might also have noticed that my gun is pointed at you."

"Drop the gun, mister. Drop it now, or I'll kill the girl."

"All right, go ahead," Smoke said easily.

"What?" the man asked, shocked by Smoke's response. "Look, you don't understand. If you don't drop the gun now, I'm goin' to kill her!"

"Yes, you keep saying that. The truth is, mister, you're in a bit of a quandary here, aren't you?"

"A bit of a what?"

"You're in a bit of a fix. If you move that gun toward me, I'll kill you. If you shoot the woman, I'll kill you. So if you are going to shoot her, go ahead and do it. If you don't drop it, I may just go ahead and shoot her myself so we can get this over with."

"I . . . I don't believe you."

"Why not? I don't know her, so she doesn't mean anything to me."

The man who was holding the woman looked at Smoke and saw the black hole of the end of the pistol pointing straight at him. His eyes grew wide in fear, and small beads of perspiration popped out on his forehead and his upper lip.

"I'll give you to the count of three to make up your mind," Smoke said. "One."

"You're crazy!"

"Two."

"No, no!" The man dropped his gun and took his arm away from the woman's neck.

Quickly, and with a little cry of relief, the woman darted away from her would-be assailant to join the suited man at the table.

"Thank you, mister. You saved my life," the woman said.

"Yes, well, this would have never come up if you hadn't been helping your man cheat," Smoke replied.

"What? Why, I never!" the woman said.

Smoke didn't know the gunman, nor the card player the woman had run to, but he did recognize the other two players, though he knew the name of only one. Ivan worked at the stable, the other player he knew only as a cowhand who worked on one of the area ranches.

"Ivan, are you a winner or a loser?"

"Ha, are you kiddin'? I'm down fourteen bucks," Ivan said. "Dobbins is losin', too," he added, nodding to the cowhand across the table from him.

"How about it, Dobbins? How much money are you down?" Smoke asked.

"I'm down twenty-two dollars," Dobbins said. "It was damn foolish of me to lose that much money. That's a month's pay for me."

"What is your name, mister, and how much have you lost?" Smoke asked the would-be gunman.

"My name is Crabtree, Buster Crabtree, and I've lost twenty-eight dollars, all to him!" Crabtree pointed directly across the table.

"And who would you be?" Smoke asked the winner.

"My name is Clemmons. Roy J. Clemmons." The man spoke with the accent of someone from the Northeast.

"You're a little out of your territory, aren't you? What are you doing in a place like Big Rock?"

"Sue and I arrived by train this morning. We are on the way to San Francisco, where I have taken employment at the Blue Chip Club. I'm sure someone like you has never been to San Francisco, so no doubt, you've never heard of the club."

"The Blue Chip Club is a gambling establishment on Lombard Street," Smoke replied.

Clemmons's eyes opened wide in surprise. "You know the place?"

"I know the place. I also know that it has a reputation for hiring gamblers who can assure the house wins by manipulating the cards."

"I-I don't know what you are talking about," Clemmons stuttered.

"Mr. Clemmons, there is no doubt in my mind but that you were cheating these three men, and I'm quite sure your woman was involved in some way. I don't approve of what Mister Crabtree did, but I can understand what drove him to do it. So here's what you are going to do. You are going to return the twenty-eight dollars to Mr. Crabtree, the twenty-two dollars to Mr. Dobbins, and the fourteen dollars to Ivan. Then each of you are going to take out whatever money you have put in the pot for this hand. Gentlemen, this game is over."

"Now, just why in the hell should I do such a thing?" Clemmons asked, angered by Smoke's demand.

"Because I'm holding a gun and you aren't," Smoke replied easily. "And I could kill you long before you can get to that holdout gun you are keeping just under that bright red vest."

"And here I thought you were my hero for saving me," the woman said as Clemmons began counting out the money, then reluctantly returning it to the other three players. "Why, you are nothing but a thief with a gun."

"Yes, ma'am. Well, some folks steal with a gun, and some folks steal by using a good-looking woman to signal what the other card players are holding." Smoke replied.

The three men began counting their money and putting it away.

"Mr. Crabtree, we aren't going to have any more trouble with you, are we?" Smoke asked.

"No, sir, I'm satisfied that all is well. And I apologize for makin' such a damn fool of myself. I also thank you for bein' the only one of the two of us to show any sense this morning."

Louis had come over to the table. "*Monsieur* Clemmons, I believe you said that you arrived on the morning train?"

"I did."

"Then it is my suggestion, *monsieur*, that you return to the depot and await the earliest train that can take you out of town."

"You've got no right to order me to stay in the depot," Clemmons said

"*Oui*, that is true. I can only offer that as a suggestion. However, as the owner of this saloon, I am telling you to leave my establishment now and never come in here again."

"Yes, well you certainly don't have to tell me that. I've no intention of remaining in an establishment, owned by somebody who would countenance robbery at gunpoint." He glared at Smoke. "Nor do I intend to stay in this town any longer than the very next train. Come, Sue, let's get out of this place."

The others in the saloon applauded as Clemmons and the woman left.

Smoke returned to his seat.

"Annie," Louis called to one of the girls who did work for him. "Bring us two more beers, would you, *mon cher*? These have grown flat."

"So, when are you going to Texas?" Louis asked when the beers were delivered.

"Just as soon as we get the horses gathered and broken, we'll be taking them to Big Jim Conyers at his ranch near Fort Worth."

"Why do they call him Big Jim?"

"Well, he's six feet seven inches tall, and he weighs nearly three hundred pounds. Does that give you a hint?" Smoke asked with a chuckle.

"*Mon Dieu*, that is a big man," Louis said.

"Yes. He's also a pretty big man in Tarrant County, and I'm not just talking about his size."

Sugarloaf Ranch

Seeing a plume of dust in the long, dedicated road that approached the ranch, Sally Jensen smiled, then stepped out onto the wide porch so she could watch his arrival. The road—on the state and county maps it was called Jensen

Pike—came from Big Rock and served at least four more ranches and half a dozen remote houses before; reaching the eastern boundary and passing under the entry arch with the name of the ranch, *Sugarloaf*, fashioned from wrought-iron letters above. But she knew Smoke had no intention of riding under the arched entry.

He left the road, then urging his horse Seven into a mighty jump, sailed over the fence almost as if on wings. After successfully negotiating the fence, he galloped into the compound before pulling the horse to a stop and leaping down from the saddle.

Sally stepped out to the railing to look down at her husband. "Well," she said with a wide and welcoming smile. "It does my heart good to know you still think of me as someone you would gallop home to."

"Sally, my love, I would soak my trousers in kerosene and ride through a forest fire to get home to you."

"What? And expose Seven to such danger?" she quipped.

"If I asked it of Seven, he would do it without hesitation. He is the greatest horse in the world!" Smoke augmented his comment by patting the hard-breathing animal on its forehead.

Sally laughed. "Smoke, you have said that about every other horse you have ever owned. And you have named every one of them Seven."

"That's true, and they were the greatest horses in the world, too."

"Don't be silly. There can only be one greatest," Sally reminded him.

Smoke held up his finger and waved it back and forth. "No, that's the schoolteacher in you talking. If you love horses, you know there can be as many greatest horses as you want."

Again, Sally laughed. "If you say so."

"How are things going here?" he asked.

"Here comes Pearlie. You can ask him yourself."

Smoke's foreman was Wes Fontane, though not one out of a hundred people who knew him knew what his real name was. He was *Pearlie* to one and all.

"Is Earl goin' to be able to get them angle irons done?" Pearlie asked as he approached.

"Pearlie!" Sally said in a chastising tone.

For just a second, Pearlie looked confused, then he smiled and nodded. "I said *them* angle irons, 'n I was supposed to say *those,* wasn't I?"

"Very good."

"So, Smoke, did—"

Smoke held up his hand. "Just say the word *those.*"

"What?"

"I already heard your question. Just change *them* to *those* and I'll answer. There's no need to repeat the whole question."

"Those," Pearlie said.

"Yes," Smoke replied, and both men laughed.

"God help me, I'm surrounded by crazy people," Sally said, but she laughed as well.

"How's the gather going?" Smoke asked.

"It's going great," Pearlie said. "We found forty-seven new colts to brand, and Cal's out there with them now. I expect they are pretty close to being done."

"What about the horses we're taking down to Texas?"

"We don't have 'em all, but we've got most of 'em picked out. Then, of course, they will have to be broken," Pearlie said. "It'll be good to see the Colonel again. Are you going, Miz Sally?"

Pearlie's reference to Big Jim as *the Colonel* was because he had been a colonel in Hood's Division during the War Between the States.

"Yes, Julia has invited me. When the train leaves next Monday, I'll be on it."

"Hey, Smoke, is Live Oak as big as Sugarloaf?"

"I think the two ranches are within a few hundred acres of each other. I'm not sure which is"—he paused and looked at Sally before finishing the sentence—"the *bigger* of the two."

"Very good," Sally said with an approving smile.

Pearlie stretched. "Woowee, I'll be glad when we're done here. I'm just about all tuckered out."

"You aren't too tired for peach cobbler, are you?" Sally asked.

"Are you kidding? Even if I couldn't walk, I'd be able to pull myself in on my belly to get some of your cobbler."

"You don't have to go to that extreme. Just be cleaned up when you come to the table."

"The only thing is, I feel bad about all the others. All the hands have worked as hard as Cal and I have, and I feel a little guilty about being the only ones to enjoy the cobbler."

Sally smiled. "You don't have to feel guilty. When I was in town, I acquired sufficient ingredients for Mr. Peabody to make enough peach cobbler for all the hands."

"Great!" Pearlie said with a wide smile. "Now, I not only won't feel guilty, I can eat here, then go out to the cookhouse and have seconds."

Connect with

Us

Visit us online at
KensingtonBooks.com
to read more from your favorite authors, see books
by series, view reading group guides, and more.

for sneak peeks, chances to win books and prize packs,
and to share your thoughts with other readers.

facebook.com/kensingtonpublishing
twitter.com/kensingtonbooks

Tell us what you think!

To share your thoughts, submit a review,
or sign up for our eNewsletters, please visit:
KensingtonBooks.com/TellUs.